PRAISE FOR KATIE ASHLEY
AND HER NOVELS

"A mixture of funny, sweet, tender, and sexy. . . . [Ms. Ashley's] got me good and hooked."
—Fiction Vixen

"'Wow' is all I can say. . . . So, if you are new to Katie Ashley, treat yourself. I promise that you will not be disappointed . . . will definitely warm your heart, make you laugh, and have you smiling long after you finish."
—Guilty Pleasures Book Reviews

"It was all fabulous. Steamy, romantic, swoon-worthy, adorable!"
—Smitten's Book Blog

"Had me laughing while it tugged at my heartstrings. . . . You know how much we loves us a HOT read, and there is plenty of heat here, ladies."
—Flirty and Dirty Book Blog

"Full of everything I love in a romance book. A sexy, scared-of-commitment leading man . . . a very relatable, beautiful woman . . . drama to last for days, and a scorching love story that left me wishing this book would never end."
—The SubClub Books

"This book was emotionally wrenching, funny, and sexy. It has a bit of everything."
—Romance Lovers Book Blog

VICIOUS

CYCLE

KATIE ASHLEY

A SIGNET ECLIPSE BOOK

SIGNET ECLIPSE
Published by the Penguin Group
Penguin Group (USA) LLC, 375 Hudson Street,
New York, New York 10014

USA | Canada | UK | Ireland | Australia | New Zealand | India | South Africa | China
penguin.com
A Penguin Random House Company

First published by Signet Eclipse, an imprint of New American Library,
a division of Penguin Group (USA) LLC

First Printing, June 2015

LIBRARY OF CONGRESS CATALOGING-IN-PUBLICATION DATA:

Ashley, Katie.
Vicious cycle/Katie Ashley.
p. cm.—(A vicious cycle novel ; 1)
ISBN 978-0-451-47491-9 (softcover)
1. Single fathers—Fiction.   2. Motorcycle clubs—Fiction.
3. Motorcycle gangs—Fiction.   4. Man-woman relationships—Fiction.   I. Title.
PS3601.S548V53 2015
813'.6—dc23   2014048122

Printed in the United States of America
10 9 8 7 6 5 4 3 2 1

Set in Bulmer MT Std Regular
Designed by Spring Hoteling

To Olivia Caroline Ashe—my long-awaited answer to years of prayers, my little miracle, my daughter: May you be as strong, sassy, and sweet as the women I write, and may you never, ever date one of the bad boys like the ones in Mommy's books.

And to Charlie Hunnam because without him and *Sons of Anarchy* this book would have never been written. Thanks for being about the fairy tale, baby.

VICIOUS CYCLE

PROLOGUE

WILLOW

Bouncing her legs on the worn leather couch, Willow happily followed along with Dora as she took off exploring. No matter where the cartoon went, it was always better than the run-down apartment building where Willow lived. At the sound of splintering glass shards crashing across the kitchen floor, Willow abandoned Dora's world, tucked her ratty teddy bear under her arm, and hightailed it out of the living room. Although she was only five, she knew all too well what was to come after the angry voices and the throwing things began. She had learned to read the signs, and sadly, she was never wrong. There weren't many places of refuge in the tiny apartment where she and her mommy lived. But there was one place she could always count on to ride out the violent storms.

To other kids her age, the dark recesses under the bed were a frightening place. But for Willow, the *known* horror that often surrounded her was far less scary than the *unknown*. Lifting up the faded blue and white patchwork quilt, she crawled across the dingy carpet and underneath the ratty mattress that smelled like smoke

1

and pee. Dust bunnies clung to her clothes, clouding her lungs and making it difficult to breathe.

Once she settled in, she pinched her eyes shut and imagined herself miles and miles away. Whenever she was scared, she went to be with her Angel Mommy. In Angel Mommy's world, everything was happy, beautiful, and pure. Rainbows stretched across the sky over castles filled with unicorns. But the best part of all was Angel Mommy herself. Angel Mommy never drank too much out of the bottles with dark liquid that made her real mommy angry and then sad. Angel Mommy never had boyfriends who yelled at Willow or smacked her in the face or on the bottom. For Angel Mommy, Willow was her whole world—the only focus of her love and attention. They would play for hours and hours, running along the grassy meadow or playing hide-and-seek in one of the castles on the hillside.

She'd first begun to dream of Angel Mommy two years before at Christmastime. After her real mommy had drunk from the bad bottles and Mommy's boyfriend had stuck himself with the scary needle, they'd started yelling at each other. Cowering on the couch, Willow had tried to hide behind the pillows. As Mommy and her boyfriend's voices rose louder and louder, they began to push and shove each other. When Mommy tripped over one of Willow's shoes, she lost her balance and fell into the small Christmas tree in the corner. Ornaments had broken and scattered along the floor.

After Mommy had screamed at Willow and thrown the offending shoe, hitting her in the face, Willow had tried to pick up the mess to make Mommy less mad. An angel in a long white robe was the only thing that hadn't broken. It had soft, dark hair that she could stroke like one of her dolls, and it also had soothing brown eyes that gave Willow the reassurance she so desperately needed. Willow hadn't let Mommy see that she kept the angel. And that very day, Willow named her Angel Mommy and always kept the ornament close to her side.

Under the bed, she let her hand creep down to her shorts pocket where Angel Mommy waited to give her comfort. Willow stroked the doll's hair as the yelling in the living room grew louder. Just as she was about to plug her ears with her fingers, there was the bang of the front door blowing open and hitting the wall, like when Mommy's boyfriend came home angry. More voices now. More yelling. More broken glass. It sounded like the living room was being torn apart.

Mommy was begging someone with a voice that Willow wasn't used to. It rang with fear, and it was usually Willow who was afraid, not Mommy. *Thump, thump, thump.* Willow's body began to shake so hard at the sound her teeth clattered. She tried to figure out what was making the noise. Was it pounding boots? Mommy didn't like when Willow's shoes made loud noises. Her now-clammy hands went to swipe at her runny nose. Holding her breath, she prayed to Angel Mommy that the man in the boots wouldn't find her. But even as she was saying the words over and over in her head, the scary person came inside her bedroom. She could tell right away from the size of his feet that it was a man. He headed to the closet. Clothes and toys began to litter the floor as he went through her possessions as if he were looking for something in particular.

Then he went over to her chest of drawers. One by one, he pulled the drawers out and tossed them to the floor. When one landed a little too close to her, she jumped and hit her head against the mattress, which made her let out a squeak. The small noise caused the man to freeze.

Willow's heart began to beat wildly, and she felt like she couldn't breathe. As she tried burrowing further underneath the bed, the mattress covering her was ripped away. With a scream, she stared up at a man who was a vision out of her worst nightmares— long, stringy black hair, an angry red scar that ran down his face and onto his neck, and a patch over one of his eyes. Willow pinched her eyes shut with fear. *Please, please, help me, Angel Mommy!*

But then Big Booted Man snatched her up and hoisted her over his shoulder. She could barely breathe, least of all cry out or scream. It was as if her voice had been snatched away the moment her precious hiding place had been invaded. Her body trembled with fear as he marched out of her bedroom and into the living room. He tossed her about like a mistreated baby doll. When they finally came to a stop, he jerked her around to where she was facing away from his chest. His arm was wrapped tightly around her waist, binding her to him.

Her voice momentarily returned at the horrific sight before her. "Mommy!" she cried. Mommy and her boyfriend, Jamey, were tied with rope to two chairs from the kitchen table. Jamey stared at her with the same aggravation he always had. But Mommy wasn't talking or looking at her. Blood trickled out of her nose and mouth; her head hung limp. When she didn't respond, Willow kicked at Big Booted Man to try to get away. "Mommy!" she shrieked.

She was rewarded with a smack to the head and face. "Shut the hell up, brat!"

Although she shouldn't have, she cried out at the pain. Her face stung as if someone were poking her repeatedly with something tiny and sharp. It sent tears to blur her eyes.

She jumped at the sound of a gravelly, harsh voice behind her. "Crank, watch yourself. She doesn't get hurt until I say so—got it?"

"Yes, sir," Crank replied.

Willow turned her aching head to see a mean man staring at her. The look he gave her made her tremble all over. His black eyes focused on her with such hatred, even though she had never met him before. "Aren't you a pretty little thing," he said.

Since she didn't dare speak, she only stared at Mean Man. He then turned his gaze from her to one of the men who were standing behind her mommy.

"Wake the bitch up," Mean Man commanded.

The man grabbed Mommy's hair and yanked her head up. She cried out, her eyes blinking furiously. When she met Willow's gaze, she sucked in a harsh breath. "Leave her out of this. She has nothing to do with my business," she said in a pained whisper.

"Ah, but you see, she is part of you two, so she's *my* business. Since you decided play rat with the Feds and fuck with my business, I'm going to fuck with yours." Without taking his eyes off of her mommy, he took a step closer to Willow. "I think it's time we showed your daughter what happens when you double-cross someone." Mean Man waved a gleaming silver knife in front of Willow's face. When the blade pressed against her neck, fear overwhelmed her, sending warm liquid dribbling down her legs.

Big Booted Man, who held Willow, pulled her back from the blade to give her a shake so hard her teeth clattered. "The little cunt just pissed all over me!" he exclaimed.

Mean Man narrowed his eyes. "Don't be such a pussy, Crank. Now, hold her fucking still—you hear me?" Crank grumbled but kept his arms tight around Willow. Mean Man glanced at Mommy and Jamey before he once again pressed the blade to Willow's neck. "Now, let's try this again, eh? If you don't fucking tell us where the shipment is, I'm going to start cutting pieces out of your kid!"

Jamey rolled his eyes and gave a contemptuous snort—the kind he usually gave Willow when she tried to talk to him about dolls or her favorite television shows. "Go ahead and slit the brat's throat. I don't give a shit."

The Mean Man's eyebrows rose in surprise. "You just playin' me, man? 'Cause I will seriously hurt the little shit."

"You heard me straight. I don't give a shit if you spill her blood all over the floor, because it won't be mine flowing out of her."

"If she ain't yours, whose kid is she?"

"She's Malloy's bastard."

Mean Man hissed at the mention of the name. "Which Malloy?"

"Jamey, don't," Mommy protested, looking scared. All her young life, Willow had wondered who her daddy was. Whenever she asked, Mommy would call her daddy bad names. She'd never even seen a picture of him. Now it seemed Mommy had been hiding who her daddy was because she was scared. Willow couldn't help wondering if her daddy was as bad as these men.

"Shut your trap, bitch," Mean Man snarled. He then jerked his chin up at Jamey. "Tell me which Malloy the brat belongs to."

"She's Deacon's."

A name. Willow had finally heard her daddy's name. For some reason hearing it made her feel like she knew him somehow. Her happiness was fleeting. Hearing her daddy's name seemed to make Mean Man very happy, and Willow imagined that couldn't be good. A smile curved on his lips. "Well, now. This certainly changes things, doesn't it?"

His knife lowered from Willow's throat. When he inched closer to her, Willow cringed back against Big Booted Man. "This seems to be your lucky day, little girl. Letting you go now is going to serve my purpose far more in the long run." Mean Man cocked his brows and stared at her. His rough hands came to cup her chin, tilting her head to look at her from several angles. "I can't believe I didn't notice it before. You're the fucking spitting image of that cocksucker."

Mommy leaned forward in her chair. "Just let her go, okay? Using her won't do you any good. Deacon doesn't even know she's his—I left him before I found out. He doesn't like kids, so he won't give a shit about her."

Mean Man *tsk*ed at Mommy. "He might not care at first, but I'll give him some time. Even if he doesn't want her, I guarantee his brother Rev will. And I'll use any leverage I can against Deacon and his brothers." He motioned to Crank. "Put her down."

Relief filled Willow when she felt the ground beneath her feet again. Mean Man crouched down beside her. "I want you to listen to me, and listen well. You tell no one what you saw here tonight, understand?"

Although Willow bobbed her head furiously to show she understood, it didn't seem to satisfy Mean Man. He leaned in to where she could feel his hot breath burning against her cheek. "If you say a fucking word to anyone about me or what you saw, I will come to you in the night and cut out your heart. Got it?"

Apart from the times when she explored with Dora or escaped with Angel Mommy, Willow spent a lot of time afraid. But, until now, she had never experienced such intense fear. The tremors seemed to flood every part of her body. Although she shook from head to toe, she couldn't make herself reply.

But somehow Mean Man was satisfied with her lack of response. He turned back to Mommy. "Does she have somewhere she can go?"

Tears streaked down Mommy's cheeks. "Yes. She stays with the lady down the hall a lot."

Willow's fear dissipated a little at the thought of Mrs. Martinez, whose warm and cozy apartment she stayed in during the times Mommy was away with Jamey or working. Mrs. Martinez always cooked something for Willow, and she even let her help prepare the food. She let Willow call her Mama Mari, and it was like getting to have a grandmother the way her friends at school did.

"Fine. She goes down the hall, and we finish this."

"C-can I at least say good-bye?" Mommy questioned, her chest rising and falling with her sobs. Seeing Mommy cry made Willow start to cry.

"Hurry it up," Mean Man replied, shoving Willow toward the chair where Mommy sat.

Clambering as best she could into Mommy's lap, Willow buried her head in Mommy's neck. Still bound tight by her fear, she couldn't seem to make her lips move to say the words she was screaming in her mind. No matter how mad and mean Mommy was, Willow always loved her. She wanted nothing more than to be hugged and kissed by Mommy, but she very rarely got what she wanted.

"I love you, Willow. You be a good girl for Mrs. Martinez. She's going to take you to your daddy. You be good for him, okay?" Willow nodded. Mommy started to cry harder. "I'm sorry I was a bad mother, baby. I hope you'll have a better one now."

Willow jerked back to stare into Mommy's eyes. What did she mean a "better mommy"? Was she going somewhere? If Willow went to live with her daddy, did that mean she would never see Mommy again? It made her cry, and her tummy twisted. "I love you, Mommy," she whispered, finally finding the words she desperately wanted to say.

"I love you, too, Willow."

"All right. Enough sentimental bullshit. Crank, take the kid down the hall. Tell the woman to get the fuck out of the building for the next few hours if she knows what's good for her."

Big Booted Man responded by snatching Willow up again and marching her to the door. As Willow gazed over her shoulder, Mean Man closed the gap between him and Mommy. Just as they started out of the apartment, Mean Man's knife went to Mommy's throat. Mommy looked straight at Willow. "I love—" Her words were cut off when the knife slid across her neck.

Willow's mouth opened in a scream, but nothing came out. As

hard as she tried closing her eyes against the sight of the red blood pouring from her mommy's neck, she couldn't. The last thing she saw as she was taken from the apartment was Mean Man turning back to her as he brought his fingers to his lips to remind her to keep quiet.

Willow knew that she would never tell. She never, ever wanted to see Mean Man again. No matter what was done to her, she would never tell.

ONE

DEACON

Real men don't cry. Yeah, that old adage sure as hell didn't ring true in my line of work. Over the years, I'd come to see that even the biggest and baddest fuckers have their breaking point. It's not just the physical torture that breaks them. Sometimes, just a threatening mind fuck involving their wives, girlfriends, or daughters cues the waterworks until they're blubbering like absolute pussies. And at the end of the day, most would rather be beaten within an inch of their lives than give in to their emotions and show weakness. Men can handle physical pain, but it's the emotional shit that truly fucks with us.

To prove my case, I give you Pussy #1: Frankie Delbraggio, or the dumb fuck sitting before me with a mixture of tears and blood streaming down his fat-ass cheeks. He was the current recipient of my wrath because he decided to pull an idiot move, thinking he could double-cross me by working with another club. He'd gotten greedy both for more money and more power in his territory. In the process, he'd become overstretched and let one of my club's gun shipments run late.

Sure, at first glance he looked like your worst enemy—a really menacing bastard with tats and piercings who you sure as hell wouldn't want to run into in a dark alley. His skin was leathered from years of hard living, and his arms, which were currently bound behind him with cable ties, were pockmarked with track marks from the heroin addiction he just couldn't beat.

As sergeant at arms in my club, the Hells Raiders, I had to be the strong arm—the main man who used physical and emotional torture to get shit done. If I let someone like Frankie get away with drag-assing his feet on shipment deliveries and wavering in his loyalty, the whole club suffered. I couldn't and wouldn't deal with that. The Raiders are my life. They've been what I lived and breathed for from the time I was a snot-nosed, thirteen-year-old punk plucked off the streets by my adoptive father, Preacher Man, or Preach, as he was affectionately known.

Standing behind Frankie to lend a hand if needed was my adoptive brother, Benjamin, or Bishop, as he was known. He chomped on a piece of gum while eyeballing Frankie contemptuously. He was probably less pissed about Frankie fucking us over and more pissed over the fact I'd torn him away from some heavy action with one of the sweet butts—aka the ladies who willingly spread their legs for club members. At twenty-three, Bishop, with his baby-blue eyes and wavy, dirty-blond hair, thought only with his dick most days. Even though he'd been patched in when he was just nineteen, he still had a lot to learn.

While I'd worked Frankie over with a few right hooks and sucker punches to the gut, I'd broken through to him only when I'd taken his wallet. Between the weed, condoms, and a few twenties was a picture. After I gazed at it for a moment, a smirk curved across my lips. Waving the picture in front of him, I said, "Mmm-mmm. Look at that pretty piece of ass."

My words caused the shakes to run through Frankie's body. His eyes, which had once held such defiance, glazed over. Bingo. This girl, most likely his daughter, was his Achilles' heel. "How old is the sweet thing? Fourteen? Thirteen?"

When he didn't respond, I slammed another right hook into his jaw. "When I ask a question, you fucking answer me. Got it?"

Frankie nodded weakly. In a hoarse voice, he replied, "Twelve."

"Ah, just a baby. Man, I bet she has one tight pussy." I cocked my brows at him. "Nothing like breaking in a fresh piece."

As his broken jaw clenched, Frankie's arms jerked against his binds. If he could have gotten loose at that moment, he would have tried his best to kill me. But even though he was playing right into my hands, I wasn't done with him yet. No, I was about to go for his jugular. "Let me make one thing clear to you, Frankie. The next time you try to double-cross me and my boys, I'm going to find your pretty little daughter. Not only am I going to take your precious baby girl's cherry, but I'm going to ass fuck her, too, while all my brothers watch. Then any one of my guys who wants a chance can have a go at her."

As if I had taken a knife to him, my words seemed to tear through Frankie's skin, nicking an emotional artery. Tears poured from his eyes as he began to imagine something so horrific done to his little girl. His massive body shook under the weight of his sobs.

I'd painted a pretty depraved and disgusting picture for him. But what Frankie didn't know was it was all a fucking elaborate lie. I didn't go for underage pussy, especially little girls. I knew my men didn't, either. If I ever got wind of something so fucking sick, I wouldn't have waited for a vote in church—our club meeting— about blowing their ass to the curb. No, I would single-handedly cut their balls off, take their patch, and send them packing. The Hells Raiders might have been a lot of things, but sick-fuck pedophiles weren't one of them.

Once I had let Frankie stew in his torture long enough, I cleared my throat. "So are we good now, Frankie? No more playing us with the Iron Lords, right?"

"Y-yes," he stuttered, as his teeth chattered from his full-body shakes.

I cocked my brows at him. "Yes, what?"

His eyes, which still shone with tears, widened. "Yes, sir, Deacon. You have my word. I won't *ever* fuck you over again. I swear on my life."

"And your daughter's?"

He cringed at the mention of his daughter. "Yes, mine and hers. I swear to God!"

"Glad to hear it." I then slid the picture of his angel-faced daughter back into his wallet. "Glad to know that your baby girl will be staying safe and sound, too."

"Yes," Frankie whispered, a tremor of what appeared to be relief going through his body.

Glancing at Bishop, I gave a nod. He took his pocketknife out of his jeans and cut the ties binding Frankie.

"Have a good one, man. I look forward to our shipment next month," I said with a shit-eating grin.

Frankie gave a brief jerk of his head in acknowledgment as he rubbed his wrists where they had been bound. With a final wave, I headed out the door of Frankie's warehouse with Bishop on my heels. As we stepped into the intense May sunshine, I felt grateful for the warmth that heated the exposed skin below my T-shirt and the leather cut, or vest, I wore that boasted the Raiders' logo. When I slid across the seat of my bike, I caught Bishop's chuckle behind me. Craning my neck to look at him, I demanded, "What?"

He shook his head with a grin. "I was just thinkin' it was good I was with you and not Rev when you started in on that kiddie-pussy shit. He would have freaked the fuck out and ruined everything."

I snorted at the mention of my adoptive brother Reverend, or Rev, as he was known within the club. Nathaniel was his birth name, but none of his brothers called him that. The only person who refused to call us anything but our given names was my adoptive mother, Elizabeth. Although Rev was six foot four and a wall of muscle, he was really a tenderhearted pussy when it came to most things. He was the gentle giant who loved puppies and kids and that rainbows-and-hearts shit. Most of the time, he had too much goodness and integrity to fit into our world. "Yeah, well, that's the reason no one ever voted him in as sergeant at arms. They knew he wouldn't be able to do shit when it came to being a hard-ass."

"True," Bishop replied, as he slid across his bike's seat. After putting on my helmet, I kick-started the engine. There was no other feeling in my life quite like the roar of the engine beneath me. The only peace I found was on the road. Although I now had the support of a loving family, I still felt like a loner—an outsider still searching for a place to make his own. Only the road offered a place for me to be my true self.

As I wound my way through the back roads toward home, Bishop stayed close at my side. When we got to the compound, there were a few scattered bikes here and there. It was only four, and members didn't really start hanging around until they were done with their straight jobs. Years ago, when the cotton mill went bust, Preach had the business sense to buy the property. At the time, it wasn't for the Raiders. No, he was holy rolling then and focused on his ministry. After growing up in the MC world, he'd found Jesus in prison when he was just twenty. When he got out three years later, he buried his biker past and became a Pentecostal preacher.

That's where he'd met my adoptive mom—she was a fresh-faced, pure-of-heart-and-body, eighteen-year-old beauty. The daughter of a church elder. She saw him as the lost black sheep she could lead into the fold.

But even after he married the virtuous woman and started spreading the good word, the biker bred into him raged and clawed to be free. Then, two years after I came to live with him, his preaching ended in a true blaze of glory. That was the night he killed one of his own flock. I'd never been given the entire story, but I did know it had to do with the man hurting Rev somehow. Preach didn't do any time—instead, the transient man just "disappeared." Most of the congregation had been made up of truly lost souls without hope or family, so it was easy to bury him in the deep woods behind the compound without anyone asking questions.

After that night, the biker emerged strong and proud, which caused Preach and Mama Beth's marriage to go down in flames. They separated after that, but they never divorced. My mother, along with my brothers and me, stayed in the village row house while Preach slept at the clubhouse that had once been his church. While she loathed the biker world, Mama Beth watched helplessly as each of us followed in Preach's footsteps by patching into the Raiders. I think the three of us boys kept her constantly on her knees in prayer. But even though we were badass bikers, we still loved and respected the hell out of her. She was the best mother a guy could ever ask for, and she never treated me any differently from her blood sons.

Once I eased my bike to a stop in front of the clubhouse, I pulled off my helmet and hung it from one of the handlebars. I didn't have much to say to Bishop or to the two prospects who stood outside the clubhouse's front door. No, I had a singular focus at the moment, and that was getting some ass. After handling a job,

I needed a release, and sex was usually how I did it. With a determined step, I headed inside.

Guns N' Roses blared from the jukebox. My gaze flicked around the room, searching for one thing in particular. Or one *person* in particular. And then I found her. Behind the bar, Cheyenne Bates bent over the worn, mahogany counter, washing down the spilled beer and wiping away the crushed peanuts and chips. Her long blond hair was swept back in a ponytail. At the perfect view of her ample cleavage, my dick pounded against my zipper. As if she could sense me watching her, she jerked her head up, her intense blue eyes meeting my gaze. A slow, seductive smile slid across her lips.

Holding up a hand, I crooked a finger at her. She tossed the rag on the counter and then hurried around the side of the bar. She teetered on her tall but sexy-as-hell heels as she closed the gap between us. She threw her arms around my neck and then hoisted herself up to wrap her legs around my waist. "Hey, baby. I missed you."

"Hmm, I missed you, too," I replied, dipping my head to nuzzle the tops of her breasts. I steered us past the other guys and down the hallway. Once I got to my room, I kept one hand kneading Cheyenne's ass while the other went to open the door.

I'd been fucking Cheyenne almost exclusively for the last year. Occasionally, a new piece of ass might turn my head when I was on a run or at a rally. But I liked the fact that Cheyenne knew exactly how to blow my mind as I was blowing my load. She wasn't one of those chicks who expected you to get them off several times before they even thought about touching your dick. She always took care of me first. I like that shit.

Once I set her down on her feet, she sank to her knees in front of me. Her fingers came to my waist to loosen my belt and then unbutton and unzip my jeans. When she sprang my cock, she wasted no time sliding her lips down my shaft until I was deep-throating her. "Fuck," I groaned, my head falling back with the out-of-this-world sensations of Cheyenne's incredible head-giving skills. The woman had a mouth like a fucking Hoover.

Taking her head in my hands, I began to flex my hips and fuck her mouth. It wasn't long until my balls were tightening up and my cum was shooting into her mouth. She sucked and licked up every drop. I stared down at her with a lazy smile. "You sure know how to treat your man good, baby."

"Mmm, I love it. My panties are fucking soaked now just from sucking you off."

The fact that she could almost out dirty talk me was another thing that made me hot for Cheyenne. Sure, she'd been a sweet butt for years and years, and she'd been broken in by every single guy in the club, including Preacher Man. Her experience made her worth my time. Of course, since I'd been fucking just her for the last year, she had it in her head I was going to make her my old lady. But that was never going to happen. Not with her or any of the other club whores—not any girl, period.

Grabbing her shoulders, I drew her off her knees. "I think it's time I felt just how wet I got you."

"Yes, please."

Cheyenne pulled off her skintight T-shirt. Like magnets, my hands went straight for her tits. After freeing them from her see-through bra, I brought one to my mouth, sucking and biting at her nipple. I alternated from breast to breast while Cheyenne panted and moaned. My hands came to her jeans. Once I slid them down her legs, I grabbed her by the waist and tossed her onto the bed. Her eyes burned with lust as I loomed over her.

After tearing off her tiny scrap of a thong, I jerked her legs wide apart and buried my face between them. Cheyenne shrieked her approval, her acrylic nails scraping through my hair. "Oh yeah, baby.

Just like that. Fuck me with your tongue!" she shouted, her hips rising in time with my tongue.

A loud knock banged at the door, and then Rev's voice followed. "Deacon, I need you out front."

I didn't even bother raising my head from Cheyenne's pussy. Instead, I shouted, "Get the fuck out of here. I'm busy." While I returned to licking and sucking Cheyenne's clit, the unwelcome interruption remained at the door. I growled in frustration when the banging on the wood started up again.

"Deacon, I'm not fucking playing, man. I need your ass out here. *Now!*"

When I pulled away, Cheyenne mewled in frustration, her legs scissoring for friction. She'd been close before we were interrupted. Craning my neck toward the door, I shouted, "If this isn't a matter of life or death, I will cut your fucking balls off!"

"It is," came Rev's muffled reply.

"Motherfucker," I grumbled, as I slid off the bed. Snatching up my T-shirt and jeans, I put them on in record speed. When Cheyenne started to get up, I shook my head. "You stay just like that."

With a sly smile, she spread her legs and ran her fingers teasingly over her pussy. "Just like this?"

"Yeah, but don't get yourself off while I'm gone. I'm the only one who gets to do that."

She scowled at me just before I turned to head to the door. When I threw it open, Rev shot me a disgusted look. "For fuck's sake, man, wipe your mouth and fix your hair a little."

Instead of arguing that I didn't give two shits what anyone thought of my appearance, I licked my lips to savor Cheyenne a little longer. Then I dragged my arm across my mouth. As we started down the hall, I jerked a hand through my hair to try to tame the mess that Cheyenne had made.

When I rounded the corner, a silver-haired Hispanic woman came into view. Her apprehension of being in the clubhouse was rolling off her in waves. Her dark eyes darted from left to right, and she nervously fidgeted with her flowing, multicolored skirt. I couldn't imagine what was so fucking important about this woman to interrupt a fuck-fest.

When her gaze landed on me, her hand flew to her throat. Her expression appeared as someone who had seen a ghost. I glanced from her to Bishop. His usual poker face had been abandoned for one of disbelief. It wasn't something I was used to seeing. I cocked my brows at him, and he slowly shook his head.

After exhaling a frustrated breath, I asked, "Now, what is so fucking important I had to be dragged out here?"

"You David Malloy?" she asked in a thick accent. Even though she had asked the question, I could tell she already knew exactly who I was.

"Sí, señora," I replied, crossing my arms over my chest.

Hearing her native tongue didn't impress her. Instead, she shot me a disapproving look, like I was being a giant smartass, and she was probably right.

"You know Lacey?"

I snorted contemptuously. "Don't tell me she sent you to try to get some money out of me or something. I cut ties with that bitch five years ago."

"I no friend of hers."

"Then what the fuck do you want?"

Behind me, Rev coughed his disapproval for my hostile tone, and I rolled my eyes. "Why are you here about Lacey?" I asked.

"She dead."

I didn't like it that my chest tightened at the news. Lacey King had been my first love—my only real love, if I was honest. We were together for three years. Her occasional drug use and drinking hadn't been an issue when we first started dating, but after her mother died in a car accident, it morphed into a true addiction. When I refused to give her any drug money, she started fucking some guys in one of our rival clubs. Because of my love for her, I didn't kick her to the curb when I found out. No, I paid for her to go to rehab. She got out, and we had one good month together. During those few weeks, I actually thought of making her my old lady.

And then she fell off the wagon with alcohol. I told her it was either the alcohol or me—she chose the alcohol and left. That had been five years ago, and I hadn't heard anything from her since. Until now.

"Let me guess. She OD'd or died of alcohol poisoning?"

The woman slowly shook her head. "She murdered."

My brows rose in surprise. "By who?"

"Police, they don't know," she replied. But from the fear that burned in her eyes, I knew there was more to the story than she or the authorities were letting on. "I bring you something of hers."

"Trust me, there's nothing of hers I want."

"You want this. It is yours, too."

I racked my brain, trying to think if there was something that Lacey had taken from me all those years ago. But I kept drawing a blank. Then, for the first time, I saw there was someone with the woman. A tiny, dark-haired girl was hidden within the many folds of the woman's skirt. "Willow, come out."

The moment the little girl stepped into my line of sight, I felt like I'd been hit by a fucking lightning bolt. My body shuddered from the aftershocks. It was as if I were looking at the female version of myself when I had been that age. "Fuck me."

"This belongs to you. Willow, she your daughter."

At that moment, the room tilted and spun, and if it hadn't been for Rev behind me, I probably would have done a pansy-ass thing like fucking passing out. I momentarily leaned on his strength until

I could recover. Although the physical evidence showed that the kid was mine, I immediately went on the defensive. "I don't know what the hell you're talking about. I don't have any fucking kids."

Wide-eyed, the little girl stared up at me. From her expression of wonderment, I knew she was putting the pieces together. Regardless of my denial, she knew the truth—I was her father. As I glared down at her, an unwanted feeling of pride coursed through my veins.

Mine.

I'd created the angelic-looking thing before me. As I mentally counted the months and years in my mind, I couldn't help but think she had been conceived during that one perfect month with Lacey. We'd fucked morning, noon, and night, so I guess it wasn't hard to imagine I'd knocked her up. I'd certainly been barebacking, and she was off all meds. I guessed now that had included her birth control.

The woman reached into the large bag on her shoulder. After taking out a piece of paper, she thrust it at me. "You on Willow's birth certificate," she argued.

Just hearing the girl's name caused a stabbing pain to shoot through my chest straight to my heart. Willow . . . My daughter's fucking name was Willow. The first time Lacey and I had ever fucked was under one of the willow trees in the field down the hill from the compound. Before we'd fucked, we'd sat under one for hours, talking and laughing. Like a lovesick pussy, I'd even carved our initials into one of the trees. Then everything had gone to fucking hell, but she'd remembered enough to name our daughter something meaningful.

"Look," the woman instructed, flashing the paper in front of my face.

I grabbed it from her and stared down at it. There it was in bold, black ink. Under "Father's Name" was David Malloy. What the fuck had Lacey been thinking? She'd put my name on a legal document, yet she'd never fucking picked up a phone to tell me I had a kid? There were a thousand things I wanted to scream at her at that moment, but I couldn't. I'd never get to have the answers I so desperately sought, because she was dead. Worst of all, she'd been murdered. What the hell had she gotten herself into?

Even with the evidence before me, I still replied, "Yeah, well, I still want a DNA test."

Rev's strong hand gripped my shoulder. "There's no doubt in hell she's yours, Deacon."

I jerked my head to glare at him. "And if she is, what the hell am I supposed to do with a kid?"

He pinned me with a hard stare. "You'll do the responsible thing and try to raise her."

"Fuck that!" I shouted before tossing the birth certificate back at the woman. Without another word, I turned and stalked out of the bar. There was no way in hell I could stay there one more minute. Suffocating panic had invaded my body.

Lacey was dead—she'd been murdered. I had a kid—a daughter I had no fucking idea what to do with. A boy would have been one thing, but a girl? You had to be tender and sweet to girls. I didn't have a tender or sweet bone in my fucking body.

My out-of-control thoughts sent me sprinting down the dirt road. My heavy boots kicked up a cloud of dust behind me. When I reached the last row house on the left, I threw open the door without even a hello. Now retired, my mother spent her days volunteering with her church. But she was always home by five, because she wanted to watch fucking *Little House on the Prairie*.

Her blue eyes appraised me from her seat on the couch. She rose to her feet, beckoning me to her. "David, what's wrong?" she questioned, fear resonating in her voice. From her expression, I could tell she was envisioning a hundred different scenarios involving the death of Rev or Bishop.

Although I wanted to put her out of her misery, I couldn't. I couldn't move—I was frozen to the fucking floor. I didn't know how to break the news to her. I just knew I wanted her to somehow make it all right. "I have a kid," I finally blurted.

Relief flickered through her eyes, and she momentarily raised her face to the ceiling as if she was thanking God that her boys were safe. For now.

When she looked to me, her brows rose in surprise. "Cheyenne's pregnant?"

I scowled at the assumption. My mother sure as hell didn't approve of my fucking around, and she didn't care very much for Cheyenne. She wanted me to find a nice girl to settle down with to make babies, not knock up the club whore who'd been on her back in all the guys' beds. But I could tell she would swallow all her negative feelings if there was a baby involved—a grandbaby for her.

"Talk to me, David," she instructed.

Finally able to move, I picked one foot up and then the other to close the gap between us. As bitchass as it sounds, just the feel of her hand on my arm brought me so much comfort. With a sigh of both anguish and contentment, I let her pull me into her arms. And even though I had the most amazing woman before me, I couldn't help letting my thoughts go to my birth mom.

Hers was the sad tale of a good girl who'd gotten involved with the wrong man. She'd been a warm, nurturing mother who kissed my cuts and scrapes and wrapped me in her arms when I had nightmares. She just hadn't planned on my abusive old man getting out of prison, hunting us down, and then strangling her one night when I was seven.

She went in the ground, he went to jail, and I went into the system. From there, I ricocheted from one shithole to another. The anger and violence I'd inherited from my old man started surfacing when I hit puberty, and that's when I went out on my own. Yeah, a thirteen-year-old kid couldn't do much for himself on the streets but steal . . . and fight.

The ring is where Preach found me. Big for my age, I fought illegally in an underground circuit. For six months, I lived a hand-to-mouth existence, busting noses and cracking jaws, thinking no one in the fucking world cared about me. But I was wrong.

Fate is a funny motherfucker. Once upon a time, my mother had attended Preach's church. In fact, Preach and Mama Beth had hidden her and me from my father when he was on one of his drunken rampages before he was sent to prison. We'd run away in the middle of the night when my mother found out he was being released. It was probably the worst thing she could have done. She might still be alive today if she had stayed. After all, we had shelter and protection when we were with Preach.

The angry part of me wanted to tell Preach to go fuck himself when he offered me his home. I had no love for holy men like him. As if he sensed that, he had rolled up his sleeves to show me his heavily tattooed arms. He'd given me his story—the good, the bad, and the ugly—and I never looked back. I once again returned to Preach's house. He then legally adopted me, and I became the oldest of the Malloy boys. For the most part, Rev and Bishop didn't give me too much shit. Sure, we got into a few scuffles and scrapes. You can't add in a teenager to a family with a nine- and six-year-old and not expect problems.

Mama Beth's small hand on my shoulder brought me back into the present. "Speak to me, son."

I pulled away to stare into her questioning eyes. "Lacey is dead. Murdered."

A tiny gasp escaped her lips. It had been five years since Lacey had been a part of my life, but Mama Beth knew her significance. "I'm so sorry."

"There's more," I croaked.

"Sit down, honey," she instructed, leading us over to the couch. Once I collapsed down on the worn sofa, I put my head in my hands.

"She had a daughter. . . . *I* have a daughter."

Mama Beth reached over to take my chin in her fingers. She tilted my head to where I had to look at her. She cocked her brows at me, silently urging me to keep talking. "With Lacey gone, she's my responsibility. Hell, my name is right there on the birth certificate. But the worst thing . . ." I raked a shaky hand through my hair. "The kid looks just like me."

Blues eyes narrowed dangerously at me. "The worst thing? Don't ever let me hear you talk negatively about this child again. You were blessed to create a life, David. There are many people in the world who are never granted that gift."

My mouth dropped open, and I couldn't help staring at Mama Beth like she had lost her mind. I had just told her the greatest nightmare of my life had come true, and she was giving me shit because I wasn't dancing in the streets with happiness. She knew just as well as I did that I had no fucking business being a father. Anger that had started bubbling inside me welled over, and I reached a breaking point. "But don't you get it? I don't want her!" I protested, rising off the couch.

"I don't think that's an option."

I shook my head. "I *cannot* be a father."

With a mirthless laugh, she replied, "You are *her* father."

"By DNA, I'm her father, but I'm not the kind of man to be a parent."

"What you mean is, you're too selfish and scared to take responsibility for your actions."

I threw my hands up. "Oh no, don't hang that shit on me. There is no way I can provide a stable environment for this kid."

Crossing her arms over her chest, Mama Beth challenged, "And just what are you suggesting?"

"I'll take her down to Child Protective Services and put her up for adoption. Hell, she'd be much better off with two parents."

"And how well did foster care work for you?"

My fists clenched at my sides, and it took everything within me not to pick up the statue of Jesus on the coffee table and hurl it at the wall. Trying to keep a lid on my emotions, I breathed in and out several times. No matter how pissed I was, I would not disrespect my mother in her home by flying off the handle. "Things might work out better for her," I finally replied.

Sweeping one of her hands to her hip, Mama Beth wagged a finger in my face. "You listen to me, David Malloy. I will not let *my granddaughter* be put up for . . . adoption." She spat out the last word like it was the most despicable thing she could imagine. Shaking her head, she added, "Not as long as I have a breath left within me."

I raised my brows at the ferocity of her statement and tone. She might have been slight of stature, but in that moment, I knew she meant business. "What are you suggesting? Raising her yourself? If that's your decision, don't be thinking I'm going to help out."

"Sit down, David," she commanded. Always the obedient boy in her presence, I took a seat again. She drew in a ragged breath before speaking. "My heart has been so very heavy with the wayward path you have been on. No matter how much love your brothers and I give, you still remain isolated and untouchable." She shook her head. "If you can't give and receive love, you're not really living." I opened my mouth to protest, but she wagged a finger at me again. "You're almost thirty years old, David. You've wasted so many years on deadly sins. It's time you found true peace in your life."

"And you think raising this kid is going to do that?" I snapped.

"She will teach you to love selflessly."

"I do love selflessly."

Mama Beth tightened her lips, giving me one of her no-nonsense looks, like she knew I was bullshitting both her and myself. "I don't think I can do this," I muttered.

"But I *know* you can."

At the sound of a throat clearing, I glanced up. Rev was framed in the doorway holding Willow's hand. She tucked herself close to his side, and I could only imagine what he had done to win her over. Great. My kid liked my fucking brother better than me. "Mrs. Martinez left. I've got the prospects bringing in Willow's things."

"To the clubhouse?"

Rev nodded. "I figured we could put one of the cots in your room there for the night. Then tomorrow we could get her a proper bed for here at the house." With a smile, he gazed down at Willow. "You pick out anything you want, sweetheart. We'll get you whatever colors you love the most. You name it, and it's yours."

Willow didn't say a word. Instead, she gave Rev a shy smile and squeezed his hand. At what must've been my confused expression, Rev shook his head. "Mrs. Martinez said Willow hasn't spoken since her mother—" He stopped when a small tremor went through Willow's body. With his eyes, Rev answered the question that was running through my mind.

Fuck. Willow had seen Lacey die. Not only did I have a motherless kid, but I had one who was so mentally fucked-up from what she had seen that she'd stopped talking. Christ, the last thing she needed was me and my world. She needed some parents like off *Little House on the Prairie* and some serious therapy.

Breaking the silence, Rev swung Willow's arm, where it was clasped in his hand, back and forth playfully. "But that doesn't matter to us. Willow, you can talk when you want to. Right, guys?"

Mama Beth rose from the couch. "That's right." She held her arms open to Willow, who stared at them with slight trepidation. "I'm your grandmother, honey. I'm going to help your daddy take good care of you."

Willow stared past Mama Beth to me. I guess she was wondering why I wasn't welcoming her into my arms. The truth was I didn't know what the hell to do. Was it creepy if I touched her? Did I even want to touch her? The longer she stared at me, the more I felt like I couldn't breathe. I needed a release—to bury myself in Cheyenne or to make a run for my bike.

But I didn't get the chance to pussy out and leave. Willow released Rev's hand and took a few tentative steps toward me. In her other hand, she held some kind of angel that looked like it belonged on a Christmas tree. She walked straight past Mama Beth to come to me. Her dark eyes—the same color and shape as mine—never left my face.

"Say something," Rev hissed.

"Uh, yeah, so I'm David . . . or Deacon—your father."

She creeped me out by continuing to stare at me. It was the same obsessed look someone might give a celebrity. I scratched the back of my neck and desperately tried to find the right words to say. "Look, I . . . I'm sorry about your mother."

At the mention of Lacey, Willow cocked her head. Without words, I knew what she wanted from me. "She was really beautiful and sweet when she was sober and clean." Choking on my emotions, I had to clear my throat. "Even though we weren't together anymore, I did love her. Once." If I was honest with myself, I would have said that there was a small part of me that still loved her. "I wish I could have known about you when you were a baby. I'm sorry things had to turn out like they did." She still continued to stare at me. "Look, I know you must've seen some bad shit . . . er, stuff, but I want you to know that you're safe here. No one is going to hurt you. Okay?"

My statement caused tears to well in her eyes. Immediately, I felt like a giant asshole for making this kid cry. And then she shocked the hell out of me. She dove at me, clambering onto my lap. My arms went around her tiny body to keep her from falling. Small hands came up to cup my face. And then she leaned forward to kiss my cheek.

Her gesture of acceptance robbed me of all coherent thought and speech. She had every reason to hate me for not being there for her. I could only imagine that her young life so far had pretty much been hell. I'd seen Lacey at her worst when she was drunk and high. I couldn't imagine she was able to be a very good mother.

But instead of rejecting her absent father, Willow reached out to me. The only thing I could do was wrap my arms tighter around her. She felt so fucking fragile in my arms. I was afraid to squeeze her too tight for fear of breaking her. When I glanced up at Mama Beth, tears were streaming down her cheeks. She wrapped her arms around her middle as if she was trying to keep herself from falling apart. Seeing Mama Beth so emotional caused tears to sting my eyes. Fuck, I didn't cry, especially not in front of anyone. I didn't dare look at Rev to gauge what he was thinking. I imagined he would be thrilled I was actually showing a soft side for once.

And finally, I gave it all up, buried my face into the soft strands of Willow's hair, and let the tears flow. As I held my daughter in my arms, I realized how life could change on a fucking dime. Today mine had done a one-eighty.

I was a father. And even if it fucking killed me, I was going to be the best damn one I could. No one was ever going to hurt Willow on my watch.

TWO

Alexandra
FOUR MONTHS LATER

"Okay, kids. It's time to take your seats," I instructed over the buzzing hum in the room. My heels clicked across the tile as I went to close the door of my classroom. That was the signal that some of my stragglers needed to make sure they got to their desks. I smiled as they bounced in their chairs, excited to see what the day held in store for them.

I'd been teaching kindergarten at Buffington Elementary for five years now. The first year I was practically a baby myself at just twenty-two. Luckily for me, the principal had complete confidence that I could handle a class full of five- and six-year-olds.

As a child, I had played school with my dolls and stuffed animals, and for many years, I wanted to be a teacher. But then, as I grew older, my desires changed, and I thought of pursuing other careers. In the end, events in my life, especially the death of both my parents, had changed my mind. I wanted an honorable profession where I felt I could make a difference, so I had followed their foot-steps into education. While my father had been a high school math teacher, my mother had also taught kindergarten. They'd spent their lives molding young minds, and I felt my career choice honored their memory.

I once again turned my attention to my group of eager students. "All right. Let's see who is here today, and then we'll go to the mat for calendar time."

As I started taking attendance, my eyes fell on an empty seat. An ache went through my chest at the sight. It was the fourth day Willow Malloy had been absent. Protocol dictated we call home after the third straight absence, and when I had tried the day before, I had received a message that the number was out of service. Although I loved each of my little students equally, there was something special about Willow. I'd realized it the moment I'd met her, and she'd stolen my heart.

It was the day before school started. The Meet and Greet had just ended. After talking with a slew of new, anxious students and their equally anxious parents, I had collapsed at my desk, rubbing my feet, which ached from the heels I'd tortured them in. After throwing my head back in ecstasy at the way the foot massage felt, I popped open my eyes to see a dark-haired little girl standing beside my desk. I'd jumped out of my skin and almost fallen out of my chair.

A warm embarrassment rushed to my cheeks that she had seen me being so goofy. Trying to play it off, I wiped my hands on my skirt and held out my hand. "Well, hello. My name is Miss Evans, and I *really* like foot rubs and hate wearing high heels. What's your name?"

The little girl didn't respond. Instead, she just kept staring at me. There was recognition in her eyes that didn't make sense, considering I hadn't seen her before. "I didn't meet you earlier. Are you in another class this year? You're going to have so much fun in kindergarten."

I still didn't get a response from her. I began to wonder if perhaps she was on the autism spectrum and nonverbal. Then a panicked woman's voice echoed through the empty hall. "Willow? Willow, where are you?"

Taking a guess that the little girl was the missing Willow, I quickly called, "She's in here."

Within seconds, an attractive older woman with salt-and-pepper hair came rushing into the room. "There you are! You had me worried to death!" she cried.

Willow only momentarily acknowledged her before turning back to me. She edged around the desk and came to stand beside me. I couldn't help my mouth falling open when she casually climbed into my lap. One of her hands came up to touch the strands of my hair. Gazing down at her, I smiled. To my surprise, she smiled back at me.

When I glanced at the woman, who appeared to be her grandmother, there were tears shimmering in her eyes. "I . . . I'm sorry. I just haven't seen her react to someone outside her world."

"It's okay. I'm sorry she gave you a scare. We were just getting to know each other."

The woman nodded. "I had car trouble, so we were late for the Meet and Greet. I was across the hall, talking to her teacher, and when I turned around, she was gone."

I held out the hand that wasn't stroking Willow's head. "I'm Alexandra Evans."

"Elizabeth Malloy. I'm Willow's grandmother."

"It's nice to meet you."

Holding out her hand, Elizabeth said, "Come on, Willow. Mrs. Gregson is excited to meet you."

Willow burrowed deeper in my lap, giving me the impression

she was going to be with me for a while. For the first time, I noticed she was clutching something in her hand. "What's this?" I asked, pointing to what appeared to be a tiny doll.

Slowly, Willow opened her hand, and I saw that it was actually a small Christmas angel. "Oh, what a pretty doll."

My compliment brought a smile to Willow's face. "You look like her. . . . You look like Angel Mommy," she whispered.

"Why, thank you." Peering down at the doll, I tried imagining the similarities. We both had long, dark hair, and we were both wearing a white dress. With a smile, I said, "You're right. I do look like her."

A strangled cry came from Elizabeth. When I glanced up, she was clutching her throat. "She hasn't spoken in four months—not to me, not to her father. Not to anyone since her mother was . . ." She glanced at Willow and nervously shifted on her feet. "Since her mother passed away."

I blinked my eyes in disbelief as a flood of painful memories flickered through my mind. The face of Charlie, my little brother, appeared before me. I was seventeen when my parents were killed in a car crash one icy December day. Charlie had been ten—the only survivor of the wreck. The shock of losing our parents, along with being trapped in the car for hours, had rendered him catatonic for six months. Even after we moved in with my aunt and uncle—the two most wonderful, loving people in the world—Charlie didn't recover. For months he remained locked in a world of his own isolation. And then one day he slowly started to come around. Now he was twenty and partying way too much at college.

As I looked into Willow's face, I couldn't help thinking of Charlie. If he hadn't been surrounded by loving, caring people, I don't know what would have happened to him. Although it was strange and I didn't understand it, Willow had bonded with me.

Since she had already been through too much, I hated to break the bond.

I smiled at Willow. "You know, I have one spot left in my class. What would you think about going down to the office and seeing if you could be transferred to me?"

Willow's dark eyes lit up with what looked like absolute pleasure. She glanced over her shoulder at Elizabeth with a pleading expression. After wiping the tears from her eyes, Elizabeth asked, "It won't be too much trouble to do that?"

"Nope. No problem at all. It should just take a few seconds to change it in the computer."

With a smile, Elizabeth said, "I think that would be a wonderful idea."

Since that day, Willow had stuck close to my side whenever she was at school. As hard as I tried, I couldn't seem to get her to make friends with any of the other children. Most of the little girls were put off by the fact she rarely talked. So instead of jabbering along with them, Willow liked to stay with me during recess, and sometimes she would refuse to go to the gym or to art. I never forced her. Instead, I just went about my usual routine during my off-time while Willow tagged along. Some teachers might have treated her differently and refused to give her any special attention. But my own tragic past made me empathize with Willow and her situation.

After speaking further with Elizabeth, I learned that Willow's mother had been murdered right before her eyes. She had then come to live with her father, meeting him for the first time. Considering only a few months had passed, Willow was still desperately trying to acclimate herself to her new life. It would have been hard on an adult, but a five-year-old? It was almost impossible.

I was brought out of my thoughts by one of my students wiggling in his seat. "Miss Evans, can we go to the mat now?"

Laughing at his excitement, I nodded. "All right, let's go work on the calendar."

That afternoon, after I escorted all the second-load kids out to the bus lanes, I came back inside and went straight to my computer. Once I logged into the attendance program, I went to Willow's name. Grabbing an apple-shaped notepad, I jotted down her address. I didn't even bother with trying Elizabeth's contact information. I wanted to go straight to the source. If I couldn't reach her father by phone, then perhaps I was just going to have to track him down at his house.

I grabbed my messenger bag and purse and headed to my car. On the way, I typed the address into my GPS on my phone. It was another scorching late-September day in northern Georgia. The backs of my legs stung when I slid across the leather seat of my Accord.

After following the directions of the GPS's monotone voice, I turned a few blocks and found myself in one of the seedier areas of town. Even though I hadn't grown up here, Uncle Jimmy had made sure to always steer me clear of the area. He'd informed me that when the cotton mills had gone out of business in the late eighties, the area had rapidly declined. Crime rates had risen with the unemployment, and it was now inhabited by transient workers and the local motorcycle gang that I had seen from time to time on the road.

When I pulled up to a gun store and pawnshop, I glanced down at my phone to double-check that this was actually Willow's address. Then I grabbed the Post-it note out of my purse to make sure I hadn't entered it into my phone wrong. I couldn't help feeling surprised that I was in the right place. Peering through the windshield, I could see that a shop had been made out of part of the old cotton mill. Next to it was the old mill's office, which appeared to have been converted into some sort of roadhouse or bar.

Unease filled me the moment I shut the car door. Two men in biker boots and leather leaned against the wall of the pawnshop. With a forced determination, I pushed myself forward on shaky legs. As I approached the men, I could feel their heated gaze burning through me, singeing my cotton sundress as they stripped me down with their eyes. A shudder of repulsion ran through me, making me feel dirty and used.

When I met their hooded gazes, I plastered a smile on my lips. "Hello," I said softly. As I reached for the door of the pawnshop, one of the men stepped in front of me. I couldn't help jumping back, my hand flying to my mouth to stifle a scream. He cocked his brows at me as he held open the door like a proper gentleman.

Embarrassment flooded my cheeks at my over-the-top reaction. "Thank you. You're very kind," I said as I hesitantly squeezed past his body into the shop. My heels clacked along the floor, and I nervously fidgeted with the strap on my messenger bag. As I glanced left and right, I didn't see anyone behind the counter. "Hello?" I called.

A black curtain was shoved aside, and a tall, hulking man stepped out. Regardless of his enormous size, the kind expression on his very handsome face immediately put me at ease. "May I help you?"

Extending my hand, I said, "I'm Alexandra Evans. I'm looking for David Malloy."

Instead of shaking my hand, the man crossed his arms over his chest and cocked his head at me. "What do you need with him?"

Something about the man's guarded tone made me uneasy. "I . . . uh, his daughter, Willow, is in my kindergarten class. She's missed a lot of days of school, and I was worried."

My response seemed to appease the man, because his muscular

arms relaxed, and he finally offered me his hand. "I'm Nathaniel Malloy, Willow's uncle."

"Oh, it's nice to meet you."

"Same to you. Deacon—er, David—is actually at the clubhouse. I can take you there."

The thought of entering the roadhouse alone made my skin crawl, so I was very thankful that Nathaniel was offering to take me. After he came around the counter, he opened the door for me. "Tiny, keep an eye on the shop, okay?" he ordered to the tallest and biggest of the guys. A nervous giggle escaped my lips at the irony of the man's name.

As I walked next to Nathaniel, his towering presence somewhat overwhelmed me. He was all man, from his large hands and feet down to the musky smell that invaded my nose and messed with my senses. If I hadn't been so out of my element, I would have been very attracted to him, even though his faded jeans, tight black T-shirt, and arms covered in tattoos screamed bad boy. But even in the few moments I had been with him, I could tell there was much more to him. The way he carried himself was like a cultured gentleman, not a hard-core biker. "Willow doesn't say much, but I know she loves going to school."

"She's probably the brightest student in my class. Besides my attachment to her, I didn't want her falling behind after missing school. Considering her potential, I think she could easily skip to first grade at the halfway point in the year."

Nathaniel's blue eyes widened. "Really?"

I smiled. "Yes, really."

"Deacon and our mom will be really pleased to hear that."

"Who is Deacon?"

Nathaniel grinned. "That's David's nickname."

"Oh, I see."

A large pickup truck rumbled into the parking lot. When a

short, bald man got out of the cab, he waved a brown envelope in his hand. "Hey, Rev. Can you come here for a sec?"

"I'm busy. Get Tiny."

The man shook his head. "This packaging needs a Malloy signature on it."

Nathaniel gave a frustrated grunt. "Fine. I'll be right there."

When he turned to me, I gave him a slight smile. "Rev?"

He responded with a warm grin. "Just a nickname."

"For what?"

"Reverend."

My brows shot up in surprise. "Oh, are you a minister?"

He cocked his head teasingly at me. "Are you a teacher or a reporter?"

I laughed. "Forgive me, but I'm used to answering questions all day. I can't help but ask some myself."

"Well, Miss . . . I'm sorry. What was your last name again?"

"Evans."

"No, Miss Evans. I'm not a real reverend."

"Then how did you get the nickname?"

"Yo, Rev!" the man from the truck called impatiently.

With a grimace, Nathaniel/Rev shook his head. "Listen, I have to take care of this. Just go on inside, and I'll be there in a minute."

Inwardly, I groaned. I didn't want to go into the roadhouse alone. I would have much preferred having Rev by my side. But when he started walking away from me, I realized I'd better head inside and out of the oppressive heat, despite feeling out of my element. As I entered the room, I took a deep breath to try to still my out-of-control nerves. Smoke hung heavy in the air, stinging my eyes and causing me to cough. Several men in leather biker cuts lounged on stools at the bar, nursing beers. Across from me, a heated pool game was taking place.

I took a few steps inside and then froze. "Are you lost, darlin'?" a big-busted woman in a halter top asked.

"Uh . . . I'm looking for David Malloy," I said.

Two men at the pool table whirled around. The shorter of the two, a tough but cute-looking blond, cocked his head curiously at me. But the moment my gaze locked on the other man, I knew he was Willow's father. They had the same dark hair, soulful dark eyes, and heart-shaped face. David, however, had dark scruff covering his face. Although he was Rev's brother, I didn't see any resemblance between the two. Although he was shorter and slightly less built, David was just as good-looking as Rev. "Mr. Malloy?" I questioned, closing the distance between us.

He tossed the pool stick on the table and took a long drag on his cigarette, then stubbed it out in an ashtray on the table. "What do you want?" he demanded.

I didn't need to glance around the room to know that every eye in the place was on us. "I really need to speak with you for a moment."

His dark eyes narrowed as they raked over my body. The next thing I knew, he leaped at me, knocking me back into the wall. One of his hands came to grip my throat while his body pinned me in place. Fear like I had never known overwhelmed me, sending my heartbeat drumming wildly in my ears. It was so loud it felt like a cannon blast going off around me. "Please," I murmured.

David glared at me as his thumb pressed harder into my throat. "They're really falling down on their job at the academy."

"E-excuse m-me?" I stammered.

With a smirk, he replied, "Don't they train you ATF bitches to hide your fear a little better? I mean, you're practically pissing your pants right now, not to mention your heart is beating ninety to nothing."

I shook my head slowly back and forth as I tried processing his words. "ATF? I don't understand."

He rolled his eyes. "A white-bread piece of ass comes waltzing into my clubhouse, wanting to talk to me alone. It doesn't take a fucking genius to realize you're a Fed."

A Fed? It took me a moment to process what he meant. Holy shit. He thought I worked for the government as an agent of some sort. Quickly, I replied, "No, I'm not."

A voice came from behind him. "Deacon, man, you're gonna get your ass jacked up even further for this."

Glancing over his shoulder, Deacon said to the young, blond-haired man, "Stay out of this, Bishop."

Bishop held up his hands. "Fine. It's your fucking funeral."

David's hand slid down my throat to the buttons on my dress. Glancing over his shoulder at the others, he questioned, "What do you bet she's wired up under her tits?"

When his hands started to rip open my dress, I couldn't hold back my scream. "No, stop! I'm not who you think I am. I swear!" I protested.

"Then just who the hell are you?" he demanded.

Before I could answer, a tiny voice came from behind us. "Miss Alex?"

The sound of Willow's voice caused David to release his hold on my dress, but his body still kept me pinned to the wall. At that same moment, Rev entered the clubhouse. When he saw me, his eyes bulged, and he broke into a run to reach us. Grabbing David's shoulders, he slung him away from me. "For fuck's sake, Deacon, what the hell are you doing?"

"I'm giving this undercover ATF bitch what she deserves," Deacon spat, taking a step back toward me.

"Christ, she's not ATF," Rev countered.

"Oh, then who the hell is she?"

"She's my teacher . . . and my friend," Willow answered in a small voice.

David, or Deacon, stared openmouthed from me to Willow. "I think that's the most I've heard you say since you got here."

Willow didn't respond to him. Instead, she came bounding over to me and threw her arms around my waist. "I've missed you, Miss Alex."

Leaning over, I kissed the top of her head. "I've missed you, too, sweetheart. I've been worried about you since you haven't been in school."

She gazed up at me, her lips pulling into a frown. "Deacon says I need to stay close to home because someone wants to hurt me." Clinging to me tighter, she whispered, "I think it's Mean Man."

I squeezed her tight. No child her age should have to go through all she had, not to mention what she seemed to be still experiencing with her new life. I knew through her grandmother that she was in outside therapy twice a week, along with the daily check-ins she did with our school psychologist. It was almost miraculous the strides she was making.

As I swayed her back and forth in my arms, I couldn't help wondering exactly how she fit into the biker world. Her father sure hadn't been what I was expecting. I'd expected someone negligent, not the surly, aggressive man who had greeted me so forcefully. How was it possible he cared for Willow? He didn't seem to have a tenderhearted bone in his body, and Willow so desperately needed tenderness in her life.

Wanting to cheer her up, I plastered a smile on my face. "I have some things for you."

"You do?" she asked, her dark eyes dancing with excitement.

Nodding, I bent down to pick up my bag where it had fallen during my scuffle with Deacon. I pulled out the card I'd had the other children make, along with some of the small art projects she had missed. "Everyone in your class is missing you. I didn't want you to get behind, so I brought some of the work you've missed. Why don't you go start on some of it while I talk to your daddy?"

She grinned. "Okay."

The busty woman held out her hand, and Willow happily took it. When they took a seat at the bar across the room from us, I exhaled a long breath. Willow's world seemed too overwhelming. "Mr. Malloy, we need to talk."

Deacon ran his hand through his thick, dark hair. "I don't know what to say."

"How about starting with 'sorry,' you asshole?" Rev suggested, glowering at him.

Deacon stared at me intently as if he were seeing me for the first time. "I'm sorry. I really thought you were someone else."

After smoothing down my dress where it had been manhandled by Deacon, I tried gathering my wits. No matter how hard I tried, I couldn't seem to form any coherent thoughts. With Willow, I was in my element and could easily find the right words to say. Her father was a different story. "Do you often welcome strangers by manhandling them?" I asked.

His brows rose at my words and tone. "I'm sorry that I mistook you for an ATF agent." He gestured to me. "It's not like we see your kind around here a lot unless they're a Fed and looking for an angle."

"I don't think I even want to ask why a simple bar and pawnshop would raise the attention of federal agents."

"No, babe, you don't."

I had to bite my tongue to keep from telling him to stop calling me something so sexist. At the same time as I was enraged by his behavior, goose bumps of attraction rose along my arms. I couldn't believe I was slightly turned on by this asshole.

He motioned me to follow him with a flick of his hand. "Come on."

After exchanging a glance with Rev, I reluctantly followed Deacon into a room to the left of the bar. When he shut the door behind us, I couldn't help jumping at the sound. A slow smirk curved across his lips. "Do I make you nervous?"

Licking my dry lips, I replied, "Just a little."

"What about Rev? Does he make you nervous?"

I shook my head. "No, he doesn't."

Deacon crossed his arms over his chest. "And why is that?"

"Regardless of his size, there is a kindness about him. Plus, he came to my rescue back there." Jerking my chin up, I said, "I couldn't imagine him ever hurting anyone."

A grin slunk across Deacon's face. "So naive, aren't you, babe?"

"It's *Miss Evans*." I took a step back from him. "Did you have a point in bringing me in here besides giving me a hard time?"

"I brought you in here so we could talk about my daughter in private." He then strode past me. After pulling out one of the chairs at a long table, he gestured for me to take a seat. Reluctantly, I walked over and eased down onto the plush leather. Instead of sitting beside me, he walked over to take the seat across from me. After he leaned back in his chair, he pursed his lips at me. "So talk."

"I'm very concerned that Willow has missed almost a week of school. She's far too bright not to be in class. I see now that she isn't sick." Leaning forward with my elbows on the table, I asked, "What is this about you keeping her out because it isn't safe?"

Deacon's expression darkened. "That's none of your fucking business."

"You may not think so, but I'm sure CPS might see things differently."

"Are you threatening me, Miss Evans?" he questioned. The harshness of his tone, coupled with his slightly menacing expression, made me burrow deeper into the chair to try to escape him.

"I—I'm just stating facts, Mr. Malloy," I replied, my voice cracking from nerves.

He shook his head. "You have a lot of fucking nerve, coming into my club and trying to run my life."

"That's not what I'm doing at all. I just want what is best for Willow."

"I think as her father I know what is best for her," he countered.

"With all due respect, you've only been her father for a few months."

Deacon shot out of his chair. "Get out!"

Even though my legs shook with fear, I held my ground. "No."

"Excuse me?"

"I said no," I whispered.

Deacon's dark eyes widened. "Would you prefer me to throw you out?"

When he started around the table, I held up my hand. "Please, just listen to me for a minute." He froze and stared expectantly at me. "Regardless of whatever dangers there are in your world or whether you're suitable to be a parent, I don't think that Willow should be taken away from you. She's been through too much trauma to be taken from those she loves. I can tell she's happy here . . . that she's loved here."

He cocked his brows questioningly at me. "You mean that?"

"Yes, I really do."

"Then why are you on my ass, woman?" he demanded.

A nervous laugh bubbled from my lips. "I'm sorry, but I have to look out for what is best for my students. I'm sure you think that what you're doing is the right thing to protect Willow, but she needs to be in school. She needs the interaction with other children. She thrives when she is in school." At Deacon's eye roll, I pressed on. "Did you know I'm recommending her to be placed in the first grade in December?"

"Is she too much of a problem for you?" he snapped sarcastically.

"Willow is *never* a problem to me. If I was totally honest, she's my favorite. I'll be devastated to lose her."

Deacon's expression lightened a little. "So what, she's really smart or something?"

"Yes. She's a very bright and capable student. She grasps concepts quicker than my other students. I think she'll excel at being challenged in the first grade rather than having to stay in kindergarten."

As he weighed my words, Deacon's hand came up to rub the hair along his chin. "I don't know what to say. I had no idea she was so smart." With a wry grin, he said, "I sure as hell don't know where she gets it from."

"I'm sure she gets a little from you and from her late mother."

The mention of Willow's mother sent a scowl across Deacon's face. "Look, you're an outsider, so I'm not going to tell you all of my business. But hear me when I say that I'm not comfortable letting Willow out of my sight right now. She needs to be here in the compound, where I know she's safe."

"Someone is threatening to hurt her?"

"Some people want to hurt me, and they'll use whatever means necessary to get to me, including hurting my kid."

I sucked in a harsh breath at the thought of anyone hurting sweet Willow. While I didn't agree with Deacon's world, I had to give him credit for trying, in his own misguided way, to keep his daughter safe. There had to be some solution to the problem.

As if he had read my mind, Deacon came around the table and sat beside me. "Is there some way to hire a tutor or something? You know, someone who could come here and teach Willow? Then you and the authorities could get off my back."

Over the years, I'd had a couple of students have to go on homebound services for lengthy illnesses. I'd been more than happy to go teach them after school. Besides the occasional relationship or get-together with friends, I didn't have much going on outside of my classroom. There was no husband to be home for, no dinner to get on the table at a certain time, and sadly, no kids to take care of. Besides my brother and aunt and uncle, I was pretty much on my own. My students were my life.

"I could do it—I could come after school to teach Willow."

Deacon eyed me with a skeptical expression. "You'd really be okay with that?"

"Sure. I'd love to teach her." Nibbling on my lip, I contemplated what needed to be done logistically to make that happen. "Since she isn't sick or suffering from an injury, she wouldn't qualify for homebound services from the county."

Deacon's brows creased. "What does that mean?"

"It just means my salary wouldn't be covered. You would have to pay out-of-pocket."

A gleam burned in his eyes. "I know I might look like a low-life biker, but I can assure you I can provide financially for whatever Willow needs."

My cheeks flushed with embarrassment, and I quickly ducked my head. "I apologize if I offended you. I certainly wasn't implying anything. I was just trying to work this all out in my head." After drawing in a deep breath to calm my nerves, I barreled on. "I've done homebound services before, so I know what all it entails. It also makes sense for me to do it since I would know exactly what Willow would be doing if she were in the classroom." Leaning forward in my chair, I jerked my head up to give him a tentative smile. "If you're not sold on me, I could recommend someone else for the job. But I can't imagine Willow being comfortable with just anyone."

"No, she wouldn't. And for some reason, she's really taken a serious fucking liking to you."

"I assume that was a compliment?"

The corners of Deacon's lips quirked. "Yeah, it was a compliment. Willow doesn't interact with anyone outside our club. And even though she's spoiled fucking rotten here, she doesn't react half as much with us as she did out there with you." He shook his head. "And, man, the fact she was talking, too."

"I'm glad she's bonded with me. I care about her very much."

"Enough to come here to this hellhole every afternoon?"

I nodded. "Yes. That much."

Deacon rose out of his chair. Thrusting his hand at me, he said, "Well, I guess you have yourself a job, Miss Evans."

Rising up to meet him, I let him take my hand in his. "I accept, Mr. Malloy."

"Then let's go tell Willow the happy news."

As I followed him to the door, I could never have imagined in that moment how being a part of Deacon and Willow's world was going to change my life.

THREE

DEACON

"That's it. Give me your best, you pussy!" I antagonized, dodging the punches that whirled at my head. Adrenaline thrummed through my veins, pumping energy through my arms and legs. No drug or drink ever got me as high as fighting. I dug the feel of my fists connecting with the hard bone of the jaw or the soft flesh of the abdomen as things escalated quickly into a whirlwind of hits.

My boots dragged across the canvas of the boxing ring as I made quick footwork. They didn't make the best choice for sparring, but when I had come down to the Raiders Gym to check on business, I hadn't expected to fill in as the chief second, or the head trainer, for Bishop.

While I'd learned to use my fists to survive on the streets, Bishop had honed his fighting skills in the ring. Before the Raiders bought the gym, Preacher Man had often brought us here to work off steam. It wasn't long before Bishop was knocking out seasoned fighters. He'd won several division titles and probably could have gone pro, but the higher he rose in the sport, the more people wanted to stick their nose into his private life—primarily the club.

To the average onlooker, the gym, with its boxing and martial-arts training, looked legitimate, but it was all a front. For the club, it was a way to manage interstate gambling on fights and races. Bishop didn't want to do anything that would bring heat down on the club, so he continued boxing in the lower divisions.

Even as stealthily as Bishop moved across the floor, deflecting my hits and throwing his own back at me, I could tell he was off his usual game. "This is turning into quite a walkover, little bro."

"Easy fight, my ass! You're panting and in a sweat," Bishop challenged.

"These jeans and boots aren't exactly lightweight."

Bobbing and weaving in front of me like a cobra, Bishop anticipated my next move. When I remained still, he shrugged. "I just had a late night—that's all."

"Dumbass, you know better than to bang club whores the night before a major training day."

"I wasn't."

"Then what kept you up?" I asked.

He dodged my unexpected jab and flashed me a wicked smile. "Guess you could say I'm hot for the teacher. I kept jerking off to Miss Evans."

I froze on the spot. "What the fuck did you just say?"

Bishop's laugh echoed around us. "Yeah, I'm man enough to admit I was jerking off rather than fucking some club whore ass." When I continued staring at him, Bishop stopped hopping around. "Come on, bro. After you've seen a fine, white-bread piece of ass like that, it's hard to take some sloppy seconds to your bed. I mean, I only got to see her for, like, five minutes, but you had your hands all over her." He closed his eyes. "Can you imagine how fucking tight she would be?"

I threw a hard right hook to his jaw before I could stop myself. Bishop staggered back. Shaking his head, he rubbed his gloved hand along his reddened jaw. "Deacon, what the fuck, man?" he demanded.

"Don't be talking like that about Willow's teacher."

"Well, I sure wouldn't do it in front of her, but I thought you and I were on the same page when it came to pussy."

Shaking my head, I growled, "Not about hers."

Bishop leaned back against the ropes. "Are you trying to tell me you don't think she's hot as fuck?"

I closed the distance between us to where I was once again up in his face. "You got a hearing problem, little brother? I said don't talk about *her* like *that*." Shoving him, I said, "You got another thing coming if you think you're going to turn on your sweet-boy charm to try and tap her ass. She's fucking off-limits. Got it?"

Bishop's blue eyes widened. "Oh yeah, I think I got it." He stood toe to toe with me. "I get it loud and clear. But maybe next time you should piss on her leg to mark her as yours."

I threw my head back and laughed. "That ain't it."

"You sure? 'Cause I sure ain't never seen you get this fucking twitchy over someone sniffing around Cheyenne."

My teeth ground together in frustration. "Doesn't the old adage 'don't shit where you eat' mean anything to you?"

"Suppose so."

"For reasons I don't even begin to fucking understand, that Miss Evans means a hell of a lot to Willow. If she gets scared off because some douche bag uses her, then that hurts Willow. Not to mention the fact that this bitch has me by the balls with CPS."

Bishop processed my words. "Okay, okay. I'll keep Miss Evans for my spank bank."

Rolling my eyes, I cuffed the back of his head. "You're a disgusting fuck."

Just as we were about to start running through a few more combinations, Archer, one of the prospects, came sprinting up to the ring. "Prez just called an emergency church meeting. Wants you guys there in ten minutes," he said, his words coming in wheezing pants from his exertion.

Snatching off the sparring mitts, I pushed away the feeling of overwhelming foreboding and hustled over to the ropes with Bishop on my heels. We slid underneath them and then hopped down. I thumped Archer on the back before heading outside to my waiting bike. I cut the usual ten-minute drive to the clubhouse into five. Bishop, followed by Archer, stayed on my tail.

When I threw open the clubhouse door, I found the inside as silent as a tomb. None of the usual retirees were lounging around the bar, throwing back beers. The pool table balls were racked and ready to go, but no one was around to play. Prez must've put the word out that we were not to be disturbed.

Off to the side of the main meeting area was the room where we held church—the name for our club meetings. When Bishop and I ducked inside, we found the others already assembled. Our meeting table was a true throwback to the old cotton-mill days. Most of the business decisions by the former cotton barons had been made around it when it was in the boardroom. Now we used it for slightly less than honorable business dealings.

My still-sweat-soaked ass slid across the plush, leather-seated chair. My old man had insisted on spending a pretty penny on the chairs. "I ain't scrimping on some piece of shit that breaks your back and pinches your nutsack. I don't want anyone squirming around during church. Your attention should be fucking focused on the club and only the club," he'd said. A smile tugged at my lips at the memory.

At the head of the table sat our grim-faced president, Caisson, or Case, for short. His shrapnel-scarred neck, arms, and legs told some of the story of how he'd gotten his road name. He'd done two tours in Vietnam as part of the Third Infantry Division. It was on his second tour that the caisson he was manning got hit and almost killed him. As army proud as he was, it was only fitting he take a name associated with his service.

He and Preacher Man had been part of the original charter members of the Georgia chapter of the Hells Raiders. They were barely twenty when they'd patched in. And even after Preach went AWOL on the MC lifestyle for many years, Case demanded that Preach take over the presidency of the Raiders when he returned. "Ain't nobody better to lead than Preacher Man," he had said.

He once again had to take over for his best friend when Preacher Man was killed. I loved my old man, but I also loved Case. At his right was the new vice president—Rev. Leaning forward in his chair, he rapped his fingers over the hardback cover of the latest book he was reading. Rev constantly battled the angel and devil on his shoulder. If he'd been born to another father, I'm sure he would have ended up a doctor or lawyer or in some fancy shit profession like that. He sure as hell had the brains. He'd even used the money from his service with Uncle Sam to get a two-year degree from the community college. In the end, the pull of our world was too much for him, especially for his loyalty. For Rev, his tender heart was both his salvation and his undoing. All the best of Mama Beth had gone into Rev, but it was often overshadowed by Preacher Man's dominating DNA.

Barry "Boone" Michaels, our treasurer, sat across from me at the table, twirling a skull-and-crossbones cigarette lighter between his fingers. He was just a few years older than me, although his salt-and-pepper hair and beard made him appear even older. We'd both gone through our prospecting period together, and we'd been patched in the same night. He liked to give me shit that as the president's son, I'd had it a lot easier. The truth was Preacher Man had them go twice as hard on me to prove my worth. He wasn't going to let any son of his get by just on who he was.

Next to Boone sat our secretary, Steve "Mac" McDonald. His tattooed hand sat poised over a notepad, ready to document everything that happened. He was forty-five. He'd patched into the Raiders twenty years ago. He was a good bridge between the two distinct generations in the club.

A tense silence choked off the air in the room. Something heavier than we had faced in a long time had gone down or was about to go down. Unable to stand the quiet any longer, I demanded, "So what's shaking, Prez?"

Case shifted in his seat like he was physically affected by the news he had. "Nordic Knights are stirring shit. Again."

A low, united growl came from all my brothers. It was an unwritten rule that clubs would have beef with one another from time to time over territory disputes and business dealings. But there was no club we despised more than the Nordic Knights. Regardless of all the alliances we had made with other clubs, we would never have peace with the Knights. There was too much bad blood between us.

"What are those bastards up to now?" Boone asked.

"We heard this from one of our insiders in the Atlanta PD. It seems the Feds reopened a case on the Knights. There was a big drug shake-up four months ago. An informant had brought them lots of information about the inner workings of the Knights drug ring in trade for immunity." Case paused to run a hand over his salt-and-pepper beard. I sucked in a harsh breath because it was one of the tics he had before unloading some really heavy shit on us. His gaze cut over to mine. "This informant had been playing as a courier for her boyfriend, Jamey Ericson, one of the Knights. Before she could testify in court, she and Jamey were murdered execution style in their apartment."

As the pieces of the puzzle slowly fit together, all the breath left my body, and I momentarily wheezed before I could speak. "Lacey."

"Yes."

"Jesus, what was she thinking?" I murmured. Since the day Willow had been brought to my door, I'd been searching for information about who could have killed Lacey. I knew she had been involved in some deep shit, considering how no one connected to her would talk, regardless of the amount of money I offered them. The person closest to her, Willow, sure as hell wasn't talking, and even if she could, she was too young to understand who the people were in her mother's world. In the end, I'd been led to believe it was a drug deal gone bad—she or her boyfriend hadn't coughed up the money they owed.

"Deacon, there's more," Case said.

"More than finding out the mother of my child took up with some Knights scum and then turned rat?"

Rev shook his head. "Maybe she needed immunity to stay out of jail for Willow's sake."

"Knowing Lacey, I have a hard time believing she was thinking of anyone but herself," I argued. Feeling Case's intense gaze on me, I glanced from Rev to him. "What?"

"He said there were a lot of mentions of a guy named 'Seagal.' "

I bolted forward in my chair as Rev sucked in a harsh breath. "He just overheard all this shit, right? What if what he's hearing as Seagal is really *Sigel*?" Rev asked.

Case grimaced. "Yeah, it is. He's out. Been out for five months for copping a deal."

"How the fuck are we just now hearing he's out? I thought we had eyes and ears all over the jailhouse," Bishop demanded.

A tense silence fell over the table. Just the mention of the name "Sigel" hit me, Rev, and Bishop especially hard. Frederich "Freddy" Spears, or Sigel, as he called himself now, was the president of the

Nordic Knights. Sigel gave the Raiders far too many fucking reasons to want him six feet under. There was the racist bullshit he spewed about being the son of an actual former Nazi soldier, but there was also the fact he was once one of our own.

Of course, he was just Freddy back then. Most of the time he was known as Fucked-Up Freddy because of his heroin addiction. Like the legendary Hells Angels, the Raiders had a bylaw about no needles in the club. You might snort crank or smoke some crack, but shooting up rained a whole different type of shit down on you and your brothers.

Preacher Man tried to intervene to help Freddy, but he finally had to kick him out of the club and take his cut. It wasn't too long before Freddy adopted a new road name, Sigel, after some sun bullshit in German mythology. It was a nod to his ties with the Aryan Brotherhood. He then formed his own club, the Nordic Knights, and did everything he could to fuck with us, including trying to move drugs in our territory. Regardless of some of our less-than-legal business dealings, we never dealt in drugs or women. Preacher Man worked tirelessly to push Sigel and his Knights out of Raiders territory.

Our true hatred of Sigel came from the fact he had our father's blood on his hands. And not metaphorically from some hit he'd put out. He'd pumped Preacher Man full of holes at point-blank range when the two were meeting under a truce flag. My fists curled in rage as I remembered cradling my father's dying body. As his sergeant, I had gone with him to the meeting.

Growing up on the streets had hardened me to where the death of a man could be swatted from your memory the same way as ridding an annoying fly from your face. The quicker you desensitized yourself, the better. I'd witnessed all manner of ugly deaths—torture scenes with bodies flayed open like cadavers on a med-school table, the charred, blackened flesh of burned bodies, the cross still wrapped around the neck of a decapitated head that had been blown off in a car bomb.

But no matter how hard you've worked to turn yourself off, nothing compares to the death of someone you love—someone who was your savior. Those emotions you've buried so fucking deep in the ground come bursting out of their grave like it's the Second Coming. In a way it is—it's the Armageddon of your soul. As the emotional torment claws at your skin, you wish for your own death. Anything would be better than the agony consuming you. If only you could find atonement by switching places—their life for your own. But instead, you find an emotional immortality that places you in a private hell on earth.

Almost three years had passed since the night we'd lost Preacher Man. I'd tried to put as much space and distance as I could between me and the memories that haunted me in the dead of night, the ones that woke me in a fit of screaming and clawing at the sheets. But just hearing the name Nordic Knights ricocheted me from the present back into that night. Like a movie reel on repeat, I watched Preacher Man's body contort as the bullets entered his chest and gut. I'd made it to his side just in time to grab his collapsing body before it hit the grimy pavement.

I shook my head to try to rid myself of the memories. But no matter how hard I tried, the harsh, metallic smell of blood entered my nose. My hands tightened on the armrests of the chair—the muscles felt stretched and weighed down the same as that night. Like a flash of lightning cutting across the night sky, I was once again back in that alley with my father dying before my eyes.

I'd struggled to keep my hold on him as the blood, mixed with pieces of flesh and intestines, made him slippery. Each time I tried to get a better hold on him, he screamed from the pain. Finally, we had gone down on the pavement together. Flailing, I had scrambled to my knees, cradling Preach's head in my lap. Trying to channel my fear, I'd focused my eyes on Preach's. The acceptance in his gaze told me that death was close. All the words of gratitude and love that I wanted to express wouldn't come from my mouth, no matter how hard I tried to speak.

As if he sensed my turmoil, Preacher Man brought a trembling, blood-soaked hand to my cheek. "I know, son," he wheezed. And then he said something on his dying breath that I still longed to understand. "Angels . . . beautiful angels with dark hair are coming for you. They are your only salvation."

With his eyes fixed above us on the sky, he exhaled a long, painful breath. And then he was gone. The realization lit every molecule in my body on fire like flipping the switch on the electric chair. I shot off the pavement with my arms and legs twitching with rage and resentment. As I lunged for the man who had taken my father's life, a gun's muzzle met me in the face.

"My beef was with your pops. Bad blood from years past. You get to live. For tonight, at least."

"You might as well end me right now, motherfucker. 'Cause if you let me walk away, I'll rain a fucking firestorm down on you!"

A smile had curled at his lips. "I'd love to see you try. When morning comes and word spreads how I took down Preacher Man without a fight, you and your Raiders won't have a fucking ally anywhere. Me and the Knights will run you into the ground."

When I had lunged at him, the barrel of the gun smashed across my cheek, breaking my nose. As tears blinded my eyes from the hit and blood poured down my face, I'd been forced to watch as Sigel had spat on Preacher Man's body.

But what Sigel couldn't have imagined, nor any of us Raiders, was that Preacher Man had been two steps ahead of him. All of our allies stayed firmly in place based on last-minute peace offerings Preacher Man had made. The greatest of his last-hour deals included cashing in a favor owed by one of the Atlanta PD—a somewhat-crooked cop who was willing to falsify a warrant that took the drug task force straight to Sigel's door. With his arrest history, he would be behind bars for at least five to ten, and I would be forced to sit on any revenge plans. Sure, I could've put out a hit for Sigel's throat to be slit or for him to be shanked. But I wanted full-on justice, an eye for an eye, with his blood on my own two hands.

By hiding his brokered deals, Preacher Man had gone against all the charter rules that forced a vote by the officers. Like a sacrificial lamb to the slaughter, he had selflessly worked to ensure the safety of the club, even if all along it was going to cost him his life. Deep down, I knew that he had instigated Sigel's imprisonment to keep me from any revenge that would come from his probable death. He must've feared I would be killed or imprisoned and wanted to protect me. He never would have fathomed my next move.

"Deacon," a voice implored, jerking me out of the past and into the present.

"What?" I croaked. Staring down at my hands, I thought of a movie Rev had made me watch. Some bullshit Shakespeare stuff that I had slept through back in high school. Like the deranged chick, I rubbed my hands furiously together, trying not to see the blood I imagined on them—the blood of Sigel's only son.

The son I had strung up and then proceeded to torture like something out of medieval times. The son who bore the wrath of the bottomless quicksand of grief for Preacher Man that I found myself trapped in. The son I'd left to bleed out on his apartment floor after I did a final act of degradation—I stripped him of his cut and took it with me.

Over the years, I'm sure Preacher Man and Case had rendered the same kind of revenge as I did. I'm not sure if they outdid my level of violence. Grief can bring a man who refuses to acknowledge emotion to his knees. It warps you into a shadow of your former self. It manipulates you into succumbing to the mental anguish you try so hard to escape from. It makes an emotional cripple out of even the strongest man around.

That was the intensity of my loss for Preacher Man. Salvation out of hell was rarely granted, but Preacher Man had been mine. So far I'd lived three lifetimes—the life before Preacher Man and the Raiders, my life with him, and now my life without him.

What I didn't want to acknowledge then or now was that the grief I had brought to Sigel would have a price. He'd left me alive once, but when he was free, would he do it again? Now that he was out, I was staring down the barrel of a gun.

The deep baritone of Case's voice once again dragged me from my thoughts. "Sigel killed Lacey," he said.

"Did he know who she was?"

Case shook his head. Then with a grimace, he added, "But he knows who Willow is."

My heart twisted as if a giant's hands had clenched around it. "He's the threat."

What I hadn't told the nosy-ass Miss Evans was a week ago I'd received a package. Within it were pictures of Willow on the school playground, eating lunch in the cafeteria, and skipping out to Mama Beth's car. While there had been no note, the message was clear—someone was after my daughter. That's when I had put Willow on lockdown within the compound. She didn't go anywhere outside, and even when she was inside, a prospect was on her ass every moment.

Never in my wildest dreams could I have imagined Sigel was behind it. But now that I knew who it was and his involvement in Lacey's murder, the why wasn't adding up. Not from Willow herself, but from the school psychologist, we knew what Willow had seen. She'd drawn pictures with a "Mean Man" who had hurt her mommy. She had been within Sigel's reach of revenge, yet he'd let her go. I didn't understand.

As if he sensed my confusion, Rev said, "He let her live because he realized you didn't know anything about her." When I flicked my gaze to his, Rev sighed raggedly. "He wanted to wait until you could have feelings for her. Then it could be personal."

"Motherfucker," Bishop muttered.

The knowledge of what Sigel intended sent jagged pain through my chest the same as if he were standing over me and stabbing me. The calculating bastard was fucking with me from a distance, just waiting until the time was right to strike. "If Sigel's truly using Willow to get to me, it could be months, even a year, before he and the Knights come at us." I glanced around the table at my brothers. "The more time that passes, the more I can get attached to Willow. Then the greater the revenge."

"Sigel has never struck me as a patient guy. He bided enough time waiting to get to you when he was in jail," Mac argued.

"But he didn't know about Willow then," I replied.

"I don't think he intends to stop with her," Rev said.

I jerked my chin in agreement. "No. I'm sure after what I did, he won't be satisfied until he puts me in the ground."

"These aren't some racist upstarts anymore. My informant says that the Knights have been stockpiling weapons. To help the prosecutor, the Feds have been allowing the purchases," Case said.

"So what do we do? Smoke them before they can smoke us?" Bishop questioned.

Mac shook his head. "With the Feds breathing down the Knights' necks, we'd be offering ourselves up on a silver platter. Any way we could fuck them up is just going to fuck us over worse in the end."

"If we're supposed to be worried about the Feds, then that would mean the Knights would have to be, too. I don't see Sigel giving two shits about jail time. When it comes to revenge, he'll take the risk," Boone argued.

"As long as Sigel breathes, both Willow and Deacon are in danger." Surprisingly, it was Rev who'd spoken. The implication of his words was clear, which went against his usually nonviolent nature. But when it came to the lives of his brother and beloved niece, Rev wouldn't hesitate to break a commandment.

Lacing my fingers behind my head, I countered, "While I'm inclined to agree with you, Rev, we can't just play into his hand. He knows once word gets around that he's out, I'll be on edge, waiting for him to come after me for what I did to his son. He's banking on the fact that Willow hasn't talked or that I have no idea he's tied to Lacey. He's getting his rocks off on this little game he's playing."

We all glanced anxiously at Case, who continued stroking his beard in thought. "I say that for appearances, we play it cool—no going in after Sigel with guns blazing. But I want us to reach out to each and every one of our allies for added protection as well as any shit they can get us on the Knights. If we're lucky, the Feds will take the fuckers out long before we have to act. Sigel is one conviction away from life. If the right side of the law can put him away, we'll ensure he dies once he's inside."

"That addresses Sigel and the Knights, but what about Willow and Deacon?" Rev questioned.

I threw up one of my hands. "What about us?"

Ignoring me, Rev stared straight at Case. "I think Deacon should have an escort at all times he's outside the compound."

I groaned. "Come on, man. You're acting like I'm a marked man."

"You are," he growled.

"With our cuts, we're all marked men every moment of the day," I countered.

Slamming his fist down on the table, Case barked, "That's enough." Rev and I both eased back in our chairs. "I agree with

Rev. Until we can get a better handle on all this, you're not to leave the compound without an escort." Before I could protest, Case swept up his gavel and then banged it. "Meeting is adjourned."

When I started to rise out of my chair, Case shook his head. "You stay."

I knew the other guys were just as surprised as I was by his request. Reluctantly, I let my ass fall back in the seat. After the rest of the guys filed out of the room, I glanced expectantly at Case. "What's eating at you now, Prez?"

"I'm worried about this teacher."

My brows shot up in surprise. "With all the shit going on with the Knights, you're thinking about her?" When Case nodded, I asked, "You worried for her or for the club's safety?"

The flame from Case's lighter illuminated his face as he lit his pipe. After taking a few puffs, he replied, "She's an outsider."

"Yes, I'm aware of her status," I replied, digging in my pocket for my own smokes.

"Just having her here in the clubhouse or at your house is trouble waiting to happen."

I hastily lit a cigarette. As I inhaled sharply, I let the sweet nicotine sting fill my senses. "She's more trouble if we keep her out."

"I know. That's the only reason why I'm letting her in here. But my issue with her isn't just the fact that she could bring CPS sniffing around in here."

"What is it, then?"

He slid a manila folder over to me. "I had someone look into her background."

"Is it that serious?" I asked, flipping the folder open.

"If you consider the fact her uncle is a retired state trooper."

I grimaced as I glanced over the papers regarding Alexandra's life. Of all the teachers I could have had snooping around, I had to have one who was tied to the law. And this uncle wasn't just someone she saw on the holidays. He had become her guardian when she was seventeen and her parents died in a car accident.

"He's a lifer here in town, and so is his wife. It won't take long for him to put two and two together about who Alexandra is working for," Case said.

"Did he ever put any heat on us when he was active?"

"No, he didn't. He even collected toys from his fellow officers for our charity runs."

I flipped the folder shut. "Then I don't think he's going to be an issue."

"I hope not." Case took a thoughtful drag on his pipe. "She's a very beautiful woman."

I snorted. "Better not let Kim hear you say that. She'll have your balls on a platter."

Case grinned at the mention of his possessive wife. While there was amusement in his eyes, he still pinned me with a hard look. "Beautiful women like Alexandra are trouble for a man like you, Deacon."

"What the fuck is that supposed to mean?" I demanded, stubbing my cigarette out in the ashtray.

"It means a woman like her can get under your skin. She's smart, independent, and good-hearted. She loves your kid, and your kid loves her."

"Jesus, Case, you sound like an old woman."

"I'm trying to give you something to think about."

"Trust me when I say that regardless of how 'beautiful' Miss Evans is, I'll have no trouble keeping my dick in my pants around her."

Case shook his head. "It's not your dick I'm concerned about. It's your head and your heart."

Shaking my head, I said, "Jesus, man. When did you grow a fucking vagina and start talking out of your ass with head-and-heart bullshit? This is me we're talking about, Case. Not Rev."

"I am serious."

"I don't know what I should worry about more: Sigel or the fact that my club president thinks I'm going to let some white-bread piece of ass turn me soft."

"All I'm saying is just be careful. And for fuck's sake, don't say or do anything to piss her off. We need her on our side."

"Fine. Anything else?"

"She doesn't go anywhere in the compound without someone watching her. She doesn't need to be hunting for the john and accidentally stumble onto something she shouldn't. Got it?"

"I'll put the prospects on her."

I rose from my chair and patted Case's back on my way out of the room. I didn't know any other way to put the man at ease. I mean, he had nothing to worry about with Miss Alexandra Evans. The woman was beautiful, yeah—for sure—but that little sweet-ass chick and I were never going to tumble in any sheets. I'd stay away for the same reasons I'd warned Bishop away. I was far less concerned about her getting a rise out of my dick than I was about her making waves for the club.

FOUR

ALEXANDRA

As I made my way across the parking lot to my car, I couldn't fight off the butterflies I felt in my stomach. I had never been apprehensive about doing a homebound job before. It didn't take much to realize what it was about this job, or who it was, that made me anxious. While I might've been looking forward to working with Willow, I was most definitely not looking forward to seeing her father again. Sure, we had found some sort of middle ground a few days before, but David, or Deacon, didn't impress me as the kind of man who stayed on an even keel. Our first meeting had been both physically and emotionally volatile. I could only imagine that it wouldn't be long before we were coming to verbal blows again . . . maybe even physical ones—at least on his end.

Once I got to my car, I turned the radio to an upbeat song and tried desperately to ignore the voices of doubt in my head. Instead, I tried to focus on some of the visualization techniques my late mother had taught me. My father had jokingly called my mother "Mary Sunshine" for her ability to see the positive in even the hardest of situations. Instead of Deacon occupying my thoughts, I focused on Willow. She needed me, so I had to be strong for her.

When I pulled up outside the pawnshop, a nervous shudder ricocheted through my body at the sight of Deacon waiting on me. After quickly turning off the car, I grabbed my bag. With my eyes firmly on Deacon, I fumbled with the door handle for a few seconds before I was able to throw it open.

When I unceremoniously tripped on the uneven pavement, which sent me flying forward before I could right myself, the corners of Deacon's lips turned up with a teasing lilt. "Glad I can amuse you," I blurted before I could stop myself. I cringed as his dark eyes widened with surprise at my response.

"I'm glad to see you made it."

Jerking my chin up, I countered, "I'm not late. I told you I wouldn't be able to get here until three."

"No, Miss Evans, you're not late." He flashed me a wide smile. "I'm just glad to see you."

"You are?" I questioned, unable to hide my surprise. Was he implying what I thought he was? Was I going to have to set him straight that while flattered, we would only ever have a working relationship?

"Yeah. Willow's been pestering the hell out of me all day about when you would get here."

"Oh," I murmured.

The shit-eating grin that stretched across Deacon's face caused warmth to flood my cheeks. I stared down at the pavement, silently willing it to open up and swallow me and my embarrassment. Deacon's finger on my chin caused me to jump. "Don't worry your pretty little head about me coming on to you, Miss Evans."

"Thank you. I appreciate that," I murmured.

"But don't think it's because of something decent within my character. You're not my type."

I sputtered with indignation at his words. "That's good to hear since you're most certainly not my type either."

Deacon merely grinned. "You know, Rev told me to tread easy when it came to you. He thinks you're some delicate little flower I could crush. But he's wrong."

"Is that right?"

He nodded. "You're a tough little thing when you have to be."

"Life has done that to me," I replied before I could stop myself.

"Doesn't it to everyone?"

The tone of his words surprised me. I realized that within his statement there was insight into Deacon's own character. I couldn't help wondering what life had done to him. But I had the feeling I would come closer to unearthing a buried treasure in my backyard than learning Deacon's secrets.

"I appreciate you meeting me today." I stared pointedly at him. "I hope I'm not taking you away from your job."

"No, you're not."

"What is it that you do exactly?"

Motioning his hand to the pawnshop, Deacon curled his lips into a smirk. "I would think my profession as an entrepreneur would be evident."

"Yes, but it's the type of businesses that you own that concerns me. After all, Ed Wigington, who owns the tire shop, doesn't have to keep his son home from my class."

"I co-own the pawnshop with my brothers along with Raiders Gym downtown."

"That's the one where boxers and MMA fighters train."

"It is."

From my uncle Jimmy, I knew a hell of a lot more went on there than just training. Allegedly, it was the legitimate front for gambling on fights. Deacon must've been reading my mind because he said, "No, Miss Evans, it's not the type of place someone like you would frequent."

"So you don't deny the rumors that a lot of illegal stuff goes down there?"

With a teasing smile, he held up one hand. "I plead the Fifth."

"Why does that not surprise me?"

"Would it be so surprising if I told you that most of the up-standing citizens of this town have tainted reputations?"

"I'm not concerned with anyone's reputations other than yours at the moment and how that reputation affects Willow."

Deacon surprised me by suddenly closing the gap between us. My breath fell in harsh pants as he loomed over me. I fought the urge to take a step back. He cocked his brows at me. "Are you insinuating that I'm involved in shady dealings?"

"Maybe."

"I told you the other day not to stick your nose into my business."

"I'm not."

"Doesn't seem like it to me."

"I'm just concerned, that's all. Somehow I can't get it out of my mind that you're like a modern-day Jesse James."

Deacon's dark eyes shone with amusement. "You think I'm an outlaw?"

Shaking my head, I countered, "Oh, I know you're one."

"Kinda makes you hot, doesn't it?"

"Excuse me?" I demanded, taking a step back.

"Good girls always cream their panties over outlaws."

"You flatter yourself. I'm certainly not"—I gulped—"creaming my panties over you." Of course, the words were a blatant lie. The proximity of him, coupled with his words and his overpowering manly scent, caused moisture to dampen my panties. When he continued to stare at me like the Big Bad Wolf appraising his next meal, I shook my head. "I thought you said I didn't have to worry about you coming on to me. Not your type, remember?"

With a wink, Deacon replied, "Maybe I lied. I'm not known for being very trustworthy when it comes to women."

"Once again, that's not surprising."

"Although most of the girls down at the Lounge would give me glowing reviews." He flashed me a grin. "That would be the gentleman's club that my brothers and I own a stake in."

Knowing that he expected a rise out of me at the mention of strippers, I merely replied, "Aren't you the Donald Trump of Eastman?"

With a shake of his head, Deacon gave a bark of a laugh. "You know, I might actually be able to tolerate you, Miss Evans."

"The feeling is mutual, Jesse James," I replied.

He held open the clubhouse door for me. "Mmm, I love it when a chick gives me a nickname."

Ignoring him, I headed inside. It momentarily felt like returning to the scene of the crime after our altercation from the other day. With the jukebox blaring a heavy metal tune in my ears, I surveyed the much smaller crowd. "Are you planning on me teaching Willow here?" I asked, trying not to sound horrified. I couldn't imagine trying to teach phonetics over the music and the clanking of beer glasses.

Deacon laughed. "No, White-Bread. I don't expect you to work in the middle of all this bullshit."

"Thank you for being so considerate," I replied tersely. I chose to ignore the fact he had once again called me white-bread.

"Actually, it was my mother's idea. She thought it might be better if you guys had a place of your own to work. Some shit about making it seem more like real school. She made us fix up one of the guest rooms."

I bit back a smile at the words about his mother. It was

amusing thinking of any woman barking out orders and him scurrying around to obey her. But I was sure if there was any woman who could bark orders at Deacon, Beth Malloy was that woman, and I admired the hell out of her for it. "That should be fine."

Across the room from us, Willow sat at one of the round tables. She was swathed in a frilly pink boa, and a glittery pink tiara sat on her head. Seated with her were two young men in their late teens or early twenties who wore cuts similar to Deacon's. The table was set for a tea party. What caused me to do a double take was the fact that the two men also sported boas and tiaras. When they met my gaze, they both appeared to be in the seventh ring of hell.

Deacon chuckled at what must have been my bewildered expression. "They're prospects for the club, so they have to do whatever we order them to do."

"And today's order of business was a tea party?"

With a shrug, Deacon replied, "Willow wanted one."

Adjusting my bag on my shoulder, I eyed him. "But why aren't you playing with her?"

He shot me a look of absolute disbelief. "Why the fuck would I do that?"

"Because she's your daughter. Fathers often play with their daughters."

Deacon shifted uncomfortably on his feet. "I wouldn't even begin to know how to play with her."

"And you think those poor guys do?"

At that moment, Willow bounded over to us. "Miss Alex!" she squealed before throwing her arms around my waist. Mine and Deacon's conversation was forgotten with Willow's enthusiastic greeting.

"Hi, sweetheart. How are you?" I asked as I squeezed her back.

"Good. I've been waiting all day to see you. I finished all the work you left me."

"You did?" I asked with surprise. While some of the worksheets were review activities of what we had been doing, I'd never expected her to finish so fast.

"Uh-huh. I'll go get them."

As Willow sprinted away, Deacon shook his head. "You bring out the fucking chatterbox in her. I swear, she doesn't hardly say two words to me."

"Do you ever try talking to her?"

His brows drew together as he brought his hand up to scratch his neck. "Not really."

"Even if she doesn't talk to you, she's a very good listener."

"What the hell would I talk about with her?" he demanded, sweeping his hands to his hips. His usual scowl was back, and he looked at me like I had asked him to solve a difficult equation rather than something as simple as telling him to talk to his daughter.

"Tell her about when you were her age."

"Those aren't happy little stories to share, Miss Evans. I wouldn't want to give her nightmares."

The intensity of his stare, along with the tormented look in his eyes, caused me to look away. "I'm sure if you just sit down and try, the right words will come to you," I said softly.

"We'll see," he grumbled before stalking away. As I watched his retreating form, I couldn't help but wonder about all the demons he held within him. Willow interrupted my thoughts by skipping up to me with a handful of papers.

"Are you ready to see our classroom?" she asked.

"I'd love to."

With a squeal, she grabbed my hand and then dragged me across the room. We reached a long hallway that was filled with doors on both the right and left sides. When we got to the fourth on the right, she flung it open. "What do you think?"

I gazed around the room. There were two old desks in the middle—a larger one for me and a smaller one for Willow. I don't know how he had managed it, but Deacon had set up a whiteboard on an easel. There was even a multicolored rug on the floor for story time. I couldn't keep the smile off my face. "It's wonderful. Your daddy did a great job setting it up."

As Willow beamed at my praise, I motioned to her desk. "Now, I think it's time we got to work."

Two hours later found Willow finishing up on the last lesson of the day. I'd worked her hard, but she had enjoyed every minute of it. You never would have imagined she had missed any school at all. As I rose out of my chair, I smiled down at her. "Okay, then. School's over for today."

Her lips curved down in a pout. "But I'm not finished."

"We'll finish tomorrow."

"Okay," she reluctantly replied, rising out of her seat. She took my hand, and we started into the hallway. When we reached the last door on the right, mortification filled me at the unmistakable sounds of a couple having sex.

I glanced down at Willow in horror, but she merely smiled. "Uncle Bishop must be exercising again."

"Exercising?"

Willow nodded. "Deacon said whenever there's a lot of loud noises in the rooms, it's people exercising. Uncle Bishop exercises a lot."

I bit my lip to keep from laughing at Deacon's explanation. I had to hand it to him for coming up with a good explanation. I'm sure with the type of men and women Willow was around, there was a lot of "exercising."

When we started toward the back door, one of the prospects who had been at Willow's tea party stepped in front of the door, blocking the exit. "I'm just going to walk Willow home," I explained.

"It's my job to do that."

"But I want Miss Alex to," Willow protested.

"I don't think there's a reason why we both can't walk her home. Do you?"

He shook his blond head. "No, ma'am."

I extended my hand. "I'm Alexandra."

Hesitating, he glanced left and right before accepting my hand. "Archer."

"Nice to meet you."

"Likewise." He then stepped aside for us to go out the door. As Willow led me down the gravel pathway, Archer hung back, giving us our space. Willow jabbered about who lived in each of the simple houses. Of course, I had no idea who anyone in the club was. Apparently, Deacon and his brothers each had a house of their own, along with their mother.

"But we always eat together. Grandma says it's because the boys can't cook."

I laughed. "That's not too surprising."

Deacon's mother's house was at the end of the pathway. It sat in the middle of a small cul-de-sac. Multicolored flower beds brightened the front of the porch. I hurried to keep up with Willow, who dropped my hand and bounded up the stairs. When I got onto the porch, I turned around to see Archer at the bottom of the stairs. "Thanks for seeing us home," I said.

He smiled. "You're welcome."

"Come on, Miss Alex," Willow cried, grabbing my hand. She barreled through the front door, dragging me behind her. "Grandma, I'm home!" she called.

"I'm in the kitchen, sugar," a kind voice replied.

When she turned around, Beth jumped at the sight of me. The last time we had met was a month ago at the Meet and Greet. As her hand swept to her chest, she gave me an apologetic smile. "Oh, Miss Evans, I'm sorry. I wasn't expecting company."

"And I'm sorry for startling you. I just wanted to walk Willow home. I wasn't expecting to come in."

"Oh, but I'm glad you did."

We were interrupted by the back door banging open. Deacon appeared first, followed by Rev. I watched in surprise as another young man came in last, closing the door behind him. At the sight of me, a grin curved on his handsome face. "Well, well, I finally get to formally meet the famous Miss Evans."

Warmth filled my cheeks at his words and the way he was looking at me. The fiery intensity of his stare was burning the clothes right from my body, leaving me naked before him. "I'd hardly say I was famous," I argued.

"In the rug rat's eyes you are," he replied.

"What do you mean 'formally meet'?" I asked.

"Oh, I saw you at the clubhouse the first day you came. You know, when my asshole of a brother had you by the throat."

I gasped at the memory while Deacon slapped the guy on the back. "This is my youngest brother, Benjamin."

"That's Bishop, actually," the blond god corrected, throwing out his hand.

The moment our hands met, I suddenly remembered the sounds of sex and Willow's words about Uncle Bishop exercising. "Did you have a nice workout?" I blurted before I could think better of it.

His brows knitted in confusion. "Huh?"

"Never mind," I replied. When I met Deacon's eyes, amusement shone in them. Unlike his clueless brother, he knew exactly what I had heard and what Willow had told me. With my embarrassment growing, I knew I needed to get out of there. "Well, I guess I better head home."

"Stay for supper," Beth said.

"Oh, I appreciate the offer, but I can't."

"'Cause you got a man you gotta get back home to?" Bishop asked, sidestepping by me to head to the kitchen sink.

As he lathered up his hands, I could feel both Deacon and Rev's inquisitive gazes burning into me. "No, it's nothing like that," I replied, feeling warmth creeping up my neck and flooding my cheeks.

Glancing over his shoulder, he asked, "Kids?"

"No. It's just me. Well, me and my dog."

After drying his hands, Bishop leaned back against the counter and shot me an impish grin. "Sounds to me like you ain't got a reason not to stay." As I opened my mouth to protest, he reached over to steal a piece of ham. Beth swatted his hand before shooing him away.

Then, with a no-nonsense look, she pointed at me with her carving knife. "Benjamin is right. Besides, it's late. You've worked double time today, and you need a good, home-cooked meal."

"I don't want to be an inconvenience," I protested.

Willow tugged at my hand. "Oh, please stay, Miss Alex!"

I couldn't help laughing at her enthusiasm. "Aren't you tired of me yet?"

"Nope. You should spend the night, too!"

A wicked grin curved on Bishop's face. "Can she stay in my room?"

My mouth gaped open at his audaciousness while Willow shook her head. "No, Uncle B. She stays with me."

Bishop winked at me. "I may fight you for her."

Before I could respond, Deacon smacked the back of Bishop's head. "Knock it off," he warned.

"Hey, can I help it if I think Miss Alex is hot?"

As Deacon and Bishop began exchanging words in a low tone, Willow tugged my hand again, bringing my attention back to her rather than the very alluring Malloy brothers. I couldn't help feeling flattered at the attention of the two handsome men. Of course, Deacon's angry growls kept me in check.

"So, Miss Alex, are you going to stay?"

When I gazed down at her hopeful expression, I didn't know how to say no to her. Accepting defeat, I smiled. "Okay, okay, I'll stay." Then I gave Bishop a pointed look. "Just for dinner."

"Yeah!" Willow squealed, doing a little happy dance around me.

Taking me by the shoulders, Beth led me over to one of the chairs. "You sit right here, honey."

I let her ease me down onto the seat. "Thank you. I really appreciate your hospitality."

"Hospitality?" Deacon repeated.

When I glanced over my shoulder at him, he shook his head. "You really are white-bread."

"Don't be inhospitable to our guest, Deacon. Just because your daughter has a greater vocabulary comprehension level at her age than you do doesn't mean you can be a jerk," Rev said.

A giggle escaped my lips at Rev's teasing of Deacon. My laughter elicited a wink from Rev and a glare from Deacon. Rev took a seat across from me. Motioning Willow to his side, he said, "Come here, rug rat, and tell me what you learned today from Miss Alex."

She wrinkled her nose as she wrapped an arm around his waist. "I'm not a rug rat," she countered in a soft voice.

He cocked his brows at her. "Oh, you're not?" he questioned, his voice laced with amusement. Willow shook her head back and forth. "Then what are you?"

"A ballerina."

"Not that again." Deacon groaned as he took a seat at one end of the table. The corners of Willow's lips turned down in a frown. At her sad face, Deacon sighed. "Look, kid, we've been over and over this. I can't let you out to go to school, so I sure as hell can't let you go to dance lessons."

"Language, David," Beth chastised.

Deacon grunted at his mother before tossing his napkin into his lap. "Whatever. It ain't happening."

Rev narrowed his eyes at Deacon's somewhat apathetic response. He reached over to ruffle Willow's hair. "Just be patient, sweetheart. We'll get you those dance lessons someday soon."

"You're in luck. I know how you can get your dance lessons right here at home," I said with a smile.

Deacon's eyebrows popped up. "How's that?"

"I can teach her."

"You?" he asked incredulously.

I drew my shoulders back. "Yeah, me. I started ballet at the age of three. I taught at the local dance studio to put myself through college."

"That makes sense. You have a dancer's body," Rev said.

My gaze jerked from Deacon's to Rev's. Bishop slapped Rev on the back. "Oh, man. You've been checking her out, too, huh?" he teased with a grin.

"Just an observation," he replied softly, without meeting anyone's eyes.

After a moment of uncomfortable silence, Deacon cleared his throat. "Okay, then, Miss Twinkle Toes. Guess you're getting your precious dance lessons."

Willow squealed with excitement, her body bouncing in her chair beside me. "I want a pink leotard, Miss Alex."

I grinned. "I think I can make that happen."

Beth set down a large platter of ham. "Well, now. I think that's everything." After she dropped down into the empty chair at the other end of the table, she nodded at Deacon. "Will you return thanks, son?"

My mouth gaped open when Deacon laced his fingers together and bowed his head. It took me a moment in my stupor to bow my head as well. Deacon's deep voice boomed through the silent dining room. "Bless this food to the nourishment of our bodies and our bodies to your service. Amen."

"Amen," echoed around the table.

We then started passing around the bowls of food. "This all looks so delicious," I said, spooning some green beans onto my plate.

"Thank you," Beth replied with a pleased smile. After she offered me some corn bread, she asked, "Now, where is it you're from originally?"

"Marietta. I moved here when I was seventeen to live with my aunt and uncle."

After nodding her head in acknowledgment, Beth chewed thoughtfully on her corn bread, and I could see the questions about my past whirling through her mind. Deciding to put her out of her misery, I said, "My parents were killed in a car accident when I was seventeen. My brother and I came to live with my mother's brother."

Beth's face fell at my admission. "Oh, honey. I'm so sorry. Such a terrible tragedy for one so young."

A knot formed in my throat, and I could only nod my head in acknowledgment. Although almost ten years had passed since my parents died, there were still times when I found it almost unbearable to think about, much less talk about. Most of my initial grieving had gotten pushed aside to be strong for Charlie.

"I believe your uncle is a lifer here?" Deacon asked, bringing me out of my thoughts.

"Well, for most of his life, I suppose. He was twenty when he got married and moved here to be with my aunt's family."

"He's a former state trooper."

My brows rose in surprise at all of Deacon's knowledge about my family. "Yes. He retired two years ago with forty years with the Georgia State Patrol."

"Ah, God's Special Police," Bishop said with a grin.

I laughed. "A lot of his local PD buddies teased him with that."

"Does he still have ties to the GSP or the local PD?" Deacon asked.

With a shrug, I replied, "I don't really know. I think he's enjoying his retirement a lot. He has a cabin in Blue Ridge, and he and my aunt spend a lot of time there." Gazing down the table at him, I smiled. "Why all the interest in my uncle's law-enforcement ties?"

Deacon swiped his mouth with a napkin. "I was hoping he might help me with a speeding ticket."

"It's judges—not patrolmen—who fix tickets."

He winked at me. "Good to know."

Something told me he didn't have any tickets that needed fixing. He was more concerned with how Uncle Jimmy might affect his club. Wanting to steer the subject away from Uncle Jimmy, I said, "This is delicious. You're a wonderful cook, Mrs. Malloy."

"Call me Beth. And thank you so much."

"I should probably hire you to teach me to cook. I'm afraid that I'm not very good at it."

Beth smiled. "I would be happy to teach you. But there would be no charge. It would be a pleasure." Gazing around the table, she said, "Since I wasn't blessed with daughters, I'd love to be able to pass on my knowledge."

"You got a granddaughter," Deacon protested.

"That's right. I do. But it's going to be a few more years before she's ready to be unleashed in the kitchen."

Willow paused in gnawing on a piece of ham to eye Beth. "But you said I'm your bestest cooking helper."

"And you are, sweetheart. But you're going to stay a helper for now rather than the cook." At Willow's crestfallen expression, Beth said, "You need to put all your energy into your schoolwork and being a ballerina."

Tilting her head to the side, Willow mulled over Beth's response. Then, as she perked up, Willow turned to me. "Can my leotard have sparkles on it?" she asked.

"I don't see why not."

"And I want a pink tutu. Do I have to wear white tights or can I have pink?" As she rambled off more and more questions, her plate remained untouched.

"Finish your green beans," Deacon instructed gruffly, showing a rare moment of his paternal side.

"Okaaay," Willow mumbled.

Deacon's brows rose while fire flashed in his eyes. "What did you say?"

Willow tucked her head to her chin, refusing to meet his eye. "Okay."

"You say 'Yes, sir' when answering me."

"Don't be so hard on her," Rev said.

Deacon pinned Rev with a hard glare. "Don't tell me how to parent my kid."

"She's only five, Deacon," Rev challenged.

At the rising voices of her father and uncle, Willow began shrinking down in her chair. Desperate to soothe her distress and ease the building tension between the brothers, I blurted, "So which one of you Malloy boys is going to take me for a ride on his motorcycle? 'Cause, you know, I'm a motorcycle virgin."

Rev's fork clattered noisily onto his plate as he stared, dumbfounded by my outburst, while Deacon's finger froze in midpoint at Rev. Bishop started coughing on the large bite of corn bread he'd swallowed. He reached for his iced tea and drained it in a long gulp.

"I do believe my request has rendered you all speechless," I mused.

"I think it's hearing the word 'virgin' come out of your lips," Bishop replied with a cheeky grin.

"What's a virgin?" Willow asked.

I giggled at the look of horror that crossed all three Malloy brothers' faces at Willow's question. "Something you'll find out about when you're older," I answered, letting the boys off the hook. My response elicited a sigh of relief from the men and a nod of approval from Beth.

For the remainder of the dinner, Willow concentrated on finishing her plate rather than asking any more questions. When she was done, she glanced cautiously at her father. "Did I do good, Deacon?" Her voice quavered a little as she waited for praise. I wondered why she didn't call him "Dad." I guessed it was something she was working up to.

At her question, Deacon's gruff expression momentarily softened. "Yeah, you did good, kid. Now go take your plate and rinse it off."

As Willow started for the sink, my gaze locked on Deacon's.

"I know I may have seemed . . . a little harsh about her eating, but she was pretty malnourished when she came here."

Knowing the situation Willow had lived in with her mother, I wasn't too surprised by that information. "I agree that she needs to eat her vegetables and she needs to show you respect. My father asked the same thing of me when I was Willow's age." I offered him a smile. "I think maybe your delivery could use just a bit of work, but other than that, you're doing very well."

A smirk curved across his lips. "Thank you, Miss Evans."

"You're welcome."

Beth rose from her seat. "All right, boys. It's time to clean up."

A chorus of groans echoed around the table. "At least let me do the dishes since you were so kind to invite me to dinner."

Beth smiled. "And deprive my sons of the task?"

I laughed at Bishop's aggravated grunt and Deacon's roll of his eyes. "No, I wouldn't want to do that at all."

"You gonna read me my bedtime story, Uncle Rev?" Willow asked.

Before he could reply, I said, "You know what? I bet your daddy would love to read you a story tonight."

Deacon's eyes narrowed at my comment while Willow's widened in surprise. "Really? *You* want to read to me, Deacon?" she asked.

"Yeah, sure, kid. Why not?"

A beaming smile lit up her face. "Okay. I'll go brush my teeth and get my pajamas on."

"Whatever," Deacon replied.

Trying to ignore his glare, I turned to Beth. "Thank you again for dinner."

"You're more than welcome. Feel free to join us anytime. You have a standing invitation every night," Beth said.

"That's very sweet of you."

As I started to the foyer, Deacon stepped in front of me. "I'll walk you back to your car."

I couldn't hide my surprise at his uncharacteristically thoughtful gesture. Of course, I also hoped he wasn't going to go off on me about my bedtime-story suggestion. "Um, thank you," I mumbled as I followed him out the door.

The flame from his cigarette lighter lit the way for us in the dark. The sound of Deacon's boots clomping across the floorboards filled the silence between us. After we pounded down the stairs, Deacon turned to me. "You know, you should really go for Rev."

"Excuse me?" I questioned in surprise. After all, that was the last thing I'd expected out of him. A harsh "You need to mind your own fucking business when it comes to me and my kid" was more what I'd expected.

Deacon took a long drag on his cigarette. "He's into you—I can tell."

Cocking my head, I eyed him curiously. "Funny. I thought you came out here to go off on me about what I did with Willow, not to play matchmaker."

"I'm not too stubborn to admit when I'm wrong about something."

"You sure about that?" I teased.

"Yeah, I'd be a dick to yell at you for just suggesting I read to my kid. I mean, that's what parents do. Well, that's at least what my mother did for me."

It was the first time he had given me any insight into his childhood. I couldn't help wondering about what Deacon was like as a little boy. I'd since learned that he was an adopted son of Beth's. I was certainly curious about his life before he came to live with the Malloys.

After silence stretched momentarily between us, I replied, "I'm glad to hear you say that."

"Now, what about Rev?"

"What about him?" I questioned coyly.

My comment earned me a scowl from Deacon. "What about dating him?"

"He seems very sweet, and he's very good-looking. But . . ."

After he exhaled a trail of smoke, his eyes found mine in the dark. "He's not like Bishop and me, if that's what you're worrying about."

"How's that?"

"He likes good women."

"And after spending a couple of hours with me, you automatically know I'm good?" I countered.

"You're sure as hell not a sweet butt."

"A what?"

He grinned. "Sorry. I keep forgetting you're not of our world, White-Bread."

"Don't call me that."

After flicking off the growing ashes of his cigarette, Deacon said, "A sweet butt is a chick who gets off by hanging around an MC club and banging any guy who wants to be with her."

Wrinkling my nose, I replied, "You're serious?"

"Hell yeah."

"Why would women disrespect themselves like that?"

Deacon shrugged. "That's their business, not mine."

"Well, you're certainly right about me not being a club whore."

"Which is a definite turn-on for Rev."

"If Rev is so into me, why didn't he walk me to my car?"

"Because he's gun-shy with women. He got his heart broken by some bitch who never deserved him."

"That's awful."

Deacon tossed his cigarette to the ground and then stomped it out with his boot. "He's better off now, but he's been through some rough times."

"It's very sweet of you to be looking out for him."

"He's my brother. I want him to be happy," Deacon replied as he led me around the side of the clubhouse. When my car came into view, I quickly dug my keys out of my purse. After I popped the lock, I met Deacon's expectant gaze.

"I think it's best if I focus solely on Willow right now and not romance."

His brows knitted tightly together. "So that's a no?"

I shrugged. "I guess it's more of a not right now. How's that?"

"Not what I wanted to hear."

With a laugh, I opened my car door. "Good night, Deacon."

"Good night, Miss Evans."

"Are you never going to call me Alexandra?"

"Maybe . . . just not right now," he replied with a crooked smile.

FIVE

DEACON

When the antique cuckoo clock in the corner of the pawnshop struck three, I pushed myself out of my chair and tossed aside the *Playboy* I'd been eyeing. Thanks to Willow's school hours and Case's insistence, I now had a new routine. Every day at three, I would stand outside the pawnshop. As I had a cigarette, I waited for Alexandra to arrive. I could count on her arriving just about the time I had lit up and taken a few drags.

I usually got treated to an eyeful of her legs, since she always wore skirts and dresses to work. A cloud of her sweet-smelling perfume would hit my nostrils as I escorted her into the clubhouse to a waiting Willow. I'd spend the next two hours shuffling around the clubhouse, keeping an eye on the door to the "classroom" that Mama Beth had insisted the boys and I construct.

Three days into this new schedule found me propped up on a barstool, bored as hell and frustrated as hell since Cheyenne had been eye-fucking me all afternoon. Finally, I gave up and escaped to the bathroom to pour some cold water on my half-mast dick.

After all, there was no way I could sneak away for a quickie with Cheyenne when I was supposed to be keeping an eye on Alex.

When I returned, Willow stood at the bar, flashing a paper at Cheyenne, who gave her a look of disinterest. In Cheyenne's world, if you didn't have a dick or a cut, you weren't much use to her. At the sight of me, she did manage to give Willow a beaming smile. For some reason, it made me angry that she couldn't give my kid any welcome attention when I wasn't in the room.

"Look, Deacon. Look what I made on my test!" Willow cried, dancing around me. I opened my mouth to say something, but she continued rattling on. "Miss Alex said this is some of the work that first graders are doing, and I'm really smart to be able to do it already."

"Yeah, that's great. Good job," I said. My words fell a little short of the foreign feeling of pride that swelled in my chest. Sure, I'd done okay when I was in school, but nothing like Willow. She was gonna be something.

Willow threw her arms around my waist, squeezing me tight. I couldn't help stiffening at her touch. She may have been with me for four months now, but I still couldn't get used to her expressions of affection. I didn't know what my fucking problem was. Both Rev and Bishop reacted easily to Willow's hugs and kisses. But here I was, her own flesh and blood, and I still felt emotionally detached from her. I was beginning to wonder if I would always feel this way.

Breaking the hug, she said, "Im'a gonna go show Grandma."

"Yeah, you do that. Get her to put it on the fridge or some shit."

Willow bounded out of the main hall and out the back door. She waved the paper at Archer as he walked her out of the compound to the house. Even within the confines of our compound, I wasn't taking any chances with her safety.

Peering around the room, I questioned, "Where's Alex?"

"Bishop asked her to go back to his room," Cheyenne replied.

"You're shitting me."

When she glanced up at me, a catlike smile curved Cheyenne's lips. "Why would I lie about something like that?"

"I meant why would she do that?"

Cheyenne shrugged. "Maybe she thinks he's hot. Wouldn't be the first girl to drop her panties for Bishop."

I staggered back in shock. Alex was alone in a room with Bishop. A girl like her should never, ever be alone with a biker, least of all Bishop. That motherfucker had totally disregarded what I had said about leaving her alone. My fists clenched at my sides. I was going to kick his ass.

Without another word to Cheyenne, I stomped down the hall. The door to Bishop's room was closed tight. I knew the right thing would be to knock, but for some reason, I didn't give a fuck about the right thing.

"Oh, Bishop, that's so good," came Alex's muffled praise.

Rage uncoiled within me, spreading through my body. Alex refused Rev and acted like she was too good for me, but she was spreading her legs for my manwhore of a brother.

I braced my hands on the doorframe and lifted my leg back, kicking the door with all the strength in me, causing it to fly open. As it banged against the wall, I stalked inside. Nothing could have prepared me for what I saw. Instead of Alex and Bishop naked and fucking, they were sitting on the edge of his bed. With a pencil in his hand, Bishop balanced a workbook on his lap. I couldn't get a good look at the workbook, but I could only imagine it was some kind of sex manual.

"What the fuck is going on here?" I demanded.

For the first time I could ever remember, Bishop blushed. The tough-ass motherfucker seriously turned the color of an overripe tomato.

Alex rose to her feet, giving me a glare that could curl paint off a wall. "I'm not sure that is any of your business."

"This is *my* clubhouse and *my* brother. Everything that goes on in my club is my business."

Cocking her head at me, Alex motioned to my cut. "I thought you were just the sergeant at arms."

I barked a laugh. "*Just* the sergeant at arms? Lady, you don't know shit about my office or what this patch means."

"I would hardly think it was your right to know everything. That sounds like the job of the president."

Staring past Alex, I eyed Bishop. "Quit stalling and answer my question, brother."

Alex went to sit back down beside Bishop. "You don't owe him an explanation. What happens between you and me is private."

"Miss Evans, you are seriously pissing me off, and if you know what's good for you, you will shut the fuck up and stay out of this!" I growled.

"Okay, okay," Bishop said, as he threw up his hands in defeat, sending the workbook fluttering to the floor. Before he could pick it up, I beat him to it.

Gazing down at the cover, I read aloud, *"Mastering the GED Exam."* I cut my eyes back to him. "This isn't a sex manual."

Bishop's embarrassment turned over to humor. "A sex manual?"

I shrugged. "What else would you be doing with her back here but fucking?"

Alex sucked in a harsh breath. "Certainly not that," she snapped.

"You don't know my brother's persuasive ability, not to mention his"—I paused to scratch my chin—"infatuation with you."

"And you do not know my moral and ethical resolve," she countered.

I flashed her a grin. "There you go using them big words. My feeble little mind can't keep up."

"Maybe you're the one who should be studying, rather than Bishop."

"Anytime you want to teach me, I'm ready to learn."

She glared at me for a moment before crossing her arms in a huff. Damn, she was so sexy when she got riled. A fiery little hellcat in a prim and prissy exterior. Turning my attention from her, I waved the workbook at Bishop. "So what's all this about?"

He gave me a sheepish look. "I wanted to finish high school—that's all."

I eyed him suspiciously. "Have you taken a few too many hits to the head?"

"No, asshole, I haven't."

"Since when do you give two shits about whether you finished school or not? You didn't seem to give a rat's ass when you dropped out seven years ago."

Bishop snatched the workbook from me. "Maybe I realized that I'm not going to be able to keep boxing forever. Besides doing club errands or working at the gym, I don't have shit for options. If I wanted to go to mechanic school, I'd need a GED."

"Mechanics? You don't need school for that. We can find you a hookup to learn hands-on. Truman can always make you a license."

With his blue eyes flashing, Bishop replied, "I want something legitimately my own for once—not something the club had its hand in."

I shook my head slowly from side to side. Was my little brother actually growing a conscience? "Is this Rev's influence?"

Bishop rolled his eyes. "Can't I have a thought of my own without being influenced by my good or bad brother?"

"Yeah, you can. It's just . . . I guess I'm speechless."

"That's a fucking first," Bishop grumbled.

Crossing my arms over my chest, I eyed Bishop. "Look, man,

I don't mean to rack your balls about this. What you're doing is a good thing for you. I could never fault you for doing that."

"You're serious?" he questioned, his blond brows rising in surprise.

"'Course I am."

A grin stretched across Bishop's face. "Thanks, bro. I'm glad to hear that."

I glanced from him to Alex. "My, my, you certainly are devoted to my family. First my daughter and now my brother. Who will you educate next?"

"Whom," she replied.

"Huh?"

The corners of her lips teased as if she was holding back a smile. "You mean *whom* will I educate next."

As Bishop chuckled, I replied, "Guess I'm the lucky one."

"Maybe you can repay the favor for all the education by granting me a favor?"

I eyed her warily. "What do you want?"

"There really isn't a proper place here for Willow's ballet lessons." She paused, nibbling on her bottom lip. I'd noticed she tended to do that when she was nervous. Usually she did it around me when she wasn't giving me lip. "I was just wondering with you owning the gym—"

"The club owns the gym," I corrected.

Her cheeks tinged a little. "Well, with your ties to the club, would it be okay if I gave Willow her lessons there? There would be sufficient mirrors, and you really can't teach proper form without mirrors."

"If she's needing mirrors, maybe you could let her borrow your bedroom," Bishop suggested with a wicked gleam in his eye.

"Fuck off," I snarled, as Alex's cheeks reddened again.

Bishop only snickered as he flipped open his workbook again

while Alex drew in a breath. "It wouldn't be every day. Most students only attend dance once or twice a week. If there was just a corner of the gym we could have, that would be plenty. I could even have Willow wear headphones to take care of doing the poses to the music."

Scratching my chin, I thought about it. I knew I would have to run it by Case, and he probably wasn't going to like the idea of Alexandra being around the gym. Of course, most of the questionable activity took place only on Friday or Saturday nights. "I suppose it would be all right. Let me talk to the guys about it, but maybe we can give it a trial run tomorrow."

Alex's face lit up. "That would be wonderful. I could just meet you guys down there at three. The lesson could run until three thirty, and hopefully, we wouldn't have to even adjust the schoolwork for dinnertime."

"I don't think Mama Beth would mind adjusting the time."

After giving me a genuine smile, Alex said, "Thank you, Deacon."

"You're welcome."

When we remained standing there, staring at each other, Bishop cleared his throat. "You mind leaving us so we can get some more work done?"

"As long as you keep those hands on your workbook and not her," I countered.

Bishop rolled his eyes. "I heard you loud and clear before, brother. Give me some fucking credit."

"Better yet, give *me* some fucking credit," Alex said.

Sweeping a hand to his chest, Bishop said, "Ouch. That hurt."

Alexandra only giggled. "You're more trouble than you're worth."

As I watched them, I slowly began to realize that neither one of them looked at the other like they wanted to rip the other person's clothes off. While Bishop might've been jacking off to her earlier, I doubt he was anymore . . . unless he had a teacher fantasy from years back. I knew then that although he was a horndog, I could trust him around Alex. She was probably the first woman besides our mother that he actually respected, which was saying a hell of a lot.

Holding my hands up in defeat, I started backing up toward the door. "All right. I'll go and let you two work."

Alex nodded. "So I'll see you at three tomorrow at the gym?"

"Yeah, sure."

After giving me a wave, she turned her attention back to Bishop. Instead of giving me a shit-eating grin that he had her attention and her fine ass sitting beside him, he ducked his head and looked at the workbook.

With a shake of my head, I went in search of Case to explain how my daughter's leash around my finger now included his gym and ballet lessons.

SIX

DEACON

"What time is it?" Willow asked for the twentieth fucking time in the last five minutes.

Gripping the ropes of the boxing ring, I growled, "Kid, you're getting on my last nerve."

"Please, Deacon," she said. When I turned away from Bishop's practice session, she gave me her best sad-faced pout. The kind that would make a regular father melt. But I wasn't a regular father.

"She'll get here when she gets here," I finally replied.

Willow crossed her arms over her chest in a huff. She'd been wired since the moment she'd woken up. Today was her first dance lesson with Alex. I don't think I'd ever seen her so fucking excited about anything. Of course, Mama Beth and Rev found her behavior cute. As for me, she was about to drive me bat-shit crazy. I couldn't tell her to fuck off like I do with my brothers when they're driving me crazy. Instead, I had to be as patient as I could be with her, which for me wasn't saying a whole lot.

When the gym door blew open behind me, I didn't have to guess who it was. Willow's earsplitting squeal told me all I needed to know. I released the ropes and started over to them. "Oh, Miss Alex. You're finally here!" Willow shrieked, dancing around Alex.

Alex grinned down at her. "I didn't realize I was that late. I had carpool duty this afternoon, so I didn't get to leave on time. I didn't even stop to change. I came straight here."

"I'm glad you did," Willow replied.

"So am I," I muttered.

With a laugh, Alex said, "Just let me go get changed." She thrust a glittery pink bag at me. "Can you get Willow ready for me?"

"You can't be serious."

Alex's eyes narrowed on mine. "I don't think it's too much to ask since I picked up all the things she would need. Besides, we don't have a lot of time to waste."

I looked from Alex to Willow. Ever since she had come to live with me, Mama Beth had taken care of bath time and getting her dressed. Yeah, she was my kid, but I didn't exactly know the rules when it came to seeing her without clothes. Although I couldn't quite put my finger on it, there was something that felt pervy about it.

Before I could argue anymore, Willow reached out and took my hand. "Come on, Deacon."

When Alex shot me a triumphant look, I scowled at her. Instead of mouthing off, I let Willow drag me back to the men's locker room. "Miss Alex can take the ladies' room," Willow informed me.

She started to barge right on, but I jerked her back. "Wait a minute. I need to make sure nobody's in there getting dressed."

"Okay."

Releasing her hand, I ducked inside. The smell of sweat and jockstrap assaulted my nose. When I saw it was empty, I held the door open for Willow. She came skipping inside. She put her bag down on one of the benches and started digging inside. Another one of her ear-splintering squeals had me jumping out of my skin. "Look, Deacon. Miss Alex got me a sparkly pink leotard just like I asked for." The contents of the bag came flying out—there were panty hose–looking things—pink, of course—some shoes, and a flimsy-looking skirt thing.

Once everything was out, Willow tore her shirt off her head and then stripped out of her jean shorts. She plopped down on the bench and held out the panty hose–looking thing to me. "Help me with my tights."

"Uh, okay," I muttered. I reluctantly took them in my hand, and then I knelt down in front of her.

"Hold out the one leg so I can get my foot in there," Willow commanded.

"I don't know—"

"Like this," she instructed, rolling the fabric down. I held it out, and she eased her foot inside. Then I did the other side. When both were at her ankles, I started wiggling them up her legs. I grimaced as I tugged them up over her pink panties. Once they were in place, I eased back on my heels.

"Now help me with the leotard."

I exhaled a long sigh. "Okay, then."

One of Willow's tiny hands reached out for my shoulder. Balancing herself with one arm, she stuck one of her pink legs into the hole of the leotard. When she swayed a little, I reached out and grabbed her by the waist, steadying her.

"Oops." She giggled as she stuck her other leg in the hole. I then took my hands off her waist and helped tug the leotard up to her chest. Then she wiggled her arms in. After I helped her adjust it, she ran over to the mirror and let out yet another ear-piercing squeal. "Deacon, look at how pretty I am!"

I couldn't help chuckling. "No false modesty for you, huh?"

She glanced at me over her shoulder. "Huh?"

"Nothing. Yes, you do look really pretty."

When she grinned, she reminded me of Lacey. While she looked just like me, she still had little mannerisms and quirks that were her mother's.

"Ooh, now I need my hair put up in a bun." She eyed me curiously. "Can you do my hair?"

Scratching my head, I replied, "I can try."

She nodded. Digging in her bag, she produced a hairbrush for me and then something to hold her hair. "Sit down," I instructed, motioning to the bench in front of me. She quickly obeyed. The moment I ran the brush through her hair, I became assaulted by a barrage of memories.

"You know the only reason why I sort of know how to do this?" I questioned, my voice choking off with emotion.

"Uh-uh," Willow replied.

"I used to brush and braid your mother's hair."

"You did?"

"Yeah, I did." I could almost hear Lacey's sultry voice begging me to brush her hair. Although it often rendered her catatonic from relaxation, it also tended to get her fired up to fuck me. Something about the tender touch of my hands on her hair turned a switch inside her.

After a moment of silence, Willow softly asked, "Did you love my mommy?"

My hand froze, stilling the sweeping motion of the brush. As I thought of the feelings I'd once had for Lacey, an ache burned through my chest. "Yeah, I did."

"Did she love you?"

"Yeah, I think she did at one time."

"You think when I grow up I'll be prettier than her?"

"Probably. Let's face it. You look just like me, and I'm pretty damn handsome." When Willow didn't acknowledge my comment,

I said, "Yes, you'll be prettier. Is that what you want, to be the prettiest?"

She shrugged her tiny shoulders. "Yes . . . as long as it doesn't make me hurt people or let them hurt me."

"What do you mean?"

"Mommy was so pretty that she let lots of men hurt her. Sometimes they hurt me. But most of the time, it was Mommy who hurt me."

Her words caused a volatile mixture of rage and pain to course through me. Hearing Willow talk about how much her mother hurt her made me wish that Lacey were still alive so I could kill her with my own bare hands. I knew firsthand what it was like to be abused as a kid, and I didn't want anyone else to have to deal with that pain, especially my own flesh and blood. Even though I knew she was fucked-up on drugs, I couldn't imagine how Lacey could hurt Willow. Of course, when I'd started fucking Lacey, I hadn't actually been looking for someone maternal. She was no Mama Beth, that's for damn sure. And even though I didn't know her that well, I knew Alex would be ten times the mother that Lacey had ever tried to be. Wait. Why the fuck was I bringing Alex into all this?

Placing one of my hands on Willow's shoulder, I said, "You know that you don't have to ever worry about being hurt again."

"Yeah," she replied tentatively.

"I'm serious. If anyone hurts you, I will put them in the ground. Do you understand me?"

Willow turned back to me with wide, frightened eyes. "Look, I didn't mean to scare you. I just want you to understand that you don't have to worry about being hurt again."

"Okay."

As I brought the brush through her hair again, I sighed. "And I'm sorry that I wasn't there to stop your mom from hurting you. I promise you it wouldn't have happened if I'd been there."

"It's all right."

"No. It really isn't." A ragged breath shuddered through my body. "You didn't deserve that, and I should've been there."

With an intuition that freaked me out, Willow asked, "Did someone hurt you when you were little?"

As I recalled the horrific memories of my past, my head began to swim, and the room seemed to close in on me. The last thing on earth I needed was for Willow to see me flake out. I was supposed to be strong for her.

I counted to ten and tried to collect my thoughts. "Deacon?" Willow prompted.

"Yeah, my old man used to beat the shit out of me after he beat my mom. Usually for no reason at all. My mom tried to get us away, but . . ."

"What happened to your real mommy?"

"She was murdered, just like yours."

"Was it Mean Man?" Willow asked in a whisper.

I shook my head. "No. It was my father."

After relief momentarily flickered across her face that it hadn't been the "Mean Man," her tiny brows scrunched in confusion, as if she couldn't imagine anything so horrible. "Your daddy killed your mommy?"

"Yeah, he did," I replied, and I hated that my voice sounded choked with emotion.

"He must've been a real bad man."

"Yeah, he was." As I swept the brush through her hair again, I said, "Guess we're a lot alike with the fact our mothers were killed, huh?"

A solemn look came over her face. "Yes, but I'm more sad for you."

My brows shot up. "Why's that?"

"Because you loved your daddy, and he hurt your mommy,

which hurt you really bad. Even though I lost my mommy, I still have my daddy." Glancing at me over her shoulder, she added, "And you would never do anything to hurt me like that."

My hands froze in her hair as I tried to process her words. In spite of all my shit, Willow thought I was a good guy—a guy who would never hurt her. I sure as hell hoped I could live up to her expectations. It was a lot of fucking pressure. "You're right," I croaked. Cuffing the back of her neck playfully to ease the mood, I asked, "When did you become so wise?"

She shrugged. "Mrs. Martinez used to say I was an old soul."

The mention of someone from her former life made me think for a minute about how she had mentioned the "Mean Man" again. The shrink she saw twice a week had warned us not to grill Willow for any information about what she had witnessed. But at the end of the day, we needed more intel. "What can you tell me about Mean Man?"

Willow immediately turned white as a sheet, and a tremor ran through her body. In a strangled voice, she replied, "No. I can't . . . I can't ever talk about him. He'll hurt me."

Even though I wasn't used to showing her a lot of affection, I pulled her into my arms. "No, baby. He won't. Me, Uncle Rev, and Bishop, and the rest of the Raiders won't let him. He can't get to you. I promise."

My words seemed to ease Willow's concerns a little because she stopped trembling. Taking her by the shoulders, I gently eased her back to where I could look into her eyes. "Maybe if we knew what he looked like, we could find him and put him in jail."

My pep talk did nothing to convince Willow to talk. She just slowly shook her head back and forth. "Okay, then, let's change the subject. All this shit is too heavy for someone your age." I swept up her long, dark hair. Twisting it around, I wrapped the hair tie around it. "There. How's that?"

Willow turned around on the bench. When she was facing the

mirror, she turned her head left and right. "It looks good. Will you put the ribbons in now?"

"You're a bossy thing, aren't you?" I teased, trying to lighten the mood.

She laughed. "Maybe."

Although it pained me greatly, I tied the ribbons around her bun. I had to admit that she looked cute as hell. Her outfit had transformed her into a ballerina. Whether or not she had any talent for it was yet to be seen.

"Okay. That's enough mirror time. Let's get you to Miss Alex," I said.

She reluctantly turned from admiring her reflection and met me at the door. When she tugged on my hand, I bent down to her level. She surprised the hell out of me by standing on her tiptoes to bestow a kiss on my cheek. "Thank you, Deacon."

"You're welcome."

Cocking her head at me, Willow asked, "Maybe soon I'll be ready to call you 'Daddy.'"

Her statement caused me momentarily to stagger back. Where the hell had that come from? Did I even want the kid to call me "Daddy"? I'd sure as hell have to be more of a father for her to call me one. I couldn't deny her words caused an ache to burn through my chest. Somehow I finally found the words to respond. "I think I would like that."

Willow smiled before bounding out the door. When we got back into the gym, I noticed two or three of the guys standing stock-still outside of the boxing ring. Instead of their attention being trained on Bishop, they stared off to the side. It took me only a moment to figure out who they were staring at.

I started to tell them to put their tongues back in their mouths, but I never got the chance. Instead, my eyes zeroed in on what they were obsessed with. Outfitted in her own skintight leotard, tights, and skirt, Alex was bent over, ass in the air, with her palms pressed to the mat. I could have never imagined something as simple as stretching could be so fucking sexy.

Oblivious to all the stares, she rose up and then brought her arm over her head. As she leaned in to the stretch, her ass swished provocatively. When she finished with the one arm, she moved on to the next one. And then she pulled a move that proved my undoing. She stretched her leg out next to her head. "Fucking hell," one of the guys muttered.

"Why are you all staring at Miss Alex?" Willow demanded, bringing me out of my fantasy of how many positions I could put the very limber Alex in.

Willow's words startled Alex. Her leg dropped down, and then she whirled around. When she saw all the men standing around, her face flushed. Trying to ease her embarrassment, I shouted, "Go on. Show's over. Go back to work or whatever the hell you were supposed to be doing!"

As the men scrambled, Willow raced over to Alex, who was now cowering in the corner. When I reached them, Alex shook her head. "I don't think this is going to work."

"Look, I can promise you what happened was just a onetime thing. There's never any women down here, so naturally they had to gawk when they saw one."

Alex's cheeks were still red. "I won't feel comfortable. . . . I won't be able to focus if I have to worry about being ogled."

"What's ogled?" Willow asked.

"Don't worry about it," I snapped.

"I'm sorry. I just can't."

"You mean I'm not going to get to have ballet lessons?" Willow asked in a small voice.

Before she could throw a fit, I held up my hands. "Just give me a minute to think of a solution, okay?"

Both Willow and Alex crossed their arms over their chests and stared expectantly at me. "The basement," I blurted.

"What?" Alex asked.

"I can set you up something in the basement."

"But it's scary down there," Willow said in a hushed voice.

"It won't be when I'm through with it. I'll put in more lights, clean out some of the junk, and put up some mirrors."

"That sounds wonderful," Alex gushed, a pleased smile on her face. I could only imagine that in her white-bread world, she hadn't had much exposure to the tough-as-shit men who train here, so I guess it made sense she'd be so put off.

"What do you say, kid?" I asked Willow.

"I think it sounds okay."

I laughed. "Just okay. Man, there's no pleasing you."

She nibbled on her lip before asking, "Will you put in a barre, too? You know, like it's a real studio."

"I think I can swing that."

Her face lit up. "Then I love it."

Before I thought better of it, I reached out and ruffled her hair. "Glad you think so."

Willow jumped back from me. "Don't mess my hair up!"

Alex laughed at our exchange. "We wouldn't want to mess up your bun." Amusement danced in her eyes when she looked at me. "Did she do that, or did you?"

"I did. Why?"

She shrugged. "I'm just surprised—that's all." With a teasing smile, she said, "You're a man of many talents, Jesse James."

"Hmm, there's more of my talents I'd like to acquaint you with." Inwardly, I cringed. Had I actually just laid some serious innuendo on her? What the hell was my problem? I was just as bad as the Neanderthals who had been panting and drooling over her earlier.

Alex's eyes widened at my suggestive tone. "Well, I think it's time that I acquainted Willow with a few basic ballet poses."

"I'll keep an eye on things for you."

After pursing her lips at me, she replied, "Why doesn't that make me feel better?"

I threw my head back and laughed. "At ease, White-Bread."

The next half hour passed without Alexandra being eye-fucked by the guys. While I eventually focused back on Bishop in the ring, I threw a look in her and Willow's direction every few minutes. Jesus, did Alexandra have patience when it came to Willow. She worked over and over with her to make sure she understood the pose things and how to hold her arms. While I would have freaked the fuck out and stalked off, Alex kept her head and never raised her voice.

When the instruction was over, Alex quickly bypassed me for the bathroom to change. "Did I dance good?" Willow asked.

"You did good, kid," I replied.

"She did *well*," Rev emphasized behind me.

After turning around, I rolled my eyes at his grammar-correcting ass and then managed to smack him in the balls with Willow's bag. "Be careful getting her home."

Bending double, Rev wheezed out a few breaths. "My pleasure," he muttered through gritted teeth.

Willow happily reached for Rev's hand. "Can we get ice cream today?"

Rev refused to meet my glare. Instead, he placed a finger over his lips. "What did I say about keeping secrets?"

She giggled. "Okay."

As they started for the door hand in hand, I shook my head. I'd seen Rev, with busted and bloodied knuckles, beat a man within an inch of his life. But you put him in a room with a kid, especially Willow, and he was a fucking teddy bear. I couldn't imagine what it would be like when he finally had a kid of his own.

Although I had indulged in a few X-rated fantasies involving Alexandra, I still thought she was a good match for him. I needed to stay on his ass about asking her out. When I'd first mentioned it to him, he'd argued that he didn't want to make things complicated for Willow. I told him he was being a pussy, and then he'd walked away. I guess it wasn't the best pep talk to get him back into the game.

Alexandra emerged from the bathroom wearing jeans and a T-shirt. She looked a hell of a lot different out of her school clothes. I also couldn't help imagining for a second what she looked like without any clothes on at all.

She slung her bag over her shoulder and threw her hand up at me before heading out the side door. Whether or not she realized it, she was easing into our world. She didn't find it necessary to ask where Willow was. She knew that someone had come to escort her home. Maybe she didn't realize whoever drove Willow was followed by two prospects for added protection. Of course, she might've had some questions as to why Archer slunk out of the gym after her. I knew Case wanted her watched regardless of where she was.

When Bishop came out of the ring ten minutes later, I decided it was time to head back to the compound. As I started out to my bike, Alex's car still sat in its space. One of her jeans-clad legs hung out of the door. The hood was up, and Archer was bent over it, assessing the damage. At the screeching sound of the car refusing to start, I knew a shot alternator was the reason she was still there. When I walked up to the car, she banged her fists on the steering wheel. "Dammit!" she cried.

"Easy, now."

Her gaze snapped up to mine. "This is the second time this week my car won't start. The mechanic who worked on it swore to me it was fixed." Under her breath, she mumbled, "Asshole."

"Come on," I said, urging her with my hand.

"Excuse me?"

"I said, come on. You're not going to solve anything by sitting there and pitching a fit."

"I was not pitching a fit," she growled.

"Easy, White-Bread. I'm not the enemy here—got it?"

She exhaled a frustrated breath. "Fine. I'm sorry."

"Look, I'll get one of the club's mechanics to come over and fix your car. Archer can wait here with it and make sure nothing happens to it. In the meantime, you can ride home with me so you can still teach Willow."

Alex contemplated my words. "Is this mechanic good, or is he just going to take me for a ride?"

I laughed at the potential double meaning of her words. "He'll do a good job, or he'll answer to me."

"And that's sufficient motivation?" she asked curiously.

Cocking my brows at her, I asked, "What do you think?"

Instead of replying, she exhaled a long breath. "Fine," she muttered before she grabbed her purse. "Feel free to take the cost out of my pay."

"I don't think that will be necessary." When she started to protest, I held up my hand. "What you do is worth far more than we pay you."

Ducking her head, she nibbled on her lip. "Thank you. That means a lot coming from you."

"You're welcome." Dammit. If fired-up, angry Alex didn't turn me on, then shy, appreciative Alex made my dick twitch.

When I got to my bike, I picked up my helmet to give to her. "Since I don't have an old lady, my bike isn't outfitted with a bitch seat. You'll just have to sit really close to me." Instead of taking the helmet, Alex remained frozen, staring at the bike.

"What's wrong?"

She shook her head furiously back and forth. "I'm not getting on that motorcycle."

"Why the fuck not?"

"Because I just can't."

"You don't strike me as the chickenshit type."

Her dark eyes flashed venom at me. "I'm not . . . chickenshit. I'm just practical. Motorcycles are very dangerous."

"What happened to you wanting to ride one?"

"That was about me finding a way to change the subject before so you and Rev wouldn't upset Willow any further by brawling at the table."

"We weren't brawling," I countered. Once again, I shoved the helmet at her. "Look, White-Bread, I ain't got the time or the energy for your particular line of bullshit. It's really pretty simple. You ride home with me and teach Willow, or you sit here in the hot-as-fuck parking lot, waiting on our mechanic, who may or may not be able to fix your car right now."

Tentatively, her hand reached out for the helmet. It didn't escape my notice that she was trembling. "You were right."

"About what?"

"I am chickenshit."

I laughed at her acknowledgment. "There's nothing to be scared of, babe. You just hold on tight to me, and I'll do the rest. Okay?" She took a step closer to the bike. Drawing in a deep breath, she slid the helmet on. As she threw a leg over the seat, I gave her my best genuine smile, to which Alexandra gave me a goofy two thumbs-up.

Shaking my head, I slid onto the seat in front of her. When her hands gripped my cut, I reached behind me to bring them around my waist. "This isn't the time to be shy. Hold on tight." I then gunned the engine. When I tipped the bike off the kickstand, Alex clung to me like a second skin. Her thighs clamped against mine, and it took everything within me to keep my dick from reacting.

Glancing over my shoulder, I shouted over the roar of the pipes. "Ya know, I would never let anything bad happen to you on my watch."

"I wish that made me feel better," she murmured.

"Trust me, Alex."

Her fearful eyes met mine. She gave a slight jerk of her head. "Okay. I trust you."

I knew it took a lot for her to say that, and it caused a weird tightening in my chest. Without another word to her, I turned back around and started easing out of the parking lot. The moment we got out onto the road, Alex molded herself against me again. I hadn't had a woman on the back of my bike since Lacey. My brothers might have a new piece of ass on their bike every week, but to me it meant too much to give a ride to just any girl. And even being as close physically as I had been with Cheyenne, I never had her ride with me. Now, just because of one fucked-up alternator, I'd broken my rule.

As we sped along the streets toward home with Crazy Ace, another one of our prospects, on my tail, I couldn't help enjoying the feel of Alex's arms around me, her fingers splayed into my chest. My mind immediately flashed to pulling her around to straddle me, arching my hips against her jeans-clad pussy. I couldn't help groaning both at the image and at my out-of-control thoughts. The last thing I needed was Alexandra to feel me hard.

She would probably freak out and fall off the bike, trying to get away from my perverted ass.

Finally, we reached the compound. I eased my bike into a spot and killed the engine. Glancing behind me, I asked, "You okay?"

Surprisingly, she grinned at me. "Yeah, I am. Once we got started, it wasn't so bad."

"Glad to hear that."

She hopped down and took off the helmet. As she handed it back to me, she said, "Maybe you'll take me riding again?"

While I was stoked she wanted to go again, I knew I had to shut her down. "Don't get ahead of yourself, babe. You had some car trouble—that's it."

Alex stared at me for a moment before bringing her hands to her hips. "Don't flatter yourself that I was insinuating I wanted anything more from you than another motorcycle ride."

Before I could say anything else, Rev came out of the club-house. "There you guys are. Willow was getting panicky."

"Sorry. My car wouldn't start."

Rev glanced between her and me. "And he gave you a ride on his bike?"

"Yes, he did."

"Wow. He doesn't ever let women on his bike."

While I shot Rev a "fuck you" look, Alex's eyes widened at me. "You don't?"

Scratching the back of my head, I replied, "I don't like to be bothered with a bitch when I'm riding."

With a roll of her eyes, Alex said, "Just when I think you might have redeemed yourself even a tiny bit, you go and say something like that."

I couldn't help chuckling as she stomped past Rev and into the clubhouse.

When he glanced at me and raised his brows, I shook my head. "Don't ask until I've had at least two beers."

He laughed and followed me inside.

Two hours and three beers later, I was still shooting the shit with the guys when Alex and Willow appeared. Putting down my fourth beer, I headed over to them. "Rev's waiting on you. Head on down to Mama Beth's."

Willow nodded. After giving Alex a hug, she sprinted for the back door, where she took Rev's hand and tugged him outside.

When I saw Alex staring longingly at one of the guy's beers, I said, "It's been a long day with some bumps in the road, so let me buy you a drink to make it up to you."

Her brows rose in surprise at my offer. "You want to buy me a drink?"

"Sure," I replied, giving her my most convincing smile.

"Is this your way of apologizing for being a dick about the motorcycle ride?"

With a shrug, I replied, "Maybe."

"Still can't say you're sorry, can you?"

I grunted. "Not really sure that I need to, but if it makes you feel better, I'm sorry."

Alex grinned triumphantly at me. "That was a pretty shitty apology, but since it's coming from you, I'll take it."

"Does that mean you'll take a drink from me, too?"

"Won't your mother be expecting you for dinner?"

I shook my head. "The boys and I have to fend for ourselves when it comes to dinner on Wednesday nights. That's when Mama Beth has her ladies' Bible study down at the house."

"How terrible that you might actually have to cook for yourselves," she mused, the corners of her lips turning up in a teasing smile.

"When it comes to cooking and cleaning, we're pretty much shit out of luck."

She laughed. "Sounds like a typical man."

Motioning to the bar, I asked, "What's your poison?"

"Depends. If I'm at home and wanting to slowly unwind, I'd go for a beer. But after a long day like today, when a quick buzz would be good, I'd go for tequila."

I snorted. "Hard stuff like tequila? You've got to be shitting me, White-Bread."

"Nope. Patrón Silver if you have it."

"I thought you'd want some white wine."

She grinned. "I'm such a paradox."

Rolling my eyes, I said, "Big words again."

"I have two sides that don't really go together or make sense."

"I would have to agree." Waving Cheyenne over, I said, "Give me two shots of Silver."

Cheyenne gave me a slight glare before reaching under the bar for the Patrón. She set the two shot glasses down on the bar a little harder than she had to before pouring in the white tequila. Without another word to me, she headed down to the end of the bar, where some of the other guys sat.

Alexandra eagerly reached for her shot glass. Raising it, she cocked her brows at me. "Bottoms up?"

With a nod, I grabbed my glass. "Bottoms up," I echoed. As I brought the glass to my lips, I eyed Alexandra, waiting for her to pussy out. Instead, she sucked down the tequila in one gulp and didn't even use a lime.

Once I finished mine, I grinned at her. "Impressive."

"Thank you."

"Another?"

"I really shouldn't."

"Come on. Live a little."

"Riding a motorcycle and getting drunk off tequila on a school night? I'd say you're a bad influence on me."

"I take that as a compliment."

She laughed. "I imagine you would." She then handed me her shot glass. "I'll take you up on your offer."

"Good." When I glanced down the length of the bar, Cheyenne once again glared at me. I didn't know what her fucking problem was. I was just having a drink with Alexandra. It wasn't like I was fucking her on the bar or something.

Without a word, she came over to me. She slammed the Patrón bottle down on the bar. "In case you two want more."

And then she stalked away. Alex glanced from Cheyenne's retreating form over to me. "I don't think she's a big fan of mine."

With a shrug, I replied, "Doesn't matter."

"When she looks at me like she wants to scratch my eyes out, it does matter." Alex ran her finger over the rim of her tequila glass. "Are you seeing her?" she questioned softly.

"Not exactly."

"What does that mean?"

Grabbing the bottle of Patrón, I poured us both another well-needed shot. Without answering her question, I raised my glass to her. "Bottoms up again."

Alex took her glass and then clinked it with mine. "Cheers." We then both downed the shots, shuddering a little as the alcohol burned our throats. "Now, answer my question," Alex demanded in a no-nonsense tone.

"Okay, but you're not going to like it." I poured myself another shot. Surprisingly, Alex slid her glass over for a refill. Once we downed yet another one, I said, "I'm not dating Cheyenne, but I've been fucking her for over a year."

Alex's dark eyes widened at my summation. "I see."

"Hey, you asked."

"Actually, I see a lot more. She wants more from you, but you're not willing to give it. Right?"

"Maybe."

"Don't you want to settle down now that you have Willow?"

"Willow doesn't need some woman forced on her to play mommy. She has Mama Beth. Besides, Cheyenne isn't mommy material. I'm not sure she's even wife material."

"That wasn't exactly the question I asked, but your evasiveness about the subject of marriage and commitment speaks volumes."

"Look, I'm always honest with the women I'm with. What bullshit fantasies they get about me is their own damn problem."

Alex rolled her eyes. "You're such a romantic."

"Well, well, who do we have here?" a voice questioned behind us.

Alex whirled around a little too fast, causing her to stagger on her feet. "I probably should have eaten something before having those three shots," she murmured.

"Maybe you should have fed the poor girl something, Deacon," Case's wife, Kim, chastised.

"You know I'm more about getting them drunk than keeping them sober," I replied with a wink.

Kim smacked my arm playfully before reaching over to hug me. As she pulled away, her green eyes shot me a questioning look. I knew she was wondering what in the hell I was doing partying with Alex, especially right in front of Cheyenne. As the president's old lady, she was in charge of keeping the peace between the wives, girlfriends, and club whores. From her expression, I could tell she thought the whole situation had trouble written all over it.

Although I wasn't one to ever want an old lady, Kim was one of the best. With her humor, over-the-top personality, and heart as big as her natural double Ds, she made a hell of a president's wife. Case had fallen head over fucking heels for her the moment he saw her dancing underage at the Lounge. At first the seventeen-year-old blond bombshell didn't warm to thirty-year-old Case's come-ons. Like me, she'd run away from foster care at fifteen and had been living hard the last two years. But once she turned eighteen and he started showing her his softer side, the one his brothers had no idea existed, he finally won her over. They married a year later, and they still couldn't keep their hands off of each other, which was also evident in their five kids ranging from three to twenty.

Besides the wrath of Mama Beth, Kim was one of the main reasons that the Raiders never dealt in any prostitution. She'd been forced down that road for a period of time when she was on the streets, and Case respected the pain she had experienced too much to take anything on business-wise besides strippers.

"Where are your manners, Deacon? Introduce me to your friend," Kim said, interrupting my thoughts.

"This is Willow's teacher, Alexandra Evans." Motioning to Kim, I said to Alex, "This is our president's wife, Kim."

Alex extended her hand. "It's nice to meet you."

"Likewise," Kim replied with a smile.

Tiny strolled up then with a clipboard in his hand. "Hey, boss man. We just got some deliveries that need taking care of."

I nodded. "Excuse me, ladies." After I hopped off my stool, I turned to Rev. "Keep an eye on her," I said in a low voice.

"Sure thing," he replied.

It took a good fifteen minutes to take care of the inventory. It needed a little extra care supervising it out to the warehouse, considering what was inside—the latest gun shipment we were holding for our Tennessee chapter of the Raiders. Once it was secured inside, I headed back to the clubhouse.

Music blaring out of the jukebox, along with the sounds of whistles and catcalls, met me when I came back in the door. I couldn't imagine what the hell was going on. Then I did a double take at the sight of Alex on top of the bar, dancing with Kim. But she wasn't just dancing. No, she was singing off-key as loudly as she could with Kim to "Pour Some Sugar On Me."

"Well, fuck me," I muttered under my breath.

About ten of the guys encircled the bar, watching and cheering them on. Of course, most had their perverted gazes fixed on Alex. Her limber body served her well in ballet as well as bar dancing. Each sway of her hips and slide of her hand down her body caused my dick to swell. It was either cut and run or get Alex the fuck off that bar. Of course, there was also a third option, which had me getting her off the bar and taking her to my room to fuck her brains out.

I chose choice B for both of our sakes. I could only imagine that sober Alex would be mortified at her behavior. Striding up to the bar, I pushed some of the guys out of my way. When I saw Rev, I smacked him on the back of the head.

"Jesus, man, what's your problem?" he shouted over the music and singing.

Motioning to Alex, I said, "I thought I told you to watch her."

Rev grinned. "I am watching her."

"Yeah, for the record, her dancing on top of the bar was not what I had in mind."

"Come on, Deacon. She's just cutting loose and having some innocent fun."

At my "you gotta be shitting me" look, Rev said, "She's just dancing. If she had started trying to strip, I would've stopped her. As far as our brothers go, you can be damn sure that no one touched a hair on her head on my watch . . . well, maybe no one but Kim."

At that moment, Alex backed her ass up to Kim and ground against her. "Sweet Jesus," I grunted while the men around me shouted their approval. When Alex finally met my gaze, I crooked my finger at her. With the grace of a supermodel on a runway, she walked down the length of the bar to me. The moment she was within my grasp, I motioned her down to where I could whisper in her ear. When she did, I grabbed her by the waist and pulled her down.

My brothers booed and hissed at my move. "Shut the fuck up!" I shouted as I put Alex on her feet.

"No. I don't want to stop dancing."

"Yes, you do."

"I'm thirsty," she absentmindedly announced. One of our out-of-town members, Tony, handed her a beer. "Thank you," she replied sweetly. She then proceeded to down the thing in a series of big gulps and then sucked down another one that was placed in her eager hands.

"I don't think that was a good idea." Now that she was off the bar, she began to sway a little. Grabbing her shoulders, I steadied her. "Okay, I think it's officially time for you to go to bed."

Alex swatted my hands away from her. "Don't be a party pooper," she slurred. Glancing over her shoulder, she cried, "More shots!"

While Rev chuckled at her enthusiasm, a song with a fast beat came on the jukebox, and Alex scrambled to climb up on the bar again. "Get down."

"But I wanna dance again."

After her beer, she could barely walk, least of all dance. When I tightened my arms around her waist, she twisted around and then shoved me as hard as a drunk girl her size could. I didn't budge, so she sent a stinging smack across my face. "Get off me!"

"I do that, and you're going to end up on the floor."

Jerking her chin up at me, she shrieked, "You're an asshole!"

"And you're a mean little drunk," I mused, my cheek still stinging.

Alex's brows furrowed. "Am I really a mean drunk?"

"Considering you just slapped me, I would have to say yes."

She gasped. "Oh my God. I'm a horrible person."

"And a mean drunk," I teased. When her chin trembled, I groaned. "Now, don't go making yourself a 'crying drunk,' too," I warned.

After sniffling, she said, "I'm sorry I slapped you, Deacon."

"It's okay. I'm man enough to take it."

When she peered up at me, she frowned. Closing her eyes, she shook her head. After she opened them again, she looked like she was staring past me. "You two don't hate me, do you?"

I glanced left and right. There was only Alex and me standing there. "What the hell are you talking about?"

Her finger waved between me and the empty spot beside me. "You and him."

"Jesus, now you're seeing double?"

She hiccupped. "Maybe."

I rolled my eyes. "Okay, you're really going to bed now." Taking her by the arm, I started leading her toward the bedrooms.

"Good night, Alex!" came a chorus of male voices.

"'Night, boys!" she called over her shoulder.

As we started down the hall, she gazed up at me. "You know, I really like your boyfriends . . . I mean brothers. Bikers are pretty cool."

"I'm glad you think so," I mused.

When we got inside my clubhouse room, Alex gazed around. "I was expecting something different."

"Like what?"

"Lots of black leather, some fur furniture, and lots of mirrors."

I laughed. "Well, there's that one," I said, motioning to the ceiling.

"Oh," she murmured, gazing at our reflection.

"I can't take the credit for putting it up. Whoever had it before me must've liked mirrors."

Alex brought her gaze to mine again. "But you didn't take it down?"

"Nah. It's pretty cool sometimes."

"Yuck."

"Don't knock it till you try it, babe."

She shot me a disgusted look before stumbling over to the bed. When she started to face-plant on the mattress, I grabbed her arm. "Wait a minute." With my other arm, I pulled down the spread and sheets. "Get under the covers."

She snorted. "Yes, Daddy."

Rolling my eyes, I replied, "Don't call me that."

In a singsong voice, she asked, "Are you gonna read me a bedtime story, too?"

"No, I'm not. I'm going to hope and pray your drunken ass finally passes out, because you're driving me crazy." Her response was to stick her tongue out at me. "Now you're also an immature drunk."

"Ugh, it's hot," she whined, kicking off the covers.

"If you can wait a damn minute, I'll turn on the fan." When I turned back around from hitting the switch, I sucked in a harsh breath at the sight of Alex ripping off her shirt. The white lacy bra was about the sexiest thing I'd seen in a long fucking time. It may not have been skimpy, but just seeing the outline of Alex's pink nipples beneath the lacy shit made my mouth run dry.

But she wasn't through tormenting me. Oh no. She had to rip off her jeans next to reveal white boy shorts. I licked my lips, trying hard to hold myself back from ripping them off of her and burying my face between her legs.

With my dick pounding against my zipper, I knew I needed to get the fuck out of there. If I didn't, I was going to do something I would regret—something I never, ever did, which was fuck a seriously drunk girl. When I turned to go, she grabbed onto my arm, pulling me to the bed. "Noooo, don't leave."

"Give me a fucking break, Alex. You can sleep it off by yourself."

She giggled. "I promise not to try to take advantage of you."

"That ain't it." No, I would be the one defiling her in a hundred different ways.

Her amusement faded. Staring up at me with those big brown eyes, she asked, "Don't you want to stay with me?"

"You wouldn't ask me that question if you were sober."

"And why not?"

"Because you would know that I'm sure as hell not the type of man who does what a woman asks."

"Even if she begs?"

"I only listen to pleading when I'm fucking."

Her nose wrinkled. "You're a disgusting pig."

"Yeah, I am, babe. And don't forget it."

"Would you at least sit on the edge of the bed until I go to sleep?"

"You're not giving up, are you?"

"I promise I won't tell anyone that you did. You can save face in front of your brothers. Besides, I probably won't remember this in the morning anyway."

I don't know why I eased down on the side of the bed. But then that small voice of conscience, the one I usually ignored, seemed to overrule any idea about telling Alex no. Every time Alex got remotely near me, I should bolt in the opposite direction. I'd never met a woman this dangerous—one who made me do shit I didn't want to do, to consider shit I didn't want to.

Stretching my legs out, I pushed myself up in the bed to where I leaned back against the headboard. Although we weren't touching, I could still feel Alex beside me. She overwhelmed me with her presence in my bed—the smell of her perfume, the fall of her hair on the pillow, the slide of her bare thigh on the comforter.

Lacey was the last woman I'd just lain in bed with without fucking. When she wasn't a drunken mess, there was nothing I loved more than to spoon against her. Sure, it usually led to a hard-on and screwing, but just the soft feel of her body did something to me—it calmed me. I was starting to feel the same way with Alex.

I don't know how long we lay there. Alex was so quiet I thought she had fallen asleep. But then she shifted in the bed. Propping her head on her elbow, she gazed up at me. "Tell me something about yourself—something you've never told anyone else."

Scowling down at her, I replied, "You can get the fuck out of here if you think I'm going to do that."

"Why not?"

I laced my fingers behind my head. "Because that ain't me, babe. That ain't who I am or who I'll ever be."

"Why are you so afraid to open up to someone?"

"I'm not," I growled.

"Yes, you are."

Giving her a hard look, I said, "If you don't stop the emotional bullshit, I'm out of here. I swear you're the most lucid drunk I've ever seen. Why can't you be giggling and acting stupid?"

"After the initial buzz, alcohol usually makes me sharper."

"Lucky me."

"I just thought we could talk a little. I mean, I'm here every day, but I barely know you."

"And I'd like to keep it that way."

Both fury and hurt flashed in her dark eyes. "You're such an asshole."

"It'll do you some good to keep remembering that," I replied.

"Fine. You know what? I'll share something first to establish trust."

"You can talk until you're blue in the face, but it ain't going to get me to tell you shit."

"You wanna know why I decided to become a teacher?"

"No, I fucking don't."

Ignoring me, Alex said, "When I was sixteen, I got pregnant by my boyfriend."

My eyes widened, and I stared openmouthed at her. That was the last fucking thing I expected to come out of her mouth. "You mean a Goody Two-shoes like you got knocked up?" When she nodded, I couldn't help but ask, "But I thought you said you didn't have a kid. You give it up or something?"

"Or something," she replied in an agonized whisper.

The electricity in the room changed. I realized that we were standing on the emotional equivalent of a cliff. If I continued talking to Alex about this, I might as well take her hand and watch the two of us jump off the edge. With the stakes that high, I don't know why I wanted her to continue the story. Cupping her chin, I tilted her face to look at me. "What happened, Alex?"

"No one ever knew I was pregnant. I didn't tell my boyfriend, and I didn't tell my parents. I wasn't very far along when I found out." She shuddered. "I was scared. So fucking scared. From the moment I saw the positive on the pregnancy test, it shattered me emotionally. It felt like I was outside my body, watching myself like I was a stranger. Everything I said or did from that moment on was someone else. I'd always loved babies. I volunteered in the church nursery and babysat for everyone on my street. But in that moment when it came to my own, I couldn't accept it." She glanced up at me to gauge my response—her eyes weary like a battle-worn soldier.

"Did you have an abortion?"

A mirthless laugh escaped her lips. "Go to a clinic and have someone kill my baby? No. I could have never done something like that." She shook her head. "I did something far, far worse." She glanced back at me, her dark eyes almost soulless. "*I* killed my baby."

I sucked in a breath of shock at her admission. "You did what?"

"It was during rehearsals at my ballet studio. We were practicing lifts with our male partners. There was this really high one where I was practically over his head. And when the idea came crashing down on me, I didn't even take a moment to try to talk myself out of it. I just acted." She drew in a ragged breath, her eyes staring past me like she was seeing into the past.

"You would think it would have to be something pretty momentous to rip a life from your body. But it was so simple. . . . Just one slip of my leg, one missed position I'd executed flawlessly time and time again. And even as I started to fall, it still wasn't too late. I could've changed my mind, twisted my body to where I could've fallen on my back. But no. I made sure I came down as hard as I could on my abdomen."

Her eyes closed like she was once again experiencing the physical pain along with her emotional torment. "With the wind knocked out of me, I lay there, gasping and wheezing for breath. Everyone came rushing over, asking me if I was all right. When I could finally breathe again, I felt sick at what I had done, so I excused myself and went home. The rest of the evening I waited for something to happen, but it never did. As I lay in bed that night, I put my hand over my sore abdomen, and then in that instant, the strangest thing happened. The most absolute acceptance and love for my future child pulsed through me. I went to sleep that night ready to tell my parents about the baby first thing in the morning."

Tears shimmered in her eyes, and I could tell she was close to losing it. "I woke up in a pool of blood. When I screamed, my parents came running. I pretended that I had screamed in pain because of really bad period cramps. After shooing my embarrassed father out the door, my mother started caring for me like I was a little girl again. She stripped me down like a child and put me into the shower. While I washed the innocent blood of my baby off of me, she changed the sheets. If she suspected anything, she never said. She just called in to work and stayed in bed with me all day, giving me the comfort I so desperately needed."

"Jesus," I muttered, unsure of what the hell to say to such a story. Part of me wanted to get the hell out of there—put as much distance as possible between me and Alex's pain. Somehow being in that room with her was harder than facing down a thug with a gun.

"A year later, on the very same day I killed my baby, my parents were killed. Sometimes I think it was a punishment for what I did— a karmic retribution that I threw away what I was given, so I had something else I loved taken from me." My mouth gaped open that she could honestly believe that. For a minute I wondered if it was the alcohol talking, but then I remembered how sharp it made her.

"Hey, now, don't be thinking shit like that." When Alex didn't look at me, I took her face in my hands, enjoying the softness of her skin. "Did you hear me? Your parents' dying had nothing to do with the baby. Bad shit happens all the time."

She didn't acknowledge anything I said. "After they died, I changed my major to education. Not only was it to honor their memory, but I thought if I could love children, I could somehow repent for what I did."

"Alex, listen to me, dammit. You were just a scared teenage girl who chose a path that maybe wasn't the best route. In the long run, what you did wasn't any different from going to a clinic. The end result would have been the same."

"I did it to myself. That makes it worse."

"But it's not." Gripping her chin, I tipped her head up to look me in the eye. "You didn't kill your parents. Shit doesn't work that way. Yeah, you killed your baby, but what you did didn't start some cosmic chain of events to punish you."

When she only sighed in response to my words, I said, "Fine.

You want something about me? I'll give you something. When I was fifteen, I killed my father."

While I thought my statement might cause her to run, to cower in fear, or at least gasp in shock, she did none of that. She simply stared at me, waiting for me to continue. "That doesn't freak you out?"

"I always knew you were an outlaw, Jesse James," she said with a small smile.

"Is that right?"

She gave a slight nod of her head. "But without you telling me the history between the two of you, I can only imagine it was justified."

The fucking eerie calm with which she said the words had the same effect as someone dousing me with a bucket of ice-cold water. "How can you of all people sit there and say that I was justified? I murdered my own flesh and blood," I countered.

Easing up in the bed, she pinned me with a stare. "You want me to be judge, jury, and executioner? Then don't just tell me that you murdered him. I may not know you that well, but what I do know tells me you would never kill someone unless you had to." Jerking her chin at me, she said, "Tell me what he did to you."

"I think you're smart enough to already know."

"But I need to hear it from you." Inching closer to me in the bed, she murmured, "I think you need to say it aloud, too."

Panic pricked its way over my skin. I couldn't help glancing at the door, anxious to make an escape. No one knew about my old man but me and Preach. There was a possibility that Preach had told Case or some of the other guys, but I doubted it.

"My adopted father, Preacher Man, left his church in the summer. That fall, he came to me one day and asked if I'd ever wanted revenge on my father. I told him of course I did—it was something I thought of each and every day. I was fucking blown away when he told me he'd been able to track my old man down—something even the cops hadn't been able to do—and if I wanted to, he'd take me to him."

"What happened then?" Alex prompted.

I shrugged almost apathetically. "We drove to Texas, so I could end him."

"There's more to it than that."

Flashing her a grin, I replied, "But then if I tell you, I'd have to kill you."

"After what I told you, I thought we had established more trust than that."

"Fine. You want the gory details so you can have nightmares and never want to be in the same room with me again?"

Lowering her eyes, she replied, "Not really."

"Then don't fucking ask me questions like that, because you won't like the answers. All you need to know is he's dead and will never be able to hurt anyone ever again."

"How did he hurt you?" she asked, her dark eyes once again finding mine. They were so fucking hypnotic I could barely look away. She had to be doing some kind of hypnotizing hoodoo to make me talk as much as I had.

"He's a waste of air to talk about."

"I still want to know."

I threw up my hands in defeat. "My old man was fucking evil incarnate. What the hell my mother ever saw in him, I'll never know. Guess she thought she could change him, save him from what he was. But he only ended up taking her down with him. When I was two, he pushed her down a flight of stairs when she was eight months pregnant. Said he didn't need another mouth to feed. Lucky for him, my sister came stillborn."

Alexandra reached for my hand, but I jerked it away. Her expression saddened both at what I had said and probably how I reacted to her. "Your poor mother."

"She tried leaving him a bunch of times. Before my grandparents kicked it, she stayed with them some, but they were both so old and sick that they weren't any help to her against my dad. He'd threaten to kill them if she didn't come home to him." I shook my head as my voice choked off with emotion. "She must've felt like a fucking trapped animal."

"Tell me about her."

"She was beautiful, with long dark hair and dark eyes. Willow's going to look just like her."

"So you look like your mother?"

"Yeah, I guess so."

I tried to recall as much of my seven years with her as I could. "She smelled like apricots because she loved to wear this apricot lotion." A shaky laugh rumbled through me at one particular memory. "One time she didn't have the money to get any lotion. So being a scrappy five-year-old, I stole some off the shelf. I couldn't understand why in the hell she dragged me back there. She made me give it to the store manager along with an apology. But then, in her own patient way, she made me understand how wrong it was to steal. More than anything, she said, she wanted me to be better than my father." Reaching into my pocket, I tugged out a pack of cigarettes and my lighter. Alexandra didn't protest when I lit up. After a long drag, I said, "After all her hard work, she probably wouldn't be too proud of me today."

"You're too hard on yourself."

"And you're obviously too naive. What part of my world don't you understand? I told you I killed my fucking father."

"Why did you kill him, Deacon?" she repeated. Although she had asked it before, it seemed to be addressed in a different way. She must've known how I felt perfectly justified in killing him, but she still wanted more. She wanted to make me dig up that emotional grave where I had long buried the reasons that drove me to murder my bastard of a father when I was still practically a kid. After all, I was seemingly loyal, and the greatest breach of loyalty was killing your own blood.

Even though I should've ignored her question and stalked out of the room, I decided to give her what she was after. Then maybe she could once and for all know what an unimaginable bastard I was.

"Because he killed my mother! He tracked her down and tortured her like a fucking animal. He couldn't just slit her throat or shoot her. No. He made her pay for running from him. He beat her until she died from internal bleeding and a fractured skull that sent bone fragments slicing into her brain." Shaky hands brought the cigarette to my lips so I could take a drag. Sometimes late at night, if things were too quiet, I could hear her screams . . . hear her begging for her life. Then finally her pleading for my life.

"Where were you when your mother was being killed?"

"Why do you have to ask so many fucking questions? Are you some kind of morbid freak that gets off on shit like this? A masochist for emotional pain?"

Instead of cowering back at my verbal assault, Alex stood firm. "Where were you?" she repeated.

"Why do you need to know? What could you possibly get by fucking knowing?"

"It isn't for me that I'm asking. It's for you."

I tossed the cigarette onto the ashtray on the table, then lunged at Alex. Taking her by the throat with one hand, I glared into her eyes with enough venom that she should have cowered in fear. "If you were a man, I'd take you down for fucking with me like this."

"If hitting me makes you feel better, frees you of the pain, then hit me."

"Don't tempt me."

"Answer my question."

"You got a death wish, woman?"

"He tied you up, didn't he?" When my nostrils flared with anger, she said, "He didn't just leave you in the car or another room. He made you watch what he did, but you couldn't do anything to help her."

Squeezing tighter on her throat, I willed her to shut up. She was too close. She knew too much. She could see me too well.

Her fingers came to my hand, her nails digging into my skin. But as I stared into her eyes, there was no panic or fear in them. Easing back, I dropped the hand from her throat. I eyed it with contempt before dropping it beside me. What the hell had I been thinking to manhandle her like that? "I'm sorry," I croaked.

"No. I'm the one who is sorry."

"You damn well ought to be after pulling the shit you just did."

"I'm not sorry for that."

"Excuse me?"

"I'm sorry for the helpless seven-year-old little boy who has been forced to carry around such a burden, such guilt, for something he couldn't control."

I practically leaped off the bed to get away from her. "Don't you fucking dare start that pity shit with me!"

"I'm sorry that you've never been able to open up to anyone before for fear that they won't love your darker parts."

"Shut the fuck up!" I stormed out of the bedroom, slamming the door behind me. Although I wanted to march straight for the bar and down a few shots, my boots remained rooted to the hallway floor.

God, the things I'd said to her—the deepest, darkest parts of myself. No woman had ever gotten that much from me. Not Mama Beth, not Lacey. Fear had always bound me from revealing too much. That if they knew the real me, they couldn't love me. Sure, they may have had their ideas about what I got up to in my business, but they never questioned me about it. Hell, no one had grilled me like Alexandra had.

For reasons I couldn't fucking understand, I didn't escape down the hall to throw some back with my brothers. Instead, I opened the fucking bedroom door and slipped back inside.

Alexandra sat on the edge of the bed, the sheet pulled up to her chest. Her brows rose at the sight of me. "Me coming back in here doesn't mean I agree with what you said."

"Okay," she said softly.

I crossed the room to the bed. "You're a fucking pain in my ass, Miss Evans."

"I'm sorry. I don't mean to be."

Jerking my chin at her, I said, "Go on and lie back down."

"You don't want me to go?"

"No, I don't."

Surprise flooded her face. "I just expected that—"

"Don't you ever shut up?"

Her eyes narrowed slightly before she flounced back in the bed, burrowing under the covers. Of course, while she was doing that, I got another flash of her bra-covered tits and those damn boy shorts. While her behavior still had me fuming, just the sight of that petite yet strong body of hers fueled other reactions in me. Damn, that woman.

Once she was covered, I walked around the side of the bed. I eased down on the mattress to honor her request of staying until she fell asleep. Of course, I kept my ass on top of the covers and as far away as I could from her. When I thought she had finally settled down, I reached over and hit the light.

"Deacon?" she implored.

"Alex, if you know what is good for you right now, you'll close your fucking eyes and go to sleep."

"I just wanted to say thank you."

"What the hell for?"

"For talking with me tonight. It means a lot."

While I would never admit it to her, it meant a lot to me, too. The smallest sliver of peace ran through me. Regardless of how small it was, I would gladly take it. "Yeah, whatever," I grumbled.

Then I allowed myself to fall asleep next to a woman without sex for the first time in my life.

SEVEN

Alexandra

Sunlight streamed across the bed, warming me from beneath the sheets. The moment my eyelids fluttered open, panic set in. Where was I? My eyes frantically spun around the room. And then it all came rushing back to me along with the feeling of a brass band pounding out a rhythm in my aching head. I groaned as the memories of getting drunk off my ass and begging Deacon to stay with me flooded my mind. It also didn't escape me that I was in just my bra and panties. Of course, I was glad to remember that it had been me who'd taken my clothes off and not Deacon.

Holy shit. I'd slept with Deacon.

Glancing over, I found the bed empty. For some reason, it bothered me more than it should have. When I rolled over, I felt the indentation Deacon had made in the bed. I guess he really had stayed just until I'd fallen asleep.

When I thought of what I'd told him and what he'd told me, I flopped onto my back and rubbed my head. I'd never imagined he would be so open and honest with me. Even though he'd done it kicking and screaming, it meant so much to me. I don't know what it was within me that needed for him to entrust something so dark to me. Even though he wouldn't acknowledge it, I could see him so much better than he could have ever imagined. He had locked himself down so tight emotionally that the only way he could fully accept and love Willow would be to let go of the ghosts of the past and the pain they still inflicted on him.

While I should have been horrified that he had murdered his father, I wasn't. After the lifetime of hell he had faced, coupled with his mother's death, he had been justified in doing what he did. I didn't know what it said about me as a person that I could overlook something so terrible in his past. Maybe it was what I had been through myself.

A knock came at the door. "Yes?" I called, pulling the covers up to my neck.

Deacon appeared with a cup of coffee and something wrapped in a napkin. "Mama Beth sent this to you."

Sitting up in the bed, I reached for the goodies. After setting the coffee down on the nightstand, I unwrapped the napkin. "Oh, a homemade biscuit. I haven't had one of these in years."

My heartbeat thrummed wildly at the genuine smile that stretched across his face. I so rarely got to see this type of smile—one that didn't hide sarcasm or a teasing remark. "She thought you might like it."

"I hope she didn't go to all this trouble just for me."

"Nah. She makes a big breakfast for us every morning."

"Where's Willow?" I asked after taking a sip of scorching-hot coffee.

"Back at the house. I didn't think it would be a good idea to let her know you were here."

I nodded as I chewed carefully on the biscuit, not wanting to overload my alcohol-soaked stomach. "She'd ask too many questions."

"Yeah." He cocked his brows at me. "Kinda like her teacher."

A nervous laugh bubbled from my lips. "Yeah, I suppose so."

Neither one of us appeared to be able to mention what had happened last night. Deacon cleared his throat. "Just so you know, your car is outside."

"It is?"

Deacon nodded. "New alternator was all it needed."

"Are you sure I don't owe you anything?"

"Nope. It's all taken care of."

"Thank you."

"Keys are in the ignition. I know you gotta get going to get to work on time."

Glancing at the clock on the nightstand, I saw it was six thirty. "Shit. I do." Just when I thought of flinging the covers back and hopping out of bed, I realized I was half naked.

As if he sensed my panic, Deacon started for the door. "Yeah, so, I'll see you this afternoon."

"Yes. And thanks again for my car."

"You're welcome." He opened the door and then closed it again. Glancing at me over his shoulder, he said, "I trust that what was said in here last night will stay just between the two of us?"

"Of course."

"Good," he murmured. Then he slipped out the door without a good-bye.

There wasn't a chance I would ever share with anyone what Deacon had told me last night. We had both been extremely vulnerable in revealing the wounds of our past. Considering the shame and immense sadness I still carried with me about my own dark period in my life, I could never betray his trust, just as I wouldn't want him to betray mine.

In the end, it was a relief for me to unburden myself. For reasons I didn't understand, it made me no longer feel so alone.

• • •

That Sunday found me miles away from Deacon's world. A smile played at my lips when I thought of what Deacon would say about my surroundings. He would classify me sitting in the driveway of the two-story, cookie-cutter Colonial house on an upscale street as being in my white-bread world. He was probably right, considering it was worlds away from the Raiders compound.

Riding shotgun up front with me was my black Lab, Atticus. His wet nose nudged against my arm to hurry me along out of the car. He appreciated Uncle Jimmy and Aunt Joy's house as much as I did. Part of the reason was he was from a litter that came from Mahalia, Uncle Jimmy's prized bird dog. I guess it was like coming back home for him, just like it was for me.

Atticus bounded out before I'd opened the door more than a crack, not even bothering to wait for me. He was on the porch, woofing excitedly, by the time I got both myself and the food I'd brought out of the car. As I made my way up the familiar porch steps, the front door opened, revealing the smiling face of my uncle Jimmy. "Well, hello, stranger! I'm glad you remembered where we lived," he ribbed good-naturedly.

I grinned. "I'm sorry. Things have really been busy lately since I'm doing homebound services."

Uncle Jimmy nodded before drawing me into his arms. I couldn't help but thank God for him. My dad's siblings lived out of state, and my brother, Charlie, and I had never been close to them. With both sets of our grandparents gone, we could have been sent to one of them if it hadn't been for Uncle Jimmy.

When I pulled away to smile up at him, I could see so much of my mother in his face. They had the same dark, wavy hair, although Uncle Jimmy's had far more gray than my mom's had had. Their blue eyes always seemed to have a warm twinkle in them that immediately set you at ease and made you feel loved. My mom had been tall like him, but where my mother was lean, Uncle Jimmy had his "law-enforcement-induced doughnut gut," as he liked to joke.

"Come on. Let's get inside," he said, holding open the door.

"Is Lydia here?" I asked.

"No. She's on some dig in New Mexico."

Uncle Jimmy and Aunt Joy's only child, Lydia, was an anthropologist. Fifteen years ago, at eighteen, she had left home, and Georgia, and had barely looked back. Now that she had two sons of her own, whom Uncle Jimmy and Aunt Joy adored, she tried to make it back to Georgia at least once a month.

After I headed into the foyer, Uncle Jimmy took the bags of food out of my hands. As I started to the kitchen, a voice from the living room called out to me. "Yo, Al. Come get this wild animal off me!" Charlie yelled. I grinned, knowing that was his way of getting me to come see him. All these years later, he still wasn't good at expressing his emotions.

I entered the living room to find Atticus sprawled out on the couch beside Charlie. Instead of being truly aggravated by Atticus, Charlie was giving him a rubdown, which caused Atticus to groan in ecstasy. "Hey, little brother. It's good to see you," I said as I flopped down on his other side.

He grinned, which caused two dimples to pop out on his cheeks. It made him adorable to me, but I'm sure they caused girls his age to swoon. "It's good to see you, too."

"How's school?"

Cocking his head at me, Charlie replied, "You mean am I studying and going to class or partying too much?"

I nudged him playfully. "I wouldn't be your overbearing big sister if I didn't ask."

"True. Very true." When he still remained evasive, I cleared my throat to prompt him. He held up his hands. "Fine. I've got solid Bs at the moment."

"Oh, Charlie, that's wonderful. I'm so proud," I replied before throwing my arms around his neck.

"It could all get shot to hell before the end of the semester," he teased.

"Not on your life, mister." I pulled back to give him the same stern look I gave my students. "Don't make me come to Athens and follow you around."

He snorted. "Look, I know you don't have a life, but even I can't imagine you doing that."

"I do have a life," I countered.

"Your group of girlfriends who does monthly margarita nights counts as a life?"

"We go out more than that," I lied.

"Right."

"Besides, I'm very busy right now with teaching. I'm even doing homebound services."

"Yeah, Uncle Jimmy told me."

My brows rose up in surprise. "He did?"

Charlie nodded. "Said he was worried about you."

I swallowed hard. "Why?" I asked, although I already knew the answer.

"'Cause of where you're teaching." With a wry smile, Charlie added, "Who would have thought my good-girl big sister would be hanging out with a bunch of dirty and dangerous bikers?"

Rolling my eyes, I replied, "They're not like that."

"You sure about that? From what Uncle Jimmy said, the Raiders have been known to have their hands in all kinds of dirty dealings, like gambling and gun running."

I shrugged. "It's just rumor. None of them has done time for anything." I knew that was a partial lie, considering Deacon's father had been in prison before he started the Raiders.

Charlie's teasing expression turned serious. "Promise me you'll be careful."

"Is that actual concern for me, little brother?" I teased, trying to lighten the mood.

"Yeah, it is."

Patting his leg, I replied, "You don't need to worry. I'm fine. I promise."

Although he nodded his head, I could tell he wasn't convinced. But before he had the chance to press me for more details about the Raiders, Aunt Joy appeared in the doorway and beckoned us to come and eat.

Thankfully, neither Charlie nor Uncle Jimmy brought up the subject of the Raiders, and I was able to have a fun, carefree lunch with those I loved most in the world.

EIGHT

ALEXANDRA

Two weeks had passed since my drunken confessional with Deacon. I continued coming to the compound every day as though nothing momentous had happened that night. I usually stayed for dinner at least two nights a week. I found myself in a peculiar dance with Rev. He continued not to make a formal move on me, but whenever I was around, he gave me all his undivided attention. Whenever I would find myself talking at length to Rev at the dinner table or around the compound, I would always feel Deacon's hot gaze on me. His behavior was so confusing. Deacon still seemed to want something romantic to happen between Rev and me, but his pointed looks told a different story. Of course, I knew better than to question him. He was the master of being evasive and turning the tables on me. Besides, I wasn't sure I could handle a relationship with sweet, respectful Rev, never mind volatile and brooding Deacon.

Today, after Willow and I had finished with our lesson, I was surprised to find Deacon waiting on us outside the door. "You got a minute?"

"Sure."

"I wanted to show you something."

Willow stomped her foot beside us. "Deacon, that's not fair!" Then she flounced past us to go to Archer's side.

My brows creased in confusion. "What's she upset about?"

Deacon chuckled. "She's pissed because she knows I'm going to show you the work I've done on the ballet studio."

"But why would she care about that?"

"Because I'm making her wait to see it until it's finished. You know, to be a surprise."

I couldn't help smiling at him for not only building the studio for Willow, but for wanting the finished product to be a surprise. Our shoes crunched down the gravel path. "Any idea when Willow might be able to return to school?"

Deacon shook his head. When he didn't say anything else, I sighed. "You want to get rid of this job already?" he asked.

"You know that I love working with Willow. I just worry about her."

With true concern etched on his face, Deacon questioned, "You think I'm hurting her by keeping her here?"

"No. She's perfectly safe and happy here. I just hate that she doesn't have involvement with other children."

He scratched the stubble on his jaw. "Maybe I can get Kim to bring her kids over more. She and Case have some close to Willow's age. Mac's got a granddaughter close to her age, too."

"I think that would be a great idea."

Deacon motioned for me to go on ahead of him up the porch steps. When we got inside, Willow sat at the kitchen table with her arms crossed and a scowl on her face.

"Hey, thundercloud face, you're going to make it rain in here," I said with a smile.

"I wanna see the studio."

"And you will when it's totally finished," Deacon replied as he opened the basement door for me.

"I'll come down with you two and see the progress," Beth said.

Knowing that now Mama Beth was also getting to see the studio made Willow fume even harder, so I gave her an understanding smile and said we'd be back up soon. I stepped carefully on the worn boards of the stairs. From my vantage point, I could see why Willow had found it frightening. But when I reached the bottom of the staircase, I gasped in surprise.

While the basement was one large room that ran the length of the house, Deacon had worked to clear out the far end. Mirrors ran the length of the far wall, and a new tile floor had been placed down. I don't know how he had known to get the kind like I'd had at the dance studio. New lights had been put up so that it didn't appear so dark and foreboding, and the walls closest to the studio space were painted pink. Willow's wish had been granted with a barre.

"So what do you think?" Deacon asked.

Gazing around the room, I couldn't keep the smile off my face. "This is . . . amazing. You thought of everything." Turning to him, I asked, "You really did all this yourself?"

With a wink, he replied, "I've told you before I'm a man of many talents."

Beth chuckled. "What he means to say is that we have a few electricians and contractors in the club who helped him."

"Thanks for giving away my secrets, Mom," Deacon said good-naturedly.

"Pride goeth before a fall," she replied.

Deacon merely rolled his eyes at her response. At the far end of the room, I noticed a pile of boxes along with some odds and ends.

"What's all this?" I asked, motioning to an old stereo system with a turntable and a box of old records.

"That's my old man's vinyl collection. I didn't know if you could use the stereo or not."

"I don't think so. Most of the music I'll use with Willow is on my iPod." I thumbed through some of the records. "Wow. There're some great classics in here."

"I didn't peg you as an oldies fan," Deacon mused.

"Oh, I grew up on the oldies. My parents used to clean house every Saturday with Motown blaring—the Temptations, the Four Tops, Martha Reeves and the Vandellas." I smiled. "These bring back so many memories."

Deacon took the album out of my hand and put it on the turntable. The familiar crack and pop of a record filled my ears before the unmistakable opening of "My Girl" came out of the speakers.

"You should teach Deacon to dance," Beth suggested.

My brows rose in surprise. "You don't know how to dance?"

He scowled at both his mother and me. "I've never had a reason to learn."

Giving Deacon a pat on the back, Beth said, "Give it a try. They have daddy-daughter dinner dances at Willow's school. Don't they, Alexandra?"

"Yes, they do."

"Just another reason not to put her back there," Deacon replied.

Beth laughed. "I'm going to start dinner. Maybe by the time it's done, you'll have learned a few steps?"

While he didn't say no, the glare on his face certainly wasn't saying yes. As Beth started upstairs, I took a tentative step forward, holding out my arms. "Wanna try?"

"If I don't, you'll think I'm a fucking pussy, right?"

I laughed. "Maybe."

With a grunt, he closed the distance between us. His arms

started to slip around my waist. "We're not slow dancing like a school dance. This is different."

"How the fuck is it different?"

"Put one of your hands on my waist. Then put the other in my hand." Once he did that, I smiled up at him. "Good job. Now you can either sway like this or do a box step."

"I think I'd rather sway," he replied, his hand tightening on my waist. Even beneath the fabric of my skirt, my skin felt inflamed by his simple touch. It was the first time we had been this close, touched this intimately, since the night we'd let our personal skeletons dance precariously around the room.

It wasn't the first time a man had had his hands on me, but something about Deacon's touch felt different. Nervousness, coupled with anticipation, tingled through my body. Although I had tried to ignore his magnetism before, there was no denying it now. While he was so incredibly good-looking, it was his strong, all-male presence that overwhelmed me. Good sense told me that a woman like me should never want to be in a room alone with a man like him, but I chose to ignore the voices of doubt in my head. Instead, I decided to just let myself feel.

As he stared down at me, the expression on his face changed. I swallowed hard at the intensity of the look burning in his eyes. I didn't know how something so innocent had changed over to something so illicit. Since the night we'd shared a bed, everything had changed between us.

The crackling pop of the vinyl changed over to another song. As the sultry beat came out of the speakers, I immediately recognized it. Dusty Springfield's "Son of a Preacher Man." At that moment, there couldn't have been a song better suited to us. I stood before a Preacher Man's son, desperately wanting him to do some of the things in the song. Just the thought sent an ache spreading between my legs.

The only one who could ever reach me was the son of a preacher man.

Deacon's eyes met mine, and I couldn't help noticing the lustful gleam flickering bright in them. "Don't look at me like that," he growled.

"How am I looking at you?" I panted.

"Like you want to fuck me."

The electricity in the air around us crackled and popped the same as the vinyl coming out of the stereo speakers. I knew I should turn and run away. I had a job to do with Willow, which didn't include fucking her father. While I knew that being with Deacon would be an unforgettable experience, it was an emotional land mine that I didn't think I could escape from unscathed. Everything within me screamed to pry myself from his tight embrace and run upstairs to the safe sanctuary of Beth's kitchen.

Being good isn't always easy. No matter how hard I try.

But as Deacon continued to stare at me like a predator would with its prey, I wanted nothing more than to be consumed. Without a word, Deacon's thumb inched slowly over my bottom lip. Acting on its own volition, my tongue snaked out to flick against his skin. Deacon's dark eyes flared before he ducked his head and crushed his lips to mine. The force took me off guard, and I staggered back. His strong arms caught me and dragged me closer to him. Just as I had imagined, he knew what he was doing when it came to kissing.

Deacon's tongue plunged into my mouth as his fingers came to tangle through the strands of my hair. When he tugged them, I moaned into his mouth, enjoying the sting of pain. My hands slid up his back to grip the tops of his shoulders for dear life. His lips, along with the strength of his body and feel of his fingers, had the ability to liquefy my bones and muscles. At any moment, I expected to melt down his body and collapse into a puddle on the floor.

When he finally tore his mouth from mine, both of our chests heaved. He gazed down at me with hooded eyes. "What do you want from me, Alexandra?"

"I want you to fuck me." Instantly, warmth flooded my cheeks. I'd never been this brazen or direct with a man before. Deacon's domineering presence had the ability to bring out a part of me I didn't know existed. Even if it ruined everything between us, everything for Willow, I still wanted him to consume me.

With a groan, he slid his hands down my back to cup my buttocks. Pressing me forward, he ground the hardened bulge in his jeans against me. I gasped at the friction the contact caused. "Please, Deacon."

Bending me back, he kissed down my neck, his tongue swirling on my skin. I shivered.

Crashing back against the mirrored wall, I gasped in both pleasure and pain. Deacon didn't apologize. Instead, his hands came to roughly palm my breasts beneath my shirt. Within seconds, he had the buttons undone and was jerking down the cups of my bra. At the feel of his scorching-hot mouth on my nipple, I moaned and closed my eyes. As he pinched the other between his fingers, I began to rub my pelvis against him, desperate for friction to ease the ache. "What do you need, babe?" Deacon questioned in a gravelly voice.

"You. I need you," I whimpered.

"Tell me what you want, and I'll give it to you."

I gave a shake of my head, warmth filling my cheeks. Dirty talk usually embarrassed me, so I couldn't imagine saying what Deacon wanted me to.

With his eyes on mine, Deacon snaked a hand underneath my skirt. When one of his fingers skimmed the outside of my panties, I bucked my hips against him only to have him pull away. Frustration filled me. His breath scorched against my earlobe as he repeated, "Tell me what you want, and I'll give it to you."

"Please, Deacon."

"Please, Deacon, what?" He pulled his head up to pin me with his gaze. "Please kiss me? Please suck my nipples? Please finger fuck my pussy so I can come?"

Wanting to resist saying such horrible things, I clamped my teeth down on my lip. But then, as the seconds ticked agonizingly by, the desire grew too great. "Please finger me," I whispered.

A triumphant grin stretched across his face. "What did you say?"

"I said to finger me," I repeated a little louder.

"Finger you where?"

"You know where!" I snapped.

"Say it, Alex."

Grabbing both sides of his face, I shouted, "Finger my pussy, Deacon! Finger me until I'm so wet, it's dripping down my thighs! Finger me until I come, my walls clamping around you!"

His eyes widened as the amusement from teasing me faded from them. "Fucking hell," he muttered, shaking his head at me. "You're going to be the death of me, woman." And then he pushed inside my panties and, thankfully, thrust two fingers inside me. We both groaned at the contact. I rocked my hips against his fingers. Just as I started building toward the edge, he pulled his hand away.

"Please don't stop," I begged.

"Don't worry, babe. I want you to finish around my tongue."

Deacon knelt in front of me, his hands disappearing underneath my skirt. His rough fingers came to grip the elastic band of my thong before he jerked and tugged it down my thighs. After lifting my left foot, he widened my legs and placed my calf on his shoulder. With a wicked gleam in his eye, he ducked his head, burying his face in my pussy. "Deacon!" I hissed.

At the first drag of his tongue across my clit, I cried out, clawing at the strands of his dark hair. My hips rocked forward as his assault with his tongue continued down the lips of my labia. One hand came to grip my skirt, pushing it up to my hips. Glancing down, I now had a fabulous view of him as he licked and sucked. When my gaze met his, I couldn't bring myself to look away.

But as I grew closer and closer to coming, my eyelids fluttered shut, and I threw my head back against the mirrored wall. I gripped Deacon's hair tighter, working my hips faster against his tongue.

"Deacon? Miss Alex?" Willow's voice called from the top of the stairs.

At the sound of his daughter's voice, Deacon froze, his face still buried between my legs. My chest heaved as I tried to catch my breath. I desperately needed for him to keep going—I needed to explode around his tongue.

"Y-yes?" I finally stammered.

"It's time for dinner."

"Okay. We'll be right up."

With the lust-filled moment of frenzy broken, Deacon rocked back on his knees. He eased my shaky leg down. Glancing up at me, Deacon slid my panties slowly up my legs and thighs. "I better go," I whispered.

"You don't want to stay for dinner?"

I shook my head. "I can't sit across from you right now and make simple conversation."

He cocked his brows at me, a grin stretching across his lips. "I got you that worked up, babe?"

Jerking my chin at the bulge in his pants, I replied, "I could argue the same for you."

He chuckled. "You got me with that one."

Turning around, I glanced in the mirror to quickly smooth down my skirt and button up my top. Once I was finished, I tried to calm my out-of-control hair from where Deacon's fingers had mussed it up. When I thought I looked presentable enough, I started for the stairs. Deacon reached out and grabbed me, jerking me to him.

"Deacon, we have to—"

He crushed his lips to mine. When he pulled away, I was once again a dizzy mess. "I didn't want you leaving here feeling used. I meant to say good night."

"Thank you and good night," I murmured.

When he let me go, I raced up the stairs. At the sight of Rev and Bishop's expectant look, warmth flooded my face. "I have to go."

"But why?" Beth asked.

"I—I have to be at my aunt and uncle's tonight," I lied.

"What a pity," she replied.

"I know. I appreciate the offer, though." I grabbed my bag and purse and started for the door. Once I got out on the porch, I exhaled the breath I'd been holding. As my shoes crunched along the loose gravel to my car, my legs still shook from my heated moment with Deacon. The breeze that swirled around me helped to cool off my inflamed skin. It seemed to take forever to get my trembling hands to work the key fob to unlock my car.

After I slid across the seat and started the car, I glanced up. A shudder went through me at the sight of Deacon leaning against the porch railing. He was lighting a cigarette, and his still-lust-filled gaze pierced through the windshield to send desire pulsing through me again. It took everything within me not to turn the car off, race back to him on the porch, and demand he take me somewhere we wouldn't be interrupted so we could finish what we had started. I could still taste myself from his kiss. Instead, I forced myself to throw the car into reverse and tear my gaze away from Deacon.

As I made my way through the familiar streets back home, my mind and body stayed connected to Deacon. Images of our passionate moments flashed through my mind, and the ache between my legs continued to burn. Before I could stop myself, I slipped a hand between my legs and started to stroke myself over my panties, just as Deacon had before. When I reached a red light, I threw my head back against the headrest. My fingers flew harder and faster as I desperately sought the orgasm I'd been denied earlier. It was only the loud honk of the car behind me that brought me back to reality. Mortified, I jerked my hand away, a warm flush filling my cheeks. What in the hell had I been thinking, masturbating while in traffic? Deacon continued to bring out parts of me I never knew existed. And God help me, I liked it.

After easing into the garage, I put the car in park. When I reached to grab my purse, I caught a glimpse of myself in the rear-view mirror. A nervous giggle escaped my lips at the sight of my mussed-up sex hair, rosy cheeks, and swollen lips. I looked exactly like I had almost been had. Immediately, I was thankful that it had been dark outside on the drive home and no one had taken a glance at me when I was stopped at red lights.

Grabbing my purse, I got out of the car. After stepping inside the house, I couldn't help leaning back against the door as I continued to cling to my sex haze. Pinching my eyes shut, I could almost feel Deacon's hands on my body, his mouth and tongue on my nipples, his hard erection digging into my core.

Suddenly, I was snatched out of my fantasy world as a sense of dread prickled over my skin. Swiveling my head over to the alarm pad, I realized it wasn't going off even though I had yet to enter the code. I peered at the screen, and my chest clenched when SYSTEM DISABLED flashed on and off.

Waves of fear crashed over my body at the further realization that Atticus had yet to greet me. Normally, his pink tongue would be slurping over every available part of me as he went through his welcome-home wiggle dance. In a shaky voice, I called, "Atticus?" When no bark of acknowledgment came, I took a few tentative steps farther into the kitchen. "Atticus?" I repeated. Silence reverberated back at me.

Realizing I needed to get out of the house, I whirled around to flee. My feet slipped in something slick on the floor, and I crashed down onto my knees. As I tried to regain my footing, my hands slid through something warm and sticky. Staring down, I realized I was in a puddle of blood. A scream tore from my throat. Fumbling and flailing, I pushed my way out of it. When my feet bumped into the door, I started trying desperately to get up, but each time I pushed on my hands, my knees slid further in the blood.

Then the kitchen light flicked on above me. I once again screamed when I caught sight of a hulking man in the doorway. He wore a sinister smile as he stared down at me with one eye. A black patch covered his other eye, and beneath it a jagged scar cut across his cheek and down over his neck.

"Hmm. Just how I like my women—on their knees and screaming," the man said.

Repulsed and horrified both by his words and his appearance, I ducked my head. A sob choked off in my throat at the sight of Atticus's lifeless body at the man's feet; a large gash at his throat had sent his blood across the floor, causing me to fall. "No, no, no!" I cried, hot tears streaking down my face. Concern for my own fate momentarily took a backseat to the horror of the loss of Atticus.

When I glanced up again, the man stood right in front of me. Holding my hands in surrender, I pleaded, "Don't hurt me. I have money here. You can have all of it—you can take my car. Anything. Just don't hurt me."

Grabbing me by the shoulders, he yanked me up off the floor. I dangled from his hands like a puppet on a string while my legs tried to find steady ground. With a sneer, he replied, "Oh, I'm going to take from you all right. But it's not going to be any money or your car. For this to matter, it has to be physical."

His threat caused my knees to weaken, and if he hadn't been gripping me so tightly, I would have collapsed down onto the floor. "Please, no," I begged. He released one of my shoulders to send a stinging slap across my cheek.

"Don't say another fucking word, or I will end you—no matter what the boss man said."

Pressing my lips together, I nodded in agreement. My mind whirled with out-of-control thoughts. Who was the boss man? Why had he given this thug orders about me?

He set me on my feet and then shoved me into the kitchen table. He pressed against me, his massive body keeping me from getting away. From the inside of his cut, the man produced a long knife—one that looked like it belonged in the military. The blade gleamed in the kitchen light. After admiring it for a moment, he brought it to my throat. At the feel of the blade pressed against my skin, I began to hyperventilate. My chest heaved as I gasped for breath.

Lowering the knife, he brought it to the buttons on my shirt. Slowly, one by one, the blade popped the buttons off until the shirt gaped open. Grabbing me by the collar, he ripped the shirt off my arms. As I brought my hands up in front of my bra, he began to shred the fabric of my shirt. He slid the knife back into his cut and took one of the strips, holding it taut between his hands.

"This should keep you quiet." Before I could protest, he had the strip over my mouth, gagging me. Now no one could hear me scream. The thought sent delirious desperation rocketing through me.

This isn't happening. It's all just a dream . . . a nightmare. You'll wake up in a few seconds.

With another one of the strips of cloth, he bound my hands. The fabric cut into my skin, and I cried out against the gag. Then he gripped my hips and hoisted me onto the kitchen table. He brought my hands up over my head and looped the binding to the chandelier. "On your knees," he commanded. I flailed around until I was kneeling on the kitchen table.

"Now, that should keep you quiet and still for what I have to do." When his hand went to his belt, I began to thrash against my bindings. I tugged as hard as I could, hoping to bring down the chandelier if I had to. Once his belt was off, he gave me an evil smile before bringing it over his head. A loud crack echoed through the room before the leather bit into the flesh on my abdomen. Tears stung my eyes as I screamed behind my gag. The next blow of the belt hit me across the breasts. I didn't even have the chance to recover before another lash broke against my back and then my thighs.

The man's harsh voice cut through my painful fog. "Rumor is you're Deacon's old lady." When I didn't acknowledge his words, he brought the belt across my cheek. After I finished screaming from the pain, his eye locked on mine. "Answer me, bitch. Are you Deacon's old lady?"

I shook my head furiously back and forth. My response was rewarded with another lashing from the belt. "He had you on the back of his bike. You spent the night at the Raiders compound, and he has a prospect follow you home. That is fucking old-lady territory."

"N-no, I—I'm n-not," I stammered from behind the gag. "I s-swear."

The man eyed me curiously before his lips curled in a sneer. "You lie. You lie to try to save yourself and to save that piece of shit you spread your legs for."

"No!" I cried.

"I'll go easier on you if you tell the truth. You see, we need to draw him out. Since he keeps that brat under lock and key, you were the next choice. He'll want revenge for us hurting you, and that's when we'll strike. So I'll ask you again, are you Deacon's old lady?"

Fearing for my life, I finally nodded my head. "Yes. Yes, I am."

When he licked his lips, fear prickled over my body like tiny knives. "Now comes the best part of the job."

While the beating had been horrible, the insinuation of what he was about to do was more than I could bear. He pushed me back farther on the table. Shoving my legs apart, he came to stand between them. His fingers grabbed at the button on my skirt, and I closed my eyes, praying for strength. Then, with everything I had left in me, I shoved him with one foot and then kicked him in the face with the other. The force sent him flying backward against the kitchen counter. Once again, I pulled and tugged against my bindings with all my strength.

When the man pulled himself up off the floor, blood pooled from his busted lip. "You fucking cunt!" he screamed. I tried scrambling away on the table, but I had nowhere to go. His fist pounded into the side of my head. The world around me spun in a dizzying flurry before the dark curtain of my nightmare came crashing down.

NINE

DEACON

As Alexandra's taillights faded in the distance, I pounded my shit-kickers down the porch steps. Flicking my cigarette butt into the bushes, I made my way down to the clubhouse. Just like her, I couldn't manage to sit down at a table full of my family right now. More than anything, I needed something to block her from my mind. Her scent clung to my body and fingers while her taste still resided on my tongue. I found myself completely fixated on her. Considering the half-mast erection I still sported, my body was still thinking of her, too. Taking an emotional and sexual stroll down memory lane wasn't something I was used to doing, and it was freaking me the fuck out. The very fact Alexandra had this much effect on me when we hadn't fully fucked was even more mystifying.

The sound of Archer's pipes roaring to life brought me out of my thoughts. Every night I had the prospect follow Alexandra home and make sure she was safe. I had instructed him to always hang back a little because I didn't want to spook her that her life might be in danger because of her association with me. Because she was also way too smart for her own good, I didn't want to arouse any more suspicion about how dark my dealings were.

I gave a nod at Bubba and Ollie as I headed in the back door. Since it was a Friday night, the clubhouse was filled with members from in and out of town. From the looks of it, all the rooms would be used.

I slid across one of the worn barstools. I didn't even have to flag Cheyenne down. Like she possessed some kind of "Deacon radar," she had been alerted to my presence the moment I'd walked in. I had felt the heat of her eyes seeking me out as I walked through the crowd, stopping to say hello to some of the out-of-town members.

With her palms planted on the bar, she leaned in, cocking her brows at me. I shook my head at her behavior. She always knew what I wanted and usually hauled ass to get it for me. "What crawled up your ass tonight? Get me the usual. Now."

Shooting me an "eat shit and die look," Cheyenne shoved her hands off the bar in a huff and then went to snatch me a beer out of the fridge. After popping the top on it, she thrust it across the bar to me. But when I reached for it, she jerked it away from me. I narrowed my eyes at her. "Seriously, bitch, what the fuck is your problem tonight?"

She slammed the beer bottle down in front of me. "I think I'm the one who should be asking that question."

"Excuse me?"

Cheyenne crossed her arms over her chest. "Are you fucking her?"

"I don't know what you're talking about."

She rolled her eyes. "Don't be an asshole, Deacon. You know exactly who I'm talking about. The little white-bread bitch who has been making doe eyes at you since the day she walked in here."

I took a pull of my longneck. "Alexandra. Her name is Alexandra," I replied.

At the mention of her name, Cheyenne's nostrils flared in rage. "I don't give a fuck what her name is. I do give a fuck about the fact that you've just waltzed in here with her scent all over you, not to mention the fact you got fucked-up hair and your lips are colored from her lipstick."

"Last time I checked, you ain't my old lady, and there ain't no 'Property of Deacon' patch on your back. So you best not be sticking your nose in my business."

My declaration caused the angry expression carved into her face to recede, and in its place, there was one of extreme hurt. "Deacon, you know how I feel about you—" she began in a shaky voice. My phone buzzing in my pocket interrupted her. I dug it out and glanced at the ID. Unease washed over me as I accepted the call.

"What's wrong, Archer?"

"Fuck, man. Some asshole shot out my back tire as I was tailing Alexandra. I skidded out. My bike is a fucking mess. Someone called the cops because I'm bleeding and shit, and then—"

"I've got it from here. Call Rev. Give him the lowdown and have him and the boys meet me there." Before Archer could say another word, I cut off the call. In a flash, I was off the stool and sprinting for the door.

"Deacon?" Cheyenne called after me.

I ignored her. As I threw open the clubhouse door, I eyed one of the older members leaning against the hood of his car, talking to one of the club whores. Pointing to the car, I said, "I need to borrow that. Now."

Without a word, he tossed me the keys. After jerking open the car door, I slid across the leather seat and cranked up the engine. There was no way I was taking my bike. I would be too vulnerable and too suspect. A car could ease up to the house without notice, while the unmistakable sound of a cycle's pipes would give me away.

I spun out of the parking lot, kicking up a cloud of dust and gravel. My hands gripped the steering wheel until my knuckles turned white. As I shifted in the seat, I felt like a caged animal. I knew in my gut that if Archer's tire had been shot out, then Alex was in serious trouble. Sigel and his thugs had somehow worked out her connection to me. *Fuck.* I couldn't focus on the extent of the danger Alexandra was in or I would completely lose my shit. I had to stay calm. I was no good to her or myself if I went off the deep end.

Instead, I focused my rage on who I suspected was responsible. Sigel. He'd been lying low, searching for a way to draw me out. When it hadn't worked with Willow, he'd moved on to someone else—someone he thought was very important to me.

In that moment, as my mind spun with out-of-control thoughts, I realized how much Alex did mean to me. She was more than just Willow's teacher. In the small, stolen moments we had spent together, I'd come to care about her more than I'd ever expected. While I wanted her physically so fucking bad, it was deeper than that. I'd wanted her body all along, and this afternoon was just an example of how much. But there was more. I wanted to end Sigel for trying to take something from me I hadn't yet gotten to claim.

When I reached Alex's street, I parked three houses down from hers. I didn't know how many of Sigel's men had her. After I killed the engine, I escaped off the driveway and started sprinting through the heavily tree-lined yards. At the corner of her yard, I ducked behind a bush to survey the scene. The streetlamp overhead gave enough light that I could see there was no car parked in Alex's driveway. However, just down the street, a dark car sat outside a house with a FOR SALE sign in the yard.

Keeping low to the ground, I hustled across the driveway. With the garage door down, I made my way around the side of the house, searching for another way into the garage or the house. I found a side door to the garage that was locked. Taking my wallet out of the back of my pants, I used one of the oldest tricks in the book to shimmy the lock open.

I slipped inside the darkened garage, stepping lightly to avoid making any noise. I was halfway around the side of Alex's car when the sound of struggling caused my chest to constrict. "You fucking cunt!" a man's gruff voice shouted. When I got to the door, I peered inside. Rage burned within me at the sight of Alex bound, gagged, and unconscious. It took everything within me not to rush forward. But I had to keep my head and use reason in the situation. I'd come armed with only a gun, and anything that loud was going to alert a neighbor and the police. That was the last thing I wanted. I was going to take care of this fucker with my own hands.

But all reasoning went out the window when the man pushed up Alex's skirt, revealing her thighs. Before his hand could go any farther, I stormed through the door. The man whirled around. Before he had the chance to raise his knife to me, I landed two hard punches in his jaw and gut. The knife clattered to the floor. When he reached for it, the heel of my boot smashed down on his wrist, grinding the heel into the back of his hand. As he cried out in pain, I brought my leg up to kick him hard in the chin. He went spiraling back.

I nailed him with two hard punches to the gut and then to the jaw. Blood spattered over my knuckles and onto my hands. I grabbed him by the hair and began slamming his face into the stove. When he finally slumped over, signaling I had beaten him unconscious, I released his hair and shoved him onto the floor.

At the sound of a whimper, I whirled around. Alex must've woken up sometime while I was beating the scum who had dared to attack her. When I met her eyes, they were wide with fear. I took a few steps toward her and held up my hands. "Alex, it's okay. It's just me. No one is going to hurt you anymore."

When I reached for her, she shrieked and shifted away from me. I didn't know what kind of fucking shock she was in. I had expected her to fall into my arms. At that moment, Rev and Bishop, along with Case and Mac, came busting into the house from different entrances.

"House and perimeter are clear," Case informed me.

"Good."

"So it was just that one fucker?" Mac asking, motioning to the man crumpled on the kitchen floor.

"Yeah. Hopefully the piece of shit is down for a while." Glancing back at Alex, I said, "But I don't know about her."

"She in shock?" Mac asked.

I nodded. "Won't let me near her. I think it's something about seeing me beating the hell out of the man."

Case nodded. "She's spooked about you."

"Wash your hands and face," Rev ordered. I almost told him to go fuck himself until I caught a glance at my reflection in the stainless-steel refrigerator. I realized then how I frightening I must look to her with blood spattered on my shirt and face, not to mention that my hands, all the way up to my elbows, were coated in it.

With a nod, I stepped past him and made my way over to the sink. My feet slid in something, and I glanced down. "Son of a bitch! That fucker killed her dog."

At the mention of the departed dog, Alex whimpered. "I'm sorry, babe. I'm so fucking sorry," I muttered over my shoulder. When she didn't respond, I went on to the sink. I ripped my shirt over my head, wiping some of the blood off my arms. As I turned on the hot water, I craned my neck to watch what Rev was doing.

Taking a knife from his pocket, he slowly approached Alex. "Alexandra, it's Rev. Will you let me cut you down?"

She stared at him with eyes like a wild animal that had been caged. But Rev didn't back down. He kept inching closer and closer to her. "None of us are going to hurt you. I want to cut you down, so we can get you out of here and back to the compound. You'll be safe there, and we'll take good care of you." Rev spoke evenly and in a soothing tone. Finally, it seemed to be getting through to Alex.

"I'm going to cut you free now." She eyed him warily, but she didn't try to move away. Rev sawed at the bindings that held her to the kitchen light fixture. When she was free, he eased her arms down, rubbing them to help the blood flow back into them. "Will you let me cut the gag now?"

Slowly, she nodded her head. He reached behind her and sliced the cloth. He peeled it gently away from her mouth. Tenderly, he rubbed her cheeks, which were lined red where the gag had been. "Go get her a blanket, B," Rev instructed.

Bishop nodded and disappeared into the living room. Now that she was down and being comforted by Rev, I dipped my head under the water to wash away the blood. I was only halfway through rinsing my face and hair when I heard Alex scream my name. I jerked up, water cascading down my back. "Deacon!" she cried again.

I didn't even bother with a towel. All I cared about was getting to her. When I reached the table, she dove into my arms, pressing her face against my bare chest. "Shh. I'm here. It's all right," I said. I tried not to wince as she dug her fingernails into the skin over my shoulder blades. I didn't think she was going to be satisfied until she had completely climbed into my skin.

"He wanted to draw you out—he wanted to use me to draw you out so he could hurt you."

Pulling back, I stared into her face. "What are you talking about?"

"The man said his boss wanted to draw you out. That he couldn't get to Willow, so he had come for me." Her wild gaze met mine. "Don't let him get to you, Deacon." She gripped my shoulders tighter. "Promise me no matter what that you'll stay safe."

"I promise," I said, fully aware I was lying through my teeth. Now that Sigel had struck against me, there was no way I could promise her I would be safe.

Bishop returned with the blanket, and I wrapped it around Alex as well as I could before I reached down to grab her up in my arms. As I cradled her to my chest, my gaze swept over to Rev and Bishop. "Will you two get some of her stuff together? Take care of the dog and all this mess. I'm going to get her back to the compound."

Bishop nodded while Rev jerked his chin over to where Alex's attacker remained unconscious. "What about him?"

My lip curled in disgust. "Case and Mac can get him back to the compound, but no one touches him except me."

"Okay," Rev replied. As I started to the door, I felt Rev's hand on my back. "Take good care of her, D."

Glancing over my shoulder, I took in his agonized expression. Part of it was worry for Alexandra, for me, and for the club. But another part held his own private anguish at the way Alex had called for me, reached for me, as if I were her only way to breathe again. The last strands of her sanity. I knew that had to fucking hurt. But the man was better than I was, always had been. "You have my word."

Once I got outside, I found Crazy Ace and an out-of-town member, Sidewinder, waiting by the bikes. "I need one of you guys on escort back to the compound."

"You got it," Sidewinder said. He slid across the seat of his bike as I started down the street to the car. I found an out-of-town prospect standing beside the car, watching over it. He hustled to open up the door for me. When I tried to deposit Alex over in the bucket seat, she gripped my shoulders and molded herself tighter against me.

"Babe, I gotta drive."

Her breath came in frightened pants against my neck. "Don't let me go, Deacon. I'll fall apart if you don't hold me together."

Crazy Ace came to my side. He took the keys from my hand and then opened the back door. "I got it, Sarge."

"Thanks, man."

As best I could with Alex in my arms, I dipped down onto the seat. Once we were inside, Crazy Ace closed the door and then slid behind the steering wheel. As we started down the road, Alex's silent tears began to fall on my bare chest. Easing her back, I stared into her eyes. "Talk to me, babe."

She drew in a ragged breath. "I'm sorry I can't stop crying. I hurt so bad," she moaned.

I knew she had to be in extreme pain from the welts on her body, coupled with the strain of being tied up. I didn't know what else that fucker had done to her. I didn't want to think what else he could have done that made her hurt. "I promise the minute we get back to the compound, we'll get you some drugs." I brushed the sweat- and tear-soaked strands of hair out of her face. "Until then, you fucking cry all you want."

My words caused her lips to tremble, and the waterworks started again. I spoke in low tones to her, reminding her of little things about her time with Willow. It seemed to soothe her a little, and her tears had almost stopped by the time we turned onto the familiar road to home.

When we got back to the compound, Crazy Ace could barely pull into the parking lot for all the people milling around. I'm sure word had spread, and now everyone was on edge. Once he put the car in park, I threw open the door, not caring if it hit anyone who was standing by. When I pulled myself to my feet, Alex cried out at being manhandled to ensure she stayed in my arms. I shoved my way through the crowd, ignoring the questions peppered at me.

"All right. Get the fuck out of the way. What the hell is wrong with you guys? Give the poor girl some air!" Kim's voice bellowed behind me. I turned around and gave her a grateful smile. She nodded and then started walking away from the car. Like the iron bitch only she could be, she led the way inside the clubhouse, knocking people aside or smacking them back if they got too close.

Once we were inside, I hustled Alex back to my room. Thankfully, someone had had the presence of mind to call Breakneck Bob, also known as Dr. Robert Edgeway. He stood outside my room with his medicine case in hand. Breakneck had been an original charter member of the Raiders. At first everyone thought he was just some preppy upstart trying to show he had a pair by riding a motorcycle. But even though he was in medical school and came from one of the finest families in town, Breakneck was the real deal when it came to a biker. He'd patched out several years back, when the hospital threatened his license for being a member of the Raiders. Now he stayed close with the club by being our unofficial club doctor.

"Hey, man. Glad you could make it," I said as I swept past him into my room.

"I'm sorry that I had to be called out for something like this," he replied. He ducked in behind me, setting his bag on the nightstand.

Gently, I laid Alexandra down on the bed. When she saw Breakneck, she clawed at me not to let her go. "Easy, now. He's one of us, but more important, he's a doctor. He needs to check on your injuries."

"Stay with me," she whispered, clutching my hand.

I nodded. "I will."

Breakneck gave Alex a gentle smile. "My name is Dr. Edgeway, but you can call me Bob. I'm going to take good care of you."

His words did little to ease Alexandra. Before he began to examine her, he dug in his bag and produced a bottle and a syringe. "I'm going to give you just a little something for the pain. It will also calm you down."

She gave a slight jerk of her head while her eyes remained firmly locked on mine. After the shot, Alex became a little calmer. He went through a bunch of procedures, from shining a light in her eyes to listening to her heartbeat. He examined the cuts and scrapes on her face and chest, proclaiming they would need to be cleaned and disinfected.

When his fingers came to her bare abdomen, Alex jumped out of her skin. "I'm just palpitating your organs to make sure there's no internal bleeding."

Gritting her teeth, she gripped my hand tighter and tighter. "Looks like you're okay in that area, but I'm afraid you've got a bruised shoulder. I can't tell for sure without an X-ray machine."

"Okay," I replied.

"Alex, I have to ask you this to see if I need to further my exam. Were you sexually assaulted tonight?"

Tears pooled in Alex's dark eyes, but she shook her head firmly back and forth. I couldn't help the sigh of relief that escaped my lips. I knew she had been through hell, being beaten and strung up like she had, but I didn't think I could bear for her to have been raped because of me.

"I'll come by and see how you're doing in the morning. For tonight, I would advise you get cleaned up and then try to get some rest. I'll wait outside until you're ready to sleep, and then I can give you something."

"Okay," Alex murmured.

Breakneck nodded and then gathered up his case. When he slipped out the door, I turned to Alex. "You want Mama Beth or Kim to help you with a shower?"

"You. I want you."

"Are you sure? I mean, I know we've messed around, but I'll have to see all of you, and you've already been through so much tonight."

"I need you to take care of me, Deacon."

I exhaled a frustrated breath. "Babe, I gotta be honest. I can beat the hell out of the scum who hurt you, but this tender-loving-care shit?" I shook my head. "I ain't cut out for it."

"You're doing just fine so far."

"Fuck." I grunted before rising up off the side of the bed. Leaning over, I drew her to me, picking her up off the mattress.

When I got to the door, she yelped in surprise. "Where are you taking me?"

"To the house."

"Okay," she whispered before ducking her head to my chest.

Breakneck followed along with us, occasionally stepping in front of me to direct people out of our way. I couldn't remember the last time the clubhouse had been so packed. But anytime an attack went out on the club in any form, members from all over started to come in.

Kim fell in step with us as we made the silent journey down the road to Mama Beth's. I wasn't surprised to see her standing on the front porch when we walked up. Worry etched across her face as I climbed the stairs.

Without a word, I walked straight to the bathroom. Before I shut the door, I glanced over my shoulder. "Rev and Bishop are bringing her things. Lay out something for her."

"Of course. Anything she needs," Mama Beth replied.

I kicked the door shut with my boot. Then I eased Alex down on the toilet. She looked so fucking fragile sitting there. With her pale skin, she looked like a china doll that might shatter to pieces. Spinning around, I turned on the shower, adjusting the temperature to lukewarm. I knew anything too hot would be hell on her skin where she'd been lashed.

Once the water was ready, I turned back around. "I need to get you undressed now."

She glanced up at me through her long lashes before gently letting the blanket fall away from her shoulders. Grimacing, I reached around her back to unhook her bra. When it came undone, Alex momentarily kept the fabric pressed against her. Taking her by the waist, I eased her to her feet. I undid the button on her skirt and let it fall down her legs.

When my fingers grazed the waistband of her panties, I realized how hard she was trembling. "Alex, I don't need to do this. Let me get Mama Beth."

"No. I want you," she replied with a firm resolve in her voice. She let the bra fall from her body. Then she reached for her panties and slid them down her legs. Once she was naked, she stared up at me. "Get undressed."

"What?" I demanded.

"You're just as dirty as I am. He's still on your hands."

I glanced down to see the reddish stain on my hands and fingers. I hadn't had much time to scrub up in her kitchen before she had screamed for me. "Fine," I replied. I'd already abandoned my blood-spattered shirt back at her house, so all that was left was to slide off my jeans. I never wore underwear.

Taking Alex's hand, I led her over to the shower. When she stepped inside, I followed behind her. The moment the water hit her battered skin, she screamed. "Just give it a minute."

"I-its l-like razor blades," she sputtered.

"I know. It'll stop stinging in a minute."

My heart ached at the tears that streamed down her face. I'd been beaten enough to know what those first few minutes of hell in a bath or a shower felt like. But she'd been so sheltered, so protected, that it was a nightmare for her. And it was all my fault.

Brushing her hair back from her face, I whispered, "Shh. It's going to be okay."

She buried her face in my chest and began to cry so hard that her body shook mine. For a moment, my arms stayed at my sides. I was unsure how to handle the situation, especially with her injuries. Then, finally, I wrapped her in my embrace. "I'm sorry, Alex. I'm so fucking sorry."

"Why are you apologizing?"

"This never would have happened to you if it hadn't been for me."

Pulling away, she stared up at me. "You can't blame yourself."

"If you hadn't been involved in my world, you would be at home right now, sleeping in your bed with your dog at your side," I argued.

With a defeated sigh, she said, "Maybe that's true. But if me being attacked saved Willow from any harm, then it was worth it. Just as it was worth it to be a part of her life . . . and yours."

Cupping her face in my hands, I said, "It'll fucking haunt me forever that I didn't keep you safe enough. I thought I was doing enough having Archer follow you home."

Her brows shot up in surprise. "You had him follow me?"

I nodded. "I wanted to make sure you got home all right." Jerking a hand through my hair, I sighed. "But you have my word that with everything I have in me, you'll never be hurt again."

"Are you sure you can promise that, Jesse James?" When I opened my mouth to protest, she shook her head. "You're an outlaw. You and your club live by a different code that I can't even begin to understand."

"That outlaw code you're talking about? I'm going to use it to ensure that you're never harmed again and that the fucker who dared to touch you pays." I stared into her face, searching her expression. "You get me?"

She sucked in a harsh breath as her eyes widened. I knew then she understood what I was going to do to the fucker who had hurt her. "No one is ever going to hurt you again," I reiterated.

"I want to believe you, Deacon. But with everything that has happened to me in my life, I'm a realist. I don't see how that's possible." In a low voice, she said, "How we're possible."

A crippling panic worked itself over my body. I didn't like what I thought Alex was saying or what she might be implying. "So what are you trying to say? You don't want to be a part of my world?"

Reaching past me, she picked up Mama Beth's body wash. Taking my hand, she squirted some in my palm. "I don't think I can take a washcloth on my skin right now. Will you be easy?"

I cocked my brows at her. "Will you answer my question?"

She raised her eyes to meet mine. "I can't right now."

"You can't or won't?"

"I just can't," she whispered.

"Fine." I swallowed the lump in my throat and took a deep breath. Although I couldn't imagine her not in my world, I had to admit that it made sense she might not want to be in it. Without another word, I rubbed my hands together to make a lather. "Turn around," I instructed.

Slowly, she pivoted to where her back faced me. As gently as I could, I reached my hands out to touch the broken and puckered skin where that bastard must have hit her with his belt. I knew the look of the marks all too well from when my old man used to beat me when I was a kid. She jumped the moment I touched her. I don't know if it was from the pain or from how intimately my hands were on her. Glancing over her shoulder at me, she threw me a shy glance. "That okay?"

"Yes. Thank you."

I washed down her arms and her lower back. When I got to her buttocks, I drew in a breath. Although sex should have been the farthest thing from my mind, I couldn't help admiring the swell of her ass, the way the globes felt when I rubbed over them. Silently, I willed myself to think of anything but sex. Instead, I focused on how I was going to pick her attacker to pieces just as soon as I could get a moment alone with him.

When I finished the backs of her legs, I stood up. "Turn," I commanded again. She obediently followed my instructions. As if on autopilot, her arms came up to cross over her breasts, modestly covering them from me. "Babe, I had my mouth on those earlier tonight, if you remember correctly."

Her cheeks flushed, and she ducked her head. I groaned and ran a soapy hand through my hair. "Shit, I'm sorry. That was a bastard move to remind you of earlier, considering what all you've been through."

"It's okay," she whispered.

"No, it's not. It's exactly why I wanted Mama Beth or Kim in here with you. I'm fucking this up and hurting you."

Her gaze jerked to mine. "How many times do I have to say that it's only you I want? I need you, Deacon. I really do."

Cocking my brows at her, I countered, "Yeah, and not five minutes ago you were acting like you were gonna bail on me and this outlaw life just as fast as you could."

Her dark eyes flashed with anger. "Can you just for a moment try to put yourself in my shoes? I didn't grow up in this world. I'm not used to bad blood and turf wars. Then I got the shit beaten out of me tonight and almost raped. I'm sorry if it's past your comprehension that I might need a minute or two to catch my breath."

My head jerked back like she had slapped me. "Jesus."

Taking the shampoo bottle, she slammed it against my chest. "Wash your hair."

I bit my tongue before saying, *No one fucking bosses me around.* Instead, I cut her a break and squirted the shampoo in my hands. As I lathered up my hair, Alexandra took the body wash and poured some in her hand. With a harsher touch than I had used, she began to wash my arms and chest. My hands stilled in my hair as I watched her work.

In that moment, I knew I didn't want her to leave. It wasn't just about feeling some bullshit need to protect her after what had happened. It was deeper than that. Little by little, she had chiseled away at my resolve not to ever care about another woman. While she was so fucking wrong for me, she was also so fucking right.

Her face was mere inches from mine when I whispered, "Don't leave."

Tilting her head, she gazed up at me. "Why?" she questioned in almost a whisper.

"Because I don't want you to."

"Why?" she repeated.

Gritting my teeth, I glared down at her. "Because I fucking don't want to see your aggravating ass go."

She blinked before turning back to the spray to rinse her hands of the soap. When she started to reach for the curtain, I grabbed her hand. "Because I care about you. A lot."

"You do?"

"Yeah, I fucking do."

"I care about you, too." Alex's hand came up to cup my cheek. "And because of how I feel about you, I really don't want to go anywhere."

My brows shot up in surprise. "Even after everything that's happened?"

"If I truly searched myself, the answer would still be yes."

With a teasing grin, I asked, "You want a little of the outlaw life, White-Bread?"

"No. I just want more of you. Regardless of the risks or the obstacles, I want you."

The seriousness of both her words and her expression wiped

the grin off my face. We were at a hell of a crossroads right now. Really it was more like standing on the edge of a cliff. "You deserve better than me," I argued softly.

"I know," she replied, the corners of her lips fluttering as if she was trying not to smile. "As long as you try hard to make yourself worthy of me, I think we'll be fine."

I couldn't help the corners of my lips turning up at her statement. It didn't stop me from countering, "I ain't never had to work for a woman."

"Maybe you never had one worth working for."

I gazed into her dark eyes—ones that were now battle worn from what she'd been through tonight—and I realized how right she was. I'd never been with a woman who was book smart and educated. I'd never had a woman who cared enough about one of my brothers that she would sacrifice more of her time to help him pass the GED. I hadn't seen one of my conquests ever talk sweet or be considerate to my mother. Nor had any of them been as kind and compassionate to my daughter.

"Maybe you're right."

Her eyes flared at my response. We kept staring at each other until I finally cleared my throat. "Come on. We need to get you out of here."

Alex gave a quick nod of her head before I stepped out of the shower. Offering her my hand, I helped her out. I grabbed a towel and handed it to her while I went about toweling myself off. Her breath came in tiny gasps and hisses as she tried patting dry her broken skin.

After wrapping the towel around my waist, I headed out into the bedroom. Just like I had asked, Mama Beth had laid some pajamas out for Alex on the bed. I grabbed them and then went back inside the bathroom. Alex held out a tube of Neosporin. "Can you do the ones on my back?"

"Yeah, sure," I murmured, handing her the pajamas. As gently as I could, I dabbed the cream over her broken skin. I knew we would need to repeat this several times a day so she wouldn't scar. She had much too beautiful skin for it to be flawed. It would also mean a physical reminder of what she had been through.

When I was finished, Alex slipped on her pajamas. I went about picking a shirt and a pair of jeans I would be willing to throw away as Alex dried her hair. I came out of the closet to find her sitting on the bed with her knees drawn to her chest. Without a word, I went over to the bedroom door and opened it. "Breakneck?" I called.

His footsteps echoed down the hallway from the living room. When he came into the bedroom, Alex eyed him cautiously. "I'm going to give you something to help you sleep. Your body and your mind need uninterrupted rest, and often after a trauma, our minds can't seem to shut down to let the body rest."

"You'll stay with me, won't you?" Alex asked me.

"Of course," I lied. The truth was, the moment she was asleep I had business to take care of—business that wouldn't wait.

She nodded at Breakneck. After digging a syringe out of his bag he stepped over to her. Alex winced as the needle entered her arm. Once it was over, she eased back to lie down in the bed. Her eyes sought out mine, pleading for me to join her.

After I gave Breakneck a grateful pat on the back, I went over to the bed. As soon as I stretched out, Alex burrowed herself against me, laying her head on my chest. I wrapped one of my arms around her, trying to give her the shelter and safety she so desperately needed. "Talk to me," she whispered.

"About what?"

"Anything. I just want to hear your voice."

As I racked my brain, trying to think of something to talk about, I finally settled on a story. "The first day I came to live with

Preacher Man and Mama Beth was both scary and happy. While it was weird having parents again, it was an entirely different story having two new brothers. . . ."

When Alex's labored breaths signaled she had finally fallen asleep, I slowly began to extricate myself from her embrace. Whatever was in the shot that Breakneck had given her had sufficiently knocked her out. She didn't even stir as I slid off the mattress and stood over her. It felt good to finally see her peaceful. Of course, her face, marred with bruises and cuts, along with the rest of her exposed skin, didn't appear peaceful. It was the badge of someone who had been through terrible trauma.

A trauma that I was going to ensure was avenged. I opened the door to find Rev and Bishop both standing outside. Just a jerk of my head answered their unasked question. I may have been caring and tender in the last two hours, but now I was ready to go to work. In silence, we walked down the hallway. In the living room, I found Mama Beth and Kim staring expectantly at us. "Can you guys go sit with Alex? I have some things I need to take care of."

They didn't bother questioning what kind of business would take me from the bedside of the wounded woman I cared for. They had spent enough time with Raiders men to know what I was about to do. Mama Beth reached up to cup my cheek, tears brimming in her eyes. While she couldn't condone my actions, I knew she grasped my reasoning. Then she trudged down the hall with Kim behind her.

We headed out into the dark night. Silence hung heavy around us. We were all weighted down with the task ahead of us. Even if Rev and Bishop didn't lay a hand on Alex's attacker, they would share in his demise just by witnessing it, and in turn, they would have blood on their hands.

When we got to the clubhouse, members still milled around. At the sight of what had to be my grim, yet determined, expression, they moved out of my way. As I pounded down the basement stairs, the familiar rush of adrenaline began to pump through my veins. Blood pounded hard in my ears, drowning out the sound of my boots on the wooden stairs.

If Willow had been frightened by the basement at Mama Beth's, she would have pissed her pants at the sight of the one at the roadhouse. Stark white walls that often had to be repainted to cover the blood stains were illuminated by a lone lightbulb that hung on a chain and cast eerie-looking shadows into the four corners of the room. On one of the walls was a rack that resembled something out of a medieval torture chamber. Next to it sat a table filled with tools of torture.

I jerked my chin at Case and Boone before turning my attention back to the task at hand. In the middle of the room, Alex's attacker was strung up to one of the hooks hanging from the ceiling. His arms, which were covered in multicolored ink, stretched taut over his head, and I knew the position had to hurt like hell after a while. But he deserved it. He deserved every fucking thing I was about to give him.

He was conscious now. He eyeballed me as I strolled up to him with a shit-eating sneer plastered on my face. "What's this fucker's name?" I questioned.

"Name on his cut says 'Crank,' but his ID says Keith McGuiness," Mac replied from behind me.

Staring him straight in the eye, I said, "Crank, you fucked with the wrong man."

He mumbled something at me behind his gag. Cupping my ear, I said, "Sorry. Can't hear you."

This time when he screamed it, I could pretty much make out the "fuck you!" but I still reached forward to one side and yanked off the gag. The force was so hard that two of his teeth popped out and clattered onto the floor. "Sorry about that. But you won't be needing those when I'm through with you."

Crank's reply was to spit a stream of blood, which spattered onto my boots. For the moment, I chose to ignore it. "Sigel sent you to rough up my girl. Thought it would draw me out for his revenge, right?"

Crank didn't respond. Holding out my hand, I waited for one of the brothers to hand me a tool. A set of pliers was placed into my palm. "You gonna answer me?"

When he continued to ignore me, I brought the pliers up to his hands. In rapid-fire succession, I cracked and broke the knuckles on one of his hands. Trying not to give me the satisfaction of his pain, he sucked in breath and panted it out, refusing to scream. Once I did the other hand, he did cry out as his hands, searing with pain, jerked and convulsed against his bindings.

"I'll ask you again. Didn't Sigel sic you on Alex so he could draw me out to get revenge?"

Once again, he only stared me down with pure venom boiling in his eyes. Over the years, I'd come across men like Crank—tough nuts to crack. Well, unless you actually cracked their nuts, and then they'd start singing like canaries. So I went back to work, but this time I replaced the gag.

After using the pliers to pluck off each of his fingernails, I handed the bloodied tool back to Bishop. He then handed me a crowbar. With almost the same stance as a golfer, I leaned back before putting all my strength into landing a solid blow into his right kneecap. A muffled scream broke through the gag, but I ignored it. Instead, I launched the crowbar into the left kneecap, shattering it on impact.

Crank now hung precariously by his arms, unable to support his weight by his broken knees. Sweat poured off his face, which twitched with the pain that ran over his body. I ripped off the gag again. "Just tell me yes, and this will go a lot easier."

Eyeballing me momentarily, Crank croaked, "Fuck you."

"No, man. I'll fuck you with the rusty end of this crowbar if you don't start talking."

"Should've slit your brat's throat when I had the chance," he spat.

"Excuse me?"

A menacing smile curved on his lips. "I could've fucked her every which way before slitting her throat, but Sigel said no."

I swallowed hard at the image he had painted—one I was all too familiar with using during torture scenes. I just sure as hell wasn't used to having the tables turned on me. Without another thought, I launched the crowbar at his lower back, nailing his kidney. He screamed, a combination of spit and blood spewing from his mouth. After nailing the other one, I allowed him a moment to ride the wave of pain. "Are you going to tell me shit, or should I just end you now?"

"End me," he groaned.

"Fine." Tossing the crowbar onto the table, I took the long bowie knife. Eyeing the tats on his chest, I shook my head. With methodic precision, I began to slice at each of the tats that represented his ties to the Nordic Knights and the venomous hate they spewed.

I don't know how much time passed or when Crank finally stopped screaming. When I glanced up at him, his eyes had glazed over, and I knew he was in the shadowy area where you have one toe still in the living and another one over the line into death. Taking the blade, I slashed it across his wrists. His once-groggy state turned over to panic as the last of his life force spurted and flowed out onto the cement and down the drain in the floor.

Glancing over my shoulder, I gauged my brothers' responses. Only Rev wore a look of disgust. I'm sure he felt I'd gone too far, regardless of what Crank had done to Alexandra. Without a word to any of them, I walked down the length of the room to the shower. After pulling off my blood-saturated clothes, I ducked under the water. As I got rid of the physical evidence of my crime, my brothers worked at getting Crank down.

Lathering up my body, I watched as they rolled him in plastic and then in a tarp. He would be deposited on the doorsteps of his clubhouse sometime tonight. It would involve a major production plan of changing unmarked cars to go into Knights territory. Most likely a runner—someone who worked for the club on odd jobs—would end up tossing the body, so that none of us would be connected to the crime by the Feds. But Sigel would know loud and clear who'd ended Crank.

After I showered, I slipped on the sweatpants and T-shirt that Archer brought to me. Although I should've gone back home to Alexandra, I headed out of the clubhouse toward the woods. Before I could be with her again, I had to get my head on straight. While there had been many kills in my life, they still all affected me. My emotions got jangled, and I would need some time to decompress.

With only my gun and flashlight, I tromped through the brush and headed into the woods to the one place I always went to find solace and healing.

TEN

ALEXANDRA

As I slipped into a groggy consciousness, my limbs felt too heavy and laden down to move. Blinking furiously, I struggled to open my eyes. The moment my lids finally flew open, everything that had happened the night before came crashing down on me like a building crumbling in on itself. A scream tore from my lips as a reel of images assaulted me. The arms and legs that I had previously not had the energy to lift began to thrash violently on the bed. My body shook and convulsed until a soothing voice to my left calmed me. "Shh. It's okay, honey," Beth said, as she took my hand in hers.

Bile rose in my throat, and when I swallowed hard, my throat raged in agony. But it wasn't the screaming from last night that had left it raw like it had been shredded by razor blades. It was a combination of the strong hands of my attacker on my throat as well as my cries of terror before Deacon had swooped in to rescue me.

Oh God, Deacon.

He had been my protector—a true knight in shining armor. His strength had saved me from a hellish nightmare. My eyes scanned the room wildly for him. "David is fine. He just had to take care of some things. He'll be back in a few minutes," Beth reassured me.

I couldn't help wondering what he was doing. I'd still been cognizant enough to remember him barking orders to Rev and Bishop about bringing my attacker back to the compound. Had he gone to torture the man for information? Maybe even kill him?

At my shudder, Beth eased the covers tighter around me. When I glanced up at her, she tenderly cupped my cheek. "I'm so sorry this happened to you, honey."

"Thank you," I murmured.

"Are you hurting anywhere?"

"I just feel achy—that's all." When I shifted in the bed, some of the lashes on my back screamed in agony, and I grimaced.

"Let me get you some of the medicine Breakneck left."

"Breakneck?"

She laughed. "I'm sorry. I still refer to him like when he was a club member. I meant Dr. Edgeway."

A small knock came at the door. "Grandma Beth, can I see Alex now?" Willow's muffled voice questioned.

I shook my head wildly back and forth as tears stung my eyes. "I-I c-can't let her see me like this."

Beth twisted the hem of her apron before meeting my gaze. "She's been asking to see you all morning. She cried herself to sleep in Nathaniel's arms because she was so worried after they brought you home. I don't think she's going to be satisfied that you're truly okay until she can see you."

"W-what does she . . . ?" I swallowed again. "What did you say happened to me?"

"David told her you were in a car accident. He thought that was the best explanation for your injuries."

"My injuries?"

Beth grimaced. "The cuts and bruises."

"Oh," I whispered.

The once-gentle rapping at the door grew louder. I could almost imagine Willow's tiny palms smacking against the wood. "Please, Grandma Beth, let me in!" she cried.

Her agonized tone broke me. Regardless of whether I had the emotional and physical strength to see her, I couldn't deny her. She had been through too much in the last year. There was only so much a child could take, and I couldn't add to her suffering.

Pushing myself up in the bed, I called, "Come in, sweetheart." I winced from the slicing pain in my throat.

The door flew open, banging back on its hinges. Willow came barreling into the room. As her dark eyes met mine, the haunted look faded slightly. Her tear-streaked cheeks stretched into a wide smile. But as she surveyed me, the smile started to dim. I could only imagine my face was pretty messed up. "Oh, Miss Alex, you have so many boo-boos. Are you going to be okay?"

Forcing a smile to my face, I nodded. "I sure am. Just a little battered and bruised, but I'll be fine."

Her dark brows creased in worry, and I could see the wheels in her head were turning. She was wondering whether to believe me. Lifting my hand, I motioned her to the bed. "Come sit with me. I know being with you will make me feel better."

She grinned as she made a beeline to the bed. "Careful," Beth warned when Willow scrambled onto the bed.

"Want to watch some cartoons?" she asked.

"I'd love to."

With a grin, she reached over to the nightstand and grabbed the remote. After turning on the TV, she settled on an old *Scooby-Doo* episode.

"Think you could eat something?" Beth asked. When I shook

my head, she said, "I have some biscuits and gravy made. They'd be soft on your stomach. But if you want some soup, I can make you some of that."

Her insistence caused an emotional ache to burn through my chest. She was mothering me, and it had been so long since I had been mothered. It was something I missed desperately. At my continued hesitation, she said, "It'll do you good, honey."

With my throat clenched at the onslaught of emotion, I merely nodded my head. Beth's face lit up at my agreement. "All right, then. Biscuits and grits or soup?"

"I can't imagine anything I'd want more than your biscuits," I said.

She smiled. "Then biscuits it is. Be back in a minute."

As Willow snuggled to my side, I bent down to bestow a kiss on the top of her head. Closing my eyes, I inhaled the sweet fragrance of her shampoo. "Love you, Miss Alex," Willow murmured.

Tears filled my eyes. "I love you, too, sweetheart. So very, very much."

Gazing up at me, Willow said, "Oh, don't cry!"

"It's okay. They're happy tears from hearing your sweet words."

Willow frowned. "I was just going to say I wish you were my mommy, but I better not if it's going to make you cry."

There was the noise of someone clearing his throat in the doorway. When I glanced up, my heart surged at the sight of Deacon's strong form. He held a tray filled with the food that Beth had insisted on me eating. "Hi," I said softly.

"Hi," he replied. His dark eyes then went to Willow. "Go on out to the kitchen and have your lunch."

Her lips turned down in a pout. "But I wanna stay with Miss Alex."

"Willow—"

"I just got to come in a few minutes ago," she protested.

"Don't argue with me. Go. Now," he commanded. His no-nonsense tone had Willow scrambling off the bed, but it didn't stop her from stomping across the room in a huff.

When she met him in the doorway, she crooked her finger at him, beckoning him down to her level. After he stooped a little, she said in a slightly hushed tone, "Miss Alex is hurt and sad, so you be nice to her."

His eyebrows shot up in surprise. "What did you just say to me?"

"Don't be mean like you usually are. Be nice."

Deacon's expression of utter disbelief brought a much-needed smile to my face. He stared down at his daughter like she was some alien life-form. The state of his shock took away any ability to chastise Willow for her words or tone. When he finally gave a slight nod of agreement, she breezed on past him into the hallway.

With a bewildered look on his face, he crossed the room to me. I sat up, propping myself against the pillows, as he eased down on the bed. "You hungry?"

"Not really. I just didn't want to hurt Mama Beth's feelings."

"Well, you need to eat. Keep your strength up and all."

I watched in surprise as he balanced the tray on his lap. Taking the spoon, he swirled it through some of the grits before scooping out a bite. When he brought it up to my mouth, I widened my eyes.

"What?" Deacon asked, the spoon hovering close to my lips.

"You just surprised me—that's all."

When I still didn't take a bite, Deacon cocked his brows at me. "Don't tell me you're going to make me do that bullshit thing like the spoon is an airplane."

I laughed and then winced from my sore ribs. "Would you really do that?"

"Fuck no."

Leaning forward, I took the spoon into my mouth, sliding the grits onto my tongue. "Mmm. Those are so good."

"Leave it to Mama Beth to make homemade grits. She acts like it's some kinda sacrilege to eat packaged ones."

"She just wants the best for her boys," I replied with a smile.

Deacon spooned me a bite of biscuit and gravy. As I chewed thoughtfully, he cocked his head at me. "What are you thinking about?"

"That no one would ever believe that Mr. Hard-Ass biker boy was feeding me."

With a snort, Deacon said, "Boy? I'm a man, babe."

"That you are."

Obediently, I took in another bite of grits. Once I swallowed, Deacon brought the orange juice to my lips. "Shit!" I cried, as the acidity entered my mouth and swished against the raw parts caused by the gag as well as me biting on my tongue and cheek.

Deacon grimaced. "I should've realized orange juice wouldn't be a good choice."

"You have a lot of experience with busted mouths?" I questioned before I could stop myself.

"Yeah, I did. Back when I used to fight."

"Don't you fight anymore?"

"Yeah, but it was different back when I was kid. It was a way of survival then." Searching my eyes for any judgment, he added, "But even now, I won't stop fighting."

"A necessary evil," I murmured. When he gave a brief jerk of his head in acknowledgment, I couldn't help asking, "What happens now?" I asked.

"You stay here until you get better."

"Then what?"

Deacon shrugged. "Then you stay here until I get tired of you."

I laughed. "I think you need to work on your hospitality skills."

He grinned. "What's with all the questions? I thought we took care of all this touchy-feely shit last night in the shower."

"We did. But I'm a little OCD when it comes to having a plan for the future."

"All your pretty little head needs to worry about is healing." With a pointed look, he added, "Because that bastard will never hurt you again. I swear it."

As Deacon brought the spoon to my lips, I pushed his hand away. At his raised brows, I asked in a whisper, "You killed him. Didn't you?"

Deacon let out a ragged sigh. "Don't ask me about my business."

I shook my head. "And don't pull a Michael Corleone *Godfather* moment on me, Deacon. I know I said I would stay, but I do have my conditions. Honesty is one of them."

"The only reason I would keep things from you would be to protect you. The less you know about the Raiders' dealings the better. Then you can never be made to testify in a RICO case."

While that made sense, I couldn't leave well enough alone. "Did you kill him?" I repeated.

The spoon clattered noisily into the bowl. The cold and calculating expression on Deacon's face caused me to shrink back against the pillows. "Yeah, I fucking killed him. When someone hurts the people I care about, I don't wait for a judge and jury—I take matters into my own hands."

While I'd had my suspicions about Deacon's dark sins, as well as having his confession about killing his father, nothing could compare to actually hearing the words come out of his mouth. He was beyond just a dark-dealing outlaw. He was a killer—he'd even killed for me.

When it all came down to it, I was in love with a murderer. Suddenly, it became hard to breathe as I struggled to comprehend how Deacon fit into my ethically and morally sound world.

"Say something," he commanded.

Staring down at the faded quilt, I replied, "I don't know what to say."

"That you can see past the blood on my hands to the real me."

"Is that side of you so easily compartmentalized?"

"Probably as well as yours with the baby," he countered.

I pinched my eyes shut at the mention of my own sins. I suppose to the world I looked like I would have a clean conscience. To some people what I had done so many years ago wouldn't be an issue. After all, there was no finite moral compass that we adhered to. Every individual, every faith, every culture often picked and chose what was right and wrong in their eyes. Depending on where you looked from, light was dark and dark was light, leaving many hues of gray. Maybe everyone fought his or her own struggle to keep the dark side from overpowering them. Maybe we were all fighting a secret war within, while Deacon just chose to fight his in the open battlefield without shelter.

With the feel of Deacon's intense stare on me, I opened my eyes. His expression told me he was sorry for bringing my past into the discussion. I knew apologizing wouldn't be easy for him. It wasn't his style. "Maybe I need a little time to process all of this. Just like you needed time to open up to Willow and to me, I need the same when it comes to your world."

"I get it. It's hard imagining yourself actually caring for someone like me."

"That's not it."

"Are you so sure? Have you given any thought to how you'll explain me to your aunt and uncle? What about the teachers you work with? How will good little Alexandra be taken when she's dating a thug?"

"Don't presume that I'm so shallow. The moment my parents were killed, I gave up giving two shits about what people thought of me. No one wants to be labeled the orphaned freak or always have someone whispering about them. It's the one reason I went away to college and never stepped back in my hometown. I never wanted to be a martyr to the tragedies in my life." Pushing myself up in the bed, I crossed my arms over my chest. "Yes, we're from very different worlds. Just like people might question me about my choice of you, I don't doubt for a minute that some in the Raiders will question you as well."

"It's none of their fucking business."

"You know as well as I do that they'll make it their business. That's what people do." Reaching out, I took his hand in mine. "At the end of the day, it doesn't matter what anyone else says. It's about you and me." I stared down at his hand, running my fingers over his. It should've been frightening to hold the hand that dispensed malicious justice. But it was also the hand that had so gently washed me last night, the fingers that had tenderly put ointment on my wounds. Warmth pulsed through me at the thought of another talent his fingers and hand had.

Deacon brought his other hand to my cheek. "Just you and me."

Leaning in to his palm, I closed my eyes, enjoying the feel of his callused fingers against my cheek. The brief moment of intimacy ended with a voice from out in the hallway. "Can I come back in now?" Willow asked.

At Deacon's grunt of frustration, I giggled. There was something so endearing about seeing Mr. Rough and Tough be utterly clueless when it came to a pint-sized girl. "Yes, you can come back in now."

Willow bounded through the open doorway, coloring book and crayons in hand. "I thought we could color together."

"I would like that a lot."

After placing her stuff on the nightstand, she crawled over Deacon and wedged herself between us. I grinned at the appalled look on Deacon's face. "You know, you could have gone to the other side," Deacon said.

"It would be harder to share crayons, then."

His brows shot up. "What?"

"Don't you want to color with us?"

Deacon opened his mouth to protest, but I gave a quick shake of my head. "Sure he does." When he stared at me like I had lost my mind, I said, "I need the company."

Unable or unwilling to argue with me on that point, Deacon merely exhaled a long whoosh of air. Glancing between Willow and me, he asked, "So what are we coloring?"

"Ballerina Barbie," Willow answered.

"I should have known," he mumbled.

As he held up a simple purple crayon, I knew without a shadow of a doubt that, no matter what other acts that hand might have been responsible for, I loved Deacon with all my heart.

ELEVEN

Alexandra

The heave and sigh of Beth's old porch swing almost lulled me to sleep. With my e-reader resting in my lap, I stared out over the railings to the woods beyond the compound. When I leaned forward to get a better view of a deer nibbling on some grass, pain shot through my back, and I sucked in a harsh breath.

Three days had passed since my attack. While the belt lashes had begun to scab over and heal, the soreness in my bones and muscles seemed to be taking a little longer to mend. Emotionally I was getting stronger. I hadn't had to take anything to sleep the last two nights. Of course, it didn't hurt that Deacon slept by my side, making me feel secure and protected.

I hadn't been back home, and I dreaded the thought of facing my kitchen again. When I closed my eyes, I could still see Atticus's lifeless form and the horrible man who had attacked me. Deacon had promised to take me home when I thought I was ready, but I wasn't sure when that would be.

It had worked out almost too perfectly that school was out for our weeklong October break, so I didn't have to worry about making an excuse to my principal about my absence. I certainly couldn't have gone in to work bruised and battered. It would have raised too much suspicion and discussion about what was happening in my private life.

Deacon's voice snapped me out of my thoughts. "Hey," he said, an impish grin on his face.

"Hey to you, too."

He walked down the length of the porch with a large wooden crate in his arms. Jerking my chin at the box, I asked, "What's in there?"

"A present for you."

My brows shot up in surprise. "You got me a present?"

"You act like I would never do something so thoughtful."

I giggled. "I am a little surprised."

With a scowl, he said, "I do have a few decent bones in my body, you know."

"Yes, I know."

After setting the box down at my feet, he scratched the back of his neck. It was endearing because I knew he usually did it when he was nervous. "I'm hoping you'll like it. If you don't want it, I can give it to someone else."

I shook my head at him. "Oh no, you don't. Besides, I'm sure I'll love it."

Once again, he tugged on the hair at the base of his neck. "I hope you do. I mean, I hope it was the right thing to do."

With my curiosity at a fever pitch, I leaned forward in the swing so I could open the box. The moment I loosened the lid, it popped open, and something lunged at me. I squealed and jumped back in the swing. When I glanced down, a wriggling, whining, black pit bull puppy sniffed at my feet.

I stared at Deacon in surprise. "You got me a dog?"

His hand started for the back of his neck again. If he kept that up, he was going to have a bald spot. "I know how much you loved your dog, and well, after what happened to him, I thought you might like another one. Boone's dog had a litter of puppies a while back, and he's the pick of them all."

As the puppy nibbled on my bare toe with his baby teeth, I laughed. "Hey, now, those aren't for eating," I said, bending down to pick him up. He stared at me with deep blue eyes, and it was instant love. "Aren't you a pretty boy, huh?"

His response was to open his mouth and yawn, bestowing the wondrous smell of puppy breath on me. I snuggled him to my chest, kissing the top of his head. When I glanced up, Deacon was eyeing me curiously. "Does that mean you like him?"

"How could I not? He's adorable."

"So I did good?"

I crooked my finger at him. With his brows furrowed, he leaned down. "You did great, Jesse James," I replied before I brought my lips to his. When I flicked my tongue against his mouth to deepen the kiss, he jerked away. My heart sank a little at his reaction, but I plastered a smile to my face to hide my disappointment. Three days ago he might've been doing wicked things to me with his tongue, but after my attack, he couldn't bring himself to touch me sexually. I might as well have been labeled "damaged goods."

The screen door banged, and Willow skipped out onto the porch. The moment she saw the puppy, her eyes widened. With a squeal, she ran over to me. "You got a puppy?"

"Yes. Your daddy got me one."

Willow scowled up at her father as she swept one of her hands to her hip. "You said I couldn't have one."

"That's right. I did. Miss Alex is an adult and can take care of a puppy, while you can't. Besides, her dog got . . ." Deacon winced, and I knew he was trying to find the most delicate way of saying what happened to Atticus. "Well, he, uh . . . He went to heaven the other night, so this is to take away some of her sadness," he answered.

"Oh, Miss Alex, I'm so sorry about your dog," Willow said, her lips turning down.

"It's okay. Want to hold him?" She nodded emphatically, so I passed the puppy over to her. He proceeded to go wild in licking her face, which caused her to burst into a fit of giggles. I couldn't help laughing at the sight. Deacon also started chuckling. It felt good to be around laughter again.

"What are you going to name him?" Willow asked in between dodging the puppy's long swipes with its tongue.

"Hmm. I don't know. Why don't you name him?"

"Really?"

I nodded. "Then maybe you can help me with him and show your daddy that you're ready for a puppy of your own."

Deacon scowled at me, but when Willow looked at him to confirm his intentions, he nodded. "Oh boy, I can't believe I get to name him." Holding the puppy up, she gazed into his eyes. "Walter," she announced.

With a laugh, I asked, "Walter? Wherever did you get that name from?"

"Mr. Walter lived down the hall from me. He used to come into Mrs. Martinez's apartment for flan." Lowering her voice, she said, "I think he was her boyfriend, but they pretended to just be good friends."

I grinned. "I see."

"Sometimes I wished he was Mommy's boyfriend because he always treated me nicer than hers did."

A low growl came from the back of Deacon's throat. I knew if he could track down each and every one of his ex's former boyfriends, he would put them in the ground for hurting Willow. To change the subject, I said, "Then I think we should honor Mr. Walter by naming this fine specimen of a dog after him."

"Can I go show him to Grandma?"

"Of course."

Grinning, she turned and ran down the porch. "Why do I have the feeling that I'm not going to see very much of Walter?" I asked with a smile.

Deacon shook his head. "He's *your* dog, not hers. You both better remember that."

"Oh, I'm sure the first time he poops in the house she'll remember he's *my* dog."

With a laugh, Deacon replied, "Yeah, probably so." When his gaze met mine, his expression turned serious. He held out his hand to me. "Come on. You need to eat something."

"If you recall since you were at the table with me, I did eat some breakfast."

He shook his head. "Barely enough to keep a bird alive. You're never going to regain your strength unless you eat."

His concern made my heartbeat quicken. Knowing I wouldn't win the argument, I slipped my hand into his and let him pull me up from the swing. Hand in hand, we walked down the porch and into the house.

TWELVE

Alexandra

Friday evening found me hanging out in the Raiders clubhouse. With two pitchers of beer on the table, we celebrated my first full week returning to teaching after my attack. While Deacon was pretty adamant about not wanting me to go, he had to get it through his head that, unlike Willow, I wasn't his to keep under lock and key at the compound. Instead, though he was reluctant, he had to entrust my safety to both Archer and Crazy Ace, who followed me to school each morning and then back to the compound each afternoon. The two prospects took turns during the day watching the school.

As I snuggled in to Deacon's side, my gaze fell on the glittering antique diamond bracelet on my arm. Deacon had also been up front with me about the tracking device. But he wanted one that was on me at all times. That's where the bracelet came in. Although he tried to make light of the gift, saying that he got it out of the pawnshop, I knew it was about more than just tracking me. It was a gift the same as Walter, who snoozed in my lap, had been.

More and more members came trickling through the door.

The alcohol flowed along with the loud music blaring from the jukebox. While Kim and some of the other wives were friendly, there was still a strong line drawn between me and most of the club women, especially the sweet butts. Kim tried to ease my concerns by saying they always acted that way when one of the men got taken off the market.

One woman in particular worried me more than the others, and that was the bartender Cheyenne. Whenever Deacon was in the room, she only had eyes for him.

Trying to get my mind off of things, I stroked the top of Walter's furry head. He opened his eyes to gaze at me drowsily before yawning. "You have such the hard life," I teased.

Deacon reached over to scratch Walter's ears. "He's spoiled fucking rotten. I'm not sure he can even walk, considering how much you and Willow carry him around. Hell, I even caught Mama Beth holding him in one arm while she ironed with the other."

I laughed. "I won't argue that he's spoiled. I just didn't realize you were jealous."

He snorted. "I'm not jealous of a fucking dog."

"If you were, it would only be natural, considering he's getting all the love and attention from the women in your life."

He cocked his brows at me. "That's a crock of shit, White-Bread."

"Whatever, Jesse James," I countered.

"Yo, D, wanna join us for a hand?" Crazy Ace called across the room.

"Yeah, deal me in." When he started to ease out of his chair, I grabbed his arm. "What?" he questioned.

"It's seven thirty. Have you forgotten about Willow and story time?"

Deacon grimaced. "Shit." Backing away from the table, he said, "Gotta take a rain check, guys." At their groan of frustration, he replied, "Trust me, I'd sure as hell rather be here with you than doing story time with my kid."

"You're a good man and father, D," Kim said, patting him on the cheek.

He gave her a shy grin at her compliment. "Thanks." Leaning down, he bestowed a chaste kiss on my cheek. "Be back in a few."

Thrusting Walter toward him, I said, "You better take him with you. Willow will pitch a fit if he's not with her at bedtime."

With a sigh, Deacon took Walter in his arms. "More trouble than he's worth," he grumbled.

When he started past the bar, Cheyenne slinked out into his path. In a pair of daisy dukes that could've passed for a pair of my panties and a halter top that barely covered her breasts, she thrust a beer into his hand.

"What's this?" Deacon questioned.

With a wink, Cheyenne replied, "Something to help you through story time."

He grinned. "You know me too well, babe."

At his familiar usage of the word "babe," Cheyenne beamed. She cut her gaze from Deacon's over to mine. A triumphant look flashed in her eyes. The familiar suffocating feeling washed over me.

"All right, missy. What's doin'?" Kim questioned over the raucous noise of the poker game.

I shrugged. "Nothing. Why?"

"Don't bullshit me. You look like someone pissed in your Cheerios."

As I gazed into Kim's deep green eyes, I could see the true concern for me shining in them. Glancing around the room, I shook my head. "Not here," I whispered.

With a nod, she threw her arm around my shoulder and led me through the kitchen and outside. After doing a quick sweep of the area, I gladly found we were alone. For once, there wasn't a prospect hanging around or one of the members straggling through the compound.

Leaning back against the brick wall, I sighed. "It's Deacon."

Her brows shot up. "Is he being an asshole again?"

"No. It's not that at all. He's completely the opposite of an asshole. He's gone above and beyond the last few weeks."

"Then what's the problem?"

I wrapped my arms around my waist and squeezed, hoping I could contain my emotions. But the tears that stung my eyes betrayed me. Kim's hand tenderly cupped my cheek. "What is it, honey?"

"Since my attack . . . he doesn't look at me the same way. If he touches me, it's always like a brother or a father. When I've tried to kiss him, he pulls away before it gets too heated. He never tries to be alone with me." As tears streaked down my face, I shook my head. "Even though I wasn't . . ." My eyes pinched shut, and I swallowed hard, unable to actually verbalize the word. "It's like he thinks I'm damaged goods now."

"Oh, baby. You've got it all wrong. Deacon still burns for you—that fire rages just as strong in his eyes now as it did before. He just doesn't know how to be himself and then how to deal with what happened to you. He's confused. I'm sure he wants to be all over you, but he thinks you need space. Shows an awful lot about him that he's willing to put what he thinks are your needs before his own."

"Oh, I think his needs are being met just fine," I spat as I swiped the tears from my cheeks.

Kim's brows lined in confusion. "Huh?"

"I think he's fucking Cheyenne." There. I'd said it. Knowing Kim, she would either deny it or confirm it. When it finally came down to it, I wasn't sure I really wanted to hear the truth.

"Now, I know that ain't happening."

Jerking my chin up, I countered, "And just how can you be so sure?"

"Because I know Deacon."

"Yeah, well, I know him, too. He's always coming to bed late, after he thinks I'm asleep, and she's hanging out here later and later." Tears burned my eyes. "I don't know what to do. I'm afraid I'm losing him."

Pulling me into her arms, Kim patted my back, soothing my frayed nerves. "I think I have an idea." She eased back to stare into my eyes. "You need to make Deacon see you as a sexual being again."

"And how do I do that? Dress like a slutty skank like Cheyenne?" I countered.

A catlike grin curved on Kim's lips. "While that might get his fires burning a little, you gotta make him explode. Nothing pisses off our clubmen more than when their brothers want a piece of their women and their women seem down with it."

My brows furrowed in confusion. "What do you mean?"

"Tell me. You know how to play poker?"

THIRTEEN

DEACON

An hour, five books, and one beer later, Willow finally gave up the ghost and went to sleep with Walter snoring like a fucking bear beside her. She could be such a stubborn little shit—something she had inherited from me. Gently, I eased off the bed. I didn't dare do anything to wake her up, so I crept out of the bedroom on fucking tippy-toes. When I got to the door, I threw a final glance over my shoulder. Warmth filled my chest at the sight of Willow sleeping so peacefully with Walter by her side and that ratty angel doll in her hand.

After easing out into the hallway as best I could in my boots, I cracked the door behind me. When I got to the living room, I found Mama Beth alone. Craning my neck, I swept my gaze into the kitchen. "Where's Alex?"

"Still up at the clubhouse."

My brows shot up in surprise. After her attack, she very rarely wanted me to be out of her sight. Normally, a chick being all clingy was a turnoff. But I welcomed it from Alex, mainly because of what she had been through because of me. For the first time I could re-member, her attention made me feel needed by someone other than my brothers. It was a hell of an ego trip, feeling like someone's pro-tector. More than anything, I enjoyed spending time with her do-ing the simplest of things. Sometimes I wondered if I had lost my mind. I'd never needed or wanted to be close with a woman since Lacey, and even being in love with her wasn't the norm for me. I knew if I mentioned my feelings to Mama Beth, she would chalk it up to me being in love with Alex, and I wasn't ready to hear that from someone else.

I couldn't imagine why she would want to stay up at the club-house when I wasn't there. Even if she knew I was coming back, she much preferred her evenings in the quietness of Mama Beth's instead of the rowdy clubhouse. "Be back in a bit," I said as I started for the door.

"Okay, son."

I hurried up the pathway, anxious to check on Alex as well as maybe get in a hand or two of poker. I needed something to get my mind off sex. I was barely getting through the longest time without any fucking pussy in my entire adult life. Of course, it was my own damn stubbornness that led to it being me and my hand. Even after all she had been through, Alexandra constantly threw little hints at me that she was ready for us to go all the way. No matter how ready she seemed, I couldn't bring myself to sleep with her. For fuck's sake, she'd almost been raped, not to mention beaten and tortured. No matter if she was consenting, what kind of epic asshole would I be to screw her brains out when she was still healing physically and emotionally? Yeah, maybe the old me would have considered it, but the new me sure as hell wasn't going to go there.

Not only did I have to contend with Alex, but Cheyenne seemed more than willing to ease my pain. Whenever I'd tried to avoid Alex's come-ons by hanging out at the clubhouse, Cheyenne was thrusting her tits in my face or coming around the bar to rub herself up against me.

Basically, it was hell, pure and simple.

When I pulled open the back door, the ruckus coming from the front room met me with a deafening roar. I was glad to hear it since it meant the poker game was still in full force, and I could try to burn off some of my excess energy.

I slid behind the bar and grabbed another beer. After I popped the top, I took a long gulp. Out of the corner of my eye, I saw Alex seated at the round table, cards in hand and multicolored chips in front of her. Slowly, I lowered the bottle as I took in the rest of the guys and old ladies. Rage rocketed through me as I got an eyeful of tits and junk. My bottle crashed onto the floor as I stalked across the room to the table.

"What the fuck do you think you're doing?" I demanded.

Gazing up at me through her lashes, Alex shot me an innocent look. "Playing poker."

I cocked my eyebrows at her. "I think you forgot one of your adjectives, Teach. You're playing *strip* poker."

Crazy Ace rose out of his chair, his nipple rings gleaming in the light. "And damn if she isn't a hustler. We thought she'd be buck naked by the first hand, but she's beating us all."

Bishop, being a smug motherfucker, had the nerve to give me a knowing wink. "Yeah, but we got her this round." Nudging Alex's shoulder, he said, "You owe us one piece of clothing, babe. Take it off."

When Alex's hands came to the button on her shirt, a raging inferno colored my vision red. Without a second thought, my hands flew out to the table edge, flipping it over and sending cards and poker chips through the air. "Game over," I growled.

"I still have to pay up, Deacon," Alex snapped before having the audacity to pop open the buttons on her shirt, revealing a lacy black bra.

Just like a fucking caveman, I reached over, grabbed her by the waist, and then hefted her over my shoulders. "What are you doing?" she demanded as I started stomping away from the table. When I didn't respond, she smacked my ass. "Answer me, Deacon."

I didn't say a fucking word until I was in my bedroom. After I kicked the door shut behind us, I stalked over to the bed and dropped her on it. As her body bounced on the mattress, she hissed like a little hellcat.

"What the fuck were you thinking?"

She glared up at me. "I just wanted to have some fun."

"By letting my brothers see you naked?"

"I was winning," she challenged.

"Yeah, well, I don't give a fuck. No one in this club sees you naked. Do you understand me?"

"And why not?"

I narrowed my eyes at her. "Don't question me, woman."

"So don't tell me what to do!"

To silence her smart mouth, I crushed my lips against hers. Instead of meeting opposition, I felt her return my kiss, her hands coming up to grip my hair, tugging at the strands. In a flash, I covered her body with mine, slamming her onto her back on the mattress. I had this desperate need to claim her, not as some territorial bullshit but out of a stronger emotion. She was my complete and total opposite, but somehow we completed each other. She was the strong, compassionate, stubborn woman I needed to soften out my rough edges. She brought out the best parts of me—the ones that so often had been hidden in the past. For her, I wanted to be a better man, a better father, a better brother, and hell, a better human being.

Alex brought me out of my thoughts by widening her legs invitingly. I didn't waste a moment slipping my hips between them. As our tongues battled against each other, I rubbed my growing erection against her core. When she groaned into my mouth, I grabbed her arms and shoved them over her head.

Jerking my lips from hers, I glared down at Alex. "You are mine. Do you understand me?"

"Yes," she panted.

Keeping her arms pinned with one hand, I let my other hand come to her breasts. "These tits are for my eyes and my pleasure only. You got me?"

"Yes, Deacon. Only for you."

After giving her nipple a teasing pinch, I brought my hand between her legs to cup her mound. "And this pussy is for my eyes, my fingers, my tongue, and my cock only."

A shiver ran through her at my words. "I only want you. You and only you, Deacon," she replied.

As I loomed over her, my hungry gaze fell on some of the yellowish bruises that remained on her neck and chest. Just like that, my wood began to deflate. Jesus, what the hell had I been thinking? Dragging her back to my bedroom and mauling her like a caveman after she'd just been attacked and almost raped three weeks ago. "Fuck, Alex. I'm sorry."

When I started to pull away, her hands flew up to cup my face. "No, don't stop!" she cried.

I shook my head as shame washed over me. "I'm sorry for treating you so fucking disrespectfully after what you've been through."

"I'm not broken, Deacon. I'm the same woman I was before the attack—the day you had me up against a wall, ready to fuck my brains out."

"I know that."

"Then why are you treating me this way?"

I sat back on my knees and jerked a hand through my dark hair. "No matter how hard I try to see things differently, I'm always going to be no good for you, Alex."

"Why don't you let me be the judge of that?"

With a glare, I countered, "Are you on some fucking suicide mission or something? A closeted S and M freak who likes pain?"

"No. It's not like that at all."

"Then why would you want me to fuck you like an animal after what you've been through?"

"Because I want to be with you. And even if it means not making love but fucking hard and fast, I still want it because it's with you. I've wanted you for so long, Deacon. Maybe even before that night in your basement. My head tells me to be leery of you. That I shouldn't want to be with an outlaw like you. But no matter how hard I try to talk myself out of my feelings for you, my heart and body rage and riot for you."

"Oh, fuck," I muttered, staring into her determined face. In spite of all our differences, she still wanted me. Regardless of the fucked-up world I lived in, a good-hearted woman like Alex actually wanted me. And not just with her body to get to see what fucking a bad boy was like. She wanted me with her heart, too. It almost overwhelmed me.

After momentarily nibbling on her bottom lip, she said, "If you can honestly say that you only want to screw me and feel nothing else but some bullshit obligation toward me, then I'll get up from here. We'll go on being friends and acquaintances, and I'll never press you about having more again. And you can go back to Cheyenne, who clearly doesn't think you two are over. Hell, maybe it isn't over between you, and that's why she isn't letting go."

"There's not one damn thing between me and Cheyenne. So you can get that out of your fucking head right now."

Alex didn't appear to believe me. "Then, if you feel for me like

I do for you, fuck me until I come screaming and clenching around you."

I groaned. "Jesus, woman, your mouth is driving me crazy."

"Wait until it's wrapped around your cock."

Lunging forward, I once again covered her body with mine. I stared down at her, shaking my head in disbelief that there was a woman like Alex who wanted me. "You don't fight fair with the dirty talk."

She gave me a teasing grin. "I learned from the best, Jesse James."

Her amusement faded when I started to slide off of her. "Deacon—"

I brought a finger over her mouth to silence her. "I don't want there to be anything between us the first time I fuck you. So get up and get undressed."

Without another word of argument, she slid off the bed. Standing at the edge, she worked the buttons of her shirt. Her eyes never left mine. When she slid it off her arms, she didn't seem to be moving fast enough. Grabbing the waist of her jeans, I pulled her closer to me, before working the button and zipper. I pushed the jeans down her body. As her hands went around her back to undo her bra, I reached for her panties and tugged them down. Once she was naked before me, I couldn't help staring. I'd already seen and touched every square inch of her body that night in the shower. But tonight was about taking care of different needs.

I brought my hand between her legs. She inhaled a sharp breath as I stroked her, feeling her clit begin to swell. My other hand went to her hip to urge her legs farther apart. When she spread her thighs, I thrust a finger into her, which caused her to gasp in pleasure. I added another finger as I began to move them in a punishing rhythm. She arched her hips forward, riding my hand. Her fingers gripped my shoulders, the nails digging into the skin as I brought her closer and closer to release. When she went over, her head fell back, and she moaned my name. It made me even harder.

She urged me onto my back. Her dark eyes burned with desire as her fingers came to the button on my jeans. After she unzipped me, she started tugging them down off my hips. When my rock-hard cock sprang free, she momentarily paused to give it an appreciative look. Once she tossed my jeans over the side of the bed, she crawled slowly up my legs. As she gripped my dick in her hands, her tongue flicked across the head. I sucked in a breath as she then dragged her tongue from the base up to the tip. She continued making teasing strokes with her tongue until I groaned in agony. "Alex, quit fucking with me and suck my dick."

Pausing, she glanced up at me. "That's not the magic word."

With a growl, I reluctantly said, "Please."

She answered my fucking plea by taking me deep inside her mouth. "Christ," I grunted, arching my hips up. Her lips worked over my length while she pumped me in her hand. She started swirling and spinning her tongue around me while I was still in her mouth. Biting down hard on my lip, I willed myself not to blow my load like a teenage kid. For a seemingly good girl, Alex sure knew how to give head.

Grabbing her by the shoulders, I urged her up. Reluctantly, she let my cock fall free of her fucking divine mouth. I kept pulling her until she straddled me. A grunt of both pleasure and frustration filled me when my cock slipped and slid through her wetness. "Wait," I croaked. I flipped her onto her back and then climbed over to reach in the nightstand for a condom. After I slid it on, I glanced down at her to see her staring almost shyly up at me.

I had never made myself feel this vulnerable with a woman before. But for reasons I didn't understand, I felt safe being open with Alex. She accepted me for who and what I was, which wasn't easy. She loved my daughter like she was her own flesh and blood.

She loved my mother and brothers just like they were her family, too.

In that moment, I knew what I needed to say. She deserved to hear it. I wasn't just taking advantage of the fact we were about to fuck . . . or have sex . . . or make love. It went much deeper than that. As I positioned myself between her legs, I once again met her gaze. "I need to tell you something."

Alex's brows furrowed in concern as she nibbled on her bottom lip. "What is it?"

"I . . ." Why in the hell couldn't I say the words? Oh, fuck it. "I love you, Alex."

Her dark eyes widened. "I love you, too. With all my heart."

With the weight of the words between us, I slammed into her. We both gasped. I withdrew and then pushed inside again. I soon found an almost punishing rhythm. Just as she began to build to climax again, I rolled over on my back, still buried inside her. Gripping Alex's hips, I raised her up. Slowly, she slid down on me, inch by inch. When she had taken all of me, she flattened her palms on my chest. Then she began to ride me.

As her tits bounced with her movements, my hands reached up to grab them, rolling and pinching the nipples between my fingers. I was rewarded with a deep moan. Rising, I brought my mouth to them. When I sucked them hard, grazing them with my teeth, Alex jerked her hands through my hair. "Deacon," she murmured.

Gripping her waist, I raised my hips, thrusting into her with a pounding rhythm. She cried out as she came around me, milking my dick with her inner walls. I couldn't hold on, and I followed close behind her. She collapsed onto my chest, burying her face in my neck. Once we had finished coming down, I stroked her back with my fingers. We remained joined, her warm breath on my neck.

"Babe?" I questioned.

"Mmm," she murmured.

"You okay?"

Raising her head, she smiled down at me with a thoroughly fucked look on her face. "Oh, I'm more than okay."

"I'm glad to hear that."

Her finger tapped against my chest. "Do you want to sleep now?"

"No. That's not what I had in mind."

"It isn't?" From her tone, I could tell she was fucking with me.

"Just as soon as I've recovered, I plan on putting you on your knees and taking you from behind."

"That sounds nice, I guess."

I cocked my brows at her. "*Nice*?"

With a shrug, she replied, "Yeah, you know, you've done doggy style once, you've done it a million times."

"Oh, that's it. You're in trouble now." She gave a shriek when I rolled her onto her back. We came apart as I began to tickle her sides, making her giggle to the point where she lost her breath.

"No . . . Deacon," she pleaded.

"Say you're sorry."

"Sorry," came her panted reply.

"Say 'no man will ever fuck me like you do, Deacon,'" I commanded.

Her chest heaved as she tried to catch her breath to repeat such a long sentence. "No man will ever fuck me like you do, Deacon."

With a grin, I said, "Damn straight. And that's because I'm a fucking sex god."

She shook her head. "No. It's because you love me."

My amusement faded slightly at her words. "You think just because you bring up love that I'll go easy on you, huh?"

"I hope you don't."

Sliding the condom off my dick, I tossed it in the trash can beside the bed. "You don't, huh?"

"I really don't."

"If you say so." I jerked my chin at her. "Get on your knees for me."

Slowly, she twisted over onto her stomach. Placing her hands on the mattress, she then shifted up onto her knees, swaying her ass provocatively at me. "Like this?"

"Fuck yeah. Just like that."

After sliding another condom on, I gripped her cheeks in my hands, spreading her apart. Just when she thought I was going to move forward and thrust into her, I bent over and flicked my tongue against her clit. "Deacon!" she cried, pushing herself back against me. With long swipes of my tongue, I began to eat her pussy. When my tongue wasn't enough, I brought my entire mouth against her, sucking her clit. She came, crying out my name, her fingers twisting into the sheets.

I didn't wait a second to pull away and then thrust into her. Gripping her hips, I kept up a relentless pace. Our skin slapping together echoed through the room along with my grunts and her pants. Leaning over her back, I whispered into her ear, "Next time I take you like this, I'm going to put my cock into your ass."

When she stiffened, I knew I had hit uncharted territory with her. "Would you let me do that, Alex? Would you let me take your tight ass?" I sent a stinging slap across one of her cheeks.

Without a moment's hesitation, she cried, "Yes, Deacon! Yes, I would."

"Damn, baby," I muttered, slamming harder and harder into her. Alex's head bowed down to where her face rested on the mattress. Her cries and whimpers of pleasure became my undoing. Knowing I was close, I slid my hand between us to rub her clit. She buried her face in the mattress and screamed as she came. I slammed into her two or three more times before I groaned and spilled myself inside her.

I slowly withdrew from her before sliding the condom off.

Alex remained on her stomach, unmoving. "Did I wear you out?" I asked as I placed delicate kisses across her back.

"I really do want to sleep now," she said drowsily.

I chuckled. "I know, baby. I'm wiped out, too."

I pulled the sheet from under her body, then climbed in beside her. At the feel of me, she rolled over to snuggle against my chest. It might've been only ten o'clock, but I happily fell asleep beside the woman I'd thoroughly fucked and who I thoroughly loved.

FOURTEEN

Alexandra

Kim had been so right about my playing poker to get Deacon's attention. Once we were together for the first time, he couldn't keep his hands off me. I had yet to sleep at my house since the attack, so the fact I was at his house every day and night left him plenty of time to touch me. And I sure as hell was enjoying every minute of it.

I went about my days in a lust haze. Morning sex with Deacon kept me thinking about him all day. He would usually show me how much he had been thinking about me, too, when he'd find a way to get in a quickie between Willow's lessons and dinner. After we tucked Willow in and did her story time, we would sometimes retire to his bedroom early. I'm sure Beth knew exactly what was going on, but she never said anything or gave us disapproving looks.

On this Sunday morning, I had once again woken up to be worshipped by Deacon. Three orgasms for me and one for him later, we lay tangled together in the bed.

"Listen, it's just going to be you getting Willow in bed tonight," he said after a long silence.

"Where are you going?"

"Out."

My brows shot up in surprise. "Excuse me?"

His eyes narrowed slightly. "Fine. If you must know, it's auditions down at the Lounge. As a stakeholder in the club, I have to be there to vote."

I snorted contemptuously as I worked to untangle myself from him. "You've got to be kidding me."

"I'm not."

Crossing my arms over my chest, I huffed, "Let me get this straight. You're telling me you're going to be auditioning strippers tonight, and I'm just expected to say, 'Have fun, honey'?"

Deacon squared his shoulders. "Yeah, I guess so."

"Do I mean nothing to you?"

"Alex, don't start this shit."

"Oh, I'm sure as hell going to start this shit." Rolling out of bed, I snatched up my discarded yoga pants and shirt. Narrowing my eyes at him, I said, "You're with me now—my man, and I'm your old lady. That means we don't look at or touch other members of the opposite sex."

"I'm not going to be touching anybody!" he shouted.

After I jerked my shirt over my head, I huffed, "You don't have to. I'm sure they'll be touching you when they're rubbing themselves all over your dick during a lap dance."

"Now, listen to me. You might be my old lady, but that doesn't mean you get to tell me what to do. So you need to pipe the fuck down."

"You are an unimaginable asshole!" I screamed.

"And you need to learn your place!" he shot back.

I shook my head, hating myself for the tears that sprang into my eyes. "I can't do this, Deacon. I can't lie in an empty bed, wondering what or who you're doing. If this is really how you feel, I don't think we need to see each other anymore."

"Dammit, Alex," he snarled, reaching for my arm.

I pulled out of his grip and started for the door. "If you go to that club tonight, don't bother coming home to me when you're done. I won't be here."

With that, I slipped out the door. I pounded down the stairs and headed for my car.

"Hey, where are you off to so early?" Kim called from the sidewalk. She was doing her morning jog around the compound. When I didn't respond, she came over to me at the car. I hurried and slipped inside, trying desperately to start the car so I could escape her.

"Alex, talk to me."

"I have to get out of here." I tried once again to put the key in the ignition, but my trembling hands wouldn't work.

"Honey, what's wrong?" When I burst into tears, she reached into the car and pulled me out. Putting her arm around my shoulder, she led me up the hill to her house. I was sobbing so hard I was shaking when she tugged me through the front door. I could only imagine the looks her kids and Case were giving me. She ushered me past the living room and kitchen onto the back porch.

"Now, what on earth is going on? I thought after your little fuck-fest with Deacon, there wouldn't be any more trouble in paradise."

Sniffling, I wiped my eyes on my sleeve. "Does Case go to the auditions at the Lounge?"

Her body stiffened. "No, he doesn't." When I opened my mouth, she shook her head. "It isn't for the reason you think."

"It isn't because you told him not to?"

She shook her head. "No. It's because it has too many bad

memories for me. I was stripping there when I met him. Out of respect for me, he doesn't go there anymore."

"Deacon's going to the auditions there tonight. He wouldn't even listen to me when I pleaded with him not to go." Staring into Kim's green eyes, I said, "I don't think I can be with him anymore."

"Oh, no. I'm not letting you give up so easy."

"I can't be with someone who doesn't care about my feelings. This may seem small now, but what happens when it's something bigger? He told me he loved me, yet he can go down and watch naked women hump a pole? It doesn't add up."

"Deacon is just being stubborn. He's never had to justify his actions to any woman. Nor has he ever had one tell him no, except his mama. You need to find a way to turn the tables on him, give him a taste of his own medicine."

With a mirthless laugh, I said, "Why does all your advice come in the form of a game?"

"Because that's what works with these men, honey. I wouldn't have told you to play strip poker to get your man to touch you again if you'd been dating a banker or even a mechanic. But you're with one of the Raiders, and they're a whole different breed of men."

"You're right," I replied. I then thought about how Deacon went caveman at the poker game when he thought his brothers were going to see me naked. I obviously couldn't stage another poker game. I had to find a different means this time. And then it hit me.

"Kim, do you have any connections down at the Lounge?"

Her brows furrowed. "What are you talking about?"

"I mean, someone you could call for a favor."

"Yeah, I guess so. Why?"

"I just thought of a way to beat Deacon at his own game."

When she realized what I meant, her eyes widened and her mouth dropped open. "Holy shit. Are you serious?"

"You don't think it will work?"

She laughed. "Oh, honey, I think it will be the most fucking epic thing ever."

Nibbling on my lip, I then asked, "You don't think it's too much?"

With a wink, she replied, "It's all in how far you go."

I drew in a deep breath before I broached a difficult subject. "Would you be willing to help me?"

The amusement in Kim's face faded. When she began to wring her hands in her lap, I regretted mentioning it. I knew it was a lot to ask of her. "Look, it was wrong of me to ask. I'm sure I can bribe one of the regulars for some help."

When I rose out of the chair, she reached for my hand to stop me. "I think I can make an exception for you."

"Really? You mean it?"

She nodded. "Besides, it's coming up on my and Case's anniversary. Might be nice to give him a lap dance for old times' sake."

I laughed. "Only if you're sure."

"I am. I wouldn't offer if I wasn't."

"So what do we do now?"

Kim grinned. "We go make the ballet dancer in you into a pole dancer."

As I paced behind the curtain in my clear high heels, I wondered what the hell I had been thinking to entertain the thought of stripping for Deacon. Sure, the club was closed to its regular clientele and only patch-holding Raiders would be allowed in. That's the only reason I even allowed myself to entertain the idea of stripping. The last thing I needed was for someone to recognize me. I could kiss my teaching career good-bye if that got out.

I peeked out into the audience, squinting to see past the glittering black mask that covered my eyes. At least ten of the Raiders sat in the first row of chairs next to the stage. Although I didn't plan on taking everything off, the G-string I was wearing along with my bra top wasn't going to leave much to the imagination. I wasn't sure I would ever be able to look at Rev or Bishop again.

But when I zeroed in on Deacon's face in the front row, rage flew through me. What the hell? He was in the fucking front row. I mean, could he have at least hung out in the back? Oh, I was going to make that asshole pay.

Kim had sacrificed her entire day to help me. She'd taught me how to work the pole, found me an outfit to go with my music, and then did my hair and makeup. She had also pulled some strings to get me the first audition spot.

Coco, the head girl, took the microphone next to me. "Okay, we're ready to begin."

Whistles and catcalls echoed behind the curtain. I could tell the men were more than ready to get the show on the road. Kim fluffed my hair and adjusted my cowboy hat once more before belting the long duster I was wearing. "You go out there and get your man."

"I'm going to try."

She smacked me on the ass before heading back into the wings. The opening chords of the music echoed out of the speakers. Cher's "Just Like Jesse James." Not the most obvious choice when it came to stripping, but it was one I had carefully picked because of the meaning it had for Deacon.

As the curtain was flung open, I had one second of sheer panic shoot from the top of my head down to my feet. And then it was gone. It was replaced by courage pulsing through me. I didn't think about who was at the end of that stage. I didn't think about the fact I was merely a kindergarten teacher who had somehow gotten off on the wrong path. I didn't think about the inhibitions that usually curbed any wild behavior.

Instead, I strutted down that stage to the pole, swaying my hips provocatively from side to side. It gave the men the smallest peek at my thighs and what else might be under my duster. Staring out into the crowd, I slowly and deliberately undid my belt, making a production out of it. When I whipped open the duster and then stripped it off, I was rewarded with bellowing approval from the men.

I slunk over to the pole, my hands gripping the metal for dear life. Because of my ballet training, I was somewhat of a natural when it came to pole dancing. I swirled and bent and twisted my body, giving them a real show.

As I was arched over on my back, straddling the pole, the one line I had been waiting for came up. At "Just like Jesse James," I rose, and then with my free hand, pointed a trigger straight at Deacon. The amused look on his face faded. Realization suddenly dawned on him of exactly who I was.

He was out of his chair in a flash.

Thankfully, I had prepared for that.

FIFTEEN

DEACON

As I sat in the cheap leather chair waiting for the strippers to come out, I felt something I hadn't ever experienced before at the Lounge. Guilt. Yeah, I'll admit I felt pretty fucking guilty coming tonight after my fight with Alex. Our first real fight as a couple, and it was over strippers.

"What's wrong with you?" Bishop asked as he flopped down beside me.

"Nothing," I grumbled. On my other side, Rev snorted. Turning in my seat, I glared at him. "You got something to say?"

"Just that you're an idiot."

"Is that right?"

"Yeah, it is. You have someone as wonderful and amazing as Alex at home, and you come down here?"

"Oh, come on, Rev. D's just watching. It's not like he's going in the back for a lap dance like he used to." Bishop smacked me on the back. "You aren't, are you?" he asked in a low voice.

"No, I'm not," I growled.

"See? No harm there."

Rev leaned forward in his seat so he could see us both. "I think there's a lot of harm in what he's doing . . . or what he's done."

After swallowing the rest of my beer, I cocked my brows at Rev. "Sounds like you've been talking to Alex."

Rev shook his head. "Actually, it was Case. He came up to the roadhouse saying that Alex was bawling her eyes out at his house before eight this morning."

I grimaced. I knew she had disappeared with Kim, and instead of going after her, I'd thought the best thing to do was to let her calm down. Then she hadn't come home the rest of the day or answered my calls or texts. I knew she was all right, though, because she was with Kim.

"Yeah, well, she's got a lot to learn when it comes to me and my business."

"You're an asshole."

"So I heard this morning."

Bishop snickered at my comment while Rev shot me a death glare. "Somebody should beat some sense into you."

"Is that right? Are you the man to do it, brother?"

"If it means keeping you from hurting Alex, I'd sure as hell do it!"

Bishop rose out of his chair to stand in front of us. "Easy, now. I don't think we've ever had brothers thrown out before a show even started."

"Whatever," I grumbled.

Rev didn't respond. Instead, he crossed his arms over his chest. "It wasn't like I meant to hurt her feelings," I finally said to fill the silence.

"She deserves better," came Rev's soft reply.

"Guys—" Bishop started in warning.

I shook my head. "No, Rev's right. She does deserve better

than me." I knew that I had no place being at the Lounge. I should have been trying to find Alexandra to make things right. I started to rise out of my seat to leave when Case pushed me back down.

"You need to stay and enjoy the show."

It took me a moment to speak, considering how shocked I was to see him. He never went to the Lounge. "I need to make things right with my old lady."

"See a little tits and ass first to get you fired up to go talk to her."

"I don't wanna see any tits or ass besides hers, which unless I make it right with her, I'll never see again." With Case practically trapping me in my seat, I sighed. "Whatever."

The music blared over the loudspeakers. It was an unusual choice. When the curtain opened and I got a look at the girl, my surprise grew even more. She wasn't like the usual girls we auditioned. This chick looked almost classy, like she had come out of the highest-paid clubs in Atlanta. I couldn't imagine what the hell she was doing here.

As she started down the stage, my dick stirred in my pants. I hated myself for having a reaction to anyone besides Alex. After she whipped open her duster and tossed it off the stage, I couldn't look away. It was like she had some magnetic pull. She had fabulous, natural tits that were barely covered by her skimpy bikini top. Her long dark hair fell over her shoulders. The color made me think of Alex's.

If I was truthful, there was so much about this girl that reminded me of Alex. With half of her face covered with the glittering mask, I couldn't tell just how much she looked like her. But her body was a dead ringer for her, too.

And then it was like a bucket of cold water doused my head. With a teasing smile, the girl pointed a trigger finger at me as the song said, "Just like Jesse James." And then I knew it was Alex shaking her half-naked ass on the stage at me. I barely had time to process my emotions before I lunged out of my chair. Alex merely watched me as I hoisted myself onto the stage. "What the fuck do you think you're doing?" I demanded as I stomped over to her.

She didn't reply. Instead, she nodded at someone over my shoulder. Before I could glance back, both Rev and Case came up onstage. A pair of handcuffs appeared out of Case's pockets. Once again, I questioned, "What the fuck do you think you're doing?"

Case and Rev gave shit-eating grins before launching themselves at me. I didn't have time to dodge out of their way before they tackled me. As I thrashed against them, I felt my arms being raised above my head. The snap of the cuffs seemed to echo over the music. When I tugged my arms, they didn't move. They had bound my hands as tight as they could to the pole. I was completely at their mercy. Or I guess I should say Alex's.

"Have fun," Case said to Alex as he headed off the stage.

"Alexandra Evans, you let me out of these cuffs right. Fucking. Now!"

She slowly shook her head back and forth. "Tonight you're going to understand that you're mine, Jesse James. More than that—I'm going to show your brothers that you and your dick are mine."

Her words, coupled with her attire, caused my cock to pound against my zipper—the fucking traitor. Whistles came from down below us. "Get him, Alex!" Crazy Ace roared.

"Make him beg!" Boone chimed in.

Glancing over her shoulder at the men, Alex gave them a sweet smile before turning back to me. "How long do you think it'll take you to blow your load in front of the guys?"

Narrowing my eyes as her, I sneered, "I'm not coming in my pants like a teenager."

She cocked her head. "Are you so sure about that?"

Bending over, she braced her hands on the floor while her ass began to work me over my jeans. I groaned at both the sensation and the image of her practically bare ass as it ground against my dick. With each upward thrust of her hips, she rubbed a different part of my cock. I wouldn't have been surprised if she was getting wet from the precum that was probably seeping through my jeans.

She rose and turned to face me. She leaned in to lick her tongue along my lips before sucking my bottom lip between her teeth, nibbling it slightly. Lifting one of her legs, she brought it around my hip. My eyes rolled back in my head at the feel of her scorching pussy through my jeans. Her hands came to my neck, and she began to ride me just like if we were horizontal. Her eyes locked with mine as tiny pants of exertion came from her lips. I'd had lap dances before, but being fucked on a pole was a whole new ball game.

I grunted and flexed my hips against her, desperately trying to find more friction. Alex began working herself harder and harder against me. Biting down on my lip, I willed myself not to give in. Grabbing strands of my hair, Alex jerked my head up to where I could meet her gaze. As the song echoed "Come on baby" around us, Alex commanded, "Come for me, Deacon. Come for me and me alone."

I couldn't fight it anymore. Throwing my head back against the pole, I let myself go. "Alex!" I yelled in a hoarse voice.

When I started coming back to myself, Alex was unlocking the handcuffs. My arms dropped down, and I winced. Ignoring the cheers and catcalls of my brothers, I shook my head at her. "You're going to get it."

"Am I?"

"Oh yeah." Grabbing her by the waist, I hoisted her over my shoulder. She brought out the fucking caveman in me. As I stomped backstage with her, Alex never protested. She merely let me carry her. "Get the fuck out of here," I growled to a bouncer who was waiting in front of the private rooms. I knew that later some of the guys had planned to audition the girls here. For now I was going to use it to take Alexandra.

Once the bouncer left us, I tossed Alex onto the couch. "You think you're pretty smart, don't you?"

"I was just proving a point."

"That I'm yours?" I demanded as I tore off my shirt.

"Yes."

"Do you think any man in there doubted that before tonight?"

"No. But I don't want any of the women who hang around here, especially Cheyenne, having any doubts that you belong to me and they should keep their hands off!" Fuck. She was worried about me and Cheyenne. Just as I was about to tell her that Cheyenne meant nothing to me, she pursed her lips at me. "Of course, it didn't hurt for you to get brought down a notch in front of your brothers."

Again, all other coherent thought left my mind except the animalistic urge to fuck the beautiful woman in front of me. I jerked off my jeans and crumpled them into a ball. I had started to use them to wipe up the mess along my thighs and hips when Alex reached out to stop me. Leaning forward on the couch, she brought her tongue to lick the cum off of me. She'd swallowed me before, but there was something so fucking sexy about what she was doing that I couldn't help shuddering.

Not wanting her to have the upper hand again, I wound some of the strands of her hair around my hand and jerked hard. She gasped in both pain and pleasure. "You deserve to be punished," I growled.

"Then punish me. Just like you were mine to do with what I wanted out there, I'm yours in here."

My cock started coming back to life. Visions of bending her over one of the chairs while I spanked her ass got me up and running. But then I really wanted to turn the tables. Just like she had claimed me outside, I wanted to claim something of hers. "Take everything off."

Obediently, Alex rose to her feet. As she undid her bra, I went over to the cabinet in the corner. Inside was everything you might imagine, from condoms to sex toys. While there was no sex for hire here, it was inevitable that it happened, and the club ensured you were prepared. I took out an unopened bottle of lube. When I turned around, Alex stood naked before me, except for the stripper heels, which she had left on.

For a moment, I could only stare at her. "You're so fucking beautiful."

Even in the dimly lit room, I saw her cheeks redden. "Thank you."

As I crossed the room to her, I said, "I don't know how you could ever think I would want someone else when I have you." Tipping her chin up, I forced her to look at me. "You're a beautiful face with a slamming-hot body, but more than that, you've got a fucking heart of gold, babe."

Her arms encircled my neck, and she drew herself against me. "It's not just you I'm worried about. Women can be very persuasive. You're a god around these parts, and every single woman wants a piece of you. Especially the women you've been with before." I winced because I knew she was talking about Cheyenne. Alex leaned her forehead against mine. "I don't know how to deal with that. I love you so much that I don't want to ever have to imagine you leaving me."

For a moment, I could only stare in disbelief at Alex. How in the hell was it possible that she was the one who was afraid of me leaving? Standing in my shoes, I saw it the other way around. I was worried that eventually my world and all my bullshit baggage would be too much for her. Surely Alex would see through me one day and decide that I wasn't worth sticking around for. Rev was right—she deserved someone better than me. But more than anything, she needed to know just how fucking much she meant to me.

"Babe, besides my mother, I've told one woman I loved her, and she left me. I don't throw that word around lightly."

"I'm glad to hear that." While her eyes looked serious and I thought she believed me, I needed to knock her fear of Cheyenne out completely. But I wasn't going to mention her by name.

"No other woman means anything to me, Alex. No. Other. Woman." She looked up at me, and I saw the moment she knew who I was talking about. She seemed to get it. She closed her eyes, took a deep breath, and a small smile graced her beautiful lips.

"Okay?"

She nodded. "Okay."

Here we were being so fucking open and vulnerable with each other when we were buck naked in the back of a strip club. Reaching between us, Alex took the lube from my hands. Her brows arched in surprise. "Is this what you had in mind for us tonight?"

"I had thought so, but now I'm not so sure."

"Why?"

Glancing around, I said, "I'm not sure this is the right place to take your ass for the first time."

She giggled. "I didn't realize there was ass-taking protocol."

I leaned down and nipped her lips with my teeth. "You and that smart mouth of yours."

"You love it as much as you love me."

Brushing the hair from her face, I smiled. "Yeah, I do."

Slowly, she started backing away from me. Then she twisted open the bottle. Pouring some into her palm, she reached out to take my cock in her hand. She worked the lube over it, coating it like a second skin. "Is that all we need?" she asked softly.

"Well, I might be prepped, but we need to work on getting you there."

"We do?"

Dropping down onto my knees in front of her, I said, "Yeah, we do." I dipped my head to where I could lick and suck her pussy. Alex gasped. As I worked her with my tongue, I nudged her legs farther apart. I continued my assault on her pussy and bought one finger up to tease along her puckered hole. I thought she might tense up or jerk away, but she kept rocking her hips to ride my tongue. I slid my finger through her wetness, then gently pressed the finger back to her hole before sliding it inside. She sucked in a harsh breath, her hips momentarily freezing. "Is that okay?" I asked.

"Mmm, yeah."

"Good." I worked my finger in and out of her while grazing her clit with my teeth. She jerked as the start of an orgasm began.

"Deacon!" she cried, throwing her head back. I had to steady her hips with one of my hands. As she started to come down, I slowly removed my finger. Taking her by the hand, I led her over to the couch.

When I sat down, she gave me a funny look. "We're going to start out this way so you can take what you can and set the pace." I pulled her down to straddle my lap. I worked my cock through her slickness to add a little extra lube. "Ready?"

"As I'll ever be," she replied with a shy smile.

Lifting her by her hips, I positioned myself at her entrance. "Okay, baby. It's up to you."

While keeping her gaze locked on mine, Alex bit her lip as she slowly eased down a little on me. She brought her arms up to grip my shoulders. I closed my eyes at how amazing she felt and willed myself not to thrust into her. She inched along at what felt like a snail's pace for me, but I knew for her it was a whole different ball game. I reached around to stroke her clit, hoping that would loosen up her a bit.

And it did. She finally sank all the way down on me. "How's that feel?"

"Full. Tight. But good."

I grinned. "I'm glad to hear that."

She winced as she started to move slowly on me. "That's good." Gradually, she began to speed up the pace. I also sped up the pace of the fingers I slid inside her. The closer she got to coming, the faster she began to bounce on me. When she cried out, I raised her hips and eased out of her.

Gently, I pushed her forward onto her hands and then I brought her legs up so she was on her knees. I stood up and then eased myself back inside her ass. She took me so much easier this time. I began to pump in and out of her. She was so fucking tight that it didn't take long for my balls to tighten and me to start to come. "Oh, Alex! Fuck yes!" I grunted. I pulled out of her to come on her lower back, branding her in yet another way as mine.

When I had finished, I pulled her to me, wrapping my arms around her. She tried to wiggle away. "I need a shower."

"I like you just the way you are—covered in me."

She rolled her eyes. "You're such a caveman."

"When it comes to you, I sure as hell am."

"Well, you've taken me in every way possible now," she said with a grin.

"I sure have. Now I just gotta give you my name, and you really will be all mine."

Alexandra's dark eyes widened. "Does that mean what I think it means?"

I chuckled. "Babe, I promise you that wasn't a proposal. So you don't have to worry how you'll come up with a better story than you got proposed to naked and covered in cum."

She shoved me away. "Ugh, you're disgusting. Sometimes I wonder what I see in you."

"The man who gives you screaming orgasms and who loves you with all his blackened heart."

"That only redeems you a little."

I grinned at her outrage. "Come on, little hellcat. Let's go get you a shower. Then I want you to find your clothes. You're sure as hell not going back out there like you were tonight."

SIXTEEN

ALEXANDRA
TWO WEEKS LATER

A few weeks back my two very different worlds had collided unexpectedly when Uncle Jimmy had shown up at the clubhouse, demanding to see me. After I had skipped out on a few family meals, he had gotten it in his mind I was being held captive by Deacon and the Raiders. Leave it to him to use his old GSP connections to have my cell phone traced.

Because I'd never been able to hide anything from him, I told him everything from my attack to my relationship with Deacon. I had expected harsh words and a severe admonishment for dating a Hells Raider, but I was surprised at how well Uncle Jimmy took it. "I want you to be happy, Alexandra. Just in the few minutes I've been talking to you, I don't think I've heard you sound so happy in such a long time."

He'd then requested to sit down with Deacon alone. Anxiety had filled me as I sat across the room from them, helping Willow with her schoolwork. Thankfully, no punches or yelling occurred. Uncle Jimmy and Deacon seemed to like each other, or at least tolerate each other. Willow, on the other hand, took an immediate liking to Uncle Jimmy, especially when he promised to take her to his cabin, where she could fish and swim in the river and play with his grandchildren. I thought Deacon would shoot down that offer, so I couldn't help being surprised when he agreed that Willow could go for a visit. Later, when I questioned him about it, he said, "Your uncle is a former trooper. He knows how to use a gun, how to be aware of his surroundings, and how to protect those around him. Their cabin is in a gated community. Willow would be just as safe with him as she is with one of us. Besides, Sigel won't be anticipating Jimmy."

Now, lounging in Deacon's lap, I stifled a yawn and fought the exhaustion that filled me. It hadn't exactly been a restful day so far. I'd risen almost at dawn to help Beth with Sunday lunch. Today had been groundbreaking in the fact that not only did I accompany Beth to church, but Deacon did as well. I'd done a double take when I stepped out of the bedroom to find him out of his cut and in a white shirt with the sleeves rolled up. Sure, he still had on his jeans and boots, but it was quite the transformation. He looked almost respectable. When he'd caught me staring, he'd given me his usual smirk.

After church, we'd come back to Beth's for the second momentous event of the day. My uncle Jimmy and aunt Joy arrived just after one for lunch, and after an enjoyable meal together, they had taken an overjoyed Willow with them for the trip to the cabin. Despite her obvious excitement, I still couldn't help feeling a little apprehensive. I would have preferred to accompany her, but I couldn't miss any more days away from school. As always, Deacon was one step ahead of me to put my fears to rest. When Willow left the compound with Jimmy, Beth pulled out behind them, going in the opposite direction. Should Sigel have someone watching, they would have followed Beth, who had a prospect following behind her. Just two hours had passed since she left, but it felt like she had been gone much longer.

"What are you thinking about?" Deacon asked, his voice humming against my ear.

"Nothing," I lied.

"Bullshit," he countered. When I glanced at him over my shoulder, he shook his head. "You're a terrible liar, Alex. Your body betrays you every time. You've been tense the last few minutes."

"Sorry. I was just thinking about Willow."

Deacon chuckled. "You missing the rug rat already?"

"Maybe a little. I'm not used to being here at the compound without her."

Nuzzling my neck, he flicked his tongue against my skin. "I'm sure I can think of something to get your mind off of her."

I giggled. "I'm sure you could."

Case poked his head out of the clubhouse meeting-room door. "You guys seen the latest invoices?"

Rolling her eyes at her husband, Kim groaned. "Babe, would you get your ass over here and relax, for once?"

"I would love to, but at the moment, I got shit to take care of before I can do that. That's the reason I got fucking 'president' on my rocker."

"You know it isn't good for your blood pressure," she countered.

"Hell, Case. It can wait till tomorrow, can't it?" Deacon asked before taking a long swig of his beer.

With a grunt, Case replied, "The rest of the shit can wait, but I gotta double-check these cargo invoices. It ain't adding up at the moment, and unless I can find an error on my part, our asses are gonna be between a rock and a hard place."

Kim popped the top on another beer. "If you promise to be done in ten minutes, I'll blow you out back."

Case's brows shot up. "You serious?"

Licking her tongue suggestively down the rim of the bottle, she replied, "Dead serious."

"Fuck," he grunted, as he stepped out of the meeting-room doorway. "Give me five minutes to go down to the house and check. As long as I know they're there, I'll let it go for the rest of the afternoon. Okay?"

Kim grinned. "Okay, baby." Glancing over her shoulder at me, she winked. "Amazing what a man will do for head, eh?"

I laughed. "Doesn't surprise me one bit."

"Is that a fact?" Deacon questioned, his hand sliding up my stomach to graze the underside of my breast.

"Yeah, it is," I replied breathlessly.

"You women think you have us pussy whipped," Deacon mused.

Cocking her head, Kim said, "It ain't all pussy whipping. We got your cocks whipped, too." As Case walked passed her, he sent a stinging smack across her ass.

Deacon eased me out of his lap and onto my feet. "I'll go with you, Prez. Once you have them, I'll lock them up in the safe for the rest of night. Make sure you keep your word to unwind."

"Thank you, D. I'm glad someone cares about my husband's well-being."

Winking at her, he replied, "I'm always going to go above and beyond to ensure one of my brothers gets some head."

It was Kim's turn to do the ass smacking as she popped Deacon. "Go on and get out of here before I change my mind and he has even more issues with blue balls."

Deacon chuckled as he hustled to catch up with Case. Just as I was about to sit down, the jukebox changed over to some old-school tunes with Heart's "What About Love?" Kim's eyes rolled back in pleasure. "Oh my God, I love this song."

"Me too."

Crooking her finger at me, she began to sing along with the song. Never able to resist a chance at karaoke, I rose out of my chair and went over to her. Bishop groaned. "If I find out who paid for this one, I'll kick his ass."

"They're not that bad," Rev said over us.

"They're not good, either," Bishop replied, which earned him the bird from Kim.

In the middle of our belting out the big finish, a loud roar ripped through the room. Windows rattled as the ground and walls vibrated. Bottles fell off the bar and crashed to the floor. It seemed to go on forever, but in truth, it probably lasted only a few seconds. When it was over, we all stared at one another, our faces a mixture of confusion and fear.

"Oh, fuck," Rev muttered at my side before turning to sprint out the back door. In one fluid motion, we all rushed forward after him. The moment I got outside, my heart felt like it shuddered to a stop. Smoke billowed out of Case's house, where orange and red flames licked and danced over what was left of the frame.

My world momentarily stilled. While I was frozen, everyone around me seemed to race around at warp speed. Raiders came out of every direction of the compound. At my side, Archer frantically called 911, and at the far end of the street, Beth's silver-headed form began hurrying to the fire.

As I tried to step forward to help, it seemed I was trudging through quicksand in the dreamlike world I found myself in. I shook my head, desperately hoping to shake myself out of the nightmare.

Deacon is in that house. Deacon is in that house. Deacon is in that house!

"CASE!" Kim screamed beside me before breaking into a run.

Although I willed my body to move, it remained rooted to that spot. Like the flick of a switch, I was transported back to the day I stood outside the mechanized ER doors. The grim-faced doctor had just delivered the news to me and my uncle Jimmy of my parents' deaths. As the doctor stood beckoning me to follow him to where he could take me to my parents' bodies, I froze. It was like if I took one step forward, then I was acknowledging what had really happened, but if I stayed still and in that spot, it wasn't real.

Today was the exact same way. I watched with eyes wide with horror as the fire truck wailed past me, screeching to a stop at the front of Case's house. Mac and Boone strained to hold Kim back. She fought hard against them, all the while screaming Case's name at the top of her lungs. I said a silent prayer of thanks that none of Case and Kim's five children were home. They had piled into the family van and left early this morning to spend the day at the mall and movies.

Beth stood beside Kim, head bent, hands steepled in prayer. Rev and Bishop stood on either side of her, blanketing her in their protection. The other club members milled around in the street, shaking their heads in disbelief, with ashen expressions on their faces.

Something scratched my legs, momentarily bringing me out of my trance. When I gazed down, Walter peered up at me, whining repeatedly. For a moment, I could only stare at him. It was like my arms ignored the message my brain was sending out. Finally, I managed to reach down and pick him up.

As I buried my face in his soft fur, my emotions finally thawed into a raw agony. Silent tears slipped from my eyes to dampen Walter's back. My chest felt like a watch that had been wound too tight. I wanted desperately to let go of the consuming emotions, but no matter how hard I silently wept, I couldn't find any relief. When my cries turned over to sobs, the pain raged through my chest so savagely, it felt like I was burning from the inside out.

When the last of the flames had finally been put out, there was little left that resembled the former duplex. Smoke still rose from the smoldering ashes. In a way it represented how the world around me now felt—blackened, devastated, in ruins. As I surveyed the expressions of those who had become my family, it seemed they were feeling the same way.

Two firemen brought me out of my thoughts as they walked past me. "When you think they'll clear us to go inside to look for the bodies?" the younger asked.

The older grunted. "Son, that wasn't no hot water heater blowing up. It was an explosion caused by a bomb. That, coupled with the temperature of the fire it causes, and you ain't gonna find shit. They'll be lucky if they even have a pile of ashes to put in an urn."

My hand flew to my mouth to muffle both my scream and the bile that rose in my throat. The older fireman cut his gaze over to me. His expression turned apologetic. "I'm sorry, ma'am. I shouldn't have said that where you could hear."

I didn't respond. I *couldn't* respond. After all, what does one say in this situation? My mind couldn't even begin to wrap itself around the idea that Deacon was alive inside the clubhouse less than half an hour ago. Now he was *gone*, reduced to nothingness. In the end, my protector couldn't save himself. The one place where he felt safe had somehow been breached. I didn't have to wonder who had done this. Sigel had finally come for his revenge, and he'd struck a devastating blow to the Raiders by taking out its president and sergeant at arms.

After the fire chief spoke to the crowd in a low tone, I watched as Rev wrapped his arms around Beth's shoulders, trying to console her. But I could hear her anguished wails from where I was. Bishop stood by, placing a hand on his mother's back. Despite Mac and Boone's efforts, Kim's body went limp, and she collapsed onto the ground. Just when I thought she had passed out, she began to pound her fists into the ground. "NOOOOO!" she screamed.

As the other members of the Raiders consoled one another, I'd never felt more alone in my life. Even though I could have reached out to them for comfort, I knew all too well how isolating grief truly was. You could be in a room full of people yet still be all alone in your own private hell. Cradling Walter to my chest, I turned and walked into the empty roadhouse, which was silent as a tomb.

I momentarily paused in front of the chair where Deacon had been sitting. I ran my free hand over the top rung, imagining his strong back pressed against it. If I closed my eyes, I could almost see him there, almost smell his scent still lingering in the air. Craning my ear, I tried desperately to hear his voice in the void.

With nothing but emptiness surrounding me, I made my way back to his room. I closed the door and then trudged across the floor. Taking my cell phone off the nightstand, I actually had the presence of mind to text my principal that I wouldn't be coming in tomorrow. The truth was I didn't know when I would go back—if I even could. I'd picked up the pieces of a shattered life once before. Even though it had made me stronger, I wasn't resilient. I didn't know if I could come back from this.

Collapsing down on the bed, I wrapped myself in the blanket that smelled overwhelmingly of him. Walter burrowed to my side, and I welcomed the comfort of his presence. Closing my eyes, I willed myself to sleep—to escape from the nightmare of my reality. To slip into an unconsciousness devoid of grief and sorrow. Where you never had to have those you love snatched away from you.

And finally I slipped away.

SEVENTEEN

ALEXANDRA

I was out of breath. My muscles screamed in agony, but I continued running. Dark woods with sinister-looking trees enveloped me. Fear like I'd never known pushed me on. I was running from something, but what, I didn't know. Images from my past flashed before me like lightning crashing across the sky. My mother handing me a bouquet of bloodred roses at one of my ballet recitals. My father grinning as he pressed the car keys into my eager sixteen-year-old hands. Deacon's intense dark eyes, a sheen of sweat across his tattooed chest, and his hips flexing at he pumped in and out of me.

Each of the happy memories burst into shards of glass when I ran through them, cutting me with an emotional pain that didn't seem to touch me physically. I reached the end of the woods only to find myself at the edge of a cliff. Whatever was coming for me grew closer and closer, and without a choice, I leaped off the cliff. As I began to free fall—

With a piercing scream, I bolted upright in bed. I brought a shaky hand to my forehead and swept back the sweat-soaked strands of hair. Clutching my shirt over my heart, I willed myself to breathe normally again. As I became aware of where I was and why I was there, I realized there was no respite. I had just exchanged one nightmare for another.

A gentle knock came at the door. "Alexandra?" Rev's concerned voice questioned.

"Yeah?" I croaked.

As Rev came through the doorway, I immediately forgot my own pain, and instead, I focused on his. Anguish marred his usually handsome face. In the last twenty-four hours he had lost so much more than me, and the strain was evident on his face. "Are you okay? I heard you shout."

With a nod, I pulled myself up in bed. "Just a nightmare."

"I'm sorry."

"After losing my parents, I should be used to it. I had them for months after they died. I guess it's only to be expected now."

"I know what you mean. I had nightmares for years after . . ." Rev trailed off, a pained expression etched on his face. "Well, anyway, I just wanted to check on you."

"What time is it?"

"A little after five in the morning."

"Haven't you been to bed yet?"

"Can't seem to lie still."

Although I had originally come to Deacon's room in the clubhouse for comfort, I didn't think I could bear to be alone any longer. "Will you stay with me until I go to sleep?"

Rev's dark brows shot into his hairline. "I don't think that's a good idea."

"Why not?"

He grimaced. "If Deacon were here, he'd kick my ass for being in bed with his old lady."

Before I could stop myself, a laugh tumbled from my lips as I imagined Deacon going ballistic at the sight of me and Rev together. At Rev's surprised expression, I shook my head. "You're right. He would be pissed if he was here, but he isn't. And considering he loved us, I think he would want us both to have a little comfort."

Rev weighed my words before he finally shut the door behind him. He closed the distance between us in two long strides. I scooted over in the bed as he eased down on the mattress. Slowly, he took off his boots. They thumped onto the floor before he collapsed back on the mattress. Without waiting for an invitation, I scooted over to him. He obliged me by raising his arm to let me snuggle up to him and lay my head on his T-shirt-covered chest.

"How's your mother doing?"

Rev tensed beneath me. "Not good. Breakneck finally had to give her a shot. She'd probably still be pacing the floors and sobbing if he hadn't."

Tears overflowed my eyes at the thought of Beth's grief, sending moisture onto Rev's shirt. Part of me thought I should be with her. But she had her boys. She and I would grieve together soon.

Everything in my world had turned as black as the charred remains of Case's house. And then out of nowhere, Willow's smiling face popped into my mind. A groan of agony escaped my lips, causing Rev's arm to tighten around me.

"Oh God, Rev, what about Willow? They're not supposed to be back until Wednesday."

"I figured we would go get her tomorrow. Tell her in person."

I couldn't even fathom what it would be like to tell her, least of all what it would do to her. In the last eight months, she had lost her mother and now the father she had only just begun to know . . . and to love. "Bless her heart," I murmured.

"Alexandra, I know it might be too soon to say this, but I need to. Without Deacon, you might think you don't have a place here anymore, but that isn't true. You're our family. We take care of old ladies. More than anything, Willow is going to need you."

I lifted my head to stare into his troubled eyes. "I wasn't planning on going anywhere. In case you missed it, I need you guys, too. I love you all."

He jerked his chin at me. "I'm glad to hear that."

Lying back down, I snuggled close to him. Silence stretched out between us as we were both overwhelmed by our own thoughts and grief. "Thank you for being here, Rev," I whispered in the dark.

"You're welcome. And thank you, too."

Closing my eyes, I let the emotional exhaustion overwhelm me once again, and I fell into a deep sleep.

When I woke again from a nightmareless sleep, Rev was gone. Flipping over in the bed, I eyed the clock. It was almost noon. I couldn't believe I'd managed to sleep that long. Throwing back the covers, I rose from the bed. My arms and legs felt weighted down with the all-consuming grief that besieged me. Sleep had been a welcome respite, but now I was back to experiencing the full range of emotions. I found the hallway quiet and empty when I stepped out to go to the bathroom. Although I desperately needed coffee, my desire for a shower won out over everything else. I turned on the water as hot as it would go before slipping under the stream.

I remained frozen, staring at the worn tile in front of me until the warm water ran out. The icy cold cascading over my head finally woke me up. I washed my hair and body in almost record time, my teeth chattering the entire time. When I got out, I rubbed the towel furiously over me, trying to warm up. I slipped on my robe and headed back to my room.

As I dressed, I heard the sound of a woman's anguished weeping. It didn't take me but a second to realize it was Kim's. Her and Case's room was across the hall from Deacon's. While in my own world of torment, I couldn't begin to imagine her agony. Case had been the love of her life and the father of her children, but more than that, he had been her salvation from a life of hell. My heart ached for her so intensely I began to feel like I was smothering.

My phone rang on the nightstand. When I glanced at the ID, my chest tightened even harder. I couldn't bring myself to answer it. The door opened, and Rev stepped inside. He eyed the phone, and I shook my head. "It's Willow."

"I figured it was when I heard the ringing."

Shaking my head, I said, "I can't."

He took the phone from me. "Hey, rug rat, whatcha doing?"

I heard her questioning voice all the way across from him. "Yeah, she's busy, so I thought I'd answer her phone." Willow then proceeded to rattle on.

"Yeah, we were thinking about coming up to get you today—" He paused at Willow's screech. "I know you just got there and you're not supposed to come back until Wednesday." His gaze flickered to mine.

Let her stay, I mouthed.

His brows shot up in surprise. "Hang on, rug rat," he said before pressing the mute button on the phone.

"She's having so much fun, isn't she?" At Rev's nod, I said, "Give her a few more days of innocent fun. Who knows when she'll be able to enjoy anything again."

After processing my words, he said, "You're right. We'll just wait to do a memorial until she gets back. We'll be busy enough with Case's." Rev unmuted the phone. "Okay, rug rat, you get your way like usual. You can come back with Jimmy on Wednesday." Tears stung my eyes at her excited squeal. A shadow of a smile played at his lips. "I'll tell her. I love you, baby."

He then ended the call. "She wanted me to remind you to give Walter kisses for her like she asked."

A sob choked off in my throat as I thought about the day Deacon had brought me the squirming puppy and Willow had given him his unusual moniker. At that moment, I couldn't stand to be in the compound one second longer. "I have to get out of here," I said, my chin trembling.

He merely nodded before offering me his hand. I slipped mine into his, and then we walked down the hall. The mood in the main room of the clubhouse was somber, to say the least. Where the men and women once talked and laughed as they drank, they now spoke in hushed tones if they even talked at all. Of course, all voices hushed at the sight of me.

"Alex needs some time away from here. Take her wherever she needs to go," Rev instructed Archer.

"It would be my honor," he replied.

His words and the reverence with which he spoke them caused the familiar suffocating pain to ripple through me. While Deacon and I were far from marriage or even being engaged, I had come to be recognized as his widow, just like Kim.

I leaned over to hug Rev. "I won't be gone long."

"Take all the time you need."

With a nod, I started out of the roadhouse with Archer at my side. When he walked over to his bike, I faltered. I couldn't imagine riding with anyone but Deacon. At my hesitation, he turned around. "If you're not okay with this, we can take your car."

As I contemplated his words, I thought about how once I had gotten over my initial fear, the open road had felt so peaceful. "No, it's fine."

"Are you sure?"

"Yeah, I'm sure."

He handed me a helmet, and I slipped it on. After I slid across the seat, my arms froze before I could bring them around him. It all felt so wrong—touching him as intimately as I had Deacon. When

Archer glanced over his shoulder, he gave me a sad smile as if he knew exactly what I was thinking. With trembling hands, I finally reached forward and brought my arms around his waist. He gunned the engine, and we took off.

"Where we going?" he called.

"Haynes Road," I shouted back.

He nodded. There was only one place I could think of where I wanted to escape to. I couldn't go back home. It held too many unpleasant memories. I would go to the one place that gave me purpose—the school.

When we arrived, it was a little after three. All the students were gone except for the ones in the after-school program, which was housed in the gym and cafeteria. After we pulled into a parking space, I eased off the bike and handed the helmet back to Archer. I couldn't begin to imagine the looks I was going to get from the teachers who remained in the building. Sure, some of them knew I was involved with a biker, and by now I'm sure they knew he was dead. I'd called my principal to ask for a few days off.

Thankfully, I'd remembered my keys, so we were able to slip in one of the side doors, rather than going in the front. When I started into my classroom, I noticed that Archer's feet seemed rooted to the floor. His posture seemed as if he were on high alert.

Even though I already knew the answer, I asked, "You don't want to come inside?"

He shook his head. "I'll wait out here."

"Okay." While I should have felt comforted with him keeping an eye on things, I also didn't want to be alone. Not even in my classroom, with its cheerfully decorated bulletin boards and posters. I slipped inside and closed the door behind me. Whoever they'd gotten to be my sub was obviously trying to survive with fifteen five-year-olds, because the room was a wreck.

With a renewed sense of purpose pumping through me, I went

to the closet and grabbed the necessary cleaning materials. I don't know how long I spent washing down desks and chairs, scraping off clumps of glue, and reorganizing my bookshelves and centers. Ironically, it seemed to do me a lot of good. For that brief respite, I was able to forget that the man I loved more than anything in the world had been killed yesterday.

Defeated by the painful cloud of grief that swelled around me, I walked over to my desk and collapsed down into the chair. Cradling my head in my hands, I wept openly and unashamedly. As I cried, images of Deacon and me together played through my mind. Him with Willow. Him with his brothers. Him in those last moments as he walked out the door to the horrible fate that awaited him.

Once I began to recover, I swiped my arms across my moistened face. A tissue came into my line of sight. "Thank you, Archer," I murmured, as I took it to dab my eyes.

"You're welcome, Miss Evans."

I jerked my head up at the stranger's voice. Every molecule in my body seemed to flare in distress. Although I wanted to scream for help, my vocal cords twisted in fear to where I could do nothing but squeak. When my gaze darted to the classroom doorway, the man held up his hand. "Don't worry about the prospect. He's only being momentarily detained. I didn't find it necessary to shed his blood today."

"W-who are y-you?" I stammered.

He flashed me a wicked smile. "I'm sure you already know the answer to that question, Miss Evans. You are a smart girl, being a teacher."

"Sigel?"

With a flourished bow, he said, "The one and only."

"What are you doing here?"

"I see you're a woman who doesn't beat around the bush. I'm

glad to see that. I hate when my time is wasted. I've come here to pay my respects for the loss of your dearly departed boyfriend."

My fists clenched in my lap. Anger outweighed my fear, and I felt like at any minute I might launch myself at Sigel.

Cocking his head, Sigel seemed to be weighing my body language. "I hope you will believe me when I say I had no idea Deacon would be anywhere near Case's house."

"And I hope you will believe me when I say that is utter bullshit."

Sigel's deep blue eyes widened at my statement. "I can see why Deacon liked you so much. You're like a hellcat, aren't you, Miss Evans?" Nausea washed over me at Sigel's use of the word "hellcat." It was one Deacon had used to tease me.

When I refused to answer him, Sigel shook his head. "The plan was to take out Case, which would enrage Deacon enough to come after me. I would then be able to get my personal revenge. Trust me that having him taken out in a simple explosion served no purpose for me." His expression darkened even further. "He received far too quick and painless a death, considering what I had in store for him."

While it was still hard to imagine that Sigel hadn't planned on taking Deacon out, his words certainly gave me something to think about. "With Deacon dead, I can't imagine what you could possibly want from me," I said in a low voice.

"You were once a very valuable commodity to me, Miss Evans. I'm sure that was made clear to you when you spent some time with my former associate, Crank."

Jerking my chin up at him, I said, "If you for one minute think you can use me to get to Willow, you might as well kill me right here and now. As long as I have a breath left within me, I'll keep that child safe!"

Sigel made a *tsk*ing noise in his throat. "You once again have missed the mark on this one, Miss Evans. I don't want Deacon's brat.

While I'm sure her death would greatly affect Rev and some of the other brothers, it would do little for me, considering her father is now dead."

"Then what do you what?" I demanded, my voice shrill.

"You know, they say it's a small world, and I wouldn't have actually believed how small it could be until you came into Deacon Malloy's life."

"I don't understand."

"No, I don't suppose you do. So let me refresh your memory. I'm sure you might've heard that cocksucker you spread your legs for mention that I had a son. A son that he murdered."

"In revenge for you killing his father," I spat back.

"Touché, Miss Evans. I suppose you subscribe to the Old Testament vengeance of an eye for an eye like your former boyfriend did." When I didn't answer him, he started a leisurely stroll around my desk, while his gaze roamed around. "You have a lovely classroom. In a way, it reminds me of your mother's."

My heartbeat shuddered to a stop and then restarted. "Excuse me?"

His eyes met mine. "I think you heard me right."

"But how is it possible that you knew my mother?"

"You see this is where our small worlds collide. Once upon a time, your mother taught my son, Andy. It was second or third grade. I don't remember exactly now."

"Second. She only ever taught kindergarten and second," I murmured softly.

"Ah, thank you for reminding me." Sigel came to face me again. "Your mother was one hell of a nosy bitch. Instead of worrying about all the snot-nosed brats she had to teach, she focused on Andy. She couldn't seem to believe that he got the bruises on his arms and legs from simply playing. She didn't seem to understand that I subscribed to a very old-school form of discipline for my children. So she turned the case over to the local CPS. I couldn't have them snooping around in my life, so we disappeared. We hopped from county to county, never going too far from my club." His soulless blue eyes focused on mine. "One thing that could be said for your mother was that she had one hell of a memory. I thought I'd put enough time and space between the former charges when I moved back and Andy started high school."

Slowly the pieces of the puzzle began to fall into place. "Was he one of my father's students?"

"My, my, aren't you smart. Yeah, he ended up having your old man. I guess over dinner or some shit, he started talking about how he was so worried about one of his students. And when he mentioned the name, your mother recognized it. That night I got a call from your father. He wanted answers and reminded me of the former case against me. My usual methods of persuasion didn't seem to work on him, even when I threatened something happening to you."

Closing my eyes, I couldn't begin to imagine what that call was like for my father. Nothing mattered more to him in the world than his wife and kids. But at the same time, he had a passion deep within him to stand up for what was right, even if it meant the potential for those he loved to be hurt.

"In the end, I was fucking tired of being forced to run, so I decided to take a different course of action."

His words caused a shiver to run from the top of my head down my spine. "But they died in a car accident," I said lamely.

"Yes, they did. A car accident brought on by faulty brakes and an unmarked car that hit them, causing them to go off that ravine."

My hand flew to my mouth to stop the scream building in my throat. The jumbled and jangled emotions filling my body made me feel like I was tied into a straitjacket and thrashing to get loose. It was overwhelming. The entire last ten years of my life were based on a lie. My parents hadn't died in an accident. They'd been murdered. Their deaths had been coldly calculated by the piece of shit who stood in front of me.

"Thankfully, your father hadn't flapped his gums to any of his coworkers, so no one knew that he had almost blown the lid on me, which would have affected my club. Of course, I hated that your kid brother was in the car. I never intended for you two to get hurt."

Tears of anguish and rage stung my eyes. As I stared at Sigel, I wondered what possible motive or intention he had for telling me this. I was already a woman on the edge because of him. I was barely surviving after losing the man I loved. It was too much. Far too much.

"W-why would you t-tell me this?" I stammered, barely able to get the words out.

"Because you're entitled to the truth. And because I hope it will influence you to do what I'm about to ask of you."

With a mirthless laugh, I countered, "How could you possibly think after just telling me you murdered my parents that I'll want to do anything for you?" This man had a very loose grip on his sanity. He was seriously delusional if he thought I could trust him.

"Because while you can't bring your parents back, your cooperation allows for your brother to remain safe, along with Malloy's kid."

I sucked in a harsh breath. "You're blackmailing me."

Sigel lifted one shoulder apathetically. "If you want to call it that. I like to think of it as insurance, or even collateral. We're both putting up something in good faith to ensure an outcome."

"After all that you've done, how can I possibly trust you?"

"You'll have to figure that out for yourself, Miss Evans." Sigel placed both his palms down on my desk and leaned forward. "I know after what happened with Case and Deacon that there will be retaliation by the Raiders against my club. But before that happens, I want you to bring me something—something the Raiders took from me."

"You want me to steal something?"

"It's rightfully mine, Miss Evans. Or at least it was my son's."

Eyeing him curiously, I asked, "What is it?"

He pushed off my desk and began to pace the room. Something about the item agitated him. Finally, he turned back to me. "In the club world, a man's cut is sacred. From the moment you're patched in, it becomes your second skin. You sew on your own patches and care for the leather. You don't ever abandon it somewhere for your brothers to teasingly take it or for your enemy to steal it." Reaching in his own cut, Sigel produced a pack of cigarettes and a lighter. I didn't bother informing him that there was no smoking on school grounds.

After taking a long drag, Sigel's eyes bored into mine. "Deacon Malloy didn't just walk up to my son and shoot him. Nor did he take a knife to him. That cocksucker tortured him for a good two hours."

If he had intended his words to have an effect on me, he got one. My stomach churned, and I had to fight against the urge to throw up. It was unfathomable to me that the Deacon I loved could do such a horrible thing to another person, even in revenge for his father's death.

Exhaling a cloud of smoke, Sigel said, "Besides making my boy suffer through two hours of torture, he did the most disrespectful thing a fellow biker can do. He took Andy's cut. That shoulda been something we buried him in, but Deacon took that from us."

"You think that Andy's cut is somewhere in the Raiders compound?"

"Oh, I know it is."

"But what if Deacon burned it or destroyed it somehow?"

Sigel shook his head. "You don't get rid of war prizes. That cut is somewhere in that clubhouse, and you're going to find it."

"What if I can't?"

"Oh, I know you will. You value your life and the life of your brother and Malloy's brat too much to fail."

"Once I bring you this cut, you swear not to hurt Willow or me?"

"You have my word."

"I'm not sure it's worth anything."

"In this case, it is. Rest assured that I'm not a double-crosser, Miss Evans. When I say something, I mean it. I'm sure your father could attest to that. I told him I would kill him if he didn't back off, and look what happened."

"Get out!" I shrieked, as rage shook through me.

A cruel laugh escaped from Sigel. "You're so very unhospitable. But I will honor your request for now." He strode over to the door before turning back to me. "You can expect to hear from me within the next few days. When I call, I will expect a prompt delivery. No stalling and no excuses. You can also get any ideas out of your pretty little head about enlisting help from the Raiders."

"I wouldn't dream of doing anything that would risk not ridding you completely from my life."

"I'm glad to hear that. I'll be in touch."

And then he disappeared just as quickly as he had appeared. As the emotional weight of Sigel's admission crashed over me, I began to hyperventilate. Gripping the edge of my desk, I wheezed in and out. *Breathe, Alex. Just breathe.*

I repeated the phrase over and over in my mind like a mantra. Then I realized I wasn't the only one saying it. Jerking my head up, I gazed into Archer's concerned face. With a weak smile, he once again repeated, "Just breathe."

Launching myself out of the chair, I wrapped my arms around him. I needed comfort as desperately as I did air.

"I'm sorry. I'm so fucking sorry I wasn't here. His men cornered me in the bathroom and held me at gunpoint until he was finished." I whimpered in protest when he pulled away. Scanning my face, he asked, "Did he hurt you? Did he touch you? Fuck, Alex, did he hurt you in any way?"

"No. He didn't hurt or touch me."

When I didn't volunteer any other information, Archer sighed. "Thank God you're all right."

"Take me home."

His brows lined. "To your house?"

I shook my head. "No, to the compound."

"You sure you're able to ride? I can call someone to pick us up."

"Just get me home now. Please."

"Anything for you, Alex," Archer replied. Sliding his arm around my hip, he pulled me to him. With my head against his chest, I leaned on his strength as we walked outside.

When we got to the door leading outside, I hesitated slightly. "It's all right. I'm right here," Archer reassured me. As I gazed up into his face, I couldn't help noticing the way his eyes cautiously scanned the surroundings as well as the way he clenched and unclenched his jaw. He looked like a man on edge, and I couldn't blame him. Not only had two of his club members been taken out, but he had just been jumped.

At the sight of his motorcycle, I faltered. I couldn't help the paranoia that something had been done to his bike.

"You all right?" he questioned.

"Do you think your bike was tampered with?"

Archer's brows shot up in surprise. "I wouldn't think so. If they wanted to harm us, they had the chance."

My mind automatically went to my parents and how when they left for school that morning, they felt they were safe in their SUV. "Just twitchy, I guess."

"Just a sec," Archer said. He then made a wide circle around his bike. "No boot prints."

"Would they even show?"

"If they'd been riding, they would have left some mark, especially considering there's patches of sediment and dirt all around the parking lot." He nodded. "It would show."

"If you say so," I replied, feeling unconvinced.

Scratching the back of his neck, Archer said, "Listen, Alex, it ain't my business, but I would imagine if Sigel came all the way out here to meet with you, there's something he wants. Something that you, and you alone, will give him." When I refused to answer, Archer said, "That fact alone would mean nothing was going to happen to you. At least not now."

With a quick nod of my head, I replied, "Okay. But I've changed my mind. I'm not ready to go back to the compound just yet."

He gave me a questioning look. "So you wanna go somewhere else?"

"No. I just need to ride for a little while."

"Okay, I can do that."

I'm sure he thought I had absolutely lost my mind since in one minute I was worried about the motorcycle blowing up and then in the next I wanted to be on it for a long time.

Without another word to him, I took the helmet and got on the motorcycle. We took off out of the parking lot. Archer drove us out of town and down one of the off-the-beaten-path roads into the more rural areas. As I rode, things became clearer and clearer in my mind. I had come to a crossroads I'd never imagined possible.

"Pull over!" I shouted over the roar of the engine.

Archer didn't glance back at me. Instead, he found a turn-around in a thicket of trees. When he stopped, I didn't immediately get off. "You need the bathroom?"

"Turn off the engine." When he obeyed me, I drew in a deep breath. "Archer, if I were to ask you for your help, would you give it without question?"

Slowly, he turned around to look at me. "I don't think I like where this is going."

I licked my dry lips. "If I were to ask your help to do something that would protect Willow and the club, would you do it?"

"It depends." He scratched the stubble on his chin. "What do you want?"

"First you have to swear that even if you don't agree to do it, you won't tell any of the Raiders."

Archer's eyes widened, and he hopped off the bike. He stalked around a moment before he began pacing. "You're putting me between a rock and a fucking hard place."

"I wouldn't dream of asking you this unless it was a matter of life and death."

My words only seemed to agitate him more, and he continued to pace. He'd almost worn a hole in the gravel when he finally stopped. He sighed so hard his body shuddered. Then he turned to me. "You have my word. Now, what is it?"

As best I could, I tried relating to him what had come to me while on our drive. He listened raptly without interrupting to question me. When I was done, he stared at me almost incredulously. "You're serious."

"I am."

"That's fucking bat-shit crazy."

"Yeah, well, that's where I am."

I expected him to resume his pacing. Instead, he walked back over to me. His blue eyes burned into mine as he stared me down. "I'm in."

I couldn't help my gasp of surprise. "You are?"

"Even though I should tell you to go fuck yourself for putting me in this situation, I get it. I really do."

"Thank you."

Shaking his head, he slung his leg over the bike. "Save the gratitude until we both come out of this alive."

I laughed nervously. "It's a deal."

EIGHTEEN

ALEXANDRA

I don't know how Archer managed to alert them, but when we arrived at the compound, Raiders came spilling out of the clubhouse to meet us. Rev and Bishop magically appeared. They escorted me inside. Instead of taking me to Deacon's room, they ushered me into the boardroom. Rev pulled a chair out for me and motioned for me to have a seat. "Talk to us, Alex," he urged.

Holding up my hand, I said, "I'm a little shaken up, but for the most part, I'm fine."

Bishop surveyed my face. "He didn't try anything physical with you, did he?"

"My virtue is safe," I replied with a humorless smile.

"It damn well better be. If he dared to lay one finger on you, we'd bring a fucking firestorm down on him," Bishop growled.

I drew in a deep breath and prepared to broach the subject I was wary of. "I need you to teach me how to use a knife."

Rev and Bishop exchanged a glance. "Alex, I'm not sure that's a good idea," Rev said.

"Would you prefer I be defenseless the next time I have a run-in with Sigel or one of his thugs?"

"We'll always protect you," Rev argued.

Cocking my brows, I said, "Like today?"

"I suppose you have a point."

"Do you realize that if I had been armed with a knife or a gun, I could have taken Sigel out? Just like that." I snapped my fingers for emphasis.

Crossing his tattooed arms over his chest, Bishop replied, "Well, that's nice to think, but you're not really the knife-toting kind."

"Basically, I'm a weak, helpless female?" I countered.

He grimaced. "I didn't say that."

"No, you alluded to it, and that's just as bad."

When I turned my gaze on Rev, he gave me a look of appraisal before nodding his head. "You need to learn how to defend yourself."

"Seriously?" Bishop questioned, his blue eyes widening.

"Alex is right. We can't ensure that we'll always be able to protect her. Even with Deacon gone, she's obviously still a target for Sigel. That's all the more reason for her to know how to defend herself."

Realizing he had lost, Bishop exhaled sharply. "If you say so."

Rev nodded. "Go to the shop and get her something she can use."

With one last disapproving look in our direction, Bishop headed out the door. Turning his attention to me, Rev asked, "Where's the first place you would think to go for if you were going to stab someone?"

Furrowing my brows, I replied, "The heart?"

Rev shook his head. "While ultimately lethal, you gotta get through a hard-as-hell breastbone to get to it. You want something that will immediately incapacitate your enemy."

Reaching out, he brought his hands to my neck. His fingers worked down the side. "You want to try to sever one of the carotid arteries here on the neck. They pump blood to the brain. Since it controls every organ function, you want to take out the main nervous system. Fifteen to twenty seconds after a hit, your enemy will be beyond help and likely unconscious. Then you're good to go."

"Isn't there a way to kill them instantly?"

"No, but without help, taking out a carotid will ensure they die. Plus, with them incapacitated, it gives you the time you need to get away."

"Okay."

Rev released my neck. "Once you've got them down, a few stabs or slices to the abdomen are good." Pressing against my stomach, he said, "Here." Then he moved his hand up slightly. "Here." And then he dropped it below my navel. "And here."

Bishop returned at that point with a shiny pocketknife. With one push of a button, a long blade flipped out. "See how this feels in your hand."

Drawing in a deep breath, I reached out for the knife. Except for cutting steak or carving a pumpkin, I'd never held such a knife in my hands. I didn't know when the time came to it if I would actually be able to use it. But I had to be willing to try.

As the steel blade caught the light, a feeling of empowerment came over me. It wasn't an AK-47 or a grenade, but I knew it would save my life. Most important of all, a jab and a cut could end someone else's life—someone who was a threat to me and those I loved. Someone like Sigel.

"You think you can use it when shit gets real?" Bishop questioned.

"Yeah, I do," I answered honestly.

He smiled. "Something tells me that you can. You're a tough little cookie."

"Thanks." I continued eyeing the knife with morbid fascination, imagining the damage it could do on Sigel. "So you guys keep war prizes from your enemies?"

When I dared to glance up, both Rev and Bishop stared at me with almost unreadable expressions. "Do you?" I repeated.

"Why do you want to know?"

Shrugging, I replied, "Just curious."

"Bullshit! What the fuck did Sigel say to you?" Bishop demanded.

"The less you know about it the better," I whispered.

Rev reached out to put his hands on my shoulders. "Alex, you need to tell us what Sigel said to you about war prizes."

Shaking my head, I bit down on my lip, trying to prevent myself from betraying too much information. Rev's grip tightened on me. "He wants something that was once the Knights', doesn't he?"

"Please, Rev."

"Dammit, Alex. I don't care what he threatened you with. You have to tell us!" Rev shouted.

"He wants his son's cut—the one Deacon took after he killed him. He's to call me in a few days, and I have to bring it to him. If I do this, he will leave me and Willow alone. But I can't involve any of the Raiders, or people will get hurt."

Rev and Bishop exchanged a glance. "It's here, isn't it?" I asked. When they didn't respond, I said, "Please."

Taking my hand, Rev pulled me out of my chair. He walked me down to the end of the room. On the left-hand side of the door was a closet. Surprisingly, he didn't reach for a key to unlock it. Instead, he opened it. When I glanced inside, I gasped. Sitting on the middle shelf was a leather cut emblazoned with Nazi symbols. I reached out to take it, but Rev held me back. "You don't take it now. When Sigel calls you about the meeting, then you'll get it."

Although I was frustrated, I didn't let my emotions betray me. "Okay. It's probably better keeping it here anyway."

"We'll expect to be involved. Even if we have to hang back when it comes to you turning it over, we'll still have your back."

I smiled. "Thank you. I appreciate that. I didn't want to have to do this on my own."

Rev and Bishop seemed relieved with my response. Slinging his arm across my shoulder, Bishop said, "Why don't you let me buy you some dinner?"

"That's awfully sweet of you, but I need to go home in a little while to get some more clothes and check on things."

Rev's brows drew together in worry. "We can send Archer or Crazy Ace there."

I laughed. "As tempting as it sounds to have the prospects pick out my clothes and raid my underwear drawer, I need to do this myself. Maybe even sleep in my own bed."

Bishop glanced between me and Rev. "You really think that's a good idea after what happened with Sigel today?"

"He won't do anything to me until he gets the cut."

"She's right," Rev replied.

"I still don't like the idea of you anywhere outside the compound," Bishop said.

I patted his shoulder. "Thanks for being overprotective."

He winked. "Anytime, babe."

Rev pressed the knife into the palm of my hand. "Just in case."

"Thank you."

Bishop whistled at Archer, who immediately came over. "I want you to go home with Alex. Keep your eyes and ears open for anything."

"You got it."

As we started to the door, I glanced over at Archer. "Aren't you tired of babysitting me?"

He grinned. "You're pretty easy compared to some of the really fucked-up things that prospects are usually forced to do."

"That's good to know."

"Besides, I like being with you."

"You do?"

He nodded. "Yeah, you remind me of my little sister."

Playfully punching him in the arm, I said, "Hey now, last time I checked, I was the one older than you."

"Yeah, but you guys act the same."

"I get it now." When Archer started to the clubhouse door, I stopped him. "Can you give me ten minutes? I need to get some of my clothes together to do laundry."

"Sure. Take as long as you need."

A moment passed between us, and Archer nodded in acknowledgment. I then made my way down the hall to Deacon's room. When I slipped inside, I went to the closet to grab my bag. After dumping everything out onto the closet floor, I brought the bag over to the bed. I took out my makeup bag and pulled out a small pair of scissors from it.

After cutting part of the bottom lining of my bag, I left the plastic flap half on. I threw a few shirts and pants inside before heading out into the hallway. When I got to the main room, I found it empty. Walking over to the boardroom door, I opened it. I knew Archer had ensured that it would be unlocked.

The room was plunged in darkness, and Rev and Bishop were no longer there. Glancing over my shoulder, I slipped inside. I hurried over to the closet. I tossed out my clothes, then threw open the closet door. Rev and Bishop were far too trusting, because the cut still sat on the shelf. I grabbed it and stuffed it under the loose flap of my bag. I put the clothes back on top of it and then zipped it up. I shut the closet door fast and then raced out of the room. Thankfully, no one was there to see me.

I tried easing my frantic breaths as I headed outside to meet Archer. He was waiting for me by his bike. "Ready?" he asked, his brows rising.

I nodded. "Yeah. I got everything."

"Good." He slid across the seat of his motorcycle while I

picked up the helmet that had pretty much become my own. After I put it on, I climbed on behind him. As my arms slid around his waist, I once again had to fight to keep my emotions in check. While each time it seemed to get a little easier being on the back of a bike, it didn't dull the pain of losing Deacon.

Later, as we pulled into my driveway, I couldn't help the tightening in my chest at the sight of the house that had once been my happy home. After my attack, I didn't think it would ever feel happy again. That, coupled with losing Deacon, made me seriously consider putting it on the market.

When I started up the walk, I realized that Archer wasn't beside me. Turning around, I cocked my brows at him. "Aren't you coming in?"

He shook his head. "Gonna do a walk around. Then I'll probably stay out here on the porch."

"You don't mean you're going to sleep in one of the chairs?"

"I won't be sleeping."

"But I have a perfectly good couch inside, not to mention a guest bedroom."

"Alex, when your protection is put on my shoulders, I take it very seriously. I ain't gonna be caught sleeping if Sigel decides to strike."

Realizing I wasn't going to break his resolve, I nodded. "All right, then. But it's looked like it was going to storm all day. If it does, you're coming inside. I won't have you struck by lightning."

He laughed. "Whatever."

"And thank you. For today. For everything."

As the unspoken hung heavy between us, he nodded. "You're welcome."

Turning around, I headed back up the walk. After unlocking the door, I purposely refused to look to my left. With my emotions already going haywire, I couldn't even acknowledge the kitchen or what had happened there. Regardless of the fact I tried to escape them, the memories of that horrible night rocketed through my mind, causing me to gasp.

Pushing myself forward, I hurried up the stairs, anxious to put as much distance as I could between me and the kitchen. When I got to my bedroom, I went straight for the bathroom. The moment I turned on the water, the tears pooled in my eyes like I had turned them on as well. After stripping out of my clothes, I slipped into the shower. Standing under the spray, I let the water wash away the tears that continued to fall. I thought by now I would be devoid of any moisture, but just like my grief seemed to have no cap to its depths, neither did my tears.

When I finished, I toweled off and slid into the silky blue robe that hung behind the bathroom door. I knew there would be no way I would fall asleep on my own tonight, not even with Archer hanging around. As soon as I took my sleeping pill, I wanted to at least order him a pizza—something to compensate for having to babysit me, even if he did say it was an easy job.

Opening the medicine cabinet, I took out the pills that my therapist had first started prescribing for me after my parents were killed. Now another tragic loss, another reason to take a blue pill to escape the torment of grief through sleep.

I closed the cabinet and reached for the glass on the counter. Something caught my eye, and I glanced up into the mirror. The bottle of pills clattered onto the counter. Both my hands flew to my mouth. Without a word, I shook my head back and forth, willing myself to wake up from the dream I surely found myself in. But nothing changed.

"Babe," a gentle voice said.

Framed in the doorway of my bathroom was Deacon.

NINETEEN

ALEXANDRA

The ability to speak had abandoned me. Instead, my body shook and trembled as I tried to come to terms with what was before me. His eyes never leaving mine, Deacon stepped into the bathroom. Taking slow steps, he closed the gap between us. When his hand came up to cup my cheek, my knees buckled. I would have sunk onto the tile if Deacon hadn't reached out and grabbed me by the shoulders. Easing me back, he gripped my waist and hoisted me onto the counter.

Turning on the faucet, he poured me a glass of water. When he brought it to my lips, I reluctantly took a few sips. I didn't know how simple water could possibly help at this moment. I needed a stiff drink.

"Y-you're a-alive?" I stammered.

He nodded.

"But how? The bomb . . . the fire."

Deacon ran a hand through his hair. "Walter had followed me and Case down there. Just as Case went inside the house, Walter took off into the woods after a deer. I knew he would get lost, and you and Willow would have my ass. I took two steps into the woods, and the explosion knocked me down."

I tried processing his words. He'd never been in the house. Walter, the gift he had given me, had saved his life. For the past two days, he'd been alive, holed up somewhere, as those he loved mourned his loss.

Launching myself at him, I began to slap his face and chest while my legs kicked him as hard as I could. "Dammit, Alexandra, what the hell is wrong with you?" he demanded, as he deflected some of my hits.

"What's wrong with me? Do you have any idea what the last two days have been like for me?" When he didn't respond, I grabbed the sides of his face and screamed, "A living hell! A hell where the man I'd loved was ripped from me and I was left to pick up the pieces!"

"I'm so sorry."

A hysterical laugh bubbled from my lips as I teetered precariously close to losing the fragile thread of sanity I had left. "That's all you can say is you're sorry? Well, fuck you, and fuck your bullshit apologies."

Shoving him aside, I hopped down from the counter and stalked into the bedroom. I got halfway to the door that led out onto the balcony when Deacon grabbed my arm and jerked me back against him. My eyelids snapped shut as I momentarily allowed myself to enjoy being in his arms again, savoring the smell of his musky scent.

When I recovered, I thrashed against him, trying to get away. "Would you just listen to me for a second? For Christ's sake, Alexandra. I didn't fake my own death to be an asshole. I had my reasons for not coming forward."

"They must've been pretty damn good reasons to hurt your family like you did."

Deacon winced at my words. "I needed Sigel to think I was

dead. After the explosion, as I lay there in the woods, I realized I was a sitting duck. If Sigel would take down my president to draw me out, he would stop at nothing. Dying was the best way to protect my family."

"Let me go," I growled through clenched teeth.

"I'm sorry for hurting you, Alex. You know how I feel about you and that I would never do anything to intentionally hurt you."

I had to get away from him. If I kept listening to him, my resolve would fade, and I would accept his apology. I would understand his reasoning. And I couldn't do that. If there was anything the last two days had taught me, it was that being involved with Deacon and his world was a hazard to my safety and sanity.

To escape him, I went with a literal knee-jerk reaction to his balls. As he groaned in pain, I pried myself out of his arms. Knowing I needed help, I threw open the balcony door. An ominous boom of thunder met me as I stepped outside. How fitting that a real storm was brewing as I found myself in my own emotional one. Leaning against the railing, I gazed down on the yard. The trees and bushes were so thick around the balcony, along with it being so dark, that it was hard to see.

"What the hell are you doing?"

Glancing at Deacon over my shoulder, I replied, "Archer's somewhere outside. I'm going to scream until he comes, so he can throw you out!"

"I told Archer to hang back and give us some privacy for the night. Then I'll go back to the compound tomorrow and explain everything to my family. I want you to come with me."

I shook my head. "After what I've been through, I'm not going anywhere with you. Not now, not ever again."

Deacon's dark eyes narrowed at me. "I'm willing to overlook that little stunt you just pulled because of how hurt you are. But hear me when I say this. Quit fucking playing, Alex."

"I can assure you that I'm not playing. I've not been playing for the last two days as I wept over you and what we had lost. I won't put myself through that ever again. I may love you, but I've got to love myself and my sanity more."

Jagged bolts of lightning sliced across the night sky, illuminating Deacon's face in the dark. He wore an expression of pure rage, but something else also flashed in his eyes.

Lust.

Shrinking back against the railing, I tried to come up with the best means of escaping him. But before I could try to run, he jerked me against him. "You're not going anywhere, Alex, so get that fucking look out of your eyes."

Once again, I found myself trapped in his strong arms. In a futile attempt, I tried shrugging away. When I dared to look up at him, his gaze burned into me, practically singeing my flesh. My traitorous body came alive under his stare, causing an ache between my legs. "Don't, Deacon. I don't want you."

"Yeah, you do."

Jerking my chin up at him, I spat, "I don't fuck people I hate."

"You don't hate me. You just said two seconds ago that you loved me."

He momentarily lessened his hold on me. His hands came to the lapels of my robe, jerking it open. He tore the silk fabric down my arms to let the material pool at my feet. As he stared at me naked before him, desire blazed in his eyes as white-hot as the lightning above us.

"I would die a thousand deaths just to get to see you like this. Just to have another chance to bury my cock deep inside you."

Even as his words caused a shudder to run through me, I made an X with my arms over my breasts, tears pooling in my eyes. "If I give myself to you again, I'm lost. I can't come back from this again. I might as well leap off this balcony."

Grabbing me around the waist, Deacon pulled me to him. "You're not giving anything. I'm taking what's mine." With one hand, he jerked his belt loose. "You are mine, Alex. Death or hell won't ever change how I feel about you." His breath scorched my forehead. "Nothing will ever change how much I love you. You own me—mind, heart, body, and soul."

Tears spilled over my cheeks at his words. "Deacon," I moaned before I crashed my lips against his. Dropping my arms, I reached between us to the fly of his jeans. Frantically, I undid the button and zipper before pushing the fabric over his hips. Once his cock was free, Deacon grabbed me by the thighs. He hoisted me up, then impaled me. I cried out at the intense sensation of him filling me. He slowly withdrew before plunging even deeper into me. My nails scoured his back until I felt the blood well beneath them.

The clouds opened up, sending a deluge of rain pouring over us. The storm raged with thunder cracking across the sky, rattling the windows. Wind howled through the trees, drowning out our moans of pleasure and the slapping of our soaked skin.

"Lean back," Deacon commanded. Obeying him, I released my hands from Deacon's shoulders. They momentarily flailed until they made contact with the slippery iron railing. My new position gave him the leverage he needed to pump harder and harder inside me. As he bent over, his mouth sought out my breasts, alternating between the two to suckle the nipples into hardened points.

"Yes, Deacon, yes!" I cried as I gazed up at him.

He was Lazarus rising—rising over me as our bodies hastily joined in a raw communion. He was the darkness, and I was the light—we were the perfect storm of opposites, raging against each other in perfect harmony. We let the tempest overwhelm us as life and death had new meaning, and we had a resurrection and rebirth.

Crying out, I came hard, clenching around Deacon's pumping cock. He followed shortly after me with a harsh groan. When the aftershocks finally started to fade, he pulled me up and wrapped his arms around me. "I love you," he whispered.

Cradling his head in my hands, I said, "I love you, too."

As he slid out of me, I hissed slightly at the burning inside me. His brows shot up in concern. "Was I too hard?"

"No. You were good. So good."

Deacon gave me a cocky grin as he set me on my feet. When he glanced down between us, he suddenly winced. "Shit, I forgot a condom."

"It's okay. I'm on the pill."

"You trust that I'm clean?" he asked almost incredulously.

While I probably should have been concerned, I nodded. "More than anything, I trust you."

His expression grew serious. "You can't imagine how much that means to me."

"That I let you go bareback?"

"No, that a woman like you trusts a man like me."

"Well, I do," I replied, raking my fingers through his hair.

"I trust you, too. More than any other woman I've ever been with." He knelt down before me to grab my robe off the floor. Using the silky material, he began to clean the evidence of our union off my thighs. When he finished, he rose back up to stare at me. The intensity in his eyes made me shiver. "One day I'd like you to go off the pill."

"Is that right?"

He nodded. "I want to make a baby with you."

I couldn't help the wave of shock that ran through my body at his statement. It was the last thing in the world I'd imagined he would want, least of all say out loud. "Y-you do?" I finally stammered.

He nodded, his thumb tracing over my bottom lip. At what must have been the fear in my eyes, he said, "You're not your past, Alexandra. You're already the best mother anyone could ever be to

Willow. You're everything I could want when it comes to being the mother of my child."

Tears stung my eyes at his words. "You're the only man I want to father my children. As much as I love Willow, I want a piece of you and me together."

He smiled. "You'll have it. And when he gets here, I hope he takes after you instead of his old man."

I hiccupped a laugh. "*Him*? What if it's a girl?"

His enthusiasm dampened a little. "I'm not sure I can take another girl. Willow is like fifteen girls rolled into one."

"Wait until she's a teenager."

Deacon threw his head back and groaned. "I can't even fucking think about that now."

A teasing smile curved my lips. "For the way you've been with women, it would serve you right if you had a houseful of daughters."

"You're killing me, babe."

Standing on my tiptoes, I brought my mouth to his. Deacon responded by wrapping his arms around my waist. Just as his tongue began to dance tantalizingly along mine, I broke away from him. "Having a baby together is a big commitment. Are you sure you know what you're saying?"

He narrowed his eyes at me. "I sure as hell do. I ain't some asshole who wants a bunch of baby mamas. I want one woman to raise my children."

"Inside of marriage?"

He swallowed hard, sending his Adam's apple bobbing up and down. If the conversation hadn't been so serious, I might have laughed at his horrified expression. Finally, he drew in a ragged breath. "Yeah, I could see it within marriage."

"You want to marry me someday?" I asked. Although there was a teasing lilt in my voice, my heartbeat fluttered wildly as I waited for his response.

Deacon cocked his brows at me while amusement danced in his eyes. "You fishing for a proposal, White-Bread?"

I shrugged. "Maybe."

"Then maybe someday you'll get it," he replied with a wink. Then he dipped his head to bestow a gentle kiss on my lips. "Ain't never wanted to get married before you. Guess it makes sense you would be the one I would marry."

"You're so romantic," I replied with a grin that hid my exultation.

"I am what I am, babe. You ain't getting anything else."

"I'll take you—just as you are." After a few breathless moments of kissing, I once again pulled back. "Are you sure you shouldn't go see your brothers tonight?"

"I should. But I want nothing more than to be alone with you." He kissed me again. "Another twelve hours isn't going to matter much for Rev and Bishop to get to kick my ass."

With a giggle, I replied, "You deserve it."

"After everything, you do understand why I did what did, don't you?"

"As much as I hate to admit it, yes, I do. I just wish there had been a way you could have let us know you were all right."

Deacon shook his head. "Appearances are everything. If my family and brothers hadn't truly been grieving, then the plan wouldn't have worked."

"Well, Sigel bought the lie that you were dead. That's for sure." The moment the words left my lips, regret flooded me. Deep down, I felt like I shouldn't have mentioned Sigel's visit to me at the school. Like I had just unknowingly taken a pin off of a grenade.

Tightening his arms around me, Deacon asked, "What do you mean? Did you see him?"

Knowing full well that Rev and Bishop would tell him about the encounter, I replied, "He paid me a visit yesterday."

"Tell me everything," Deacon demanded.

One of my favorite poems had always been Robert Frost's "The Road Not Taken." As I stood there in Deacon's arms, I faced my own crossroads. One way would be the easy route where I told Deacon about Sigel wanting the cut. That way would lead to a showdown that would end with one or both of them dead. I had just gotten Deacon back. I didn't intend to lose him again.

The second path entailed the plan I had masterminded on the back of Archer's bike. It involved me not only lying to the man I loved, but it meant putting myself into extreme danger to ensure the safety of the ones I held dear. In the end, it wasn't as hard a choice as I had thought it would be. It was the reason why I'd stolen the cut tonight. Only I would face Sigel when it came to handing over the cut.

"He wanted me to know that I didn't have to worry about him coming after me or Willow. That with you out of the picture, the slate was clean," I lied.

Deacon's brows furrowed. "He came to your school just to tell you that?"

"I think he knew he wouldn't have a shot to talk to me anywhere else that wouldn't be overrun with Raiders. Maybe it was a ploy to make the Raiders back off of me. I don't know."

"I don't know, either, but whatever it is, I sure as hell don't like it. I'm assuming Willow is still safe with Jimmy and Joy in the mountains?"

"But how did you know Willow was still there and not with us?"

He gave me a shadowy smile. "I have my ways of checking on her."

"Some sort of GPS like in my bracelet?"

"Yeah."

After I bent down to pick up my now-soiled robe, Deacon reached out for me. His expression was grave. "Alexandra, you wouldn't lie to me about Sigel, would you? I know you might think you were protecting me, but more than anything, I need you to be honest."

My heartbeat thrummed so wildly in my ears that I was sure Deacon could hear it. Swallowing the lump in my throat that threatened to choke me, I replied, "Why would I lie to you?"

"You tell me."

"From what I've seen of your world, Deacon, there wouldn't be any benefit in keeping something from you. As much as I would like to be noble and protect you, I know how stupid and naive that would be. At the end of the day, I need your protection far more than you need mine, so you need to know everything to protect me, right?"

After he searched my face for what seemed like an eternity, Deacon's tense expression began to fade. I fought the urge to exhale in relief. Instead, I decided to change tactics by forcing a smile to my face. I cocked my head almost provocatively at him. "Thanks to you, I need a shower, and you could probably use one, too."

A sly grin slunk across his face. "Is that an invitation?"

Wagging my eyebrows, I replied, "Of course."

"Then get your sexy ass in the shower."

"My pleasure."

With my chest constricting in agony, I followed Deacon into the bedroom. My one request of Deacon was to always be honest with me. And here I was being completely dishonest as well as deceiving him. Regardless of the sick feeling in the pit of my stomach, I wasn't going to back down. I had to do this for me, for Deacon, and for Willow.

But I couldn't think about what lay ahead just now. I needed Deacon. I needed to be held by him, loved by him, fucked by him. And that outweighed everything else on my mind.

TWENTY

DEACON

The moment I walked through the clubhouse back door, my brothers launched themselves at me and quickly overtook me. It wasn't just Rev and Bishop either. Most of the hometown charter, including the prospects, had a go at me. There was pushing, shoving, punching, and some fuckers even low blowed me by kicking me in the shins and the balls. When it was all over, I had a busted lip, what would be a shiner in the morning, and probably some bruised ribs.

But I wouldn't have taken anything else for having my brothers welcome me back to life in the only way they really knew how. I sure as hell didn't think I would come in to hugs and tears. That shit was for pussies and the Raiders women.

"I think this calls for a round to celebrate," Bishop said, jerking his chin at Cheyenne. When I followed his gaze to her, I registered the grief-stricken expression on her face. While she was glad to have me back, she knew she would never have me. My body and, most important, my heart now belonged to Alexandra. Breaking eye contact with me, she got busy pouring beers.

"We're going to need to sit down in the next hour for church. We need to get you up to speed on all that's happened the last couple of days," Rev said.

"Sure, man. Whatever we need to do." I took in the newly sewn PRESIDENT patch on his cut.

Glancing over Rev's shoulder, I saw Kim sitting on one of the barstools. In her black jeans, black boots, and black T-shirt, she looked every bit the part of a biker widow. My throat clenched like someone had grabbed me by the neck and cut off my air supply. I would have rather faced down Sigel in a dark alley than have to see her. Picking up one of my feet, I slowly made my way over to her.

When I reached her, tears streamed down her cheeks. "Thank God you're alive," she said before she began sobbing hysterically. She threw herself into my arms. She pressed her face into my chest, her cries becoming muffled. But in my head, I heard them just as fucking loudly as if a cannon were going off around me.

"I'm sorry, Kim," I murmured into her ear. "I'm so fucking sorry."

Pulling away, she stared up at me. "I know you are."

"I want you to know I didn't run out on him. Because of Alex's wild-ass puppy, I didn't even get in the house."

Kim pressed her palm against my cheek. "Oh, honey. I know you wouldn't have ever sacrificed Case. You loved him as much as he loved you."

I groaned as the tears I forcefully fought burned my throat and stung my eyes. "I did love him. I loved him like a father—like I loved Preacher Man." I took her hand from my face and placed it over my heart. "I swear to you that I will protect and provide for you and his kids. Anything you need, you just ask."

Kim's expression momentarily darkened. Instead of sadness, anger burned in her eyes. "The only thing I ask of you is to never, *ever* let one of my sons patch into this club. No matter how bad they want what their daddy had, you don't let them in." She shook her head. "I won't lose my babies like I lost their daddy."

My mind went to their thirteen- and fifteen-year-old sons, Ben and Eric. Since they were little, they'd been at every Raiders family function. They often begged Case to let them come during the week. All they had ever known was a father who was an MCer. I couldn't imagine even trying to deny them when the time came. I hoped that by then Kim's grief would have lessened and she would change her mind.

But in this moment, I had to do whatever I could to comfort her. "You have my word."

"Thank you, Deacon," she replied, leaning up to bestow a kiss on my cheek.

A beer was thrust into each of our hands. I searched the crowd for Alexandra. When I found her, I motioned for her to come to me. With a shy smile, she wove in and out of the people to join me.

Bishop raised his glass. "To my brother Deacon, who I always knew was a pussy, but since he seems to have nine lives, he now confirms it."

Laughter went up around the room. Before we could take a sip, Bishop held up his hand. "And to the memory of one of the finest fucking presidents the Raiders ever had. To Case."

"To Case," echoed around the room.

With tears streaking down her cheeks, Kim set her beer down on the bar and headed down the hallway to her and Case's old room. "I'll go to her," Alexandra said.

"Thanks, babe."

I downed my glass in three foamy chugs. Then I headed straight to the boardroom. I knew that Rev wouldn't rest easy until he was able to unload everything on me. My brothers followed me one by one into the room.

A freaky feeling, almost like a trippy flashback, pricked its way over me as I watched Rev take a seat in Case's old chair. I'd never given much thought to how much Rev looked like Preacher Man until I saw him sitting there with a gavel in his hand. I took my usual seat. Bishop eased in beside me.

Even though I'd been gone only three days, a lot of shit had happened. We had Case's funeral to deal with. It had been decided to wait until the weekend, so that more out-of-town members and other clubs could pay their respects. Selfishly, I almost wished that I had missed the whole damn thing. I didn't want to have to deal with all the emotions that I knew the final good-bye would bring up. A double dose of guilt ate its way through me. Guilt for my feelings about not wanting to give Case the proper respect as well as the fact that it could have been me boxed up in an urn. I'd outsmarted the Grim Reaper many times, but this last time, I could feel his hot breath on my neck.

"I say we hold off on patching in the prospects and voting on officers until next week. I don't want it to look like we're business as usual when we're in mourning for Case," Rev said before glancing around the table to gauge our reaction.

Mac nodded. "I second that."

Once it was unanimously decided that we put off any official club business, the meeting was adjourned. After the others filed out, Rev and Bishop stayed behind with me. "Although I'm glad as hell you're alive, I could kill you for putting us through what you did," Bishop said.

I laughed. "I know, brother. If there had been any other way, I swear to you, I would have taken it. But it was the best way to get an edge on Sigel."

"How do you think we should handle the issue of the cut?" Rev asked.

Creasing my brows, I asked, "What cut?"

Rev and Bishop exchanged a glance. "Didn't Alex tell you about Sigel demanding she bring him Andy's cut?" Rev asked.

I inhaled a sharp breath. "No, she didn't."

"That's why he came to see her at the school. He wants her—and only her—to bring it to him," Rev replied.

When I didn't respond, Bishop said, "We weren't ever going to let her go into it alone, man. Don't think that just because you were gone, we would have sacrificed her. We've been racking our brains about how to wire up that fucking cut to explode on Sigel."

At that moment, I couldn't think about or focus on anything other than the fact that Alex had lied to me. Rising out of my chair, I shook my head. "I need to go to talk to Alex. Figure out what the fuck is going on."

Rev's expression turned cautionary. "Don't be hard on her. I'm sure she just didn't want to worry or upset you right after she got you back." With a pointed look, he added, "She's been to hell and back, brother."

"I understand." It wasn't like I was going to storm back to my room and throw shit around until Alex came clean with me. I just wanted to know every single detail about what had happened in her meeting with Sigel. I hoped she hadn't left anything else out.

What happened next was something I would have never, ever imagined. The kind of knock-you-on-your-ass shock. Life threw me one hell of a fucking curveball, and the woman I loved was the very one to pitch it.

TWENTY-ONE

ALEXANDRA

After trying my best to comfort Kim, I felt terrible that I had to leave her with some of the other club women so that I could go get ready for Parents Night. Although my principal had assured me that it would be all right for me to miss it, I wanted to go. Even before Deacon's resurrection, I had planned to be there for my students and their parents.

A quick shower later, I stood in front of Deacon's chest of drawers, putting on my underwear. The shrill ring of my phone caught me off guard, causing me to jump. But when I glanced down at the ID, a stone-cold dread rocketed through me. With trembling hands, I picked up the phone. "H-hello?" I croaked.

"Miss Evans, your time is up. I want the cut. Tonight."

"Okay."

"I assume that means you got it."

"Yes, I did."

At my hesitation, Sigel asked, "Then what is the problem?"

"The only thing is it's Parents Night at my school. I've promised my principal I would be there."

"That won't be a problem at all."

"It won't?"

"No. In fact, I think it works better than any plan I had in mind. I had already anticipated meeting you somewhere there was a crowd—somewhere your Raiders brothers couldn't try retaliation without incriminating themselves. A school full of parents and children is positively brilliant."

His voice made my skin crawl. "You promise that no one will get hurt?"

"Miss Evans, it hurts me that you doubt my sincerity. Besides, like the Raiders, I don't want to do anything that would bring attention to me from the authorities. I would think shooting up a school would rank pretty high on the list of having the police and ATF on my ass."

"If you say so."

"Go on and perform like a good show pony. I'll call you with the location within the school to meet me."

He ended the call. As I pulled the phone from my ear, I stared down at it. Although I'd known this day was coming and coming soon, nothing compared to actually having the wolf outside the door. When you devise a plan, it always seems good in theory. Sure, you might experience some what-ifs, but in your mind, it gets executed flawlessly.

Yesterday when I asked Rev and Bishop to teach me how to use a knife, I'd had ulterior motives. While I wanted to learn how to protect myself, my real motive was much darker. On the way back to the compound, a sinister thought from the dark side of my psyche began to push and shove its way into the front of my mind.

I had stood before a mental scale of justice and weighed Sigel's sins. He had taken two of the most important people in my life away. He had almost killed my brother. At that time, I'd thought he had killed the man I loved, but instead, he had killed the president of his club.

As long as Sigel breathed, he would be a threat to Willow, Charlie, and to me. Now that Deacon wasn't out of the picture, as Sigel thought, he would finally have the showdown that they had been building toward. I didn't want to face that reality again so soon after having him back. I wanted to save Willow from the fate of being an orphan.

Sigel had to die.

And I was going to kill him.

Tonight I would continue to be Willow's protector and then my parents' avenger by taking justice into my own hands.

Clutching the phone, I didn't hear Deacon come into the bedroom. The sound of his voice caused me to jump. "Who was that?"

"Oh, just Uncle Jimmy," I answered.

"Is he wanting us to come get Willow ASAP because she's driving him crazy?"

I laughed. "No, nothing like that." After I set the phone down on the chest of drawers, I asked, "Your meeting go okay?"

"Well, it did up until I found out you'd lied to me."

My hand froze as I reached to pull my skirt off the chair. I couldn't bring myself to look at him. "What do you mean?"

"I found out from Rev and Bishop that more happened in your meeting with Sigel than you told me."

I swallowed hard. Frantically, I searched my mind for a way to defuse the potentially volatile situation I found myself in. "Oh, that," I replied, with a flippant wave of my hand.

"Yeah, that."

Turning toward him, I sighed. "I'm sorry, Deacon. I'd just gotten you back. I wanted to enjoy the time I had with you, not have you getting needlessly angry. There was nothing malicious or calculated in what I did."

Lies. All lies.

Deacon's accusing gaze turned over to one of hunger. He seemed to appreciate my lacy black and pink panty and bra set. In that fraction of a second, I knew what I had to do. "You're looking at me like you want to devour me," I said in a throaty whisper.

"I do."

"Mmm, maybe I should give you a quickie. Whet your appetite a little until I can get back."

"I like the sound of that."

"Get on the bed," I commanded.

Deacon's brows shot up at my authoritative tone. "Excuse me?"

"Just taking the reins, cowboy. I need to top you so I don't mess my hair up."

He grinned. "Just don't forget who's the real boss around here."

"Oh, I'm well aware of that one."

When he flopped back on the bed, I took a shaky step forward. With trembling fingers, I opened the nightstand drawer. Instead of taking out one of the gold foil packets, I grabbed the handcuffs that we'd played with at the Lounge.

Swinging them around my fingers, I winked at him. "Let's play a little cowboy and bad cop together."

Deacon's eyes widened. "What the hell has gotten into you?"

I shrugged. "Just glad to have you back—that's all. Got a lot of fantasies to enact together."

"If you say so, babe," he replied with a chuckle.

"Raise your arms." He hastily complied by bringing his arms over his head. His hands reached out for the intricately designed rails in the iron bed. It was now or never. Once I handcuffed Deacon, there was no going back with him or with Sigel. Deacon held up a code of loyalty and honesty, and I was breaking that. I wasn't sure he could ever forgive me for what I was about to do.

I couldn't help but wonder if I was looking into the eyes of the man I loved with all my heart for the last time with love between us. I was standing on the tracks, staring down a runaway train.

The clasp of the handcuffs echoed around the room. For a moment I kept my hands wrapped around them, unblinking and unmoving. Then I slowly pulled away. I took a step back and then another. Deacon's brows crinkled. "What are you doing?"

Ignoring him, I grabbed my skirt off the chair and slid it on. When I went for the silky blue blouse with the ruffled front, Deacon asked, "Is this part of the game?"

Tears burned my eyes as I worked frantically to button the blouse. When I was finished, I glanced at him. "I'm sorry."

"What do you mean? Alex, what the hell is going on?" His tone had turned from amusement to desperation.

"I have to do this, Deacon. It's the right solution. Really it's the only solution where you and Willow don't get hurt."

"You're not making any sense." He jerked at the handcuffs and winced. "Get me out of these."

I turned away from him to start digging in my suitcase. At the very bottom, I slid aside the lining and stared down at Andy's cut. With trembling fingers, I took it out. I rose from the floor and then turned back to Deacon. His eyes left mine and drifted down to my hands. With widened eyes, he demanded, "What the fuck are you doing with that?"

"I took it from the war prize closet."

Deacon sucked in a breath so fast it sounded more like a hiss. "Alexandra, I want you to get me out of these handcuffs *right fucking now*!" When I gave a slight jerk of my head, he growled. "Don't you even think for one minute you're going to go alone!"

"There was something else I left out about my meeting with Sigel—something I didn't even tell Rev or Bishop." I drew in a deep breath. "Sigel caused the accident that killed my parents."

Deacon stared at me in disbelief. "What? How?"

I glanced down at the cut before telling him about how my parents' love of children had caused their deaths. When I finished, I dared to meet his eyes again. "Besides you and Willow, I now have a stake in this I never imagined. A chance for justice in my parents' murders."

"Alexandra, you cannot take a man like Sigel down. You are walking to your death, you stupid, stubborn woman!" Deacon shouted.

Dropping the cut on the chair, I bent down and picked a silk scarf out of the pile of clothes I had tossed out of the suitcase. It was one I had worn to teach in many times. Tonight it would serve another purpose. When I started over to Deacon, he momentarily appeared relieved. He thought I had finally come to my senses. Instead, my trembling hands took the scarf and gagged him. He bucked and fought against me, but somehow I got it tied.

Tears dripped down my cheeks when I finally allowed myself to look at him. "I'm so sorry, but I had to do this. I did it for you, and I did it for us."

He stared at me with eyes that burned with rage and venom. I didn't even want to imagine what he would have done to me in that moment if he had gotten free. I had to turn away from him as fast as I could. I couldn't bear to have him looking at me that way during what might be the last minutes I had with him.

Instead of allowing myself to break down, I swiped the tears from my eyes. I grabbed the cut and shoved it down in my messenger bag. In a moment of vanity, I grabbed my makeup bag as well, so I could repair the damage of my tears. Once I slung the messenger bag over my shoulder, I headed to the door. With my hand hovering over the doorknob, I willed myself not to look back. Instead, I said, "I love you."

Then I walked out the door.

TWENTY-TWO

ALEXANDRA

As soon as I arrived at the school, I was herded into the cafeteria for a presentation by the principal. Facing the massive crowd, I found myself sandwiched between my fellow kindergarten teachers. My legs shook with nerves as I tried to focus on what was being said. In the end, I couldn't tell you one word my principal spoke. Instead, I kept scanning the parents' faces, searching for Sigel or anyone from his club. I hated that he had chosen the school for us to do our business. It wasn't just about the one clean part of my world, my school, getting sullied. It was more about the fact that I feared people getting hurt regardless of Sigel's promise.

At seven thirty, we were dismissed to our classrooms, where for the next hour we would meet with parents. On the walk to my room, teachers chattered around me, but I couldn't join in. Instead, I tried focusing on keeping the frayed and tattered strands of my sanity from coming completely undone.

When I got inside my classroom, I thankfully found relief. With parents to greet and students to talk with, my worries about Sigel were forgotten. I was able to genuinely and enthusiastically talk about each student's progress and graciously take the compliments from their parents on how I was doing teaching their child.

The sound of my principal's voice on the intercom made me jump. "Ladies and gentlemen, it's now eight thirty. We would ask that you wrap up your questions and conversations and make your way to the exits. Thank you again for attending Buffington Elementary's Parents Night.'"

I walked the last remaining set of parents to my classroom door. Just as I waved good-bye, my cell phone rang. I glanced warily at it over my shoulder, then hurried to grab it. "Hello?" I questioned breathlessly.

"Come down the D hall—the wing of the school that hasn't been finished. Go to the last bathroom on the hallway. I'll be waiting."

When the call ended, I took a deep breath. I went over to my bag and took out the cut. After I laid it on the desk, I reached inside for the knife. I slid it into one of the inside pockets of the cut, one that I could keep my hand on at all times. With a determined step, I walked out my classroom door. As the herd of parents and children streamed through the main lobby, I eased my way through them, feeling a little like a salmon swimming upstream.

While people came out of the B and C hallways, the double doors to the D hall were empty. Because of overcrowding, the school had been forced to open early, before the last wing was completed. Glancing over my shoulder, I saw no one was watching me as I stood before the closed doors. I pushed them open and stepped into the darkened hallway.

The only light to guide my way came from the emergency signs. My heels echoed along the silent hallway. The snap and pop on the tile reminded me of gunshots. I counted down the first and second bathrooms. When I reached the third door, I faltered. I couldn't seem to bring my feet forward or my hand to push open the door. Fear clutched me in a viselike grip. Closing my eyes, I prayed for strength and for courage. Of course, the irony in praying with regards to plans to kill someone was not lost on me.

Think of Willow. Think of Deacon. Think of your parents.

Drawing in a deep breath, I pushed forward on the door. Light flooded my eyes, causing me to squint. As I glanced around, I saw the main area was empty. Passing the urinals, I headed for the stalls. The sound of my heels once again grated on my already-frayed nerves.

"Sigel?" I finally questioned, my voice echoing back to me.

With a trembling hand, I reached out to push open the first stall's doors. It was empty. I went on to the next one. "I'm here, Miss Evans." Sigel spoke in a low tone. The voice had come from the handicapped stall two down.

Knowing where he was didn't speed me up. Instead, I crept even slower down to the stall.

I opened the door. He casually leaned against the wall. His face was devoid of any emotion. I couldn't help craning my neck around. "Where are your goons?"

"They've been ordered to stay back. Keep their eyes and ears out for any Raiders scum."

"They won't find any," I replied.

"I hope not."

As I thrust out the cut to him, I frantically kept my grip on the knife, fearing my sweaty fingers would slide and drop it. When he started to reach for it, the world around me slowed to a crawl. For just an instant, I stepped outside of myself, surveying the situation.

The woman I saw was a caged animal with a feral gleam in her eyes. She swayed like a cobra in a life-and-death dance, waiting for the right moment to strike. The man fixated all his attention on the sacred object in front of him. As his hand ran over the leather, tears pooled in his eyes.

It was in that moment that everything changed, and the woman I had been before was forever changed.

With Sigel's emotions paralyzing him, I acted on his momentary weakness. A physical strength I didn't know I had propelled me forward. Snatching out the knife, I gripped the heavy blade in my fist, my knuckles turning white from the tension. Pulling my arm back, I then launched myself at Sigel's neck.

I had no idea what stabbing someone entailed. Would the knife cut through the skin easily, or would it be hard? The force with which I plunged the knife into Sigel's artery buried the blade. Blood spewed from the wound. As I stood there with my knife in his neck, Sigel's wide-eyed gaze slowly swept from the cut to my eyes.

"You should have never underestimated me," I told him.

Not wanting to risk that he could survive the injuries I'd inflicted, I didn't jerk out the knife. Instead, I braced myself and sliced through the tendons and muscles on his neck as his arms flailed up to stop me until I hit his collarbone and could go no further.

Sigel's expression flickered between emotions like a flashing sign. Grief to disbelief to pain to rage. Just as I started to pull the knife out, Sigel's gaze met mine. We momentarily stared each other down. Then he lunged at me, his hands coming around my throat. I gasped and wheezed for air as I swung my arm with the knife blindingly forward. It caught Sigel in the biceps, causing him to momentarily loosen his grip.

I stabbed him once again before he knocked my arm back, sending the knife clattering to the floor. Just as he began to squeeze my throat harder, Sigel's knees gave way. Collapsing to the floor, he dragged me down with him. His hands abandoned my neck, and I rolled to the side to gasp for breath.

When the world around me started to turn black, I fought with everything within me to keep conscious. With my breath coming easier, I began to attempt to crawl away, to reach the knife that was just out of my grip. Once I had it in my hands, I staggered to my feet.

Staring down at Sigel, I eyed the mutilations on his body, which I'd inflicted with the borrowed knife—I'd had no idea such a ferocity was hidden within me. In a way, it frightened me more than consoled me. Although it was for those I loved most, I had transitioned far too easily into the outlaw realm.

When Sigel's gaze flickered to mine, a cruel smile formed on my lips. I wasn't quite finished with him yet. "Just so you know, Deacon Malloy is alive and well."

A gurgling rattle of a laugh escaped Sigel's bloodstained lips. "Expect me to believe that?" he rasped.

"You should. Why would I have any reason to lie? He never got into the house that day. He was off in the woods, chasing our puppy. He hid out at my house for two days. Then he had his own resurrection. He's at the Raiders compound right now, handcuffed to a bed." I narrowed my eyes at Sigel. "I wasn't going to let him fuck with my revenge on you."

Recognition slowly flashed across his face, and I knew then he believed me. And with sick vindication, I got to watch Sigel take his last breath with the revelations that he would never get his revenge on Deacon and that he had been taken down by a woman.

My knees gave way, and I sank down onto the bloody tile. A commotion above me startled a scream from me. In a cloud of dust and debris, Archer collapsed down beside me from the ceiling. Once he recovered, he reached out for me. "Are you okay?"

"I-I'm f-fine," I stammered.

Archer glanced over my shoulder. "Fuck me. You actually did it."

"Yeah, I did." That statement caused a tremor to run through me. My abdomen clenched, and I turned and emptied the contents of my stomach onto the floor at Archer's feet. "I'm sorry," I moaned, when I saw what I had done.

"It's okay." He rose to his feet and then pulled me up.

On shaky legs, I surveyed the gap in the ceiling tile where Archer had come through. "Your idea really worked, huh?" To keep out of Sigel's eye and suspicion, Archer had relied on his electrician father's background. Through my bracelet, he had tracked my movements from above me in the school's ceiling. I didn't want to begin to know how he had broken into the mechanical closet, but he had found a way.

He grinned. "Yeah, it did. Fix it back for me, okay?" He then gripped me around the waist and hoisted me up. I slid the tile back into its place. We couldn't leave it as it was. It wouldn't corroborate with our story.

When he set me back down on my feet, he placed a chaste, tender kiss on my cheek. "I'm so fucking proud of you."

"Thank you," I murmured, my emotions still overwrought from what had just happened. Then I realized that precious time was ticking. "Come on. We gotta get busy."

He nodded. I handed him the bag, and he took out a clean pair of clothes—a janitor's uniform, actually. I didn't bother looking away as he stripped. I'd been through too much tonight to care about any false modesty. Instead, I took the knife, gritted my teeth, and then slashed cuts along my arms and legs. A wildfire of pain burned its way through my limbs as the metallic smell of my own blood entered my nose.

Once Archer was finished changing, he threw his old clothes back into my bag. What he planned to do with it, I didn't know. When he was done, he looked at me, and regret instantly filled his eyes. "You have to," I protested, knowing he was having second thoughts about the second part of our plan. The part where he had to make it appear like I had been attacked.

"Deacon will kill me when he finds out."

I shook my head. "You have to do it." My fingers gripped the sides of the sink. "Now, Archer!" I commanded. The words had barely left my lips when his fist connected with my cheek. Pain ricocheted through my face and head. Before I had a chance to prepare for the next blow, it felt like my lip was splitting apart.

Staggering back from the sink, I tried to get my bearings. Then I felt Archer's hands on my waist and neck. I couldn't help noticing that his fingers were trembling. "Jesus Christ, forgive me, Alex," he said.

Then he went for the grand finale. A disabling move I had never heard of, but Archer's martial-arts background had served him well. I needed to be unconscious to truly sell our story of Sigel's attack, but Archer refused to knock me out. He had demanded to find an alternative. As the pressure he was applying above my clavicle increased, I began to feel light-headed. The harder he pressed, the more it caused the world to spin around me.

And then everything went black.

TWENTY-THREE

DEACON

You know the old cliché that says that your life flashes before your eyes before you die? Well, in the last three days, I'd stared down the sins of my past twice. Once when I was knocked onto the forest floor from the impact of the blast that took out Case. Then the other when I was chained to a bed and forced to watch the woman I'd come to love more than life itself walk out of the room to an uncertain fate.

I don't know how long I screamed behind that gag. I never fully grasped what a helpless feeling it is not to be heard. As I tried pushing myself up on the bed, the metal of the cuffs sliced into my wrists, sending blood trickling down my arms. Over and over again, I jerked my arms, hoping the rails would break, but the damn things might as well have been reinforced steel.

Finally, I resorted to throwing myself back against the bed, which banged the headboard against the wall. A sheen of sweat covered my body as I banged and banged. When the door flew open, a red-faced Bishop stomped in, his face buried in some mechanical manual. "Dude, would you pipe down? I'm trying to study for my exam."

When he finally looked up, the manual clattered to the floor. His mouth dropped open almost as far as his eyes widened, and if the situation hadn't been so serious, I might've laughed at his expression. He jerked the gag away from my mouth. "What the fuck happened to you?"

"Alexandra," I growled.

"What did you do? Get ready for some kinky sex and piss her off? Man, she's a feisty one."

"Just get the fucking keys out of the nightstand and get me out of these."

Bishop started rifling through the top drawer. Finally, he produced the key. Once I was out of my metal prison, I grabbed a towel off the floor. Pressing down on my wrists, I tried to stop the bleeding.

"You gonna tell me what the hell happened?" Bishop pressed.

"I need to find Alex. ASAP. You think Archer can put a tracer on her phone?"

"Archer went with Alex when she left half an hour ago."

"Fuck!" I growled as I threw open the bedroom door. I stalked down the hall to the bathroom. While I wrapped my wrists in Ace bandages, Bishop eyed me suspiciously.

"What's going on?"

"I don't have time to explain. I need to find Alex. Now."

"Tell me why she handcuffed and left you?"

"Alex lied to me about her meeting with Sigel. She didn't tell me that he had asked for the cut."

Bishop's brows furrowed. "Why would she do that?"

"Sigel ordered Alex to bring him the cut. When I found out what she was going to do, she handcuffed me to the bed, so I couldn't go with her."

"You're fucking kidding me!"

"I wish."

"Where is she now?"

"She had this Parents Night thing at the school. I don't know if she was meeting him afterward. . . ." Then it hit me. Sigel would want a safe place to get the cut—a place with a lot of people and witnesses to foil any retaliation the Raiders could plan. "Fuck. He's meeting her at the school."

I raced out the door with Bishop close on my heels. All I could think of was getting to Alex, damn stubborn fool that she was. I hoped to hell I wasn't too late.

Without a word to any of the other guys, I hopped on my bike and tore out of the driveway. Bishop and Rev caught up with me halfway down the road. When I got to the school, my heart shuddered to a stop. My eyes were blinded by the glaring blue and red lights of the police car and ambulance. Once I parked my bike, I started scanning the crowd for any Knights. The only cut I saw belonged to Archer, who was talking to a police officer.

At the sight of me, his face drained of color. For a moment I felt that my knees would give way and I would collapse onto the pavement. Alex couldn't be gone. I couldn't even begin to imagine a world without her smile, her caring heart, her laughter. It was unbearable, and I fought for breath. It felt like someone had roundhouse kicked me in the chest. I wasn't a praying man, but in that moment I started begging and pleading.

And then Archer held his hands up to me as if cautioning me not to freak out. He said something else to the officer, and then he strode toward me. "Deacon, she's fine. A few cuts and bruises, but she's going to be fine."

Doubling over at the waist, I braced my hands on my knees and gulped in air. "Thank God you were here to protect her."

"No, man. She took Sigel out on her own."

Jerking my head up, I stared at Archer in both disbelief and horror. "What?"

And then Archer began to tell a story that was almost too hard to believe. Before I showed myself to her after the explosion, a plan had been masterminded by Alex to ensure that Sigel would never hurt Willow again. A plan for which she had enlisted the help of both Rev and Bishop, although they'd had no idea what her true intent was. No, only Archer knew the truth. He had risked both his life and his place in the club by helping Alex.

As he talked, I tried wrapping my mind around Alex and Sigel in that stall. How someone like her had managed to take down a notorious MCer simply with a knife and some courage blew my mind. When Archer finished, he shook his head. "I'm sorry, man. I thought it was the best thing for the club and for your family. Even when you came back from the dead, so to speak, it still made sense."

"It made fucking sense for someone defenseless like Alex to take on someone like Sigel?" I demanded, the blood boiling in my veins.

Surprisingly, Archer didn't back down. Instead, he narrowed his eyes at me. "Would you let go of your bullshit pride for a minute and truly think? He never saw it coming. He never imagined her capable of it. Any of the rest of us? He would have seen us coming a mile away, including you."

I still couldn't wrap my head around it or allow myself to condone what happened. "Where is she?" I demanded.

"They took her over to one of the ambulances."

Jabbing a finger into his cut, I said, "We are *not* through talking about this."

He nodded. "I understand."

I hated that there was a part of me that could see the reason and brilliance behind Alexandra and Archer's plan. However, there was a much stronger part that was mad as hell and wanted to take the kid down for his utter stupidity and wavering loyalty. Sure, he'd been brave and done everything within his power to keep Alexandra safe, as well as the club. Regardless of his protection, he had still allowed my old lady to be in danger, and I wanted to kill him for that. And yeah, the fucking irony wasn't lost on me.

I weaved my way through the crowd of onlookers. Beyond the yellow police tape, I saw the ambulance with its back doors open. Moving around the taped-off perimeter, I came through the other side. With a blanket draped over her shoulders, Alex sat on the floor of the ambulance. An EMT worked on cleaning some lacerations on her face. While she stared straight ahead, her body suddenly tensed, and her gaze jerked from staring down at the pavement to scanning the tree-lined woods. I shouldn't have been too surprised that she could sense me.

Her brows rose in surprise as if questioning my next move. I couldn't answer her because even I didn't know what to do. Finally, I dug my cigarettes and lighter out of my cut and lit up. When the EMT finished, Alex said something to him before rising to her feet. Slowly, she began walking toward me. My feet began to move of their own accord, and I met her halfway.

I winced when I got a good look at her in the light. While Archer had apologetically told me that he'd had to beat her up to keep the cops from asking questions, I sure as hell didn't like the looks of his handiwork on her face. Her right cheek was turning black, and her lip was busted and swollen.

A million different scenarios had raced through my head about what I would do or say to her when I saw her again. But at the moment, she rendered me speechless. When she reached for me, I took a step back. "If you were a man or one of my brothers, I'd beat the hell out of you right now for what you did earlier."

"Can't you understand I had my reasons?"

"Reasons? You handcuffed me to a bed, went behind my back

with a club member, and then risked your own life trying to take down my greatest enemy. That seems without any fucking reason to me."

Her dark eyes narrowed at me. "Is it always only about you and your own personal revenge and vendettas, Deacon? Can you for a moment think about what it was like for me when I found out Sigel murdered my parents? The way I see it, I had just as much reason to take him out as you did."

"You sure as hell didn't! After what he did to Preacher Man, *I* deserved to take him out, not you. Dammit, Alex. You knew how much it meant to me!"

"If we're tallying up body counts for revenge, he took out both my mother and my father. I think I had the greater claim."

"They were just civilians. We had a club history that—" My words were cut off when Alexandra hauled off and slapped the hell out of me.

"You unimaginable bastard. How dare you stand there and spout that bullshit to me? Yeah, my parents weren't in your precious club. They were honorable and decent people who lost their lives simply for standing up for what was right—a kid who was being abused." She shook her head. "You know, I expected you to be fighting mad when you saw me again, but this is beyond my realm of comprehension."

Leaning closer to me, she hissed, "I killed a man tonight. With my own hands. Hands that used to cut construction-paper hearts and point out sight words to innocent children. I did it for my parents, but I also did it for you. If I had died tonight taking out Sigel, you would still be alive for Willow. I made a sacrifice for you. And even though you're an undeserving asshole, I would do it again so that sweet little girl wouldn't be parentless."

As I weighed her words, I realized what a stupid, egotistical, self-centered bastard I truly was. Staring at her, I could only shake my head. After all, what could you say befitting a woman who had gone toe to toe with a psycho to save your life and your daughter's?

At my silence, Alex sighed. "Once they discharge me, I'll come by the compound to get my things."

I blinked my eyes in disbelief. "Why would you do that?"

With a mirthless laugh, Alex said, "You can't be serious. Did you actually think after the way you just behaved that I was going to suck it up and come home with you?"

"Well, yeah."

"Incredible," she muttered before turning away.

I couldn't let her go. I cared too much about her. Willow cared too much about her. "Alex, wait."

Ignoring me, she kept walking. Desperately, I tried to think of what might get her attention. Then I blurted, "Marry me."

Her steps faltered on the pavement. Slowly, she turned around to stare openmouthed and wide-eyed at me. "What did you just say?"

"I asked you to marry me."

"I think I liked it better when I thought I was hearing things."

Scratching the back of my neck, I closed the gap between us. "I'm sorry. I'm so fucking sorry for the way I treated you earlier. It's just . . ." I licked my lips, as my mouth had run dry from fucking nerves. "You scared the hell out of me going after Sigel and leaving me where I couldn't help you. It isn't in me to have women on the front lines, least of all my old lady—the woman I fucking love. I didn't know how to deal. You were right to call me a bastard and an asshole because I was—I am. No matter how hard I try, I always seem to fuck things up when it comes to you." Shaking my head, I said, "Jesus, I'm blabbering."

"Keep going," Alex urged.

"You're also right to call me a selfish bastard. Before Willow, I thought only of myself, and then she came along and opened me up a little. Then you came barging in and forced me to put my own needs and desires behind those I cared about." Reaching out, I touched her unmarred cheek. "And I do care about you, Alexandra. When I thought that I might lose you to Sigel, I thought I would die—I wanted to die. I don't want to live without you. I love you too much."

"You really mean that?"

I nodded. "Yeah, I do."

Time ticked agonizingly by as she seemed to weigh her words. "I have one condition."

"Name it. Anything." When she nibbled on her lip, signaling her nervousness, I took her hands in mine. "What is it?"

"I want you to make the Raiders legitimate. If I'm going to be your wife, then I want to be married to David Malloy, not Jesse James."

Her demand was something I hadn't anticipated. While I knew she had every reason to request it, I wasn't sure I could make it happen—or if I truly wanted it to happen. "I'm not the president, babe. I can't make that decision."

"No, but I know it would be something Rev would support."

"We'd still have to have a majority vote in church."

"Then make it happen. Convince your brothers that too much blood has been spilled and too many lives lost to continue on the way you are."

"Being an outlaw is all I've known since I was thirteen years old." Feeling like a pussy, I tried not to let Alex see the fear that ran through me. It unfortunately didn't escape her notice, because she brought her arms around my neck.

"You can do this. I believe in you."

For reasons I didn't begin to understand, I started to believe that we could turn the Raiders around. It wouldn't be easy. It would take time, and there would probably be repercussions for our actions. But for her and for Willow, I was willing to try.

Smiling down at her, I said, "You're my angel—my dark-haired angel." The moment the words came out of my lips, I staggered back.

"Deacon, what's wrong?" Alex asked with alarm.

But I was no longer with her. Instead, I was holding Preacher Man's body. His words echoed through my mind. "Two dark-haired angels are coming for you. They will be your salvation."

Alex stared up at me in confusion. "What?"

I realized then that I had said the words aloud. "Preacher Man told me that right before he died. At the time, I couldn't imagine what he meant. But now . . ." I stared down at her beautiful face filled with love and concern for me. "Now I understand. You and Willow—you're the dark-haired angels. You're my salvation." I pulled her closer to me, needing to feel her against me. "You're my salvation," I repeated.

"And you're mine," Alex answered.

I would take her home to my compound, where once again I would look after her as she healed. Tomorrow I would get to see my other angel, my daughter. As a unified family, we would work to make the Raiders legitimate. I knew that there were still threats looming over us, including the Knights, now floundering without their leader and sergeant at arms, who would retaliate against us.

In the end, I hoped to never again have to lose another person I loved to the violence I'd bred.

TWENTY-FOUR

DEACON

For the first time I could remember, I sat at Mama Beth's table with a plateful of delicious food in front of me, but I couldn't eat. I didn't have an appetite to save my life. My stomach felt like it had been hog-tied.

It seemed that neither Rev nor Bishop, sitting across from me, could eat either. Mama Beth cleared her throat, causing us all to glance up from staring at our plates. "Boys, you really need to eat. You're going to need your strength today."

It didn't matter that her "boys" were grown men. She was still looking after us just like we were kids. And just like she said, I knew I needed my physical strength to try to get through the emotional hell that was going to be Case's funeral.

To appease Mama Beth, I picked up a biscuit, sopped up some gravy, and then took a bite. She gave me an appreciative smile before turning her attention back to Rev. I knew he felt the burden extra hard today. After all, he was the new president. He had to somehow manage to lead the Raiders through the shitstorm of grief.

Since we hadn't patched in another officer yet, Bishop would be keeping his role as road captain. That job became even more difficult today, as he had to coordinate the route from the funeral home to the cemetery with out-of-town charters as well as other clubs paying their respects. It was an awfully big job, but I knew he could do it.

After glancing at her watch, Mama Beth said, "You best go get the girls. They need to get ready."

I nodded and rose from my chair. Alex and Willow's ballet lessons had become almost therapeutic for them both, so I hadn't been too surprised when they escaped down to the studio as soon as breakfast was over.

As I opened the basement door, classical music floated up to me. My boots pounded down the stairs, but when I got to the bottom, I paused. No matter how many times I saw Alexandra dancing, I couldn't help feeling like I'd been kicked in the gut and in the balls. She had that much effect on me. Maybe it was the skimpy leotard she wore, or the way her body stretched into positions that made my dick pound against my zipper. Most of all, I couldn't help feeling completely dumbstruck that this talented, courageous, and sexy-as-hell woman wanted to be my wife.

I wasn't the only one mesmerized by Alex's performance. In her pink leotard and pink tights, Willow stood stock-still with wide eyes as Alexandra danced on those shoes with the pointy toes. I knew in her mind she was dreaming of the day she could wear them, too. A smile tugged on my lips as I thought about the day I'd finally let her into the studio. She'd taken the basement stairs so fast I thought she was going to end up in a heap at the bottom. She had then proceeded to squeal so loud I thought the mirrors would shatter. After inspecting the barre and dancing around for a minute, she raced to my side, threw her arms around my waist, and squeezed me tight. "Thank you, Daddy," she had said, sufficiently melting my heart.

After doing a final leap thing, Alex met my gaze in the mirror.

Her cheeks warmed, and she ducked her head. "I didn't realize you were there."

Crossing the room to meet her, I reached out to grab her chin and tip her head to meet my eyes. "Don't be embarrassed. I love watching you dance."

She gave me a shy smile. "And I think I know the real reason why."

While I laughed heartily, Willow's brows furrowed. "Why?" she asked.

As Alexandra's blush grew, I merely ruffled Willow's hair. "Because I like to see her looking pretty."

Willow seemed to buy my answer. "I look pretty when I dance, too. Don't I, Daddy?" She twirled around for emphasis, causing me to smile.

"Yes, you look very, very pretty." Jerking my chin toward the stairs, I said, "Go on and get cleaned up."

"But I can't get my dress on by myself," Willow protested. Before Case's death, she had never liked to be separated from Alexandra and me because she thought she might miss something. But now it was about so much more. She had become even clingier since she had returned from the mountains. In fact, she had slept in our bed the last two nights, which really dampened our continued reunion sex.

"Grandma Beth will help you," I replied.

Always the softie of the two of us, Alex said, "We'll be up in just a minute, baby."

While that seemed to appease Willow a little, she still gave me her best pouty face before finally trudging over to the stairs.

Once the basement door closed behind her, Alex's hand came up to cup my cheek. "Are you holding up okay?"

With a lump the size of a boulder in my throat, I could only nod. Since my mother's murder before my eyes as a kid, I'd had insurmountable trouble with the death of those I loved. It was like I couldn't bear to deal with the grief and pain. I just wanted to escape and ignore it.

Case had been more than my brother and club president—he had been a father figure to me. His death had shattered me. Not only did I mourn for him, but it brought back all the pain I'd tried to repress from Preacher Man's death and my mother's murder.

Sensing that I was hovering over an emotional cliff, Alexandra pressed herself against me. As her arms came around my neck, the comfort only she could bring washed over me. "Did you write down what you're going to say?" she questioned softly.

I nodded. "I just hope I can say it all. You know, without punking out by crying like a fucking pansy."

She rubbed reassuring circles over my back. "No one is going to think less of you for shedding tears for Case. All your brothers loved him," she reasoned.

"Babe, no offense, but that's such a chick thing to say."

Pulling her hands away, she stared up at me. "When it comes down to it, don't be afraid of showing your emotions."

"I'm not afraid." When she cocked her brows at me, I sighed. "You just don't understand."

"No, I'm sure I don't. Your world is still so new and confusing to me." She patted my chest above my heart. "But the one thing I do know is I love you."

I smiled down at her. Even without her saying it, I could feel her love for me. I knew it would give me the strength I needed to get through today. "Come on. Let's go get you in the shower," I said.

"Do we have time for you to join me?"

Man, did I love this woman. She knew how to appeal to me on each and every level. With a wink, I replied, "We'll make time."

EPILOGUE

REV

SIX MONTHS LATER

With my back against the trunk of a massive oak tree, I kept a watchful eye on the crowd before me while I took a sip of champagne from the crystal flute in my hand. Grimacing, I fought the urge to spit it out on the grass, but I figured that would be considered completely uncivilized by the crowd that surrounded me. Like my brothers, I was a beer or hard-liquor man. But my new sister-in-law was in charge of this party, and she had kept it classy, just like she was.

I found her in the crowd. God, she was beautiful. I don't think I'd ever seen her more beautiful than today—her wedding day. The top of her white satin dress hugged her like a second skin, showing off the fabulous curves that had attracted my brother. As they danced under the tent as man and wife, his hand rested a little lower than the curve of her back. I wasn't quite sure how through all the yards of fabric he was able to cop a feel of her ass, but if anyone could find a way, it would be Deacon.

Shaking my head, I couldn't help but grin at the sight of him in dress pants. He'd balked at a suit or tux. The black pants and long-sleeved white shirt were the compromise he and Alexandra had reached. After the wedding, he'd slipped his cut on over the shirt. I'm not sure what Alex's relatives or friends thought about that one. Most of them were just glad she was happy and safe after what had happened to her.

She had faced a lot of scrutiny after Sigel's death. Of course, everyone pitied her as the woman viciously attacked by a felon. The plan that she and Archer had concocted had been bought hook, line, and sinker by the cops. Not once did they doubt that Archer, who had slipped into a janitor's uniform, had heard Alex's cries and come running. He had been hailed a hero for taking down Sigel. Of course, no one in the school could remember him working there before. When he disappeared after that night, many wanted to believe he was some kind of guardian angel.

No matter how much blood you have on your hands, you always remember your first kill. Just like the rest of us, Alex struggled with what she had done. She suffered from screaming and kicking nightmares, she couldn't sleep without drugs from Breakneck, and she'd started losing weight.

It was a dark time for all of us, seeing her suffer. Thankfully, after a few weeks of torment, she started to pull out of it. She started to realize her daily validation for what she did when she looked at Deacon and Willow.

Speaking of Willow . . . My gaze momentarily left Alexandra to search out my niece. A smile played at my lips at the sight of her. Already a little diva in the making, she had requested her flower girl dress be pink and poufy. And of course she had gotten her way. Her long dark hair cascaded down her back in waves, while a headband of pink roses sat on her head. At her feet was the almost-grown Walter. He looked less than thrilled by the sparkly pink leash and collar that Willow had put on him for the day. When Deacon had seen him, he'd rolled his eyes and said, "I guess I'm going to have to get you a girl dog soon, or you'll make an absolute sissy out of Walter." Of course, Willow had been thrilled by the prospect of a dog of her own.

As I scanned the crowd of wedding guests again, an ache burned its way through my chest at the way Alex glanced up into my brother's face with such intense love in her eyes. In that moment, I wished she had just once looked that way at me. But there had never been more than friendship for us. I'd known that even when Deacon had tried to push the two of us together. I'd known it from the first time I'd seen her look adoringly at him.

Even though I loved him, I couldn't help feeling jealous of Deacon. I wanted the love of a good woman more than anything in the world. I wanted to be a husband and a father. Yet for some reason, my simple wants went unfulfilled.

When Deacon's hand swept around Alexandra's waist to tenderly rest on her abdomen, I had to turn away. It hurt too much to see such happiness. Although he or she was very much unexpected by their parents, I had no doubt how much Deacon and Alex would love their future child. Willow was already beside herself with excitement about being a big sister.

I swallowed the rest of my champagne and went in search of more. After I grabbed another flute from a snooty waiter with a tray, I went back to my spot beside the tree. I was surprised when Bishop walked up to me, a serious expression on his face. I'd expected him to already be banging one of the wedding guests.

"Need to talk to you," he said in a low voice.

"Can't it wait?"

He shook his head. "No, brother. It's bad."

"Not here, then."

We started away from the tent and the happy-go-lucky wedding guests. When we got to the parked cars, I leaned against one and nodded.

"Breakneck just called."

"Why the hell isn't he here?"

"He needs a favor."

"Shit," I muttered as I dug in my pocket for my cigarettes. "He knows we're going straight, doesn't he?"

Bishop nodded. "I made that very clear to him."

One of the stipulations of Alexandra marrying Deacon had been that the direction of the Raiders needed turning around. With Case's death fresh in our minds, it hadn't been too hard for Deacon to convince us that things needed to change. Every one of us officers at the table had lost more people than he cared to count due to club violence. If things kept on like they had been, we would have been extinct in a few years.

"Then what's the deal?"

"His daughter has been kidnapped by the Highway Henchmen."

I exhaled a cloud of smoke. "Jesus, how the hell did they find her here?"

"They didn't. She was at Texas A&M. Once they found out who she was, they started making demands to Breakneck."

I couldn't even begin to imagine what Breakneck was going through. "He wants us to put out the word or what?"

"This is where shit gets kinda weird."

My brows shot up in surprise. "What do you mean?"

"He said to tell you specifically that he knew she was being . . . raped. That you would understand that."

I turned away from Bishop's questioning gaze. With bile rising in my throat, I fought hard to keep my dinner down. Fucking Breakneck! I wanted nothing more in that moment than to beat his ass for dredging up the long-buried shit of my past. I also knew he was desperate for help, and in his desperation, he thought the best way to reach me was to appeal to that broken eleven-year-old boy he had treated.

Bishop cleared his throat. "Look, man. It's not fair he's playing on your tender heart. We can put out some feelers, do the best we can to find her."

I shook my head. "No. I'll handle this myself."

"Excuse me?"

Flicking the cigarette onto the grass, I stomped out the glowing embers and met Bishop's wide eyes. "You heard me."

"How in the hell are you supposed to lead the club straight when you're about to go death wish on the Henchmen?"

Grabbing him by the collar, I stared him down. "Don't question me on this, Bishop. You keep what was said between us. Don't go flapping your jaws to the other brothers. This stays contained—you got me?"

"Wait a minute. Does this have anything to do with what happened the night Pop killed that guy and left his church?"

I had to fight the urge not to close my hand tighter around Bishop's throat. "Once again, don't question me."

Releasing him, I stalked off into the night. I had some calls to make, favors to call in, and packing to do. I'd be leaving before dawn. The unlikely hero had some avenging to do.

ACKNOWLEDGMENTS

To God for all the amazing blessings in my life both personally and professionally.

To my agent extraordinaire, Jane Dystel, who worked so hard and tirelessly to make a publishing deal a reality for me and for me to be happy with the deal.

To Kerry Donovan, my editor at NAL, who believed in *Vicious Cycle* from its inception. It's been a pleasure working with you to make this series a reality.

Thanks forever and always to Kim Bias for talking me down from the ledge, talking me through the plot points, and generally making my books and my life so much better. Love ya hard!

To Marion Archer. I could not and would not put out a book without your feedback. Most of all, thanks for the prayers and support.

To Paige Silva for your unfailing support as a friend and as an assistant. I couldn't do this business without you, least of all life!

To Kim Jones—my sister from another mister. I can't thank

you enough for your friendship, humor, and smile. Most of all, thanks for letting me take you up on the offer to see a real MC at work. The men and old ladies of HIDW are some of the nicest and most welcoming people I've ever met. It was a truly honor getting to be with them.

Cris Hadarly: my dearest friend and greatest book supporter. Thanks for being along for the ride these past two years. I love you lots.

Jen Gerchick, Jen Oreto, and Shannon Furhman: Thanks for your unfailing support of me and my books. Thanks for your early eyes on *Vicious Cycle* and the constant cheerleading.

To Raine Miller for always encouraging me in this business to stretch and take risks. Thanks for your friendship.

To my street team, Ashley's Angels, thanks for the love and support!

To the ladies of the Hot Ones—Karen Lawson, Amy Lineweater, Marion Archer, and Merci Arellano—thanks for your friendship and book support. It means the world to me.

To my naughty sistas of the Smutty Mafia: Thanks for keeping me sane and making me laugh!

To Kristi Hefner, Gwen McPherson, Brittany Haught, Kim Benefield, Jamie Brock, and Erica Deese for being the bestest friends a gal could ever ask for. I thank God for having you all in my life for so long.

Rev

THE PRESENT

As I escaped my tormented unconsciousness, I came awake to find someone shaking the hell out of me. Flipping open my eyelids, I stared up into the concerned blue eyes of my brother Bishop. His hands gripped my shoulders so tight, I figured there would be marks left. "What the fuck, man?" I questioned, flinging him away.

He tumbled back on the mattress. "You were having one hell of a nightmare."

I sighed as I rubbed my shoulders where his hands had been. "Yeah, well, that doesn't mean I want to wake up to your ugly mug with morning breath in my face," I replied, trying to ease the palpable tension in the air.

Bishop didn't laugh. He didn't make a move to get off the bed either. He continued staring at me like he hoped he could somehow work his will into making me talk. He'd been giving me the same stare for the past few days we'd been on the road. Whenever we'd stop for food or to gas up our bikes, I would find him staring at me, chewing his bottom lip like he wanted to say something. He had been desperate since three nights ago when Breakneck's personal tragedy allowed Bishop a tiny glimpse at my long-buried secret.

Breaking the silence between us, I asked, "What time is our meeting with the El Paso Raiders?"

"Seven."

I glanced over my shoulder at the glowing digital clock on the nightstand. "That doesn't give us much time to make it across the state. Better get crackin' and hit the road. You want the shower first?"

"Nah, you can have it." As I rose off the mattress, Bishop said, "I'll go grab us a quick breakfast."

"Thanks, brother."

When I started across the threadbare carpet to the bathroom, Bishop's words froze me. "Rev . . . you know it doesn't matter to me what the fuck happened to you—it ain't gonna change a damn thing about the way I feel about you. No matter what, you're my big brother and my prez."

Since I was both too emotionally conflicted and too stubborn to respond, I ignored him and pushed on into the bathroom. After locking the door behind me, I gazed at my reflection in the mirror. Two days of driving across Georgia, Alabama, Mississippi, and Louisiana with minimal sleep had taken its physical toll. That, coupled with emotional stress, had left dark circles under my eyes. After packing up to leave so abruptly, I hadn't bothered with a razor, so my beard was growing in. I looked like the hell that raged inside me.

Turning on the water full blast, I then stepped inside the shower. I placed my palms flat on the tiles and stood with my head under the stream. Rolling my shoulders, I tried to ease my tense muscles.

Two days ago felt like two years and another world ago. It was hard to imagine just forty-eight hours ago I'd been dancing and drinking at Deacon and Alexandra's wedding. Then one phone call from the Raiders' unofficial doctor, Bob "Breakneck" Edgeway, had changed everything.

Whenever I closed my eyes, I had my pick of which face would haunt me. It was either the sinister evil of my rapist or the fresh-faced innocence of Breakneck's daughter. It had been five years since I had seen Sarah at any of the Raiders' events. She'd been an awkward thirteen-year-old girl in braces who had spent most of the BBQ fawning over Eric, our then-president, Case's, teenage son. Now she was a college freshman at Texas A&M. From the picture Breakneck had texted me, she'd grown into an auburn-haired beauty with an innocent smile—the kind of girl low-life traffickers always had a jonesing for.

The criminal profiling of the scum who bought these women indicated that they didn't want fake-breasted, slutty types. They could pay for those any day on the streets or at the strip club. No, they seemed to want the unattainable female—the one who would never give them the time of day unless they were forced. And sadly, Sarah fit that bill.

We didn't have much to go on other than it was the Highway Henchmen who had taken her and were making financial demands on Breakneck to get her back. Apparently, she had spilled the beans that her old man was a biker. Usually, girls kidnapped for trafficking never got a chance of being ransomed back to their families. Instead, they were sold to the highest bidder into a life of sexual slavery. The thought that Sarah now faced that future both turned my stomach and enraged me.

After scrubbing off yesterday's grit and grime with the hotel's cheap brand of soap, I made fast work of rinsing. The moment I turned the water off, I heard my phone ringing in the bedroom. Throwing a towel around my waist, I hurried out of the bathroom to grab it. When I saw who was calling, I grimaced. "Yeah?"

"Where the hell are you?" Deacon demanded without even a hello.

"I'm touched that you thought to call me while you're on your honeymoon."

Deacon's low growl came in my ear. "Don't fucking change the subject, asshole."

"I was just trying to be nice."

"Yeah, you're just being a prick is what you're doing. Now, I want a fucking straight answer."

"Last time I checked, big brother, *I* wore the president's patch." I knew my words were the equivalent of poking a rattle-snake ready to strike. Regardless of whether I was the president of the Hells Raiders, I still owed Deacon an explanation.

"Fine, motherfucker, then answer me as your newly patched vice president, why my two brothers bailed on my reception to hit the road and are now in Texas?"

Defeated, I leaned back against the counter. I knew I couldn't evade his questions anymore. "It's complicated."

"I'm listening."

Slowly, I began unraveling the story of Sarah's abduction, and how we were going to get her back from the Henchmen.

When I finished, Deacon merely muttered, "Fucking hell."

"Yeah, that pretty much sums it up."

Deacon exhaled a long sigh into the phone. "Man, I can't believe you just left here without taking it to the table. You're the president, for fuck's sake. While it's admirable of you to do this for Breakneck, this situation isn't just about you. It involves the entire club."

"You can tell the guys I'll deal with any repercussions when I get back."

"I just hope it doesn't get any worse."

Pushing off the counter, I demanded, "What's that supposed to mean?"

"Look, I know you and your code of honor. You'll do whatever you have to do to get Sarah back."

"You say that like it's the wrong thing to do."

"It is when the Raiders are trying to go legit."

Even though he couldn't see me, I shook my head in disbelief. "What the fuck is wrong with you? We're talking about an innocent girl's life here—one of our brothers' kids. Have you forgotten that Raiders protect their own, regardless of the cost? You would do anything if someone had Willow or Alexandra. Hell, you have before."

"Do *not* bring my wife and kid into this," Deacon hissed.

"Sarah is Breakneck's kid, so for his sake, I'm willing to do anything to get her back. If that means some blowback on the club, then I'll fucking deal with it."

"No, we'll *all* end up fucking dealing with it."

I exhaled a frustrated breath. "I know you have a lot of pressure from Alexandra for the club to go legit. But I guarantee if you told her what was happening, she would be behind me all the way, regardless of what the repercussions might be to the club."

When Deacon cursed under his breath, I knew I had finally gotten through to him. "You're a stubborn motherfucker," he grumbled.

With a laugh, I replied, "I learned from the best, brother."

Deacon snorted. "Yeah, well, just be careful."

Since I knew Deacon wasn't an overly emotional guy, I couldn't help feeling a little touched by his concern. "I will. But at the end of the day, this is something I have to do."

"Trust me, I get it. I don't have to like it, but I sure as hell get it."

"We'll be back as soon as we can."

"Call me the minute you have her."

"I will."

After Deacon hung up without a good-bye, which was so often his style, I went to get dressed. But no matter how hard I tried, I couldn't shake the overwhelming feeling of dread crisscrossing its way over my skin. Although I would never have admitted my fears to him, I knew Deacon was right. Getting Sarah back was going to have serious blowback on the club.

At the time, I just couldn't imagine how severe.

Katie Ashley is the *New York Times* and *USA Today* bestselling author of the Proposition series and the Runaway Train series, as well as several New Adult and Young Adult titles. She lives outside of Atlanta, Georgia, with her two very spoiled dogs. With a BA in English, a BS in Secondary English Education, and a master's in English Education, she spent eleven years teaching middle school and high school English until she left to write full-time.